THE SEVEN PRINCESSES

smiljana coh

RP|KIDS
PHILADELPHIA

FOR SOFIA, LILI, AND NORA

ISBN 978-0-7624-5587-4
Library of Congress Control Number: 2015958244

9 8 7 6 5 4 3 2
Digit on the right indicates the number of this printing

Designed by Frances J. Soo Ping Chow
Edited by Marlo Scrimizzi
Typography: Caligula Dodgy, Chronicle Text, Helvetica Neue, and MrMoustache

Published by Running Press Kids,
An Imprint of Perseus Books, LLC.,
A Subsidiary of Hachette Book Group, Inc.
2300 Chestnut Street
Philadelphia, PA 19103–4371

Visit us on the web!
www.runningpress.com/rpkids

Once upon a colorful kingdom . . .

there lived a king

and queen,

and their seven spectacular princesses . . .

Orellia

Rosamund

Azzurra

Amaryllis

Hazel

Indigo

Violet

Each princess was kindhearted, quick-witted, and highly skilled,
but they could not have been more different.

Rosamund loved
math and building.

Orellia loved instruments
and music.

Amaryllis loved fashion design
and sewing.

Hazel loved gardening.

Azzurra loved animals.

Indigo loved swimming.

Violet loved drawing, painting, collaging, sculpture, and basically anything involving the arts.

The seven princesses did *everything* together.

There was no better sound in the kingdom than the sound
of the princesses laughing and playing.

But they didn't *always* laugh and play together.
Sometimes they had terrible fights.

One day, they had the biggest fight in the entire history
of princess fighting.

There was no worse sound in the kingdom
than the sound of this fight.

Orellia insisted Amaryllis got sequins inside her trombone.

Azzurra shrieked because Indigo had been swimming in her swan pond.

Hazel shouted because Azzurra let her potbellied pigs dig up her turnips.

Rosamund said Orellia's music was much too loud.

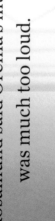

Indigo lost it because Violet's paints were taking up way too much space.

Violet painted a less-than-flattering portrait of all the sisters fighting.

Amaryllis demanded Hazel stop cooking stinky Brussels sprouts.

Rosamund never wanted to
SEE her sisters again.

Orellia never wanted to
HEAR her sisters again.

Amaryllis wanted DIFFERENT sisters.

Hazel wished she just had
her GARDEN.

Azzurra wished she just had
her ANIMALS.

Indigo wished
she could swim AWAY.

Violet wished
she was ALONE.

So each princess had her own tower built . . .

. . . and each princess stayed inside by herself.

At first it was just fine.

But after a while, something started to change.

The princesses started to forget all the fun
(and not-so-much-fun) they had shared together.

Once it had seemed there was no worse sound in the kingdom
than hearing the princesses fight.

But it turned out there was.

The silence was much worse.

The silence lasted and lasted.

It lasted right up until one extra gray day,
when Violet found an old picture.

The picture made Violet remember all the spectacular times
the sisters had spent doing everything together.

She had an idea.

Violet folded the picture into a paper plane,
and flew it right into Indigo's tower window.

When Indigo got the picture, she remembered the time
the sisters laughed so hard they split their seams and got cheek cramps.
She felt so happy inside, she quickly sent the picture to Azzurra.

When Azzurra got the picture, she remembered how the sisters jumped
in the royal leaf piles until sunset. That made her so excited,
she passed the picture on to Hazel as fast as she could.

When Hazel got the picture, she remembered the play they performed, when they all dressed up as the seven dwarfs. That made her laugh like she hadn't in years! She *had* to send the picture to Amaryllis right away.

When Amaryllis got the picture, she remembered horseback riding on the beach with her sisters, splashing in the sea. That made her heart pound so hard, she wanted to share the picture with Orellia at once.

When Orellia got the picture, she remembered the legendary piñata party she and her sisters threw. She was so over the moon, she *had* to get the picture to Rosamund pronto.

When Rosamund got the picture, she remembered how once, when the sisters were little, they connected all their block towers together.

And this gave her an idea.

Rosamund quickly got to work building swirly slides,
twisty tunnels, colorful catwalks, and bejeweled bridges
so the princesses would never be separated again.

Finally the seven princesses were reconnected.

They laughed and played, rejoiced and remembered, together in harmony.

And once again, it was the best sound
in the whole colorful kingdom.

That night, Rosamund gave Orellia a royal karaoke machine,
and they turned the volume all the way up.

Orellia glued sparkling sequins all over her oboe on purpose.

Amaryllis ate all of her Brussels sprouts for dinner.
Then she asked for seconds.

Hazel made a special spot in her majestic garden
just for Azzurra's potbellied pigs.

Azzurra had a statue of Indigo built in her swan pond.

Indigo made less-than-flattering faces on purpose,
which made Violet laugh and laugh.

And Violet hung up the picture that had brought
the seven princesses back together . . .

... which hangs inside the castle to this very day.

The End

THE ART

OF

SHIP and BOAT

HANDLING

BY

CAPTAIN R.D. MOSS

For information on this publication or to order a copy
write to: ONBOARD MARINE COMPANY
P.O. Box 29
Brashear, Texas 75420

Published by Onboard Marine Company

PRINTED IN USA by Taylor Publishing Company

About the Author

Captain R. D. Moss began his seafaring career early in 1943 when he enlisted in the U. S. Maritime Academy at St. Petersburg, Florida. Following seamanship training he sailed on deep sea vessels (tankers, freighters, towing, etc.) where he served as Able Seaman, Deck Maintenance, Bosun, and Mate.

In 1947 he turned from ocean vessels and worked for ITT and G & H towing companies as Deck Hand, Mate Relief Master and Master of Harbor and Coastal Towing Vessels, engaged mostly in ship assistance. Here, he learned the intricacies of towing and working in close quarters from men with many years experience in this field.

In 1951, Captain Moss was employed by the Houston Pilots Association to act as Master of the Houston Pilot No. 3, where he served while learning from the senior Pilots until he was appointed Deputy Pilot in 1955. In this post, Capt. Moss was taught ship handling by a group of pilots, some whose experience dates back to the beginning of the Houston Ship Channel.

In 1966, Capt. Moss resigned from the Houston Pilots and re-joined ships plying from Gulf and West Coast Ports to Viet Nam and the Far East.

In 1970 he was hired by Tidewater Marine to operate vessels in the oil and mineral trade industries and worked for numerous companies around the world handling vessels in those trades. His last employers in this field were Jackson Marine and Halliburton.

The years of combined training and experience of the men who contributed to the success of this book totals into the hundreds of years.

Captain Moss' interest in pleasure boats dates back to his early childhood. At the age of ten, he attempted to build his own boat from a hollow log which had been used to feed hogs on the family farm. This attempt failed, however, when his father saw what was happening to the feed trough and used a board to show disapproval. While Captain Moss is a staunch supporter of pleasure boats for fun and relaxation, he is equally concerned about safe operation much the same as with cars and trucks.

Early in 1944 he was an Able Seaman on board the S/S Jacob S. Mansfield which sailed from San Francisco and stopped at the port of Los Angeles to pick up twelve persons employed by the Disney Studios who were going to report coverage on the building of the Burma Road. They were bound for Calcutta, India where the military would transport them to the Burma Road area.

Among the group picked up were reporters, photographers, writers, and two artists. Mr. V. Stark was one of the artist. He asked to paint Moss's picture while enroute and the other artist chose one of the officers on board.

The voyage included fuel stops in Honolulu and Freemantle, Australia, thence to Calcutta. Mr. Stark did the painting in one of the storerooms below decks and while working one night in the Indian Ocean, not many days out of Calcutta, the S/S Jacob S. Mansfield ran upon an enemy submarine lying on the surface, apparently charging its batteries. A crew member, about the same time that the general alarm went off, came and yelled to the others that a Sub was dead ahead. As Mr. Stark jumped back he jerked the picture off the easel onto the deck covered with saw dust. It took him almost the rest of the voyage to clean up and complete the painting.

As for the submarine, it so happened that a wolf pack of them had moved in and a large number of ships were sunk in that area. The S/S Jacob S. Mansfield managed to outrun the one it had encountered. Several weeks later they left Calcutta in a large convoy under heavy naval vessel support.

Mr. Moss has not heard from Mr. Stark since.

LEGEND OF SYMBOLS

> Dead Slow Speed

> Slow Speed

>> Half Speed

>>> Full Speed

⊣ Stop

--→ Thrust

⊱ Angle of Rudder

→ Current or Wind Set

FOREWORD

A boat is always in motion or subject to be in motion unless it is completely aground or setting in drydock; when it is secured at a dock it becomes restless with wind and water disturbance.

The illustrations and diagrams depicted and explained here are designed to prevent the mariner from bumping heads with nature's elements — always a losing battle. It seems to the author that panic and bad judgment cause more accidents and fatalities than all other elements combined.

Hence, if one knows what is happening and what is going to happen while maneuvering a vessel, there is little time and no need for panic or misjudgment.

It is necessary to advise, however, that there is no such thing as complete perfection in this profession. Neither is it possible to cover all positions of maneuvers that one may encounter. Every circumstance will dictate the amount of engine speed and rudder angle necessary for that particular task.

The only certainty in boating is that conditions and results can be uncertain. At the precise time a mariner thinks he has all the answers down pat, a vessel will mysteriously do everything except that which is expected. There is always a reason for this erratic behavior, but most of us have a tendency not to look for the reason until the vessel has sailed as though it has a mind of its own.

However, the mariner who is knowledgeable enough to know that he does not know everything, and pays heed to wind, current, bottom configuration, speed, pressure and suction effect between vessel and dock will have a happy and successful career.

It should be noted that all conventional vessels constructed with fixed rudder(s) and propeller(s) operate on the same basic principle as outlined in this book. Size, weight, draft, hull configuration, hull and superstructure above the water, and horse power ratio make the difference in maneuverability.

TABLE OF CONTENTS

TABLE OF CONTENTS

TABLE OF CONTENTS

CHAPTER 1

THE ART OF MANEUVERING

Tug boat assistance when maneuvering large vessels in close quarters is recommended and sometimes absolutely necessary in order to avoid delay and possible damage. However, there are times and places in the world where they are not available. For that reason this chapter deals solely with handling them without assistance.

As shown in Figure 1-A, it is apparent that anything moving in a small circle tends to migrate from that circle, and the faster the movement, the harder it is to keep the object within the circle. It is called centrifugal

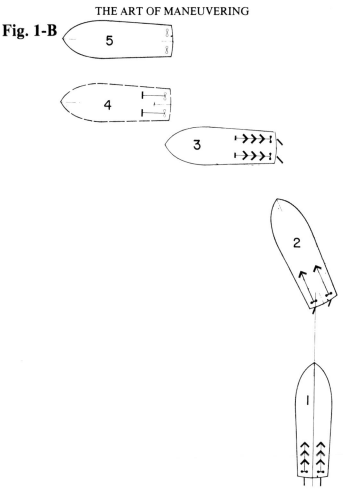

Fig. 1-B is at the top.

Fig. 1-B. *1. Full speed ahead. 2. Slow ahead — hard left rudder. 3. Stop and full astern. 4. Stopped. 5. Movement broadside.*

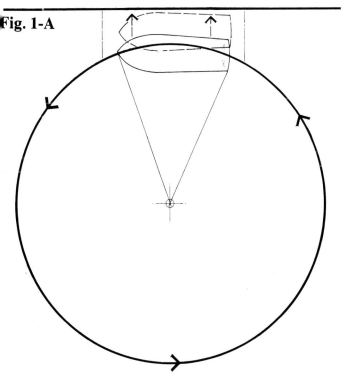

Fig. 1-A

force. Consider a discus thrower, who whirls and releases the discus in the direction in which he wishes it to travel. The faster the whirl, the further the discus will go.

Although a vessel has no physical mooring to hold it within the circle, the above principle can be an advantage or disadvantage — depending upon the person handling the vessel, as shown in Figure 1-B.

A vessel traveling on a straight course will lose considerable headway when her rudder is put hard over and she is put into a tight turn due to the friction of the turn and drag of her rudder. A single screw vessel with a right hand turning propeller will turn faster to a left rudder because of the rotation of her propeller to the pitch ratio. There seems to be no appreciable differ-

ence in the direction of turn on either twin or triple screw vessels. However, if the engine on the inside of the turn is stopped and/or backed these vessels will turn and stop sooner unless their hull is near the bottom or bank on the inside of the turn, and then they will most likely sheer off and go in the opposite direction, or they may go aground. (Figures 1-B1 & 1-B2) (Page 10).

A vessel running light with normal seaworthy trim will swing, lose headway and stop sooner than a deep loaded vessel because of the weight involved. A vessel with a lot of drag will swing and stop sooner than a vessel with little or no drag. (Drag equals the difference in the deep draft aft and the light draft forward). A vessel DOWN BY THE HEAD (deepest draft forward) will swing faster, but takes longer to stop because the propeller(s) cannot get a grip in the water. If they are extremely deep by the head, vacuum cavitation around the propeller(s) may be experienced.

This turning procedure can be an advantage from a dead stop in the water in close quarters especially if there is turning room for the vessel. The best results are obtained by making at least a 90 degree turn or more.

Fig. 1-B1

Outer sea bouy

Fig. 1-B2

Outer sea bouy

Fig. 1-B2   1. Steady on course — full or half ahead. 2.-Slow or dead slow ahead — hard left rudder. 3. Taking suction from shoal water. 4. Vessel sheering out of control to starboard. (Note: If the shoal is a gradual slope the ship will most likely go aground and stop).

Fig. 1-B1   1. Steady on course — full or half ahead. 2. Hard left rudder — slow or dead slow ahead (stop engines on motor-ship). 3. Over the ground speed should be slowed to 4 or 5 knots on light vessel in ballast.

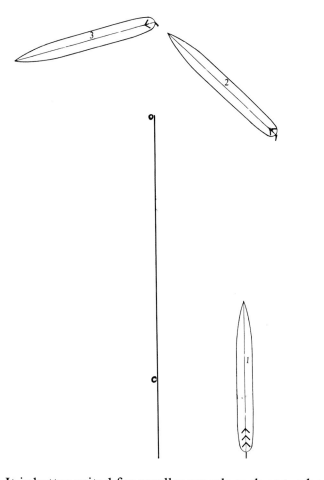

It is better suited for smaller vessels such as tug boats and yachts, but can be used successfully on just about any vessel, especially those that do not have bow thrusters or flanking rudders to assist.

It is necessary to exercise care and good judgment so that the proper amount of broadside movement is obtained to prevent damage to the vessel or dock. This is no great task, and after a little practice it will become second nature. However, when first learning this maneuver plenty of room should be left between the

vessel and dock until you get a feel of the amount of broadside movement that is obtained at different speeds.

Great care should be taken with large ships and other vessels such as drilling rigs and large floating plants because of the weight involved. In a harbor where the docks form a sheer wall and the water has no way to escape, there is little danger of doing damage (especially with a medium or deep draft vessel) because of the pressure of water that builds up between the dock and the vessel as it moves broadside. In fact, if the maneuver is performed too fast it is quite likely that pressure will cause the vessel's broadside movement to stop within several feet of the dock and start moving away. If the vessel is not exactly parallel to the dock at that time, the end that is farther from the dock will move away faster. If the stern is closer and the engines are used the suction effect of the propeller(s) will most likely cause the stern to try to come in hard contact with the dock.

However, when docking at a pier or pier head extending out into the water on piles with no bank to offer this compressed water cushion, the broadside movement will continue at or about the same rate and can do extensive damage to the pier and/or vessel.

DOCKING ON THE INSIDE OF THE TURN

Now, let's consider what can be done when a vessel wishes to dock on the inside of a turn such as right angle wharfs or piers as shown in Figures 1-C & 1-C1. It would be necessary to get lines on the dock quickly to keep the vessel from going broadside away from the dock, and it would also be very necessary to take care

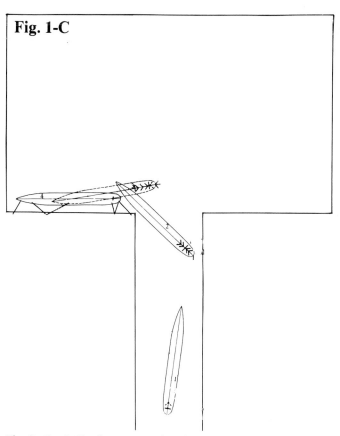

Fig. 1-C 1. Engines stopped and put slow or dead slow ahead. 2. Half astern — stop and half ahead with hard left rudder. 3. Stop and full astern — stop and slow or dead slow ahead with variable rudder to bring vessel alongside. 4. Forward spring line out first.

not to break these lines before the broadside movement is stopped and the vessel can be heaved alongside. Also, because the movement will necessarily have to be slow, a single screw vessel with right hand propel-

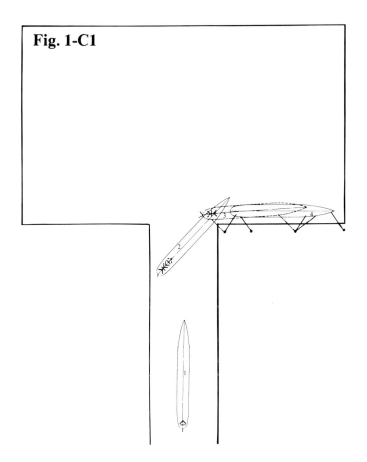

Fig. 1-C1 1. Slow or dead slow ahead and stop engines. 2. Hard right rudder — dead slow ahead — stop and half astern — stop and dead slow ahead. 3. Slow astern — stop and slow or dead slow ahead — variable rudder. 4. Forward spring and stern breast lines out first.

ler will most likely back to port and the stern may go away from the dock before a line can be passed ashore. As shown in Figure 1-D (Page 12), when there is sufficient room, a vessel can come astern and gain sternway before coming ahead with hard left rudder to land as if docking on the outside of a turn.

Figure 1-E (Page 12) shows how a stern spring line leading aft can be put out as the vessel is stopped or nearly so, and surged off under a strain (don't hold enough strain to break it) and the vessel's engines can be worked ahead on dead slow to bring the vessel alongside.

Figure 1-F illustrates using the port anchor going port side to the dock which works fine in good weather with little or no current. Notice the anchor is dropped even with the end of the dock and paid out so the vessel can work against it and steer the vessel alongside.

Fig. 1-D

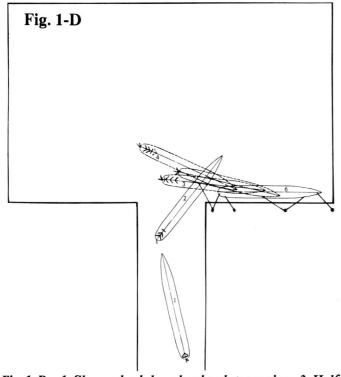

Fig. 1-D   1. Slow or dead slow ahead and stop engines. 2. Half ahead — hard right rudder. 3. Stop and full astern. 4. Hard left rudder — half ahead — slow to dead slow ahead — variable rudder. 5. Slow or dead slow ahead to bring vessel alongside. 6. Forward and stern spring lines out first.

Fig. 1-E

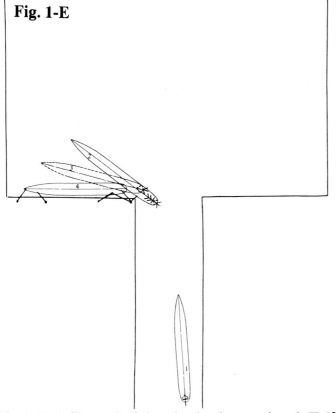

Fig. 1-E   1. Slow or dead slow ahead and stop engines. 2. Half astern and stop — slow or dead slow ahead — variable rudder. 3. Slow or dead slow ahead — variable rudder to bring vessel alongside. 4. Stern breast line out first.

Fig. 1-F

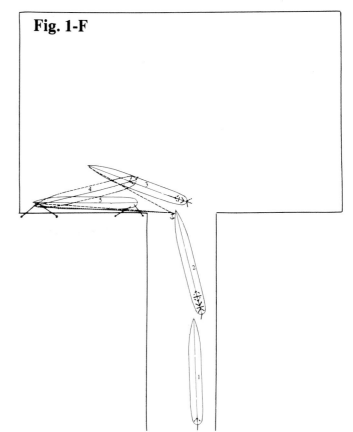

Fig. 1-F   1. Dead slow or slow ahead. 2. Slow or half astern — slow or dead slow ahead — drop port anchor. 3. Surge off anchor chain — slow or dead slow ahead — variable rudder to bring vessel alongside. 4. Hold anchor chain — put forward spring line out first.

In this and subsequent diagrams, if the anchor cannot be heaved in after the vessel is secure, the chain should be slacked off until it is on the bottom and leading up and down so that other vessels will not get fowled in the chain, and the anchor can be picked up when the vessel sails.

Figure 1-G (Page 13) illustrates the procedure if there is an on dock wind. The port anchor is dropped further offshore from the dock so that the anchor chain will lead under the hull and slacked off as necessary to let the vessel steer alongside to make fast.

Figure 1-H (Page 13) illustrates the use of the starboard anchor with an off dock wind. Again the anchor is dropped directly off the end of the dock in approximately the same place as when the port anchor is used in good weather, but the starboard anchor chain leading under the hull will breast the vessel up against the wind so that she can steer alongside the dock.

It is not uncommon to find unprotected piers extending out to where tidal currents and quite often river currents can run directly underneath as shown in Figure 1-I (Page 13). These piers will generally have some sort of cushion on each corner for a vessel to lay against when docking, which is no trouble when docking on the up current side. The vessel can be steered

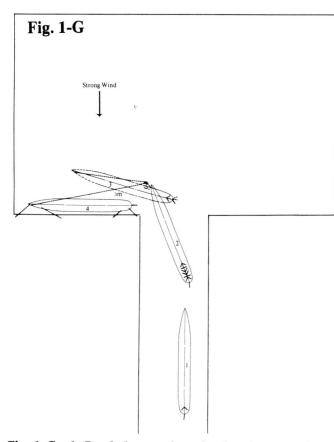

Fig. 1-G

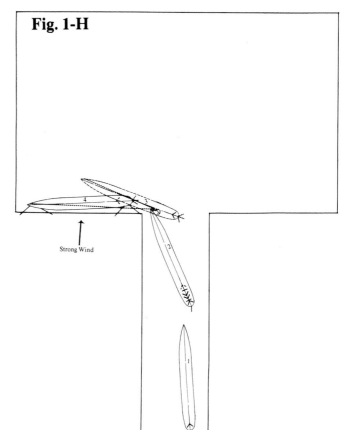

Fig. 1-H

Fig. 1-G   1. Dead slow or slow ahead and stop engines. 2. Dead slow or slow ahead — stop and half or full astern — stop and dead slow or slow ahead — drop port anchor. 3. Slack anchor chain — dead slow or slow ahead — variable rudder to bring vessel alongside. 4. Hold anchor chain — forward spring line out first.

Fig. 1-H   1. Slow ahead and stop. 2. Dead slow or slow ahead — left rudder — stop and half or full astern — stop and slow or dead slow ahead. 3. Slow or dead slow ahead — slack anchor chain — variable rudder to bring vessel alongside. 4. Hold anchor chain — forward spring line out first.

Fig. 1-I

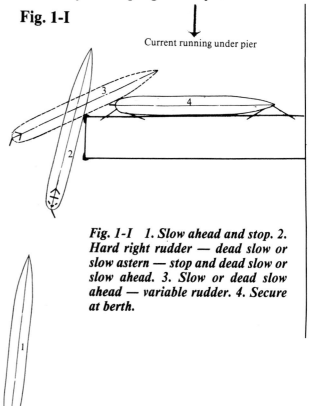

Fig. 1-I   1. Slow ahead and stop. 2. Hard right rudder — dead slow or slow astern — stop and dead slow or slow ahead. 3. Slow or dead slow ahead — variable rudder. 4. Secure at berth.

against the current while working her toward the cushioned corner until her hull touches gently about halfway between her bow and midship. She can then be moved ahead on dead slow or slow ahead with her rudder toward the dock enough to keep the current on her port side. When the current pressure becomes greater on the bow than on the stern, she will fall alongside. She can then be eased forward with her engines and midship rudder until she is in place. All that will be lost is a little paint and is generally found to be safer than trying to hold her off with tugs.

With a strong current, docking on the off current side is just about impossible with a large vessel, especially if she is loaded and there are no tugs to hold her and push her up against the current. If tugs are available, they can hold her long enough to get lines on the dock and she can generally be heaved alongside with the assistance of the tugs pushing. Otherwise it would be advisable to anchor and wait until the current has slacked or assistance is obtained. If the current is not too strong, the off dock anchor may be dropped off the end of the pier as shown in Figure 1-J (Page 14), and the vessel can be steered alongside close enough to put out spring and breast lines for heaving alongside and securing.

Fig. 1-J

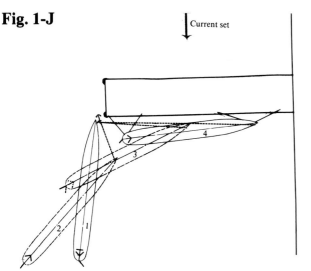

Fig. 1-J   1. Drop starboard anchor — slow astern. 2. Dead slow or slow ahead — variable rudder — surge off anchor chain. 3. Engines ahead — variable rudder — surge off anchor chain. 4. Hold anchor chain — spring line out first — secure at berth and leave anchor chain laying on bottom.

HEADING WITH CURRENT AND BACKING INTO DEAD WATER SLIP

It should be explained here that working a ship with the current broadside where the current is against the entire length of the hull at a right angle, is nearly impossible unless the vessel has tug assistance with enough power to hold her in that position. And even then it is difficult.

If the current is worked at an angle to the hull, either from the bow or the stern, it relieves this broadside pressure and will prove to be safe and efficient.

A large vessel running with the current and stopping and backing into a protected slip with slack water not effected by the current is both touchy and somewhat dangerous, but it can be done if it is necessary and there is no tug assistance available as illustrated in Figure's 1-K and 1-L. The person doing the handling has to decide within a matter of seconds which anchor to use in order to do the best job. The dockside anchor will hold the bow up against the current better if properly let go and placed to hold. However, they must be sure that the bow of the vessel has turned far enough against the current so that the vessel does not swing in the opposite direction which will cause her to head into the slip and current. This would create the necessity of going some place and turning around and starting all over again. It also puts a tremendous strain on the anchor windlass as it binds against the hull of the ship. However, any good ship handler takes these things into consideration.

On the other hand, we take the off dock anchor which will certainly hold the bow, but will not give any way out if the anchor drags or the vessel is not in the proper position to land against the pier properly.

Fig. 1-K

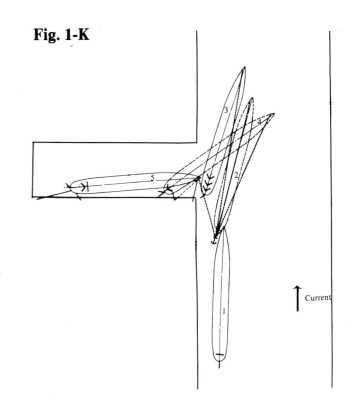

Fig. 1-K   1. Engines stopped — drop port anchor and slack anchor chain. 2. Full astern — rudder midship — surge off and hold anchor chain. 3. Heave on anchor chain. 4. Slow or dead slow astern — variable rudder — line on dock to hold stern. 5. Dead slow or slow ahead to stop in berth.

Fig. 1-L

Fig. 1-L   1. Stop engines — drop port anchor and slack anchor chain. 2. Full astern — hold anchor chain. 3. Heave anchor — slow astern — variable rudder. 4. Stop and slow ahead — hard right rudder — stop and half or slow astern. 5. Stop and slow ahead to secure in berth — stern and forward spring lines out first.

TURNING LARGE VESSELS IN CONFINED QUARTERS WITHOUT TUG ASSISTANCE

It is assumed in the two following illustrations that there is no dangerous current or wind set, and that the vessel has a right turning propeller. If a vessel has a left turning or right turning reversible pitch propeller, the procedure would be reversed and the vessel would turn on a left rudder instead of a right rudder.

Figures 1-M and 1-N illustrates going into a basin or similar place where there is enough room to turn. The anchor is put down where you want the bow to be positioned after turning. As illustrated here the starboard anchor would be used because it would be on the inside of the turn and the ship would continue turning to starboard when backed.

Notice in Figure 1-M, the anchor is dropped in the middle of the channel as the vessel enters the basin and is allowed to pay out until her stern is clear and the engines are put astern. The anchor windlass should then be locked in and commence heaving on the anchor. In the meantime the ship can come slow ahead and slow or half astern while she is turning. Remember,

the bow will always come back to where the anchor is unless it is drug over the bottom.

If there is enough room in a clear channel to turn, it can be done a little differently as shown in Fig. 1-N. The vessel can be angled toward her port bank while dropping her starboard anchor in the middle of the channel and letting the chain pay out until the vessel has taken a sheer off the bank and the engines are put full astern. At this time the windlass can be locked in and begin heaving on the anchor, while the ship keeps clear by coming ahead and astern as necessary.

Fig. 1-N

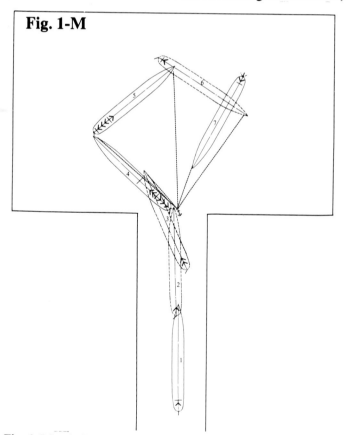

Fig. 1-M

Fig. 1-M   1. Slow ahead and stop engines. 2. Drop starboard anchor and slack off chain — dead slow ahead — hard left rudder. 3. Half ahead — hard left rudder — slack anchor chain. 4. Stop and full astern — slack anchor chain — stop and half ahead — hard right rudder. 5. Stop and full astern — hold anchor chain and heave on anchor — stop and slow ahead — hard right rudder. 6. Stop and slow astern. 7. Slow ahead — variable rudder — stop engines and heave up anchor.

Fig. 1-N   1. Slow ahead — drop starboard anchor and pay out chain. 2. Slow ahead — stop and full astern — stop and slow ahead — hard right rudder — surge anchor chain. 3. Slow ahead — hard right rudder — stop and half astern — stop engines — heave on anchor. 4. Hard right rudder — slow ahead and stop engines. 5. Dead slow ahead and stop — heave in anchor.

Fig. 1-O

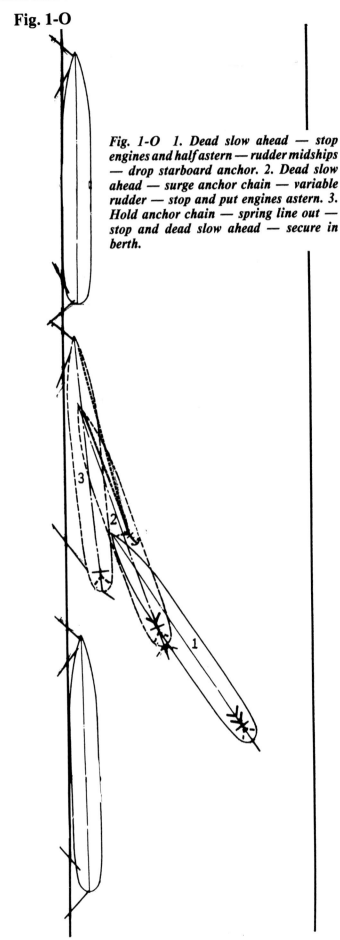

Fig. 1-O 1. Dead slow ahead — stop engines and half astern — rudder midships — drop starboard anchor. 2. Dead slow ahead — surge anchor chain — variable rudder — stop and put engines astern. 3. Hold anchor chain — spring line out — stop and dead slow ahead — secure in berth.

USING ANCHOR TO DOCK PORT SIDE TO THE DOCK BETWEEN TWO VESSELS IN CALM WEATHER

Figure 1-O illustrates the safe way of putting a ship between two that are already secured. If the Captain or Pilot is well acquainted with the vessel and knows what kind of response to expect when the engines are put astern, the docking can be done safely enough without using an anchor (if nothing goes wrong, and there is always that chance that something will). It is always safest to take that extra few minutes and put the anchor down rather than have the embarrassment of writing a report trying to explain after damage is done. The off dock anchor should be used and of course it can be dropped at your near approach to the dock or sooner. However if the anchor is dropped too soon, it will have to be drug over the bottom. Once it drags it will generally ball up with mud and will not hold again but will act as a drag in helping to stop the headway. If it is dropped too late and does not have enough scope to hold, the same thing will happen.

TURNING AND DOCKING STARBOARD SIDE TO THE DOCK BETWEEN TWO SHIPS USING PORT ANCHOR

This maneuver may look complicated, but it isn't if the weather is half-way decent and the vessel is kept under control.

As shown in Figure 1-P (Page 17), the port anchor is dropped when the bow is about two thirds along the length of the dock where the vessel is to go. It is dropped as near the dock as possible, leaving room for the vessel's stern to clear the dock and ships that are secured at the adjoining berths while the anchor chain is being payed out and the vessel is turning.

When the stern is clear, the engines can be put astern to stop the headway while the anchor windlass is locked and started to heave in while the engines are put slow ahead with a hard right rudder to keep the vessel turning. Only enough anchor chain should be heaved in to take out the slack and let the stern of the vessel stay clear of the ship moored astern.

When the bow has swung all the way around to where it is approximately at a forty five degree angle away from the dock, the ship's rudder can be used to hold the stern near the dock with engines turning slow or dead slow ahead while the bow is heaved alongside with the anchor. Remember, as long as the engines are not worked strong enough ahead to drag the anchor, the ship can literally be steered alongside the dock.

Fig. 1-P

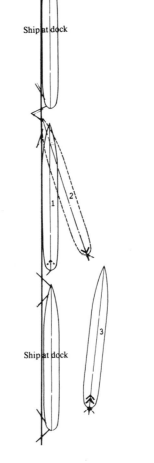

SAILING A SHIP SECURED PORT SIDE TO DOCK WITHOUT TUG ASSISTANCE

Under normal conditions with little or no current or wind, a ship which is secured port side to the dock can be sailed as illustrated in Figure 1-Q.

One should make sure that one or two good strong spring lines are tight and made fast forward, and a head line to keep the ship from drifting astern while all of the stern lines are taken in. If there is a breast line leading around the bow, it can be heaved on to help break the stern away from the dock while coming dead slow ahead on the engines with a hard left rudder.

When the stern is well out into the channel and clear of everything, all of the lines can be let go forward and the engines can be put astern with a midship or hard right rudder. Since she will back to port, she should be positioned in the middle of the channel by the time she has backed a ship's length or less.

Fig. 1-Q 1. Dead slow ahead — hard left rudder — hold spring line — heave on head line. 2. Stop engines — let go head and spring lines — slow or half astern — midship or hard right rudder. 3. Half ahead — variable rudder to steady up in channel.

Fig. 1-Q

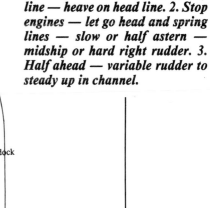

Fig. 1-P 1. Drop port anchor — dead slow ahead — right rudder. 2. Pay out anchor chain — dead slow ahead — variable rudder to keep stern clear. 3. Surge anchor chain — slow ahead — variable rudder to keep stern clear. 4. Hard right rudder — slow or dead slow ahead — heave on anchor. 5. Slow or dead slow ahead — variable rudder to keep stern in position. 6. Dead slow ahead — surge anchor chain — variable rudder to bring vessel alongside. 7. Dead slow ahead — hold anchor chain — forward spring line out first — secure in berth.

If the ship is deep loaded, in most cases she can sail by holding one or two strong spring lines leading forward from the stern and heaving on an offshore stern or breast line while coming dead slow astern for a short time on the engines. This will force her bow out into the channel and when it is clear, the lines can be taken in aft and the engines put ahead with a midship rudder, or enough left rudder to keep the suction from holding her stern against the dock while gathering headway. (Figure 1-R).

This procedure can be used with success when sailing a loaded ship which is secured starboard side to the dock as well.

SAILING A LIGHT SHIP WHICH IS SECURED STARBOARD SIDE TO THE DOCK WITHOUT TUG ASSISTANCE

As mentioned earlier, only ships with right hand turning propellers are shown in these illustrations. Ships with left hand turning propellers and variable pitch right turning propellers back to the starboard.

Figures 1-S and 1-T (Page 19) illustrates two ways on how a light vessel which is secured starboard side to the dock may be sailed safely.

Figure 1-S shows off docking in the same manner as if the vessel were secured port side to the dock. However, when her stern is clear, it is helpful if the engines are put full speed astern until she gains some stern way and the engines can be put on dead slow astern while leaving the rudder hard right to help pull her stern to starboard.

In Figure 1-T, the ship needs to be moved as far forward as possible slacking off on the forward spring. The stern spring should be held on the dock as her stern comes away and this can be slacked off some, but not enough for the ship to be able to come into contact with the vessel secured astern. When the stern is breasted out, the engines can be put slow astern while letting go everything forward. As the stern is swung in toward the dock by the after spring, the bow will come out into the channel.

The crew handling the stern spring will have to be on their toes and take this line on deck before it can be caught in the ships propeller.

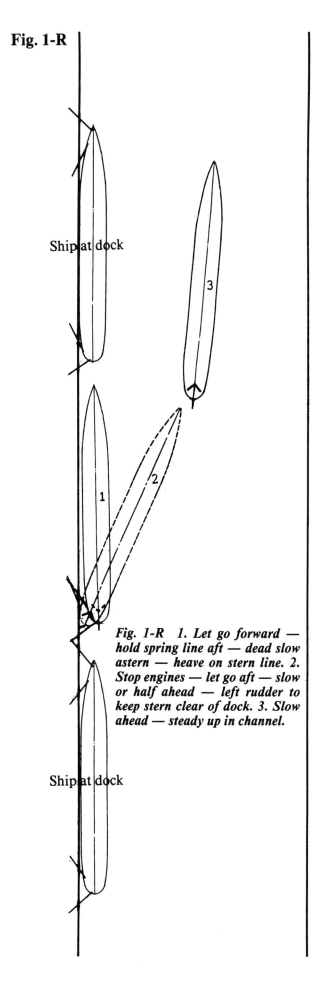

Fig. 1-R

Ship at dock

Ship at dock

Fig. 1-R 1. Let go forward — hold spring line aft — dead slow astern — heave on stern line. 2. Stop engines — let go aft — slow or half ahead — left rudder to keep stern clear of dock. 3. Slow ahead — steady up in channel.

Fig. 1-S

Fig. 1-T

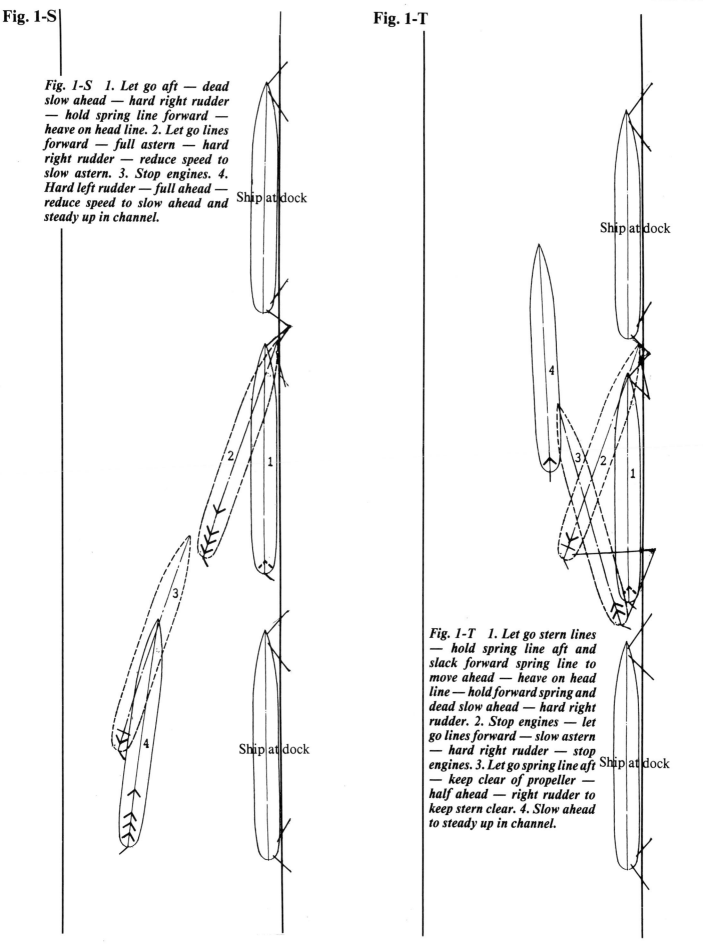

Fig. 1-S   1. Let go aft — dead slow ahead — hard right rudder — hold spring line forward — heave on head line. 2. Let go lines forward — full astern — hard right rudder — reduce speed to slow astern. 3. Stop engines. 4. Hard left rudder — full ahead — reduce speed to slow ahead and steady up in channel.

Ship at dock

Ship at dock

Ship at dock

Ship at dock

Fig. 1-T   1. Let go stern lines — hold spring line aft and slack forward spring line to move ahead — heave on head line — hold forward spring and dead slow ahead — hard right rudder. 2. Stop engines — let go lines forward — slow astern — hard right rudder — stop engines. 3. Let go spring line aft — keep clear of propeller — half ahead — right rudder to keep stern clear. 4. Slow ahead to steady up in channel.

CHAPTER 2

THE PIVOT POINT

The pivot point of a vessel has become quite a controversial subject among some mariners and writers on the subject. It is agreed, however, that it is a point somewhere between the bow and stern where a vessel turns on a vertical axis, and will vary with the trim of a vessel, its speed through the water, from a dead stop to full ahead, from full ahead to stop, the vessel's horse power, etc. At any rate this point will generally be about one-third of the length of the vessel measuring from the bow, to about one-third of her length measuring from her stern. It can, however, move further toward the bow, or further toward the stern under some conditions.

It's not hard to understand that if a vessel displaces the same amount of water from one end to the other on both sides her pivot point would be directly in the middle when stopped dead in the water and equal pressure is applied on each end on opposite sides. The only exception of course would be the obstruction of her propeller and rudder on the stern and the configuration of her bow.

On a vessel with normal seaworthy trim under way full speed through the water, the pivot point is considered to be about one third of her length measuring from the bow. Since the propulsion system of a vessel is on the stern it is understandable that the stern will do the turning as the propeller and rudder power forces it against the water pressure and the bow is forced through the water.

On a vessel down by the head where the water pressure is greatest, the pivot point will be well forward, and a vessel down by the stern with little draft forward, the pivot point may be somewhat different depending on the direction and force of the wind. If there is a strong wind on the starboard side and she is turning to the port her pivot point will be further aft. If she is turning to starboard under the same conditions, it will be further forward. A vessel with good seaworthy trim will have a pivot point well aft when going astern.

On a tug drawing 14 feet with a barge which is drawing only a foot or two, the pivot point will go all the way back to the tug when stopped dead in the water. If however, she is put full ahead with a hardover rudder, and there is no wind, the pivot point will move forward of the mid section of the barges. If the barges are light and setting on top of the water, it will move all the way forward and the barges will drift broadside away from the turn. If she is turning away from the wind, the opposite will be experienced and the pivot point will move aft toward the tug. If she is backed, the wind will carry the barges around and she will back into the wind.

The Pivot Point is an important factor in safe and effective handling of any vessel and will be mentioned in later chapters.

To help in understanding the function of vessels with different drafts under way and stopped, it will be well to study diagrams shown from Figures 2-A through Fig. 2-G (Page 21) which shows the approximate pivot point on vessels with a different trim.

It should be remembered that a ship with ballast on the stern and drawing no water forward, will back into a strong wind, no matter what her backing characteristics are. This is simply because there is no resistance forward and the wind will carry the bow like a sail.

There are seven diagrams designating the pivot point on vessels with different trim, and each of them will read as follows: A — from stopped in water to full ahead. B — normal maneuvering speed ahead. C — underway but stopped in water.

Fig. 2-A

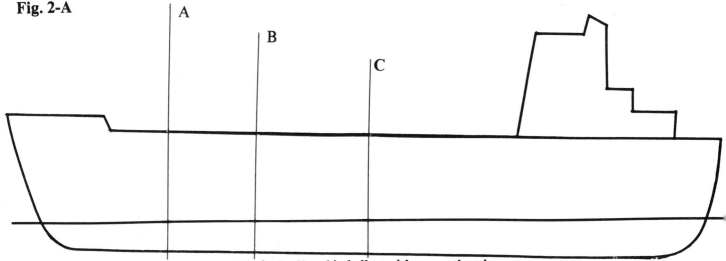

Fig. 2-A   Vessel in ballast with seaworthy trim.

Fig. 2-B

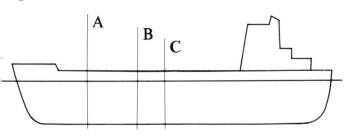

Fig. 2-B   Fully loaded vessel with normal trim.

Fig. 2-C

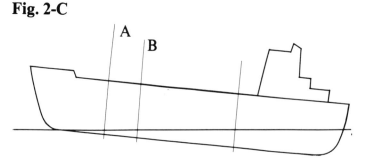

Fig. 2-C   Vessel down by the stern.

Fig. 2-D

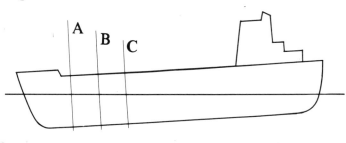

Fig. 2-D   Vessel down by the head.

Fig. 2-E

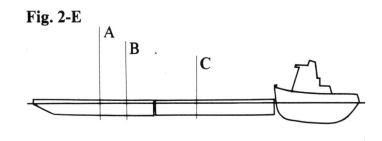

Fig. 2-E   Tug with loaded barges.

Fig. 2-F

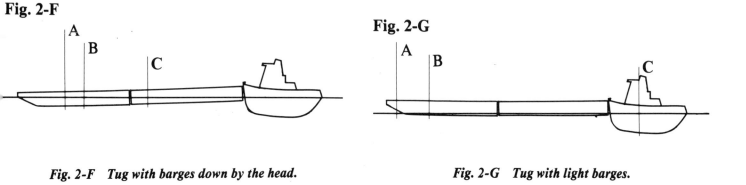

Fig. 2-F   Tug with barges down by the head.

Fig. 2-G

Fig. 2-G   Tug with light barges.

CHAPTER 3

HOLDING UP IN NARROW, LIMITED DRAFT CHANNELS

In discussing "Narrow, Limited Draft Channels" we will consider channels with a width of 250 to 500 feet and a deepest depth of 40 to 50 feet.

Wind does not affect deep draft vessels in narrow channels to any extent. However, broadside currents are a different matter and must be held up against in order for the vessel to steer and handle properly.

In many cases strong winds coming from any direction affect light vessels more than currents. However, when both are coming from the same direction (which is experienced more often than not) good judgement is necessary in order to keep the vessel from drifting aground. When the wind and current are broadside or nearly so, and the vessel is allowed to drift aground, it is almost always necessary to obtain assistance in order to refloat and get under way again. "See Figures 3-A & 3-A1". (Page 22)

Loaded vessels act differently under the above circumstances. With good headway they will run from the bank seeking deep water no matter what the wind and current may be doing. If however, they are stopped and

Fig. 3-A

Ranges

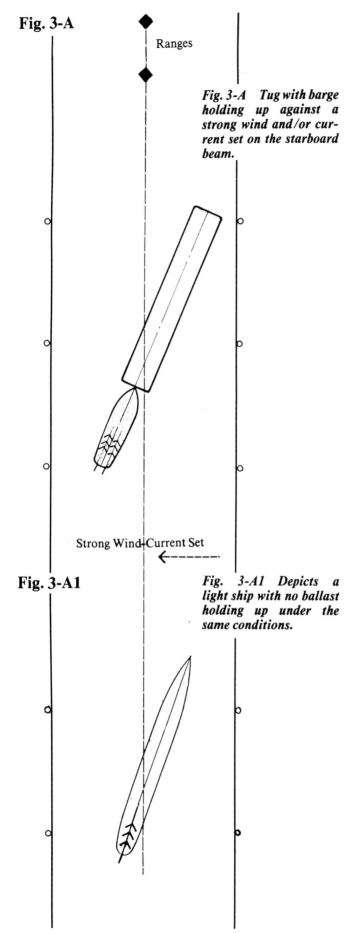

Fig. 3-A   Tug with barge holding up against a strong wind and/or current set on the starboard beam.

Strong Wind Current Set

Fig. 3-A1

Fig. 3-A1   Depicts a light ship with no ballast holding up under the same conditions.

the wind and current are allowed to press them against the bank, it is difficult and sometimes impossible to get them under way again without assistance. Figures 3-B and 3-C (Page 23) illustrates loaded vessels making good headway and out of position in the channel. Notice how they will take rudder against the bank when they are too close to it. If the engines were to be stopped or the rudder put midship they would take off across the channel as if they had been given rudder to do so.

The best thing to remember is that a properly trimmed vessel with good steerage way will take rudder toward the place of most resistance and will run to that place of least resistance. Their propeller wash which is moving the water away from a bank or shoal water and even from another loaded or partially loaded vessel, will cause the stern to move that way, and of course the bow is bound to be going in the other direction. This is called suction effect. Especially with good headway, the water cushion between the bow and bank as it rushes by is forcing the bow away, while the propeller on the stern is eliminating this pressure by washing the water away.

Figure 3-D (Page 23) illustrates the approximate angle which a vessel with good draft will need to be held up against a strong broadside current and set.

Vessels with very little draft and tugs with light barges need to be very careful about letting their stern come against a bank, shoal water, or even another vessel because very little suction effect exists and they will swing around to the point of least resistance when the stern has touched.

In determining the amount of drift the easy way is to put the vessel on a straight course and instead of looking at the bow just turn around and look at the stern. By doing this, you can readily see the amount of drift. Then by observing ranges ahead or astern, it is not difficult to determine the course necessary to steer in order to stay in the proper position in the channel.

With good headway, the rudder indicator is your best friend. Except under extreme conditions, the vessel will take rudder toward a bank when the stern is close, and the closer the stern comes to the bank, the more rudder she will take in that direction. At night and in poor visibility, constantly glancing at the rudder indicator can mean the difference of going aground or staying underway.

About the only exception to the above will be when a vessel is setting on top of the water with no draft forward and not enough draft aft for her propeller to get a good grip in the water while having a strong wind and set abeam. Under these conditions she will take rudder toward the wind and will most likely be going broadside about as fast as she is going forward. Even then

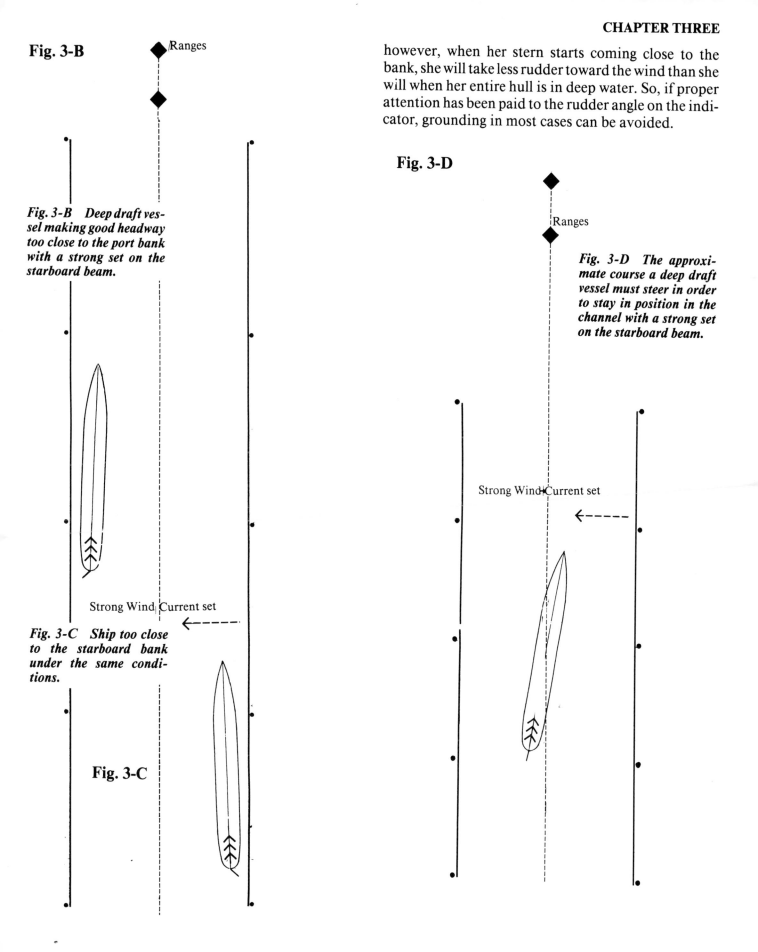

Fig. 3-B

Ranges

Fig. 3-B   Deep draft vessel making good headway too close to the port bank with a strong set on the starboard beam.

however, when her stern starts coming close to the bank, she will take less rudder toward the wind than she will when her entire hull is in deep water. So, if proper attention has been paid to the rudder angle on the indicator, grounding in most cases can be avoided.

Fig. 3-D

Ranges

Fig. 3-D   The approximate course a deep draft vessel must steer in order to stay in position in the channel with a strong set on the starboard beam.

Strong Wind Current set

Fig. 3-C   Ship too close to the starboard bank under the same conditions.

Strong Wind Current set

Fig. 3-C

CHAPTER 4

PASSING IN NARROW CHANNELS

OVERTAKING AND PASSING ANOTHER VESSEL HEADED IN THE SAME DIRECTION IN NARROW LIMITED DRAFT CHANNELS

This maneuver can be executed safely and efficiently even with large ships as long as the overtaking vessel is light. This is almost always the reason for the situation to exist except when the overtaken vessel is waiting for a berth or having mechanical difficulty. Which in either case they should be stopped and at anchor, or at least have tug boat assistance.

It should be understood a vessel wishing to pass another vessel under way, is required to give the proper signal and the vessel that is to be passed must answer that signal if they agree to be passed, as explained in the navigation and pilot rules.

As depicted in Figure 4-A, vessel (A) is overtaking vessel (B) and wishes to pass by sounding one whistle (that is by leaving vessel (B) on her port side). (A) should come up close to the stern of (B) and swing to starboard while (B) swings to her port. As the bow of (A) clears the stern of (B), (A) should increase her engine speed while (B) should maintain bare steerage way. Both vessels should keep their sterns in deep water until they are at least abeam of each other before they feel the suction from their respective banks. If this is done and vessel (A) has (B) on or aft of her beam, she will be well clear by the time both vessels have sheered back into the middle of the channel.

Two large deep draft vessels can pass in this manner, however this is not recommended unless the vessel being passed has tug boat assistance, or at least drags one or both anchors until the other is past and clear.

Fig. 4-A   A — Slow ahead. B — Dead slow ahead with bare steerage way — left rudder. A-1 — Full or half ahead — swing to starboard. B-1 — Swing to port. A-2 — Variable right rudder. B-2 — variable left rudder — slow ahead. A-3 — Variable rudder. B-3 — Variable rudder. A-4 — Steer toward center of channel. B-4 — Steer toward and steady up in center of channel. A-5 — Steady up in center of channel.

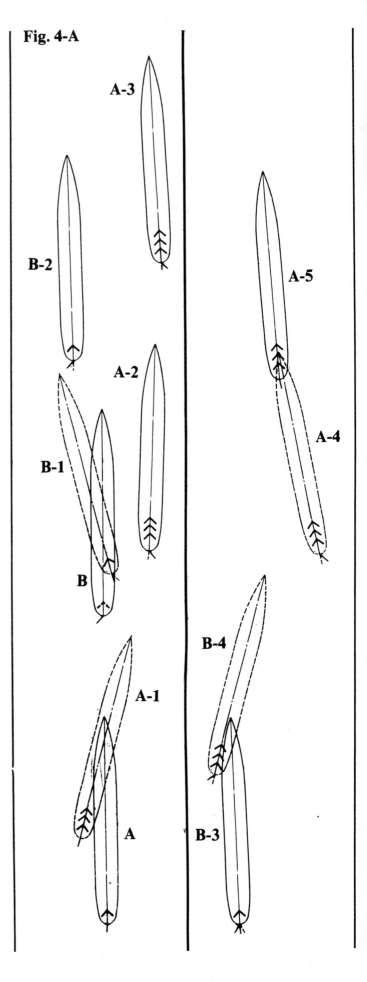

Fig. 4-A

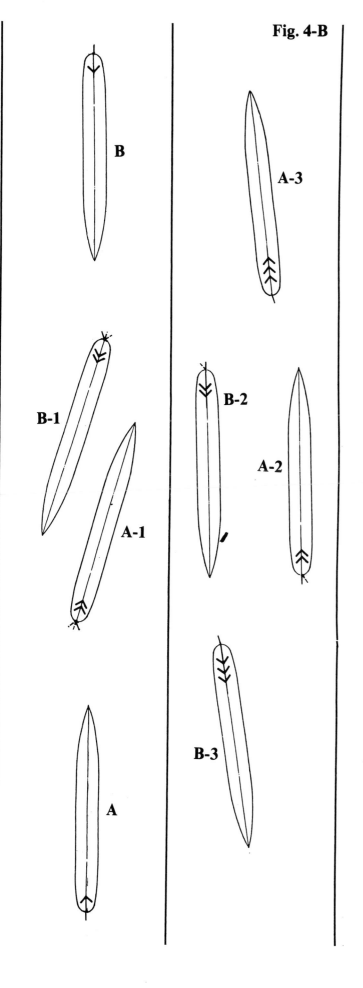

Fig. 4-B

MEETING AND PASSING HEAD ON IN NARROW LIMITED DRAFT CHANNELS

This situation is not so touchy as in the overtaking and passing situation. A vessel is advised however never to move over to the edge of the channel until she is ready to meet and pass. Once she has taken a suction and sheered back toward the middle of the channel, nothing will stop her until her stern is back in deep water. The larger and deeper the vessel and the more speed she has, the harder she will sheer.

Any good ship handler who is moving a vessel down the middle of a channel and observes another vessel he is meeting holding against the bank will stop, go aground, anchor, or do most anything necessary to keep from having a collision.

The problem with most of these ship handlers who try to hold a vessel against the bank, are subject to panic when meeting another vessel and find that their rudder is already hard over toward the bank. They may then stop their engines, drop one or both anchors, put the engines full astern, and go crossways in the channel in front of the vessel they are supposed to meet and pass safely.

The ironic part of this is that if anyone lives to tell about it, these people are always in the right because they did drop both anchors and backed her full speed, while the other vessel which was in complete control has no place to go but into the bank or stop with her engines and anchors.

It is good practice to try to always maneuver a vessel in a position so that she can be run aground on the right hand side of the channel if there is no other choice. However, if circumstances make it necessary in order to avoid a collision, either bank will do. (Figure 4-B).

Fig. 4-B A — Steady in center of channel. B — Steady in center of channel. A-1 — Swing to starboard. B-1 — Swings to starboard. A-2 — Variable rudder. B-2 — Variable rudder. A-3 — Steady up in center of channel. B-3 — Steady up in center of channel.

CHAPTER 5

NAVIGATING NARROW LIMITED DRAFT CHANNELS WITH SHARP BENDS AND TURNS

CUTTING THE CORNER

It has already been explained that a deep loaded vessel will run from a bank or shoal water. We know from reading the Navigation and Pilot rules that a vessel is supposed to (when it is safe and practical) stay to the right side of the channel. There is no way of knowing if a bank has caved off or a shoal has built up that cannot be seen beneath the water. It is not hard to visualize what would happen if another vessel were approaching from the opposite direction as shown in Figure 5-A.

HOLDING DEEP IN THE BEND

On a loaded vessel navigating a narrow channel with her hull near the bottom, turns in bends in the channel can best be made by moving the vessel to the outside part of the bend and start feeling suction off of that bank before the turn is to be made.

For example, if a loaded vessel is approaching a right turn with good headway and is taking 10-15 degrees of rudder against the port bank (outside part of the bend) just prior to making the turn, she will immediately start to turn when the rudder is put midship. Depending on the ship's size and speed, it will take very little right rudder if any to complete the turn and head down in the middle of the channel. If this procedure is practiced when there is no traffic, it gives the pilot a good feeling of the suction effect on that individual vessel, and is helpful in meeting and passing other traffic. (Figure 5-B).

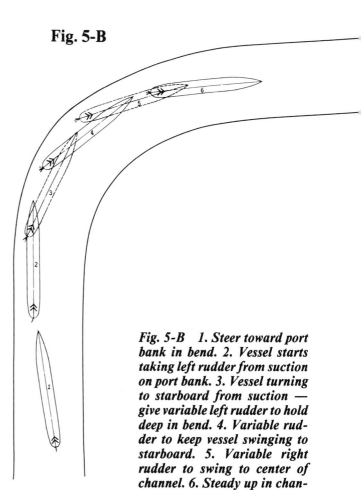

Fig. 5-A

Fig. 5-A   Ship taking suction off starboard bank.

Fig. 5-B

Fig. 5-B   1. Steer toward port bank in bend. 2. Vessel starts taking left rudder from suction on port bank. 3. Vessel turning to starboard from suction — give variable left rudder to hold deep in bend. 4. Variable rudder to keep vessel swinging to starboard. 5. Variable right rudder to swing to center of channel. 6. Steady up in channel.

MEETING AND PASSING IN THE BEND

With the bridge-to-bridge communication that we have today there is really no need for this sort of thing to happen but it does. There is no big problem as long as both vessels conduct themselves properly.

In Figure 5-C, we have vessels (A) and (B) approaching each other. (A) Should be holding left rudder against her port bank as she approaches the bend, and (B) should start taking right rudder against her starboard bank as she comes down into the deep part of the

port bank to be in position to make the next turn. Of course the starboard anchor can be put on the bottom to help hold her bow, which is better than climbing the bank, but in most cases it will be necessary to pick it up before the next bend can be made as illustrated in Figure 5-C.

Figure 5-D illustrates the ease with which two vessel can meet and pass if they arrange to do so between the bends. In this manner it leaves both vessels in position to have the deep part of the bend for making the next turn.

Fig. 5-C

Fig. 5-D

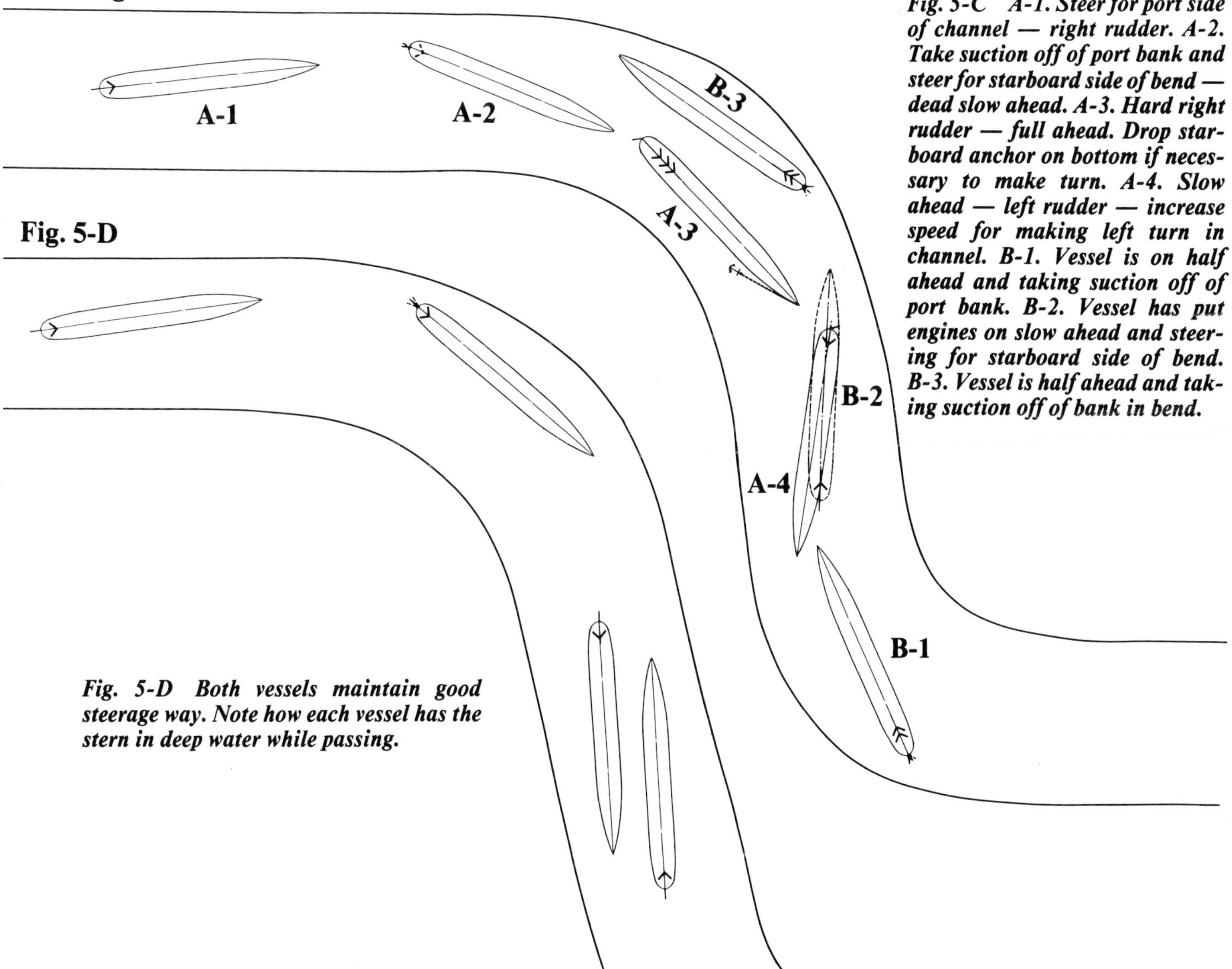

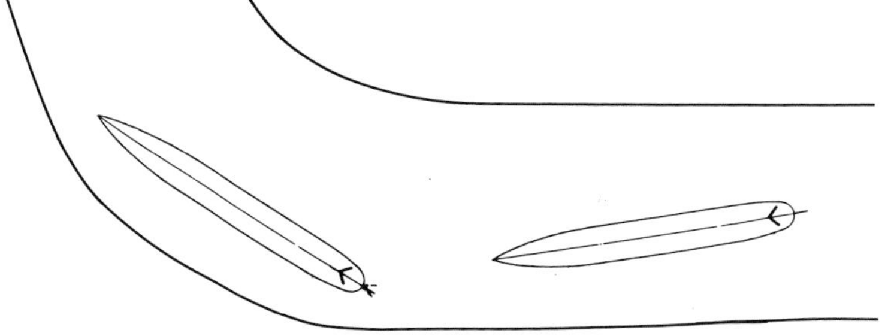

Fig. 5-C A-1. Steer for port side of channel — right rudder. A-2. Take suction off of port bank and steer for starboard side of bend — dead slow ahead. A-3. Hard right rudder — full ahead. Drop starboard anchor on bottom if necessary to make turn. A-4. Slow ahead — left rudder — increase speed for making left turn in channel. B-1. Vessel is on half ahead and taking suction off of port bank. B-2. Vessel has put engines on slow ahead and steering for starboard side of bend. B-3. Vessel is half ahead and taking suction off of bank in bend.

Fig. 5-D Both vessels maintain good steerage way. Note how each vessel has the stern in deep water while passing.

bend. As (B) starts sheering to her left making the turn in the deep part of the bend, (A) should be sheering to her right toward the inside part of the turn. For vessel (B) there is no trouble at all. She should wind up in the middle of the channel after the turn just the same as if no other vessel had been there, but the pilot on vessel (A) could have a problem if he is not on top of the situation. The vessel may need all the engine ahead power she has immediately while abeam, or just after passing (B) in order to keep from sheering too far toward her

CHAPTER 6

REFLOATING A GROUNDED VESSEL

In many cases, when a vessel is grounded at only one part of her hull and the rest is in deep water, she can refloat herself by pumping her fuel, water, and ballast to that part of the hull that is in deep water. This procedure is generally used when there are no tugs available or no assistance is desired. However, if she cannot refloat herself and a tug or tugs are necessary, the following illustration should be helpful.

In almost all cases a vessel which has run aground should be taken off as near as possible in the opposite direction as she was headed when she went aground. There are cases however, where a vessel has jumped over a shoal. If there is not enough rise in tide to float her back over this shoal, the only thing to do is lighten her in order to get her free. If her rudder and propeller(s) are on the shoal, the possibility of doing damage to both exist if the engines are used.

Figure 6-A shows a vessel aground on the bow (which is usually the case) with one tug assisting.

If this were a steep bluff bank, there is a good chance that it would cave off by swinging the stern back and forth with the tug and ship's power allowing the ship to slide off and float free. If this is not the case and she is aground on a sloping bank, the tug should try to swing her stern back and forth as much as possible to break the hull's suction against the bottom, then pull in the opposite direction from which the ship was heading when she went aground. If this procedure does not free her, and there are no other tugs available, the tug can run either one or both anchors out alongside the hull, as shown, and heave on the anchors(s) while backing the ship and having the tug pull as before.

When two or more tugs are necessary, this writer has had success by having them put a hawser out from the stern of the tug to the bow of the ship and head toward the stern of the ship, as shown in Figure 6-B. The wash from the tug's propeller(s) tends to wash the bank away from the ship's bow if the ship is not fully loaded. If the ship is heavily loaded however, the tug's propeller wash will not even come close to where the ships bottom is grounded.

If aground in or near a fairway, and there is sufficient room, ships passing at full speed are very helpful in breaking the bottom suction. However, in asking a ves-

Fig. 6-A   Tug has run out both of ships anchors and is pulling from the stern.

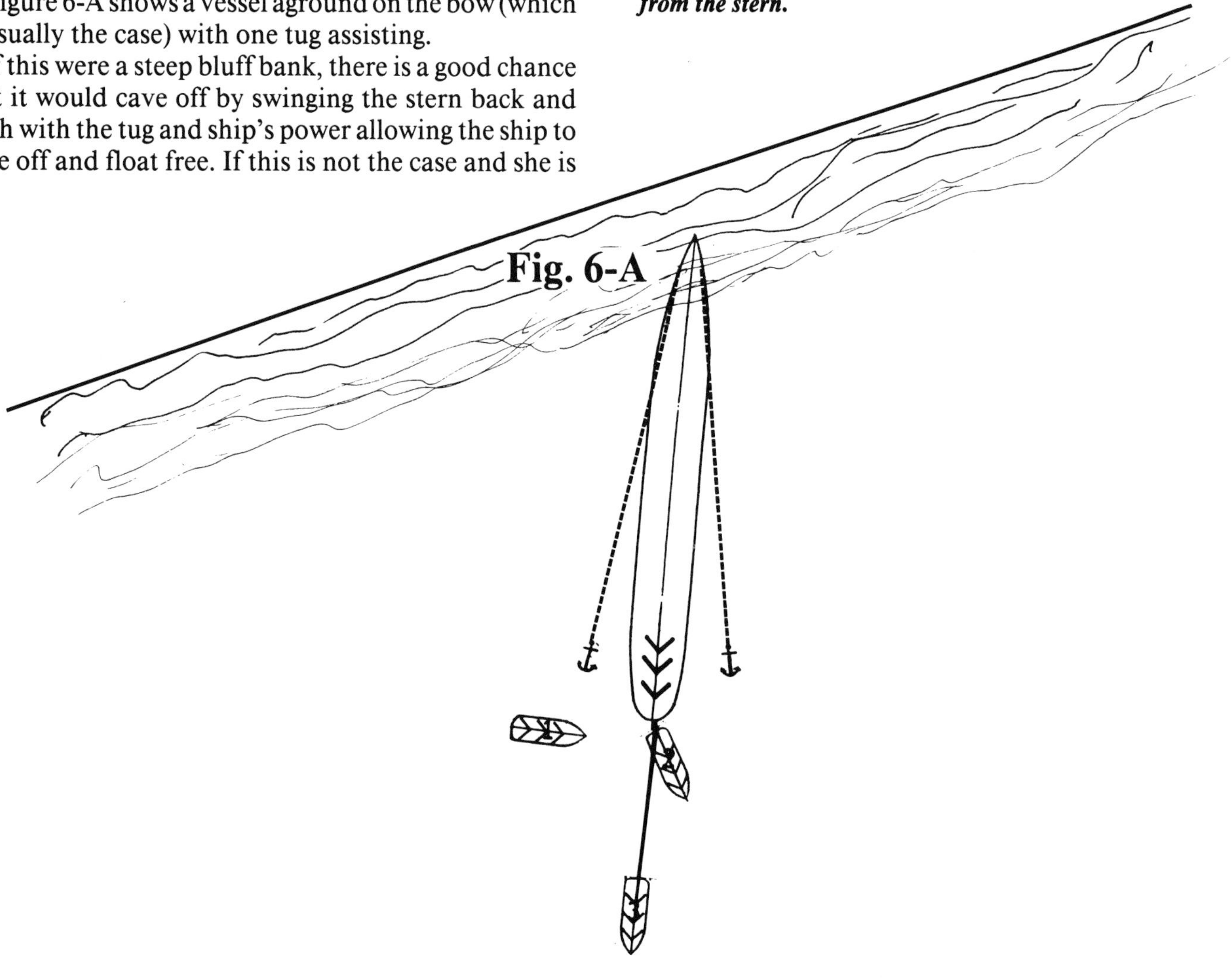

Fig. 6-A

sel to come by full speed, care should be taken not to back the ship or work the tugs full speed until the passing vessel is sufficiently clear, to ensure that the grounded vessel does not back out in front of the vessel going full speed. A ship, especially a loaded one, moving full speed in a narrow channel builds up a good bit of water ahead of it, much the same as a rise in the tide. As she moves over the ground however, she drags a large swell behind her.

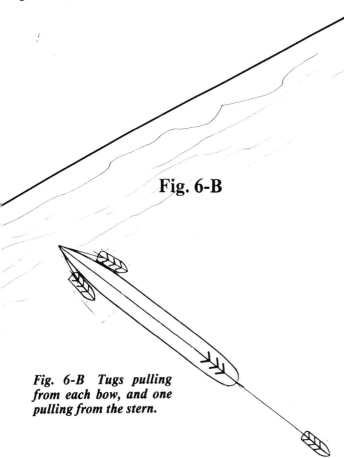

Fig. 6-B

Fig. 6-B Tugs pulling from each bow, and one pulling from the stern.

COASTAL GROUNDING

Grounding a large ship on a sea coast presents somewhat of a different problem.

If grounding occurs on a jetty, rock shoreline or hard coral, most likely the outside hull will be torn open. If the ship is constructed with a double bottom which may not be ruptured, she may still be able to float herself to port if she can be freed. If possible, a quick inspection of her hull to see if it is punctured would be the thing to do, and if it is safe she might free herself by coming astern on the engines. If not, the best thing to do is to ballast her down as much as possible in order to keep her from working up and down and surging with the sea and swells (which are generally always there) until assistance or further preparations can be made. Always, the amount and time of the rise and fall of tide should be determined immediately.

If the ship is grounded where there is a sand or clay bottom the procedure would be basically the same. There can always be an uncharted wreck or obstruction on the bottom, but if there is not, the movement of the water will most likely keep her working further ashore if she is not ballasted down to rest hard on the bottom.

REFLOATING THE HARD WAY WITHOUT ASSISTANCE

With today's modern ships and modern seamen, this procedure may seem to be obsolete and more unnecessary than the old time methods. However, these methods still work and deserve explanation here.

The old-timers used wooden timbers or spars to lash and hold two life boats together but spread apart enough for an anchor to hang between the two of them. (Remember, in those days there were very few motor life boats if any, to move these boats and they had to be moved by people with oars rowing in order to carry the anchors out and place them in the proper position for freeing the vessel).

Of course, finding wooden spars or timbers on board that would be long enough or strong enough to carry an anchor would be unlikely, but there should be pipe or small cargo booms that could be cut to do the job as shown in Figure 6-C. (Page 30).

Remember, the life boats will need to carry the anchor line in addition to the anchor and pay it out as the boats move through the water. Since in most cases the ship's anchor chain will be too heavy, a large cable or coil of line will do the job and can be carried to the anchor windlass for heaving when the anchor is set. Nylon line would work well as long as it does not chafe and cut, because it is lighter and more pliable than cable and will stretch to keep a constant strain on the anchor. The more modern ships with mooring winches would also handle the job nicely.

Fig. 6-C

Fig. 6-C Running anchor with two lifeboats lashed together.

Good judgement would dictate the continued operation. If it is felt that the vessel can float herself when the anchor line(s) have been heaved tight, she should pump out the ballast where her hull is grounded. If this is not the case however, she should wait until just before the next high tide before trying to free herself so that her hull does not work against the bottom.

TEMPORARY REPAIR TO RUPTURED HULL

Regardless of where a rupture or tear may occur where water can enter along the underwater part of the hull (other than a large gaping hole) it can be plugged long enough to permit the patching of the hole from the inside of the vessel. This is done by using a plate, timber or cement shored up from the inside that will hold long enough to move the vessel into drydock.

A mattress, folded tarpaulin or pillow (depending on the size of the rupture) can be used to hold out most of the water while these temporary repairs are being made. A mattress with a line made fast to each corner can be used, with two of the lines passed under the hull and two lines held on the deck to be payed off as the mattress is pulled toward the rupture. (Figure 6-D).

When the mattress nears the rupture, the water entering the vessel will take it directly to the hole, and the lines can be made fast to hold it there while repairs are being made.

Needless to say, this procedure should be followed immediately after the rupture occurs.

Fig. 6-D

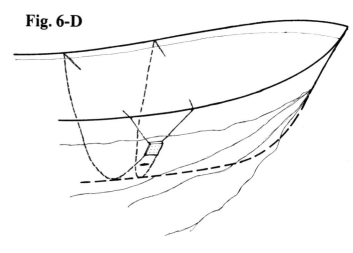

Fig. 6-D Placing mattress over rupture in hull for emergency repairs.

CHAPTER 7

BOW-THRUSTERS EXPLAINED

The more modern ships and many smaller vessels constructed since about 1955, are equipped with "Bow-Thrusters" as a means of helping them maneuver in close and difficult places. Needless to say, they are a great help when they work. However, one should first learn to work without them so that when they break down, there will be no interference with the operation of the vessel.

The standard Bow-Thruster is nothing more than a flared tube or pipe running thwartships, (horizontal, from one side of the vessel to the other) fitted well forward and near the bottom of the vessel's hull, with a propeller centered over the keel facing the tube openings to act as a pump to force water from one side of the vessel to the other. (Figures 7-A and 7-B). Of course the water coming out of the side of the vessel under pressure forces the bow in the opposite direction. They are mostly wheelhouse control with easy access to one or more single control levers that controls both the direction and speed the propeller will turn. If properly installed the bow will go in the direction the lever is pushed. It should be understood however, that the owner or builders may install the control(s) so that they operate differently and in different locations. Some owners and builders make it a practice to install a control at the bow-thruster engine, along with a telegraph, and/or telephone so that it can be operated by orders from the bridge in an emergency.

On a vessel with good steerage way, the bow-thruster is of little or no use at all because the water cannot make

Fig. 7-A

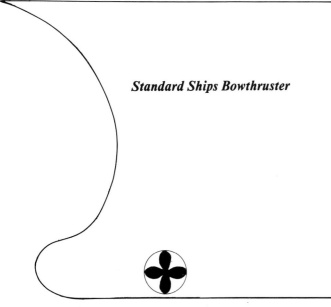

Standard Ships Bowthruster

the right angle turn into the tube as fast as it is forced out on the opposite side and the propeller can only cavitate, (pumping a mixture of air and water) which is extremely hard on the whole system and accomplishes nothing.

The standard bow-thrusters are very helpful on large ships for docking and off docking when tug boat service is limited or not wanted.

Their function however is limited compared to tugs because many of them do not have sufficient power. They will not help a ship lose headway, nor will they help to hold a steady course until the ship has come to almost a complete stop.

The standard bow-thruster is helpful on large sea going tugs when maneuvering to handle offshore drilling rigs, lay barges, anchors, etc. However, they are of more benefit to the offshore supply and support craft because these vessels generally are much larger, and with the exception of the combination Offshore Supply/Towing Vessels, have less power than the deep sea tugs.

Bow-Thrusters will be discussed in later chapters pertaining to maneuvering these vessels.

Fig. 7-B

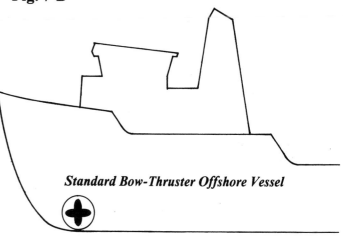

Standard Bow-Thruster Offshore Vessel

Over the years there have been more efficient bow-thrusters and maneuvering devices designed, and some of these are on the market today. However, it seems the cost of this sort of equipment, and its somewhat unproven effectiveness, makes it undesirable to present day ship owners.

This writer designed one such maneuvering system some years ago (illustrated on pages 32, 33), and a few similar systems are installed and in operation at present.

Instead of water being forced from one side of the ship to the other, it is taken in, or forced out of the bow and/or bottom of the hull, and on either or both sides of the bow as desired, while the water force is kept in a circular motion. Thus, by manipulating valves and fins, the thruster also acts as a stopping and turning device, plus broadside movement as needed. It would also help increase headway if desired.

Shown here, and page 33, are illustrations of some of the modes of operation of this system.

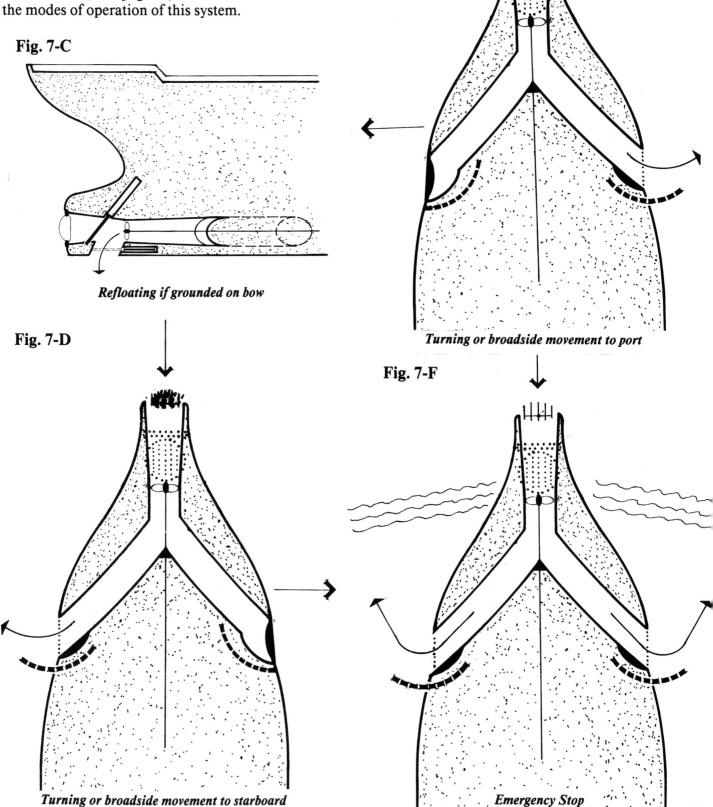

Fig. 7-C

Refloating if grounded on bow

Fig. 7-D

Turning or broadside movement to starboard

Fig. 7-E

Turning or broadside movement to port

Fig. 7-F

Emergency Stop

Fig. 7-G

Fig. 7-H

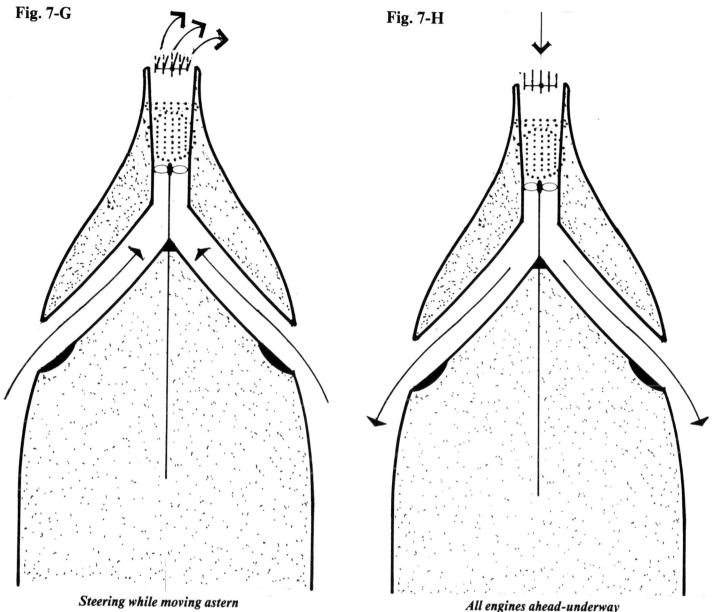

Steering while moving astern

All engines ahead-underway

CHAPTER 8
HANDLING SHIPS WITH STANDARD BOW-THRUSTER

DOCKING PORT SIDE TO

If a ship is docking port side to the dock and has ample room, a vessel with a bow-thruster would dock in the same manner as any other vessel under the same circumstances. However, if she is going between two other ships with possibly ten feet clearance on each end, it should be done as illustrated in Figure 8-A. (Page 34).

She should come in at an angle toward the dock at a very slow speed and swing her bow away with right rudder which swings her stern in toward the dock, making sure that the stern will clear the ship astern. The bow should be clear of the ship tied up ahead so that if the engines going astern does not stop her headway she will have some place to go. The bow-thruster should be able to hold the vessel in this position after her stern is nearly in position long enough for a stern line and spring line aft to be put on the dock. After this is done and the lines are tight, the bow-thruster can then push her alongside.

DOCKING STARBOARD SIDE TO

Since the ship backs to port, the procedure should be the same whether the ship is going to an open dock or docking between two ships.

With very little headway, the vessel should approach the dock at an angle and swing the bow away, the same as when docking port side to. When the engines are backed, the bow-thruster should thrust the bow away from the dock in order to hold her stern up to the dock close enough to put out a stern and spring line aft. After this is done, and the lines have a strain, the bow-thruster can thrust her alongside. (Fig. 8-B).

On occasion it will be found that a bow-thruster on a large ship is more efficient than a tug on the bow. For instance, if a ship is going into a narrow slip to secure where other ships are tied up, leaving little or no room

Fig. 8-A

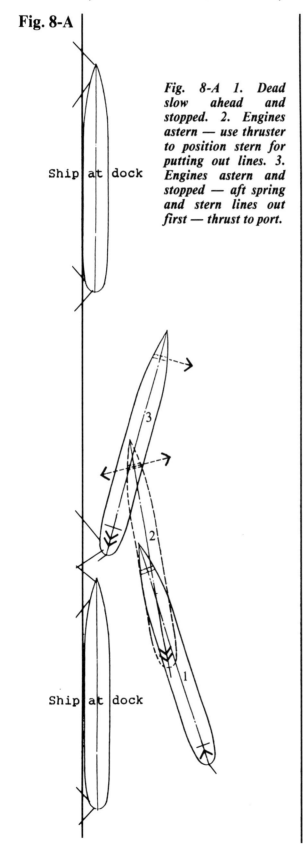

Fig. 8-A 1. Dead slow ahead and stopped. 2. Engines astern — use thruster to position stern for putting out lines. 3. Engines astern and stopped — aft spring and stern lines out first — thrust to port.

Ship at dock

Ship at dock

Fig. 8-B

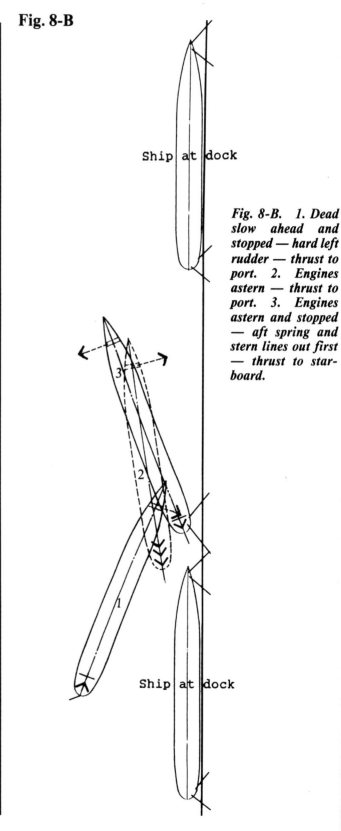

Ship at dock

Fig. 8-B. 1. Dead slow ahead and stopped — hard left rudder — thrust to port. 2. Engines astern — thrust to port. 3. Engines astern and stopped — aft spring and stern lines out first — thrust to star-board.

Ship at dock

for a tug to secure on the bow and maneuver into position, the bow-thruster is very beneficial. (Figure 8-C).

In slack water, she can pivot off the end of the slip and with very little headway, she can steer herself to her berth while making use of the bow-thruster as needed.

If a head current exist in a maneuvering situation such as illustrated in Figure 8-C1, the starboard anchor would be the proper one to use. It should be dropped off the upstream end of the slip. If a stern current exist, the port anchor dropped a little down-stream of center of the slip would be more useful. (Fig. 8-C2) (Page 36).

Fig. 8-C

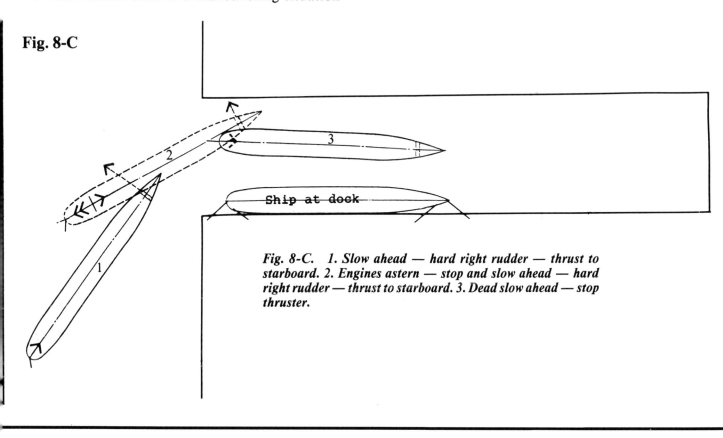

Fig. 8-C. 1. Slow ahead — hard right rudder — thrust to starboard. 2. Engines astern — stop and slow ahead — hard right rudder — thrust to starboard. 3. Dead slow ahead — stop thruster.

Fig. 8-C1 Current

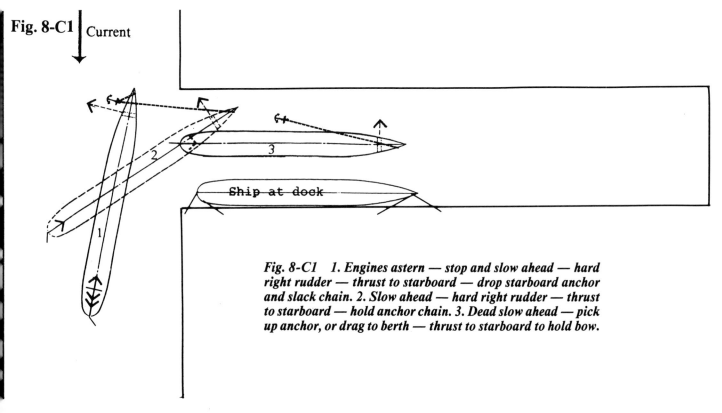

Fig. 8-C1 1. Engines astern — stop and slow ahead — hard right rudder — thrust to starboard — drop starboard anchor and slack chain. 2. Slow ahead — hard right rudder — thrust to starboard — hold anchor chain. 3. Dead slow ahead — pick up anchor, or drag to berth — thrust to starboard to hold bow.

Fig. 8-C2

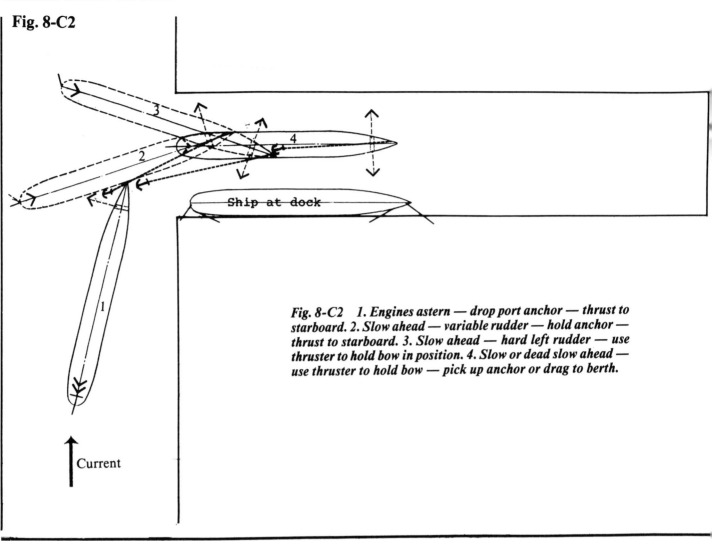

Ship at dock

Fig. 8-C2 1. Engines astern — drop port anchor — thrust to starboard. 2. Slow ahead — variable rudder — hold anchor — thrust to starboard. 3. Slow ahead — hard left rudder — use thruster to hold bow in position. 4. Slow or dead slow ahead — use thruster to hold bow — pick up anchor or drag to berth.

Current

OFF DOCKING SHIP EQUIPPED WITH BOW-THRUSTER

Figure 8-D (Page 37) illustrates taking a ship away from the dock when there is slack, calm water and wind.

All lines can be taken in except a spring and head line, and if desired, the head line can be heaved on while the bow-thruster pushes toward the dock to bring the ships stern out into the channel. When the stern is well out into the channel, the head and spring lines can be taken in and the bow-thruster can push her bow away from the dock into the channel and all that is necessary is to come ahead on the engines and stop the bow-thruster.

If the ship is light and there is a strong off-dock wind, the only thing necessary to do is to get the ship moving with good steerage way as soon as she is clear to keep her from drifting across the channel.

On the other hand, if there is a strong on-dock wind, it may be necessary to back her out into the channel, while keeping in mind that the faster the vessel moves through the water, either ahead or astern, the less effi-

cient the bow-thruster is. (Figure 8-E) (Page 37).

Off docking from a channel side dock with a stern current is no trouble at all.

Hold a spring line forward, and let the bow-thruster push the bow against the dock, breasting her stern out. As the current catches her stern and swings it into the channel, the engines can be put astern while letting go the spring line and reversing the bow-thruster to thrust the bow away from the dock and clear of the ship secured ahead. Then the engines can be put ahead for normal steerage way and the bow-thruster stopped. (Figure 8-F) (Page 38).

Off docking with a head current from the same position as in Figure 8-F is almost as simple, except the procedure is reversed, as shown in Figure 8-G. (Page 38)

All lines are cast off and taken in except the stern spring line aft. The bow-thruster, if needed, can thrust the bow out away from the dock and as the current catches the bow, the stern spring line is taken in, and the engines put ahead with rudder toward the dock to

Fig. 8-D

Fig. 8-E

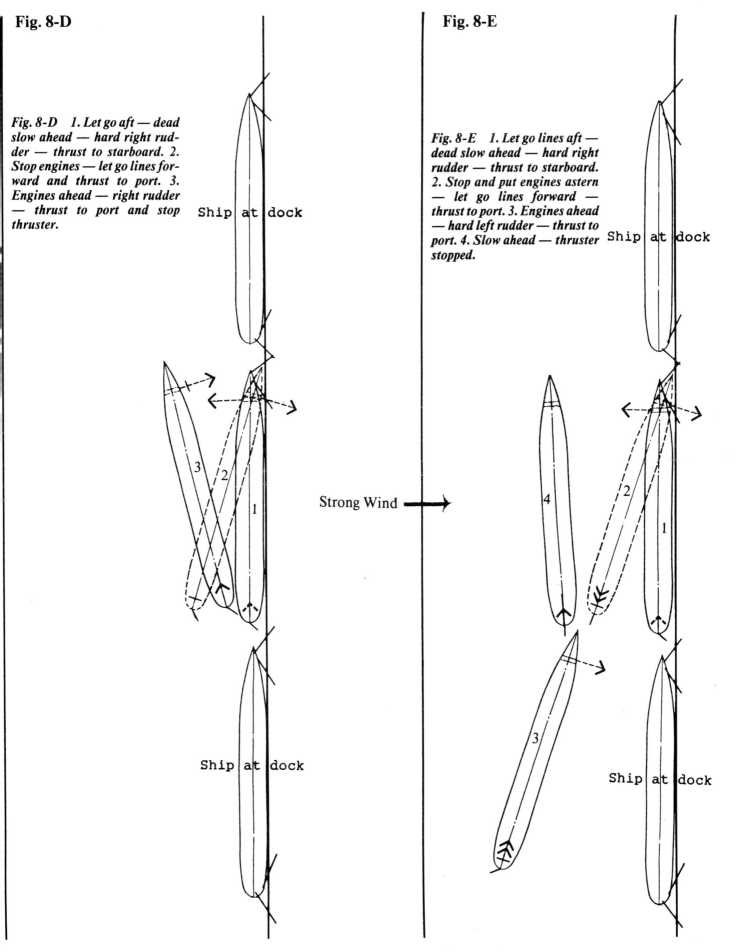

Fig. 8-D 1. Let go aft — dead slow ahead — hard right rudder — thrust to starboard. 2. Stop engines — let go lines forward and thrust to port. 3. Engines ahead — right rudder — thrust to port and stop thruster.

Ship at dock

Fig. 8-E 1. Let go lines aft — dead slow ahead — hard right rudder — thrust to starboard. 2. Stop and put engines astern — let go lines forward — thrust to port. 3. Engines ahead — hard left rudder — thrust to port. 4. Slow ahead — thruster stopped.

Ship at dock

Strong Wind →

Ship at dock

Ship at dock

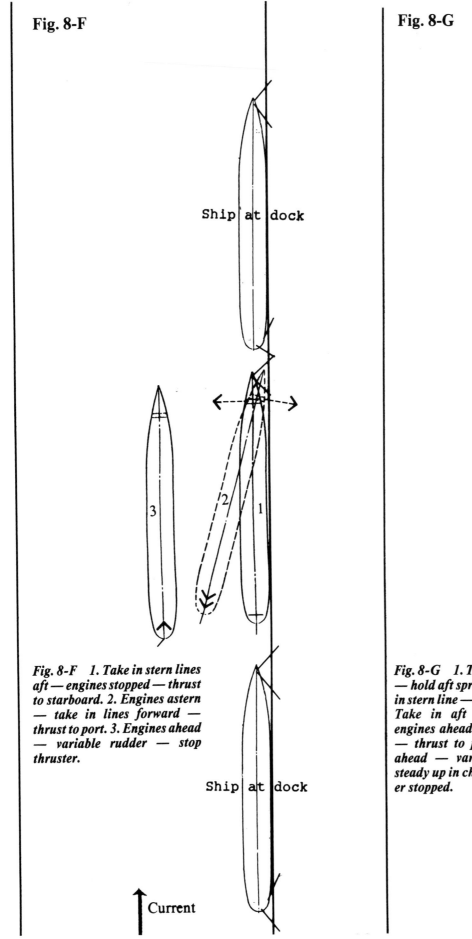

Fig. 8-F

Fig. 8-G

Current

Ship at dock

Ship at dock

Ship at dock

Fig. 8-F 1. Take in stern lines aft — engines stopped — thrust to starboard. 2. Engines astern — take in lines forward — thrust to port. 3. Engines ahead — variable rudder — stop thruster.

Fig. 8-G 1. Take in head lines — hold aft spring line and take in stern line — thrust to port. 2. Take in aft spring line — engines ahead — right rudder — thrust to port. 3. Engines ahead — variable rudder to steady up in channel — thruster stopped.

Ship at dock

Current

Fig. 8-H

keep the rudder and propeller clear of the dock. If the current starts to carry the bow out into the channel too fast, it may be necessary for the bow-thruster to thrust the bow toward the dock in order for the rudder and propeller to clear.

Moving from a slip with slack water, into the channel with a strong current, is another matter altogether. Figure 8-H presents the easy way of doing it if circumstances and conditions permit.

The bow of the ship can lay against the corner of the dock as she is eased out into the current. The bow-thruster can push the bow against the current to ease the strain on the dock and the ships hull. As the ship moves slowly into the channel and the pivot point is past the corner of the dock, her engines can be put full ahead with a hard right rudder and the bow-thruster can be reversed to push the bow to starboard, in order to pick the ships stern up off of the dock as she swings to head with the current.

Figure 8-H1 (Page 40) illustrates the more difficult way of getting out into the current and channel.

The ship should work toward the current side of the slip at as much of an angle as possible, and as the current starts to come against the bow, the thruster should start pushing the bow against it while the ship moves slowly out into the channel. When the ship is far enough out of the slip so that her stern will clear, her engines can be put full ahead with a hard right rudder while the bow-thruster is reversed to push her bow

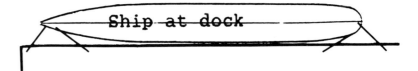

Fig. 8-H   1. Take in all lines — dead slow ahead — rudder midship — thrust to port when bow is in current. 2. Full ahead — hard right rudder — thrust to starboard. 3. Thrust to starboard and stop thruster — full astern — rudder midships — stop — engines ahead — variable rudder. 4. Slow ahead to steady up in channel.

Current

around to starboard, and the ship's engines are put full astern to make her pivot and straighten up with the channel. The engines can then be put ahead for maneuvering and the bow-thruster stopped.

Fig. 8-H1

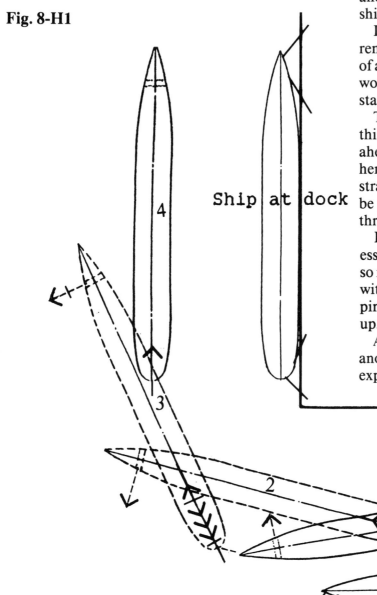

Ship at dock

Fig. 8-H1 1. Slow ahead — thrust to port. 2. Full ahead — hard right rudder — thrust to starboard. 3. Stop and full astern — rudder midship — stop and slow ahead — variable rudder — thrust to starboard and stop thruster. 4. Slow ahead to steady up in channel.

Current

Ship at dock

Note: If it is doubtful about the bow-thruster being able to hold the bow against the current as the ship moves out of the slip, the starboard anchor can be dropped and drug to help hold the bow. This will also help to keep the ship from gaining too much headway while turning. Care should be taken not to get so much anchor chain out that it cannot be picked up when the ship is straightened out and underway in the channel.

If the ship is leaving the slip to encounter a head current in the channel, she would keep her bow at as much of an angle to the current as possible. The bow-thruster would start pushing against the current as her bow starts into the channel.

The ship's characteristics of backing to port makes this maneuver much easier. Her engines can be put full ahead with hard right rudder and as her stern clears, her engines can be put full astern to make her pivot and straighten out with the channel. Her engines can then be put ahead to steady up in the channel and her bow-thruster stopped.

Here again, the starboard anchor can be used if necessary, but there is a difference. If there happens to be so much chain out that the anchor cannot be picked up with the ship under way, there is no problem in stopping and drifting back with the current until it is picked up. (See Fig. H-I Pg. 41)

A ship leaving a slip and having to maneuver past another ship secured in the slip on her port side, can experience difficulty in straightening up in the channel when heading into the current. As illustrated in Figure 8-J (Page 42), if her engines are stopped and put astern for very long, she will straighten up and start to go broadside, or to her starboard. When this happens, it may be necessary to drop her port anchor and swing around with the current in order to get under way and steady up in the channel.

Fig. 8-I

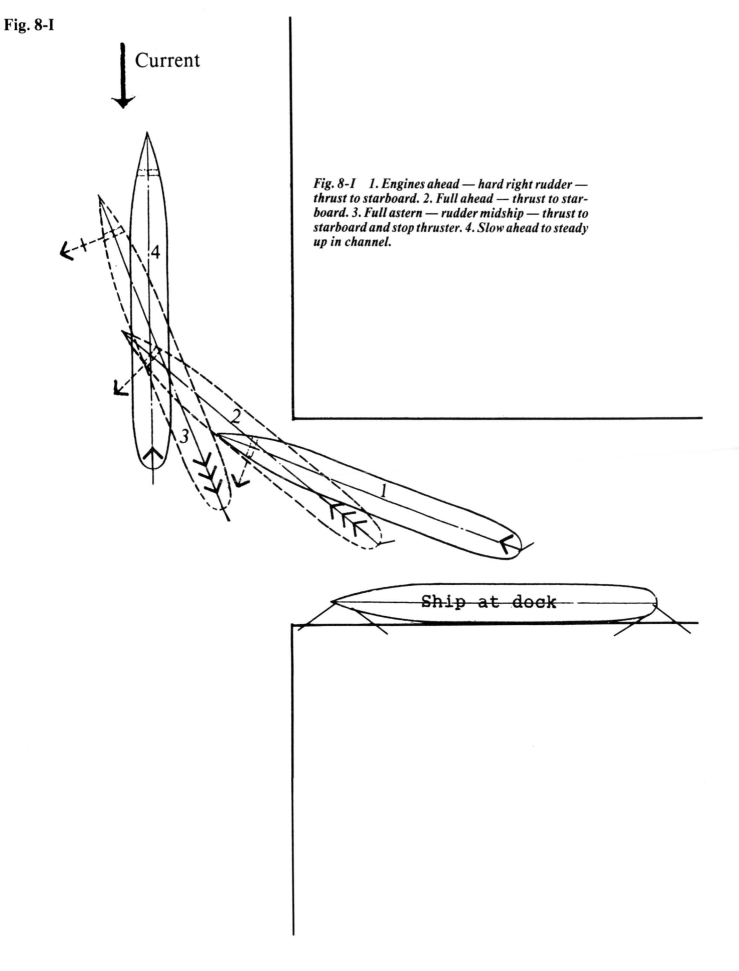

Current

Fig. 8-I   1. Engines ahead — hard right rudder — thrust to starboard. 2. Full ahead — thrust to starboard. 3. Full astern — rudder midship — thrust to starboard and stop thruster. 4. Slow ahead to steady up in channel.

Ship at dock

Fig. 8-J

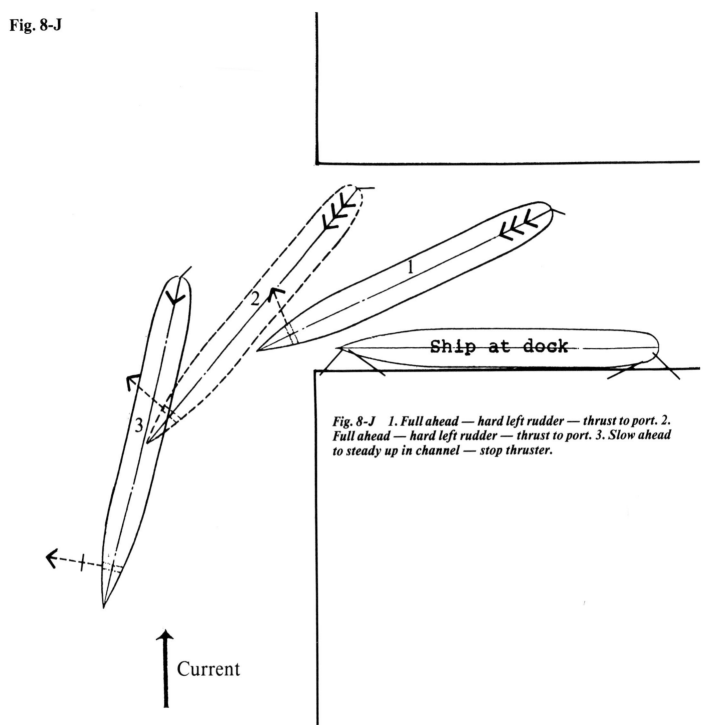

Ship at dock

Fig. 8-J   1. Full ahead — hard left rudder — thrust to port. 2. Full ahead — hard left rudder — thrust to port. 3. Slow ahead to steady up in channel — stop thruster.

Current

CHAPTER 9

HARBOR TUGS DEFINED

Tug boats engaged primarily in assisting ships in harbors around the world vary in size, design, and power. Also, techniques in ship handling may vary from one country to another, depending on design of harbors, piers, and currents that exist, and also the style and practice of ship handling which has been practiced and handed down from one generation to another.

With a few exceptions however, tugs, no matter what the design or power, have the same characteristics. They may have one or more engines turning one propeller which turns clockwise or counter clockwise, which is called in the U. S. (right hand, or right turning) or (left hand or left turning), and one rudder. If the tug has a right turning propeller she will back to port, and if she has a left turning propeller she will back to starboard. (See figures 9-A and 9-A1).

A tug may have (twin screw) two or more engines turning two propellers and have two rudders. One propeller should turn clockwise and the other counter clockwise. They may either turn outboard, or inboard. Meaning, if the starboard engine turns to the right and the port engine turns to the left, they will be turning outboard when going ahead which is characteristic of most tugs. Turning in the opposite direction when going ahead of course would be inboard turning propellers, since a right turning propeller backs to port and a left turning propeller backs to starboard. This does make some difference, but since the propellers are set so close together off the center line of the keel on tugs the difference seems negligible. The fact is, since the propellers do set off the center line of the keel, when the starboard engine is backed she will back to port, and when the port engine is backed she will back to starboard. (Figures 9-B and 9-B1).

When a twin screw tug is assisting a light draft vessel away from the dock and very little power is needed, figures 9-C and 9-C1 (Page 44) illustrate the tug's engine and rudder control necessary for keeping the tug at a right angle to the ship with only one line from the tug to the ship. If there is any doubt, a good ship handler will never go for this in order to just save a few minutes, or to save the tug crew a little work by putting out more lines.

There are some exceptions worth mentioning. A tug may have two propellers and one rudder in line with the keel which is a nuisance, because the rudder cannot take advantage of the propeller wash for steering. Or, a

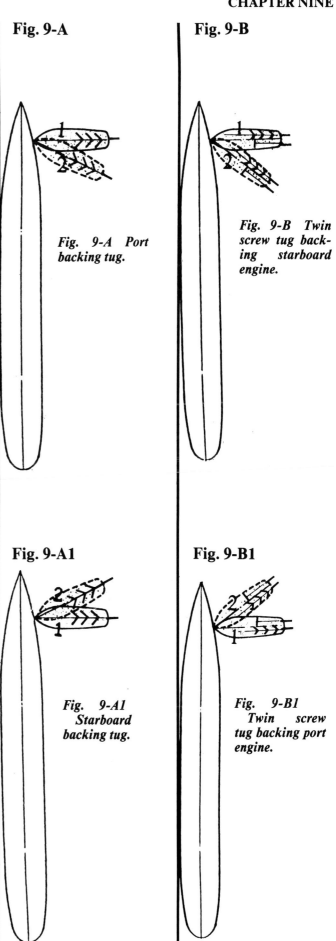

Fig. 9-A
Fig. 9-A Port backing tug.

Fig. 9-B
Fig. 9-B Twin screw tug backing starboard engine.

Fig. 9-A1
Fig. 9-A1 Starboard backing tug.

Fig. 9-B1
Fig. 9-B1 Twin screw tug backing port engine.

Fig. 9-C

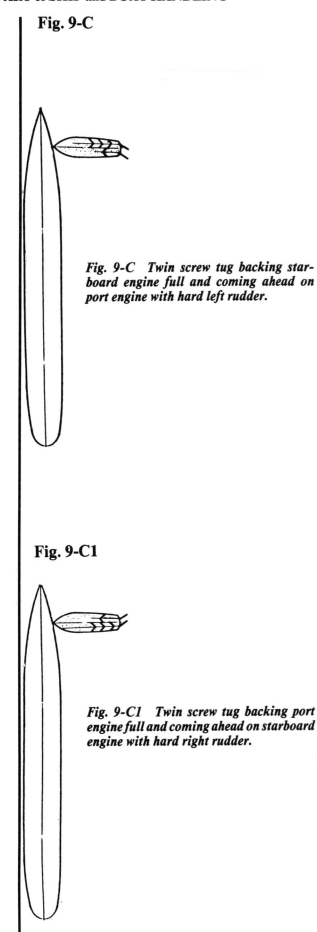

Fig. 9-C   Twin screw tug backing starboard engine full and coming ahead on port engine with hard left rudder.

Fig. 9-C1

Fig. 9-C1   Twin screw tug backing port engine full and coming ahead on starboard engine with hard right rudder.

tug may have three propellers with rudders only at the two outside propellers and none at the center propeller. This is alright as long as one or both of the outside propellers are turning ahead, but if only the center propeller is turning there is very little rudder power.

Most of the Tug Boat Companies engaged in doing harbor work design their tugs for competing in other fields of the towing industry as well. This service is mostly coastal and ocean towing of barges, drilling rigs, and ocean salvage.

A few of these tugs may be equipped with bow-thruster and even flanking rudder, which is of little or no use in ship handling, but they do help in maneuvering the tug itself until it is made fast to a ship. Also, in some ports such as the Panama Canal, specially designed tugs are in service. Their propeller(s) rotate horizontally so that they will pull in the direction the propeller(s) are facing, no matter which direction the tug is heading. Since this writer has had no experience in handling this sort of vessel, no instructions can be offered about its performance.

CHAPTER 10

ONE TUG'S EFFECT ON SHIPS AND LARGE VESSELS MOVING THROUGH THE WATER

TUG ON THE BOW OF A SHIP

A tug on the bow of a loaded deep draft ship has little or no effect regardless of how the tug is laying alongside because of the draft and weight of the ship compared to the tug. However, if moving some distance and wishing to make good headway, it will be necessary for the tug to work alongside and lay parallel to the ship or run the risk of either breaking her lines or swamping. When the ship begins to make good headway, the tug should put her engines ahead to ease the strain on her headlines and drag on the ship. (See Figure 10-A) (Page 45).

Figure 10-A1 (Page 45) does not consider weather or current. In most cases, a tug hanging on the bow of a light ship will cause the ship to take rudder away from the side on which the tug is made fast, and the ship will make leeway toward the tug side, since the tug is acting as a drag.

Depending on the type, size, and trim of the vessel, a tug made fast on the starboard bow and lying at an angle to the ship, may cause it to take right rudder toward the tug, since the tug may be acting as a rudder on the bow. If this happens the ship will be making some leeway to port.

Fig. 10-A

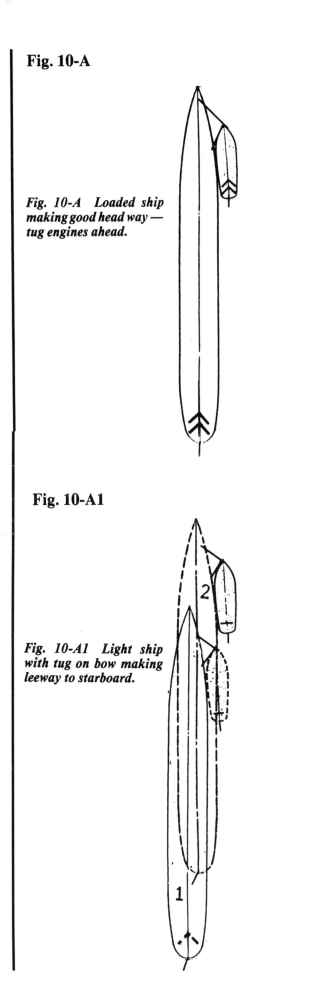

Fig. 10-A Loaded ship making good head way — tug engines ahead.

Fig. 10-A1

Fig. 10-A1 Light ship with tug on bow making leeway to starboard.

A good rule of thumb is that when a vessel carries continuous rudder to either side, she is prone to make leeway away from the side to which she is carrying rudder. (Figure 10-B).

Fig. 10-B

Fig. 10-B Tug laying at angle on ships bow — ship making leeway to port.

There are exceptions. If more pressure is applied aft of the pivot point than forward, she will be making leeway toward the direction in which the rudder is carried, unless she is carrying rudder against the bank. For instance, a vessel down by the head, with a tug laying on her quarter at an angle, will experience this leeway, and also a vessel down by the head and having a strong wind on her beam. (Figure 10-B1) (Page 46).

TUG ON SHIP'S AFTER-QUARTER MAKING GOOD HEADWAY

A ship moving any distance under her own power, should never leave a tug made fast on the quarter even if it is lashed up.

The tug interferes with the flow of water around the stern and the ship will not steer well. A loaded ship especially if making good headway, is subject to swamping or capsizing the tug because of this suction effect around the stern of the ship. Also, if the ship takes a run and the tug falls around at an angle, it will

Fig. 10-B1

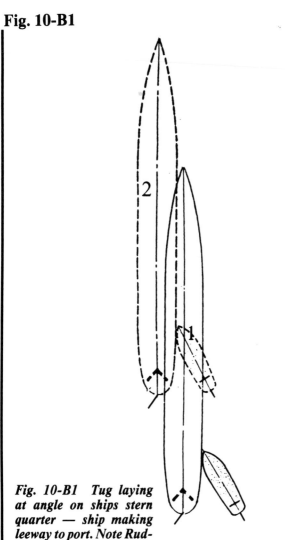

Fig. 10-B1 Tug laying at angle on ships stern quarter — ship making leeway to port. Note Rudder Angle.

Fig. 10-C

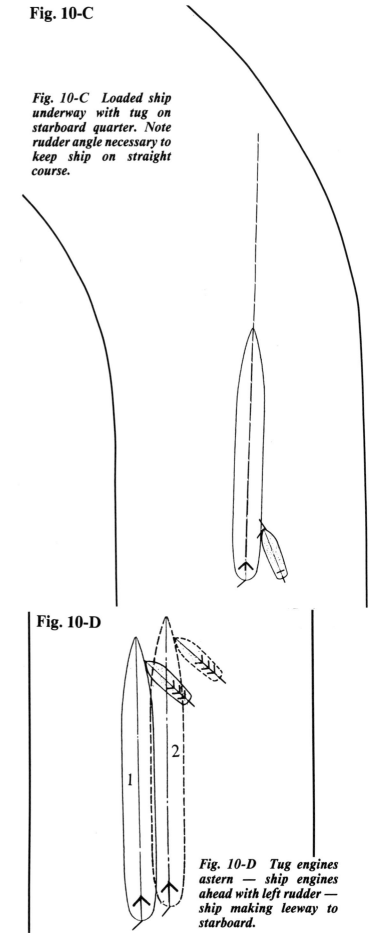

Fig. 10-C Loaded ship underway with tug on starboard quarter. Note rudder angle necessary to keep ship on straight course.

Fig. 10-D

Fig. 10-D Tug engines astern — ship engines ahead with left rudder — ship making leeway to starboard.

act as a rudder and the ship will in most cases go out of control. (Figure 10-C).

MAKING A SHIP MOVE BROADSIDE

When it is desired to make leeway (walk a ship broadside) with a tug on the bow, it can be done as shown in Figure 10-D. For instance, if the tug is on the starboard bow and you wish to go broadside to starboard, the tug can be backed and the ship's engines can be put ahead with a hard left rudder. The ship would need some room to move ahead and should not be backed unless it is necessary. When she is backed the stern will go to port and it would be necessary to come ahead on the tug. She will then start making leeway to port, and possibly gain a little headway from the tug pushing until the tug has worked around to a ninety degree angle to the ship.

Loaded ships will work in this manner unless they are on or near the bottom, but their broadside movement would be so slow it would be negligible. (Figure 10-D).

If a light ship wishes to move broadside to port with a tug on her starboard bow, she will do so more readily than she will to starboard by coming ahead on the tug and ahead on the ship's engines with a hard right rudder, then backing the engines to stop her forward movement. Since the ship backs her stern to port, care should be taken in close quarters not to get too much headway or broadside movement unless there is plenty of room to come ahead on the engines with a hard left rudder and back the tug to stop this broadside movement. The ship should not have so much headway that the tug cannot stay at or near a ninety degree angle to the ship. (Figure 10-E).

CHAPTER 11

HANDLING AND DOCKING SHIPS WITH ONE TUG ASSISTING

DOCKING PORT SIDE TO THE DOCK AT AN OPEN BERTH

With a light or medium draft ship there is no problem as long as the ship does not have too much headway, and she approaches the dock at the proper angle.

The tug can take care of the bow, and since the ship will back to port, she should not need to be backed more than one time to kill her headway and the engines can be stopped while a breast or stern line is put out and a strain taken to hold her stern alongside. If a line is not put out from the stern it will not stay alongside unless there is sufficient wind or set to hold her there. (Figure 11-A).

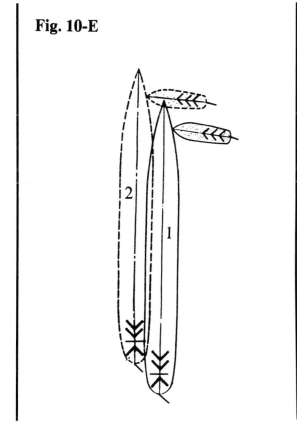

Fig. 10-E

Fig. 10-E   Tug engines ahead — ship engines ahead and astern with hard right rudder — ship making leeway to port.

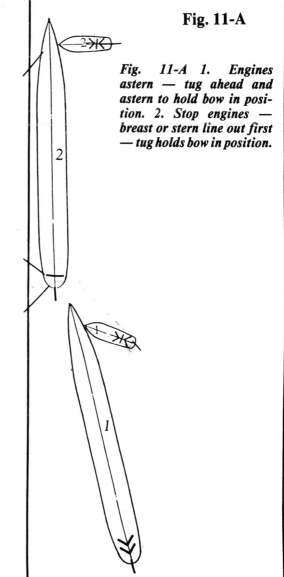

Fig. 11-A

Fig. 11-A 1. Engines astern — tug ahead and astern to hold bow in position. 2. Stop engines — breast or stern line out first — tug holds bow in position.

As will be mentioned often, great care must be taken when putting out stern lines not to get them in the propeller, and if at all possible, the propeller should be stopped when these lines are put out. If one or more of these stern lines get caught in the propeller while it is turning, it means employing a diver, going into drydock, or both. At the very best, it will generally mean needless delay and expense.

DOCKING PORT SIDE TO THE DOCK AT OPEN BERTH WITH LOADED SHIP

First it should be explained that all harbors and channels have a certain amount of settlement on the bottom which is neither liquid nor solid. A loaded ship can maneuver through it, but not nearly as efficiently as if she were floating free. In busy harbors and channels with limited depth where there is a lot of deep draft traffic the settlement tends to stay more liquified, but becomes more dense along docks and outside traffic areas.

If these harbors and channels have a soft bottom, many of the larger ships have a tendency to overload simply because they can carry more pay load. With a rock bottom of course, they don't dare because of the chance of tearing their bottom out.

Before approaching a dock with a loaded ship that is near, or dragging the bottom, it is always best to find out if a deeper loaded ship has recently sailed from this berth. If there has been, she will have wallowed out a hole against the dock and when the ship approaches she may try to knock the dock down with which ever end gets to this hole first, because this is the place of least resistance.

The ship should approach the dock at a slight angle, with no more headway than what is needed to keep her in position, along with the assistance of the tug. If in doubt, the starboard anchor should be put down to act as a drag. As the bow approaches the dock, the engine can be given a kick ahead with a hard right rudder with the tug backing to start her stern swinging toward the dock, and then put her engines astern to stop her headway while lines are put out from the stern. Of course, if her stern starts coming toward the dock too fast, her engines will have to be put ahead with a hard left rudder while coming ahead on the tug. (See Figure 11-A1).

DOCKING LIGHT SHIP WITH NO BALLAST GOING PORT SIDE TO THE DOCK WITH STRONG STERN WIND

An extremely light ship with only about half of her propeller in the water and little if any draft forward, can cause a lot of problems if she gets out of control in close quarters with a strong wind. If it is blowing direct-

ly down the channel on the stern, the ship will gain headway even with the engines stopped. If it is necessary for her to stay well off the docks until she gets to her berth, she should work at an angle so that the wind will be on her starboard quarter when she is stopped dead in the water. (Figure 11-B). (Page 49) With her in this position, the tug will fall around at a right angle and can keep her at enough angle for the wind to carry her up to the dock as she backs her engines enough to stay in position. Stern lines should be put out as soon as possible and before the bow comes alongside.

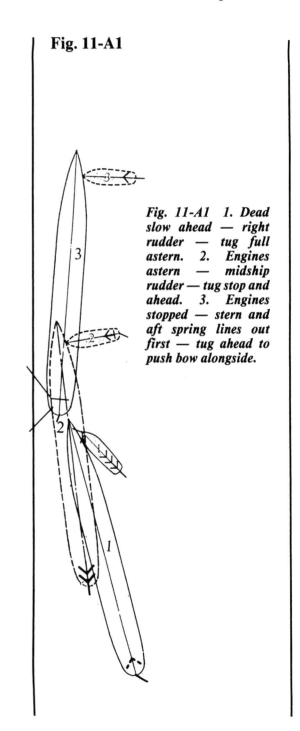

Fig. 11-A1

Fig. 11-A1 1. Dead slow ahead — right rudder — tug full astern. 2. Engines astern — midship rudder — tug stop and ahead. 3. Engines stopped — stern and aft spring lines out first — tug ahead to push bow alongside.

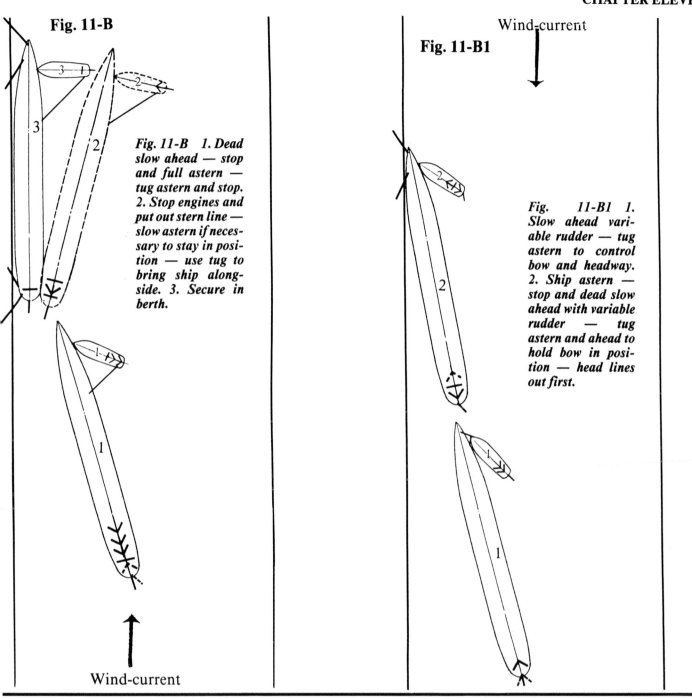

Fig. 11-B

Fig. 11-B 1. Dead slow ahead — stop and full astern — tug astern and stop. 2. Stop engines and put out stern line — slow astern if necessary to stay in position — use tug to bring ship alongside. 3. Secure in berth.

Wind-current

Wind-current
Fig. 11-B1

Fig. 11-B1 1. Slow ahead variable rudder — tug astern to control bow and headway. 2. Ship astern — stop and dead slow ahead with variable rudder — tug astern and ahead to hold bow in position — head lines out first.

DOCKING LIGHT SHIP WITH NO BALLAST GOING PORT SIDE TO THE DOCK WITH A STRONG HEAD WIND

Docking head into the wind is not so difficult as docking with a stern wind. It should be mentioned however, that when there is a gale blowing, a good deal of the time there will be rain, or some other kind of precipitation to add to the discomfort and limit visibility. The discomfort must be ignored, but under extreme conditions, there will be times when some very accurate guess work (sixth sense or feel for the ship & condi-

tions) must play a part.

Figure 11-B1 shows landing the bow first and getting a head line out. While the ship approaches at an angle, the tug should hold the bow, while the ship using her engines and left rudder should hold her stern against the wind until the bow is against the dock and a head line is out. After this is done the tug can be stopped or worked slow ahead, while the ship can give her engines a kick dead slow ahead with hard right rudder to bring her stern alongside.

DOCKING LIGHT SHIP WITH NO BALLAST PORT SIDE TO THE DOCK WITH BROADSIDE WIND BLOWING ON DOCK

As can be seen in Figure 11-B2, under these conditions it is not a matter of docking, but of docking too fast.

The ship will approach the dock at more of an angle and let the tug land her bow gently against the dock. When this is done, the tug can come ahead to keep her stern from landing too hard.

Remember, the anchors are always there if needed. If there is any doubt that the tug will be unable to hold the bow, the port anchor can be put out with a shot or two of chain as you start to approach the dock. (ONE SHOT OF CHAIN = 90 FEET).

The best way to find out if the tug can do the job, is to try it before the ship makes her approach to the dock.

There are many illustrations in this book of putting the stern of a ship up to the dock first, but it does not apply here. It has been done with success, but on numerous occasions it has not, and under these extreme conditions, it cannot be recommended, even if docking between two ships. With her propeller half out of the water, there is too much of a chance of getting it into the dock.

DOCKING LIGHT SHIP WITH NO BALLAST PORT SIDE TO THE DOCK WITH STRONG OFF-DOCK WIND

As can be seen in Figure 11-B3, (Page 51) the wind is forcing the ship away from the dock. There is not much of a chance of putting her up to the dock and keeping her there long enough to put lines out, unless lines are put out from her stern first while the tug holds her bow.

It generally is advisable to go a little past the berth and back into place, so that the tug will stay at a right angle to the ship.

If one feels it is necessary to put an anchor out here, the starboard anchor would be the proper one. The anchor should be dropped as near the dock as possible so that the chain will lead under the hull toward the dock, and will help to breast her in while keeping her from gaining headway.

DOCKING PORT SIDE TO THE DOCK BETWEEN TWO SHIPS

It is more than likely that anyone involved in handling ships for any length of time, has docked one or more ships as illustrated in Figure 11-C. (Page 51).

As long as the vessel is under absolute control and the engines can be depended upon to back, it is definitely the quickest way to do the job.

However most ships under the U.S. Flag are equipped with steam geared turbine engines, and there

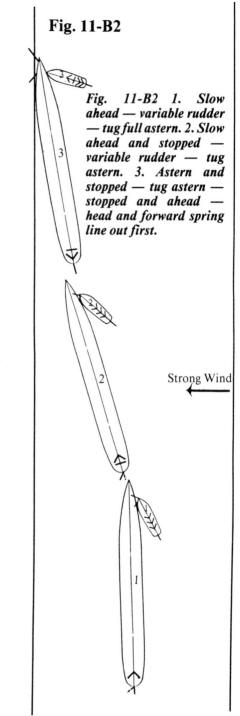

Fig. 11-B2

Fig. 11-B2 1. Slow ahead — variable rudder — tug full astern. 2. Slow ahead and stopped — variable rudder — tug astern. 3. Astern and stopped — tug astern — stopped and ahead — head and forward spring line out first.

Strong Wind

is a delay in getting the things going from ahead to astern, and no two engineers take the same amount of time. When there are only a few feet to work with, it is best to ring this type of vessel dead slow astern well before her stern is clear of the ship aft.

This type of engine does not stop the moment the telegraph is rung stop. If the engine is left on half or full astern until the vessel is completely stopped or starting to gain sternway, don't expect the engine to stop and go ahead immediately. It will not do it, and under these conditions a few seconds can be a life time.

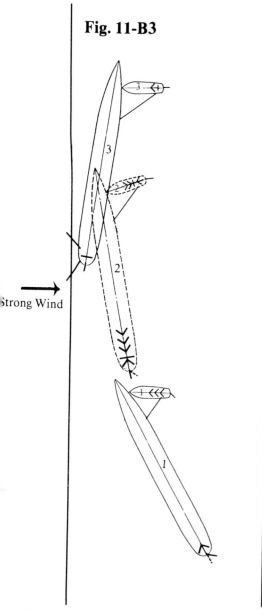

Fig. 11-B3

Strong Wind

Fig. 11-C

Ship at dock

Ship at dock

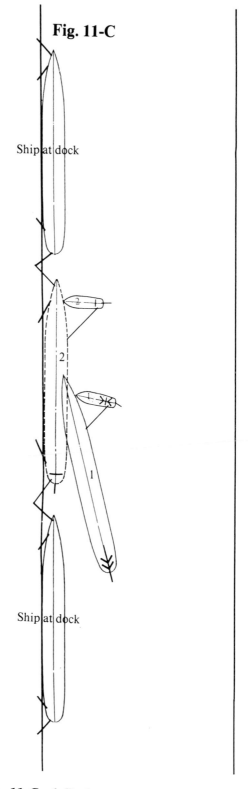

Fig. 11-B3   1. Slow ahead — variable rudder — tug ahead. 2. Slow ahead — stop and full astern — variable rudder — tug ahead — stop and astern to hold bow in position. 3. Engines stopped — stern and aft spring line out first — tug pushes bow alongside.

Now in contrast to the steam turbine, there is the Steam Turbo Electric, and the Diesel Electric engines which are not often installed because they are more expensive to operate. However, these engines should answer ahead or astern bells immediately.

The most common engine used in foreign flag vessels is the motor. These motorships will start and stop immediately if they start at all. Unless they are equipped with a braking device to stop the propeller, they will not back at all if they are moving half or full speed through the water, which of course would not be the case here. The thing that does make a difference here is the fact that dead slow on these ships is no less

Fig. 11-C   1. Engines astern — tug ahead and astern to hold bow in position. 2. Forward and aft spring line out first — tug stopped.

than three or four knots, and a lot of them will not run less than six to eight knots. As can be seen, putting them astern in advance will not work, and you can be assured that if they just cough and sputter when the telegraph is put astern, there is an uneasy feeling.

The safest way to make this maneuver is illustrated in Figure 11-C1 as long as the lines are kept clear of the propeller, and if at all possible it should be stopped while these lines are put out and the propeller cleared.

As can be seen, if anything at all goes wrong the tug is in position to assist, and the ship is under complete control. It may take a few minutes longer, but it is much easier on the nervous system.

It is the only safe way to handle ships that are con-structed with the bridge situated forward close to th anchor windlass and forward of the flare of the bov even if the ship is going to an open dock. When this typ of ship approaches the dock with the bow at an angl the bridge extends out over the dock and it is next t impossible to tell how far the hull is from the edge of th dock.

GOING STARBOARD SIDE TO THE DOCK A AN OPEN BERTH WITH ONE TUG ASSISTING

Since the ship will back to port, she needs t approach the dock as slowly as possible while mair taining control, as shown in Figure 11-D.

Her stern needs to have a good swing toward th dock by backing the tug and coming ahead on the shi with a hard left rudder. Then while the tug continues t back, the ship's engines can be put astern to stop he headway and lines can be put out from the stern.

A port-backing tug on the port bow of a ship shoul always have a stern line out to the ship to prevent i from backing around under the bow, where it would b useless, if not harmful in getting the ship secured.

Fig. 11-C1

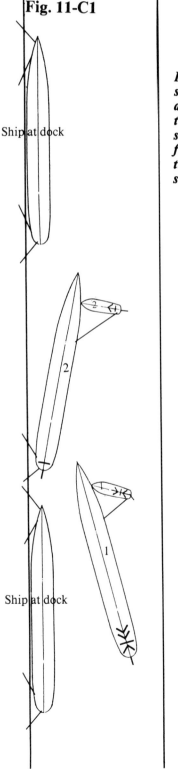

Ship at dock

Ship at dock

Fig. 11-C1   1. Slow ahead — stop and astern — tug ahead and astern to hold bow in position. 2. Engines stopped — stern and after spring lines out first — tug holds bow in position and brings vessel alongside.

Fig. 11-D

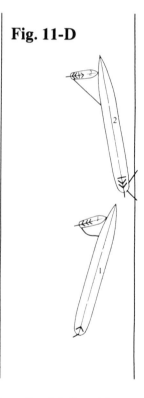

Fig. 11-D   1. Slow ahead left rudder — tug full astern. 2. Engines astern and stopped — stern and after spring lines ou first — tug astern and ahead to hold bow and bring vesse. alongside to secure.

GOING STARBOARD SIDE TO THE DOCK WITH A STERN CURRENT:
CURRENTS DISCUSSED

This is accomplished much in the same manner as docking with a stern wind, however, the current is more easily judged because it keeps more of a constant pressure on the ships hull.

It is absolutely necessary to have the ship swung at an angle so that the current will be on the port quarter of the ship when she is backed, as shown in Figure 11-E. If the ship is kept at the proper angle, the current will dock the ship. However, lines must be put ashore from her stern right away because the stern will not stay there when the bow comes alongside and the current gets between her and the dock.

The speed of the current and the ship over the ground determines the angle at which the ship should be positioned when she is stopped off her berth.

A good knowledge of local current action is very helpful, if not essential in doing a good job and keeping a ship out of all kinds of trouble. If in a strange harbor, local charts and current conditions should be studied because they all have their own identities pertaining to geographic location, rise and fall of tide, river currents, and currents caused by freshets and heavy rain fall, weather, etc..

If local information is not available, the best thing to do is determine about how fast the vessel is moving over the ground in comparison to her engine speed. By observing the shoreline and dock area and floating objects in the water to see how fast they are moving by the hull, both near the vessel and along the shoreline, will give you a good idea of what the current is doing in both places.

Stronger currents will generally be found in the deepest water of a harbor, river, or channel, with less current near docks and in shallow water. Where there are sharp bends, and the force of the water making the turn starts a whirlpool hydraulic effect, it is not unusual to see the water running in the opposite direction or be at a standstill near the shoreline or dock area.

DOCKING STARBOARD SIDE TO THE DOCK WITH HEAD CURRENT AT OPEN BERTH

This maneuver is done in almost the opposite manner in which it is done in Figure 11-E when docking with a stern current.

The vessel is angled toward her berth with the current on her port bow. If the angle is too great, and she is falling toward the dock too fast, she can come ahead on the engine with a left rudder, or back the tug, or do both. The current will take her alongside the dock where head lines should be put out first to hold her in, and to keep her from gaining sternway with the current.

Fig. 11-E

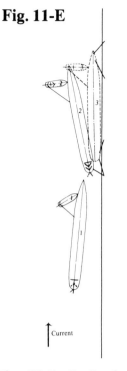

Current

Fig. 11-E1

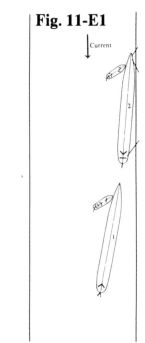

Current

Fig. 11-E 1. Dead slow ahead and stopped — variable rudder — tug astern to hold bow and slow ships headway. 2. Engines astern and stopped — stern lines out first. 3. Tug ahead and astern to hold bow in position and bring vessel alongside to secure.

Fig. 11-E1 1. Slow ahead — variable rudder — tug astern — stopped and ahead to hold bow in position. 2. Engines astern to stop headway — tug stopped and slow ahead to hold vessel against dock — head line out first.

If the strain on the head lines tends to hold her stern away from the dock, the engines can be given a kick ahead with a hard left rudder to bring the stern alongside for securing. (Figure 11-E1).

DOCKING STARBOARD SIDE TO THE DOCK BETWEEN TWO SHIPS WITH SLACK WATER

Going port side to the dock between two ships is illustrated in Figure 11-C where the stern goes to port when the engines are backed. As explained in that section, it is not the safest maneuver to execute, and going starboard side to the dock is even worse, as shown in Figure 11-F. (Page 54).

In this case it would be absolutely necessary to come ahead on the ship's engines with a hard left rudder to bring her stern in to the dock in order to put out lines. Or, she could put out head lines and let the tug move aft and push her stern in, which would be the safest unless there is traffic and/or she tries to turn broadside because of the water being disturbed.

One or more good spring lines can be put out forward to work the engines against, b. if these lines break or

THE ART of SHIP and BOAT HANDLING

fail to hold, and the ship is only ten feet or so from the vessel ahead, it is almost impossible to stop the engines and get them going astern before damage is done.

It is suggested that illustration 11-F1 be followed when docking starboard side to the dock between two ships.

The ship can swing her stern in close to the dock by coming ahead on her engines with a hard left rudder and backing the tug on the bow. The tug should have a stern line out to the ship so that it will stay at a right angle to the ship, and will be able to hold the ship in position while lines are put out aft.

If the bow goes past the vessel secured ahead, which in some cases is desirable, it will not matter because the tug can keep the ship in position while she is backed into place.

DOCKING STARBOARD SIDE TO THE DOCK USING ANCHOR AND ONE TUG ON PORT QUARTER

Some circumstances and conditions may suggest this procedure, especially when a ship is deeply loaded. It can be done with no problem as long as the ship does not have too much headway.

When she is angled toward the dock, the port anchor can be put down with a shot or two of chain. As she approaches her berth, the tug can be put ahead and the ships engine put astern. When possible, the tug should be allowed to work around at a good angle to the ship before the ships engines are backed. (Figure 11-G).

GOING STARBOARD SIDE TO THE DOCK IN A SLIP

In Harbors where slips are constructed to join outside or channel side docks, the corners are generally reinforced in some way so that ships can be breasted against them in order to turn and dock inside the slip. When there is a current in the channel, the water inside of the slip is generally calm except for the turbulence created at the entrance to the slip.

The following eight illustrations consider maneuvering only in a dead calm with no current or wind, and docking by turning without breasting against the corner. However, there should be no harm done by breasting against the corner if it works better for the person handling the ship. As will be seen, there will be current and/or weather or other conditions which will make it necessary to breast against the corner in order to dock inside the slip.

It should be remembered also, that ships keep getting larger as new ones are constructed, while docks and slips never do unless they are torn down and rebuilt.

Figure 11-H illustrates approaching the slip on the

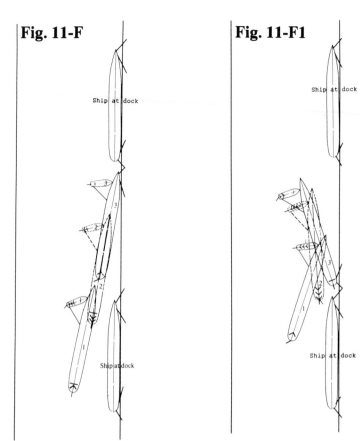

Fig. 11-F   **Fig. 11-F1**

Fig. 11-F 1. Dead slow ahead and stopped — use tug as needed to keep bow in position. 2. Engines astern and stopped. 3. Dead slow ahead — hard left rudder — strong spring line on dock — tug stopped — secure at berth.

Fig. 11-F1 1. Slow ahead — hard left rudder — tug full astern. 2. Engines full astern with midship rudder — tug full astern. 3. Stop engines — stern and spring lines aft out first — tug stopped and ahead to bring vessel alongside.

Fig. 11-G

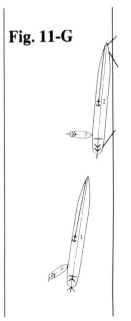

Fig. 11-G 1. Slow ahead and stopped — variable rudder — tug stopped and ahead. 2. Drop port anchor — tug ahead — ship astern and stopped — forward spring and head line out first.

Fig. 11-H

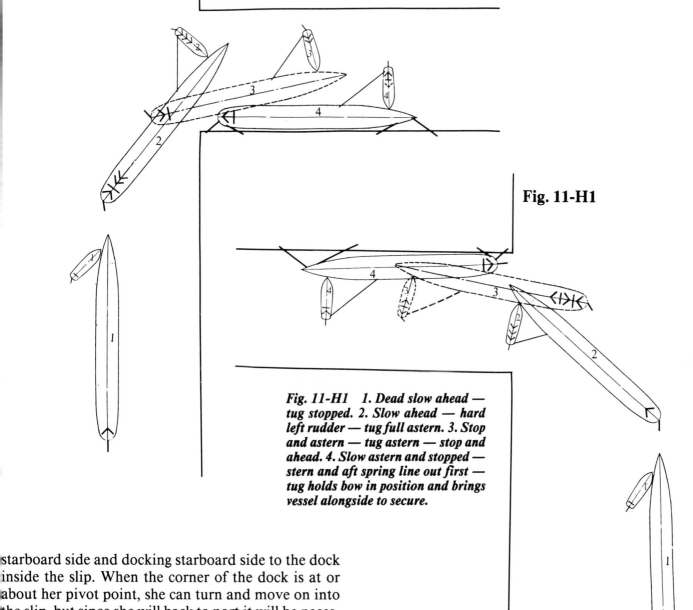

Fig. 11-H   1. Slow ahead — tug stopped. 2. Hard right rudder — stop and astern — tug ahead. 3. Slow ahead — left rudder — tug ahead. 4. Slow astern and stopped — stern and aft spring line out first. Tug brings vessel alongside to secure.

Fig. 11-H1

Fig. 11-H1   1. Dead slow ahead — tug stopped. 2. Slow ahead — hard left rudder — tug full astern. 3. Stop and astern — tug astern — stop and ahead. 4. Slow astern and stopped — stern and aft spring line out first — tug holds bow in position and brings vessel alongside to secure.

starboard side and docking starboard side to the dock inside the slip. When the corner of the dock is at or about her pivot point, she can turn and move on into the slip, but since she will back to port it will be necessary to put out a breast or stern line before her bow comes alongside. When the pivot point (midship) is past the corner of the dock, the engines can be given a kick ahead with a hard left rudder to bring her stern up to the dock for putting out a line and taking up the slack, while the tug holds the bow. Care must be taken not to break this stern line, and when possible more than one line should be put out from the stern, while making sure not to get them in the ships propeller.

Figure 11-H1 illustrates going starboard side to the dock when approaching with the slip on the port side. The tug backing will help to keep from gaining too much headway as she turns to head into the slip, and as

she turns she can experience some broadside movement to her starboard with the tugs assistance on the bow. However, as soon as the stern is close enough, breast or stern lines must be put out because the stern will not stay there after it has come alongside the dock. The tug should be able to handle the bow for securing.

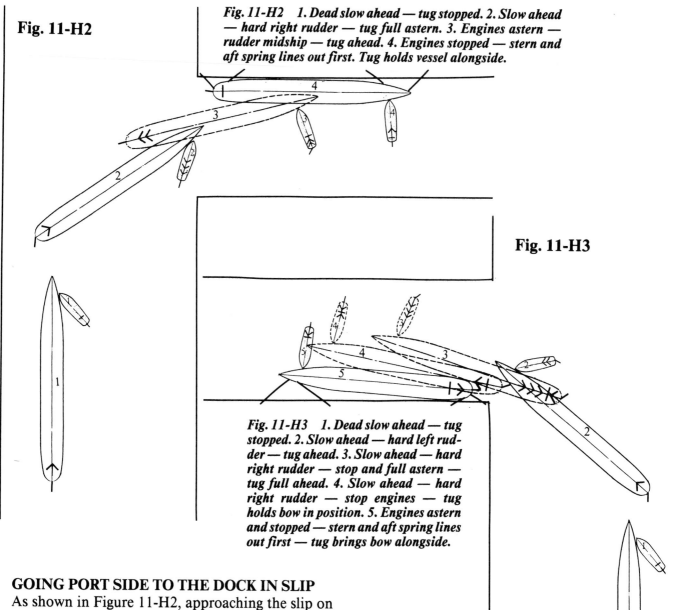

Fig. 11-H2

Fig. 11-H2 1. Dead slow ahead — tug stopped. 2. Slow ahead — hard right rudder — tug full astern. 3. Engines astern — rudder midship — tug ahead. 4. Engines stopped — stern and aft spring lines out first. Tug holds vessel alongside.

Fig. 11-H3

Fig. 11-H3 1. Dead slow ahead — tug stopped. 2. Slow ahead — hard left rudder — tug ahead. 3. Slow ahead — hard right rudder — stop and full astern — tug full ahead. 4. Slow ahead — hard right rudder — stop engines — tug holds bow in position. 5. Engines astern and stopped — stern and aft spring lines out first — tug brings bow alongside.

GOING PORT SIDE TO THE DOCK IN SLIP

As shown in Figure 11-H2, approaching the slip on the starboard and going port side to the dock is as simple, if not more so, as docking port side to the dock at an open berth. The tug backing on the bow will keep the ship from gaining too much headway as she turns into the slip. The ship backing her engines to stop her headway will cause her stern to go to port, and she will walk broadside up to the dock as the tug comes ahead to hold her bow.

It should be remembered however, that lines should be out and tight by the time the ship comes alongside or she will not stay there. It should also be remembered that the water in these narrow slips has no place to go except out, and if it is overly disturbed by too much propeller wash, it creates eddies that makes a ship go crazy.

Figure 11-H3 illustrates approaching the slip on the port and going port side to the dock.

As she turns into the slip, it is necessary to keep her port quarter close to the corner of the dock where breast or stern lines can be put out first as she nears her berth where she will be secured. Since she backs to port, this can be accomplished by backing and coming ahead with a right rudder as the corner of the dock comes abeam of and passes her midship or pivot point. The tug should be able to take care of the bow while the stern lines are put out and she comes alongside the dock.

APPROACHING SLIP ON PORT AND DOCKING STERN FIRST, PORT SIDE TO THE DOCK

As shown in figure 11-I, the ship comes close to the mouth of the slip and as soon as her stern will clear the corner of the slip, the engines are put full astern with the tug backing full speed so that the ship will pivot as she is backed into the slip. The tug can be used as necessary to keep her in position to come alongside the dock, however, no head line should be tightened up before stern lines are out and tight. The tug can always handle the bow, but the stern will not stay alongside unless lines are out to hold it.

GOING STERN FIRST AND DOCKING STARBOARD SIDE TO THE DOCK IN SLIP

When docking in this manner, as shown in Figure 11-J, the starboard quarter of the ship must be kept close to the dock in order to put out stern lines before the bow comes alongside the dock.

If the ship is kept in the proper position, the stern spring which leads forward can be put out as the stern goes by to act as a breast line and hold her stern in. As she is backed into her berth for securing, there should not be much danger of getting a line caught in the ships propeller. A stern line should be put out however, before the bow comes alongside the dock.

Approaching the slip on the starboard and docking starboard side to the dock is illustrated in Figure 11-J1 (Page 58). As can be seen in almost every case, it will be necessary to turn the ship around and back her into the slip in the same manner as if she were approaching with the slip on her port. Care should be taken however, not to work the ship's engines any more than necessary, in order to keep from disturbing the water inside the slip before she is backed into place and lines are on the dock.

Fig. 11-I

Fig. 11-I 1. Slow ahead variable rudder — tug astern. 2. Full astern — rudder midship — tug full astern. 3. Engines ahead and astern — right and midship rudder — tug holds bow in position. 4. Slow ahead and stopped — aft spring and stern lines out first — tug holds bow alongside.

Fig. 11-J

Fig. 11-J 1. Slow ahead — tug stopped. 2. Slow ahead — hard right rudder — stop and full astern — rudder midships — tug full ahead. 3. Slow astern — tug holds bow in position. 4. Astern and ahead — variable rudder — tug holds bow in position. 5. Slow ahead to stop in berth — stern and aft spring lines out first — tug holds bow alongside.

GOING STERN FIRST AND DOCKING PAST SHIP SECURED AT OUTSIDE BERTH IN SLIP

In many harbors it will be found that there is not enough room for a tug to lie at a right angle or even a forty five degree angle facing the bow, and pass by other vessels secured at the outside berth of a ship.

As illustrated in Figure 11-K (Page 58), if she is going port side to the dock, the tug should put out two head lines on the starboard bow. The ship should go a little past the slip before backing and gaining a little sternway, while the tug pushes against the bow and works around to put out a stern line to lash up facing

Fig. 11-J1

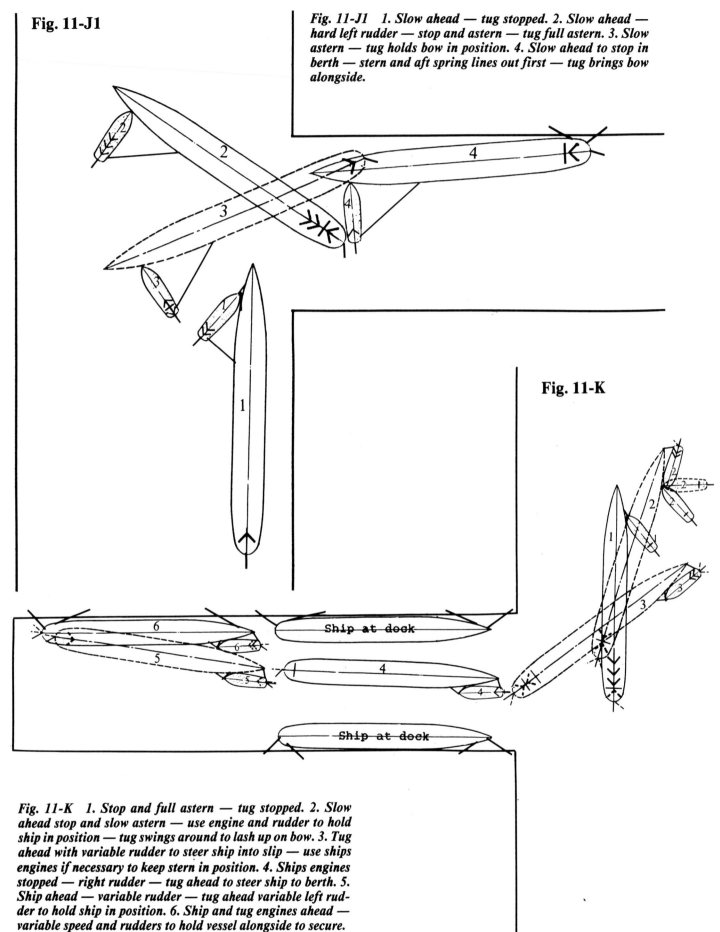

Fig. 11-J1   1. Slow ahead — tug stopped. 2. Slow ahead — hard left rudder — stop and astern — tug full astern. 3. Slow astern — tug holds bow in position. 4. Slow ahead to stop in berth — stern and aft spring lines out first — tug brings bow alongside.

Fig. 11-K

Fig. 11-K   1. Stop and full astern — tug stopped. 2. Slow ahead stop and slow astern — use engine and rudder to hold ship in position — tug swings around to lash up on bow. 3. Tug ahead with variable rudder to steer ship into slip — use ships engines if necessary to keep stern in position. 4. Ships engines stopped — right rudder — tug ahead to steer ship to berth. 5. Ship ahead — variable rudder — tug ahead variable left rudder to hold ship in position. 6. Ship and tug engines ahead — variable speed and rudders to hold vessel alongside to secure.

the ship's stern.

With the tug properly lashed up in this position, it takes up very little room, and will act as a propeller and rudder on the ship's bow.

When the ship has been worked into position to back into the slip she should not use her engines before the tug has her near her berth, unless absolutely necessary, in order to keep from disturbing the water in the slip to such an extent that the tug may not be able to control the bow.

When the vessel secured at the outer berth is clear, the tug can angle the ship's stern toward her berth, and when she is nearly in place, the ship's engine and rudder can be used against the tug's engine and rudder to stop her sternway and bring her alongside while lines are put out.

Here again, if the stern spring line leading forward is put out first and some care taken, there is little chance of getting the line in the ship's propeller.

GOING STERN FIRST AND DOCKING PORT SIDE TO THE DOCK IN A SLIP WITH STERN CURRENT

The size of the ship and slip to be docked at, plus the speed of the current, has to be considered as to the safety of the maneuver illustrated in Figure 11-L.

For all practical purposes, the tug should only have one short head line on the ship, and the tug will not be of much help until the ship has stopped sufficiently enough for the tug to work around at a right angle under the bow.

When the ship's stern has gotten into the dead water of the slip, there will be a moment of truth whether the tug can hold the vessel up against the

current enough for the ship to back on into the slip. It can readily be seen if she is falling toward the dock too fast, making it necessary to come full ahead and back out into the channel, or if she will fall down gently against the corner of the dock. It is absolutely necessary for the tug to be able to work around to a ninety degree angle or more, in order to keep from getting pressed between the ship and the outer berth where it would be of no use at all, and a great deal of damage could be done to the tug, dock, and ship.

Before this is allowed to happen, the ship should come full ahead back into the channel and start all over. However, in most cases if headway is kept at a minimum, the maneuver can be carried out without mishap, even if the ship has to land against the corner of the dock well aft of midship.

When the ship has been backed far enough into the slip to be out of the effects of the current, the tug can be moved to the starboard side to hold her against the dock while she is secured at her berth.

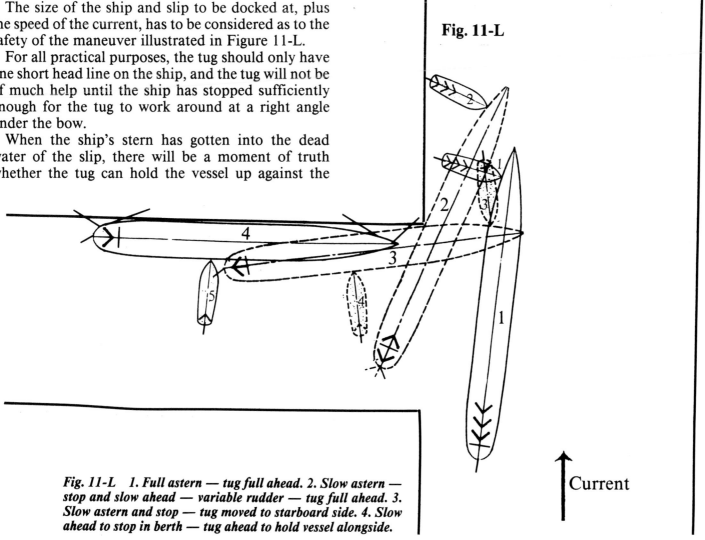

Fig. 11-L

Current

Fig. 11-L   1. Full astern — tug full ahead. 2. Slow astern — stop and slow ahead — variable rudder — tug full ahead. 3. Slow astern and stop — tug moved to starboard side. 4. Slow ahead to stop in berth — tug ahead to hold vessel alongside.

Figure 11-L1 illustrates the same circumstances as in figure 11-L, except it will be noticed that there is another vessel secured to the outside berth adjoining the slip. Here again, the size and draft of the ship, the amount of room to work in, both in the channel and slip, and the force of the current, must be taken into consideration before attempting these maneuvers.

All sorts of things can go wrong, such as misjudging the force of the current, the backing power of the ship's engines, and the tug's ability to hold the bow, or the anchor dragging can lead to trouble.

Once the ship is committed to backing on into the slip, there is not much more she can do except just that.

The best thing to remember is that the further she moves into the slip, the more she will move out of the force of the current. As she moves astern in the slip, breast lines can be put from her quarter to hold the stern alongside while the tug moves to the starboard side to hold her in place for securing at her berth.

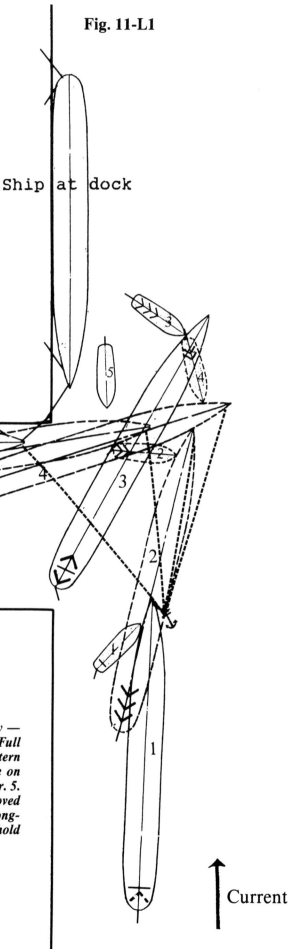

Fig. 11-L1

Ship at dock

Fig. 11-L1 1. Ahead and stopped with bare steerage way — tug stopped — drop starboard anchor and slack chain. 2. Full astern — tug ahead — surge anchor chain. 3. Engines astern and ahead — hard right rudder — tug ahead — heave on anchor. 4. Engines astern — tug ahead — heave on anchor. 5. Slow astern and stopped — stop heaving anchor — tug moved to starboard side. 6. Slack anchor chain for bow to stay alongside dock — slow ahead to stop in berth — tug ahead to hold vessel in place.

Current

GOING STERN FIRST AND DOCKING STARBOARD SIDE TO THE DOCK WITH A STERN CURRENT

The maneuver shown in Figure 11-L2 is even more difficult than in figure 11-L1. In this situation the tug has to be depended upon to catch the ship's port bow from a head-on position by the time the ship has stopped moving ahead and beginning to back into the slip. If the tug does not do this before the bow of the ship moves down with the current to come into contact with the opposite side of the slip, the ship will have a problem keeping her stern in position.

It is necessary for the ship to keep her starboard quarter up close to the dock while backing into the slip, and stern lines should be put out and a strain taken as soon as she nears her berth. When this is done, the tug can push her bow alongside.

Many ship handlers prefer to have the tug make fast alongside before approaching the slip as shown in Figure 11-L2A (Page 62), and there is nothing wrong with this. It only means that the ship must stay further out into the channel away from the slip before backing in.

Figure 11-L3 (Page 62) illustrates putting the starboard anchor out, and placing the tug on the port quarter until stern lines are put out and then moving the tug forward to push the bow into place.

If the anchor is properly placed so that it does not drag, this is just as efficient as any way to handle this maneuver. It should be remembered however, that if the anchor is placed so that it cannot be heaved in after the ship is secured at the dock, it can cause trouble when the ship leaves the dock.

HEADING INTO A SLIP AND DOCKING STARBOARD SIDE TO THE DOCK WITH A HEAD CURRENT

The ship should land gently against the corner of the dock as near the midship section of the hull as possible as shown in Figure 11-M.

The tug on the port bow can then push full speed ahead, and as the ship starts to head into the slip her engines can be put slow or dead slow ahead with a hard right rudder to move her on into her berth.

As the ship moves into the slack water of the slip, and her stern starts to lose the force of the current, she will need to put her rudder hard left to hold her stern in to the dock. As she moves into her berth the stern lines need to be put out as soon as possible to act as breast lines, and slacked off until she is in place.

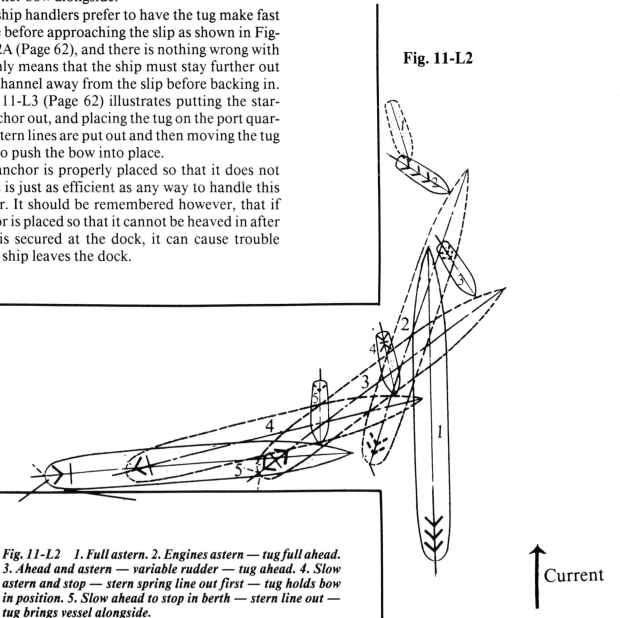

Fig. 11-L2

Current

Fig. 11-L2 1. Full astern. 2. Engines astern — tug full ahead. 3. Ahead and astern — variable rudder — tug ahead. 4. Slow astern and stop — stern spring line out first — tug holds bow in position. 5. Slow ahead to stop in berth — stern line out — tug brings vessel alongside.

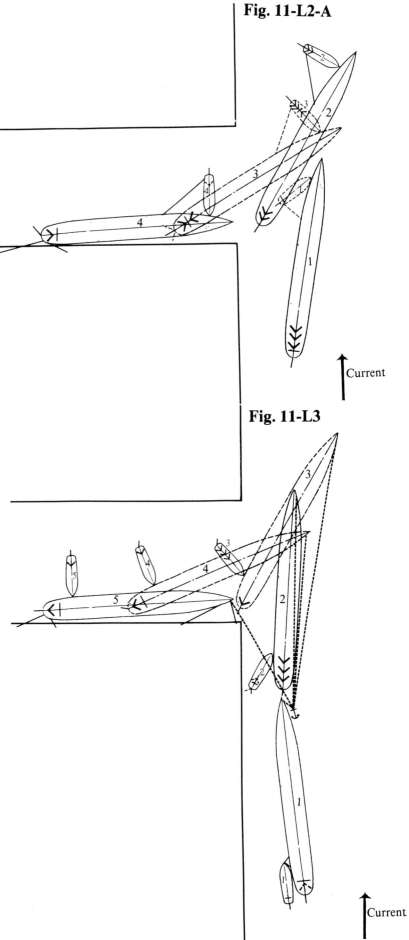

Fig. 11-L2-A

Fig. 11-L2-A   1. Full astern — tug stopped. 2. Engines astern — tug ahead. 3. Ahead and astern — variable rudder — tug holds bow in position. 4. Slow ahead to stop in berth — aft spring and stern lines out first — tug brings bow alongside.

Current

Fig. 11-L3

Fig. 11-L3   1. Engines ahead and stopped with bare steerage way — tug stopped — drop starboard anchor and slack out chain. 2. Full astern — surge anchor chain — tug slow ahead. 3. Slow astern — heave anchor — tug full ahead. 4. Slow astern and stop — tug holds stern in position. 5. Stop in berth — forward spring and head lines out first — tug holds stern alongside — secure and heave in anchor or slack chain to lay on bottom.

Current

Fig. 11-M

Current

Fig. 11-M 1. Dead slow ahead — tug stopped. 2. Engines astern and stopped — slow ahead — hard right rudder — tug full ahead. 3. Dead slow ahead and stopped — variable rudder to hold stern alongside — tug holds bow in position. 4. Slow astern to stop in berth — after spring and stern lines out first — tug brings bow alongside.

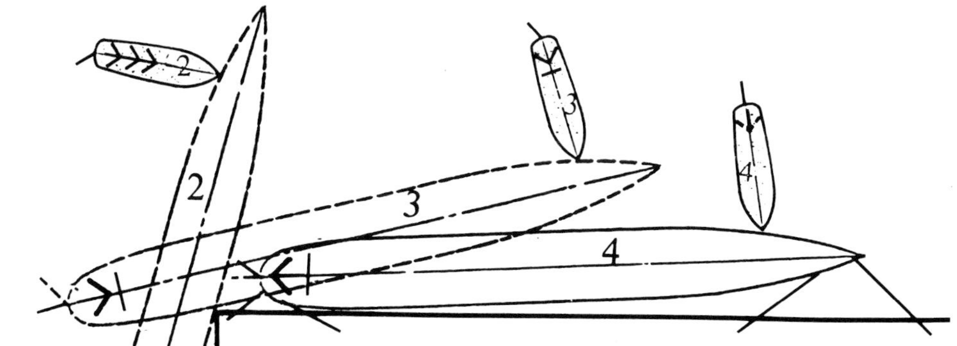

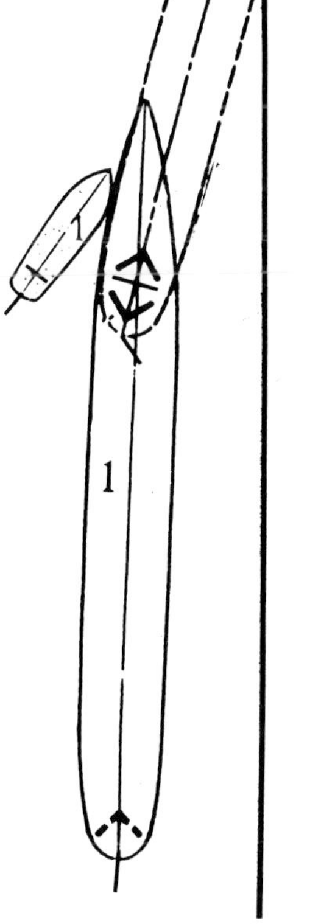

If the current is too strong, or the ship is too large to dock as shown in Figure 11-M (Page 63), she can generally be handled by putting her port anchor down off the end of the dock and letting the tug push her around on the starboard quarter which would enable her to move into the slip as shown in Figure 11-M1. (Page 64)

The port anchor chain leading under her hull toward the dock should hold her bow in to the dock until lines are put out and the tug can move around to the port side to hold her while she is secured at her berth.

Another procedure that may be used is to put the port anchor out off the end of the slip, and let the tug put a hawser on the stern to pull it up against the current as the hull rests against the corner of the dock while she moves into her berth. The anchor dragging should hold the bow, and when the ship has moved far enough into the slip to lose most of the current effect, the tug can let go the hawser and push against the hull to hold her alongside until she is secured. (Figure 11-M2) (Page 64).

Docking a ship inside a slip with a strong head current where another ship is secured to the dock outside the slip, is a somewhat difficult maneuver as shown in figure 11-M3. (Page 65)

The port anchor can be dropped well out in about the center line of the slip with one or two shots of chain in the water, while the tug can put a line out on the starboard quarter as far aft as possible.

The ship should keep the current at as small an angle on the bow as possible until it is in the slack water of the slip, while the tug holds the stern up off of the ship secured outside. As the anchor is drug along the bottom it should also drag toward the ship's berth, but it will not drag enough to breast her bow in to the dock. As soon as the stern is clear, the tug will need to move to the port side to push the ship against the dock for her to secure at her berth.

DOCKING HEAD IN, PORT SIDE TO THE DOCK WITH A HEAD CURRENT

The tug would be placed on the starboard quarter in this maneuver, as shown in Figure 11-N (Page 65), also,

Fig. 11-M1

Current

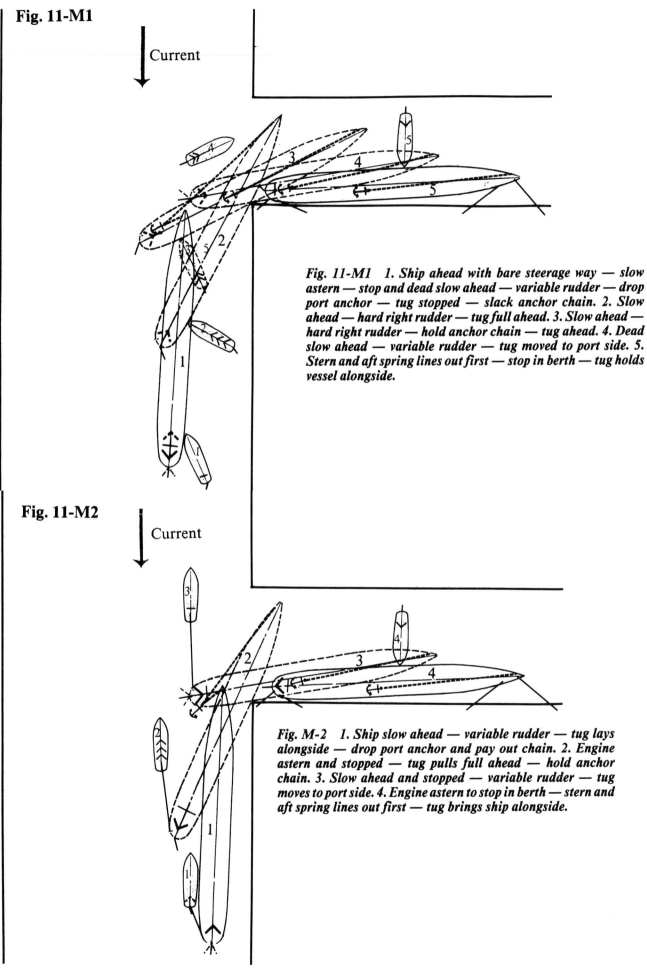

Fig. 11-M1   1. Ship ahead with bare steerage way — slow astern — stop and dead slow ahead — variable rudder — drop port anchor — tug stopped — slack anchor chain. 2. Slow ahead — hard right rudder — tug full ahead. 3. Slow ahead — hard right rudder — hold anchor chain — tug ahead. 4. Dead slow ahead — variable rudder — tug moved to port side. 5. Stern and aft spring lines out first — stop in berth — tug holds vessel alongside.

Fig. 11-M2

Current

Fig. M-2   1. Ship slow ahead — variable rudder — tug lays alongside — drop port anchor and pay out chain. 2. Engine astern and stopped — tug pulls full ahead — hold anchor chain. 3. Slow ahead and stopped — variable rudder — tug moves to port side. 4. Engine astern to stop in berth — stern and aft spring lines out first — tug brings ship alongside.

Fig. 11-M3

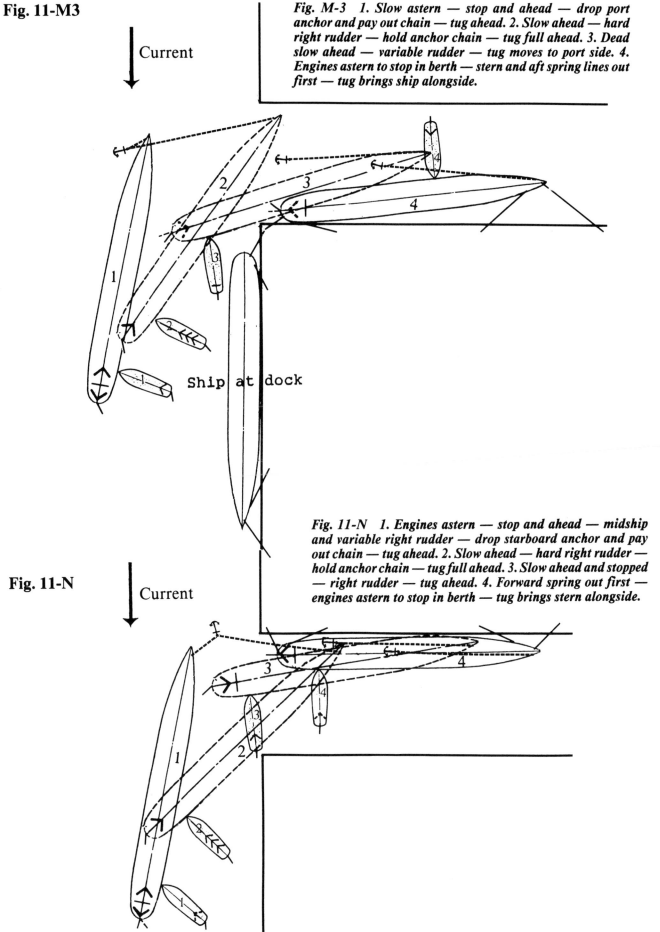

Current

Fig. M-3   1. Slow astern — stop and ahead — drop port anchor and pay out chain — tug ahead. 2. Slow ahead — hard right rudder — hold anchor chain — tug full ahead. 3. Dead slow ahead — variable rudder — tug moves to port side. 4. Engines astern to stop in berth — stern and aft spring lines out first — tug brings ship alongside.

Ship at dock

Fig. 11-N   1. Engines astern — stop and ahead — midship and variable right rudder — drop starboard anchor and pay out chain — tug ahead. 2. Slow ahead — hard right rudder — hold anchor chain — tug full ahead. 3. Slow ahead and stopped — right rudder — tug ahead. 4. Forward spring out first — engines astern to stop in berth — tug brings stern alongside.

Fig. 11-N

Current

but the starboard anchor should be used instead of the port.

The bow should be worked up in line with and off the corner of the dock, and the starboard anchor dropped while the ship drifts astern with the current and a shot or two of chain is let out and the anchor set. The ship can then head at an angle into the slip and slack water while the tug pushes the stern up against the current. The anchor chain leading under the hull toward the dock should breast her bow in while head lines are put out. The tug can bring the stern alongside to hold her in position until she is secured in her berth.

MOVING AND MANEUVERING STERN FIRST WITH A TUG LASHED UP ON BOW

A tug lashed up on the bow and facing aft on small and medium sized vessels can offdock, move stern first, and dock them with no trouble at all if properly executed.

Larger and deep draft ships are another matter, and this cannot be recommended without more tugs assisting.

As can be seen in Figure 11-O, when the tug is lashed up on the port bow of a ship facing aft we have a propeller and rudder on each end of the vessel.

Although the tug's propeller and rudder is not on the center line of the keel of the ship, it can do a good job if properly lashed up with no slack in the lines.

Off-docking is no problem because all that is needed is to hold the forward spring line on the ship and back the tug, which will breast the ships stern out into the channel. Then all that is necessary to do is let go the forward spring and come ahead on the tug. If the tug needs left rudder to bring the ship's bow away from the dock and the ship's stern starts to fall back alongside, all that is needed here is to put the ship's engine ahead with a right rudder and she will move broadside away from the dock.

Since the tug is pushing the ship stern first, and the tug's propeller and rudder is off balance with the center line of the keel of the ship, the tug can most likely steer her much better if the rudder of the ship is put toward the tug, (in this case it would be hard left rudder) in order to help offset this off balance.

When a tug or tugs are moving a ship stern first in a channel, the stern of the ship is treated as the bow and the bow as the stern. Meeting and passing signals should be given in the same manner.

When a ship is being pushed stern first with one or more tugs it is best not to get too much sternway on the ship. If the tug or tugs lose control and the ship takes a sheer toward the bank, or anything else, and the ship has to come ahead on her engines, she will sheer that much faster until she has lost most of her sternway.

Fig. 11-O 1. Let go stern lines — hold forward spring line — tug full astern — engines dead slow ahead — hard right rudder. 2. Stop engines and stop tug — let go spring line — tug ahead — variable rudder to keep bow clear — ship engines astern and stopped — left rudder. 3. Tug engines ahead and steady up in channel — ship engines stopped with midship or left rudder.

Fig. 11-O

Fig. 11-O1 1. Tugs slow ahead — ship engines stopped. 2. Tug ahead hard right rudder — ship ahead — left rudder. 3. Tug ahead — right rudder — ship ahead — left rudder — fore and aft spring lines out first — secure in berth.

Fig. 11-O1

Figure 11-O1 (Page 66) illustrates docking starboard side to the dock with the tug lashed up on the port bow, the same as it was when off docking in figure 11-O.

The tug should angle the ship toward the dock, and when she approaches her berth, the ship can come ahead on her engines with a left rudder, and if the tug uses right rudder while still coming ahead, the ship can move broadside up to her berth while lines are put out and kept clear of the ship's propeller. It is only a matter of matching the ship's propeller speed and rudder angle to the tug's propeller speed and rudder angle, and the tug must do what it is told (no more and no less) for the person handling the ship to be able to do this.

When a tug or tugs are moving a ship from one dock to another stern first, and the ship is going to dock port side to the dock after off docking as shown in Figure 11-O, she must work out into the channel and have the tug move from the port bow to the starboard bow and lash up. This is no problem as long as the tug has winches to heave her lines in and lash the tug up securely without having to push on the ships bow. If however,

Fig. 11-O2

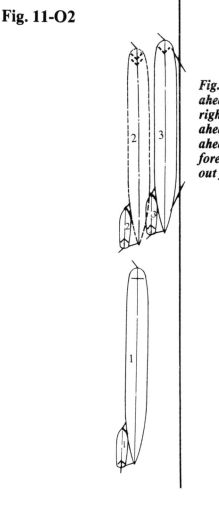

Fig. 11-O2 1. Tug ahead — ship stopped — right rudder. 2-3. — Tug ahead left rudder — ship ahead right rudder — fore and aft spring lines out first.

the tug is not equipped to lash herself up properly, it can be a real show in close quarters, and the ship may have to drop an anchor in order to stay out of trouble.

Figure 11-O2 illustrates how a ship can be made to go broadside by adjusting the propeller speed and rudder angle on both the ship and the tug.

It can be understood that because of the tug being lashed up off the center line of the keel of the ship, that if the tug is backed, the ship's bow will go to the port (toward the dock) and the stern to the starboard (away from the dock).

CHAPTER 12

OFF-DOCKING WITH ONE TUG ASSISTING

OFF DOCKING AND TURNING WHEN SHIP IS SECURED PORT SIDE TO THE DOCK

Figures 12-A and 12-A1 (Page 68) illustrates taking a ship offdock and turning her in a basin with calm weather conditions and no current.

The tug on the starboard bow can breast the stern of the ship well out into the channel, and then the tug can back the bow away from the dock and out into the channel. In the meantime, the stern of the ship will be going back in toward the dock, so the ship can put her rudder hard left and come ahead on her engines as her stern nears the dock. When the ship's engines come ahead with left rudder it starts a broad-side movement to starboard, but as the ship gains headway, the tug will fall alongside and offer less broadside pull, but more headway restriction on the ship's movement ahead.

If there is a strong ondock wind, and the ship is exceptionally light with no ballast, this can be a touchy situation, but if there is any other way to do it with one tug, this writer does not know of it. If the Pilot and/or Captain feels the ship's power plus the tugs power on the bow can do the job safely there is no reason not to get on with it. However, the ship's engines must be depended upon to come ahead with full speed if necessary, and the tug must be depended upon to hold the bow out into the channel and clear of any obstruction, including traffic.

With the ship going to a turning area after sailing, the tug should move to the port bow if the ship is turning in slack water because of the characteristics of the ship's stern going to port when her engines are put astern. However, if there happens to be currents that will effect her stern when her engines are backed, it will be best to leave the tug on the starboard bow and turn on a left rudder as shown in Figure 12-A2.

Fig. 12-A1

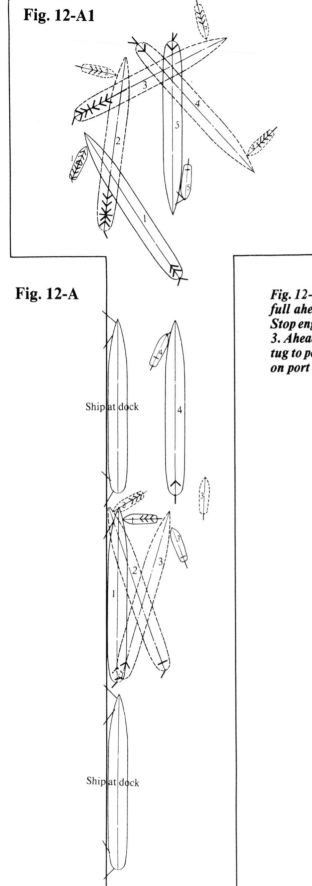

Fig. 12-A

Ship at dock

Ship at dock

Fig. 12-A1   1. Hard left rudder — tug full astern — hard right rudder — tug full ahead. 2. Stop and full astern — tug full ahead. 3. Half ahead and full astern — hard right rudder — tug full ahead. 4. Slow ahead — variable rudder — tug full ahead and stopped. 5. Half and slow ahead — steady up in channel — tug stopped and laying alongside.

Fig. 12-A   1. Take in stern lines — hold spring line forward — full ahead on tug — hard left rudder — dead slow ahead. 2. Stop engines — let go spring line forward — full astern on tug. 3. Ahead on engines — left rudder to keep stern clear — move tug to port bow. 4. Slow ahead — steady in channel — tug fast on port bow.

Fig. 12-A2

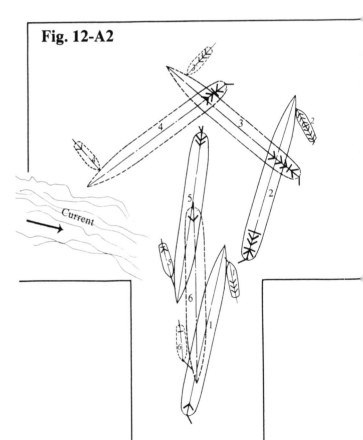

Current

Fig. 12-A2   1. Slow ahead — hard right rudder — tug full astern. 2. Hard left rudder — slow ahead stop and half astern — tug stopped and full ahead. 3. Slow ahead stop and full astern — tug full ahead. 4. Ahead and astern — hard left rudder — tug ahead. 5. Half ahead variable rudder — tug astern and stopped. 6. Slow ahead and steady up in channel — tug stopped.

SAILING AND TURNING OFF THE DOCK

If there is sufficient room for the ship to turn as she sails from her berth, it can generally be done as illustrated in Figure 12-A3. Currents and weather conditions however, may suggest a change from this simple procedure.

If the tug puts a stern line out from the tug to the ship, it should be able to breast the ship's stern out far enough into the channel for the ship to back away from the dock and turn. The main thing to watch is the ship's bow as she starts to back away from the dock. If there is slack water, it will be best to stop the tug for a few seconds until the ship's bow starts to come away from the dock. If there is a head current, it most likely will be necessary to back the tug as the ship starts astern in order to keep the bow off the dock until she can turn. (Figure 12-A4). If there is a stern current, there will most likely be no need to stop the tug's engine at all, but let it keep pushing dead slow ahead until the ship's bow clears, and then let it push full speed to turn and get under way. (Figure 12-A5) (Page 70).

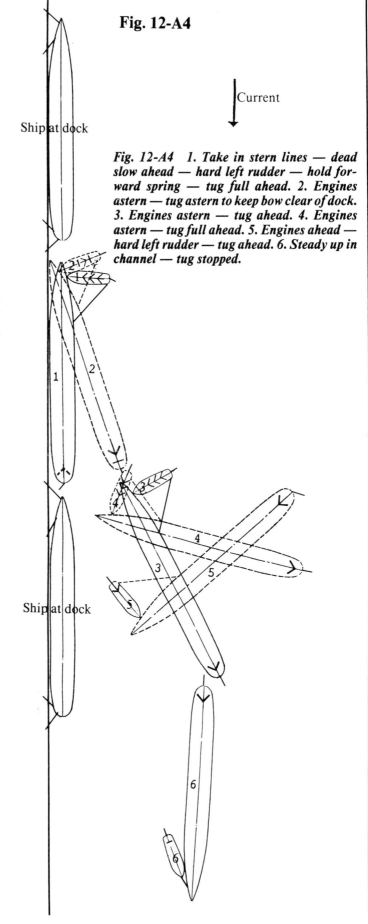

Fig. 12-A4

Current

Ship at dock

Fig. 12-A4   1. Take in stern lines — dead slow ahead — hard left rudder — hold forward spring — tug full ahead. 2. Engines astern — tug astern to keep bow clear of dock. 3. Engines astern — tug ahead. 4. Engines astern — tug full ahead. 5. Engines ahead — hard left rudder — tug ahead. 6. Steady up in channel — tug stopped.

Ship at dock

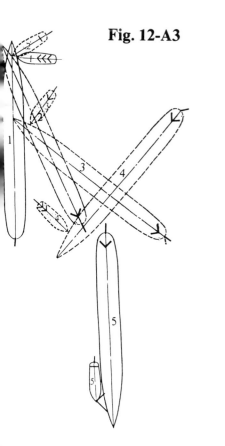

Fig. 12-A3

Fig. 12-A3   1. Take in stern lines — hold forward spring line — tug full ahead. 2. Take in forward spring line — stop tug — engines astern. 3. Tug keeps bow clear of dock. 4. Engines ahead — hard left rudder — tug ahead. 5. Steady up in channel — tug stopped.

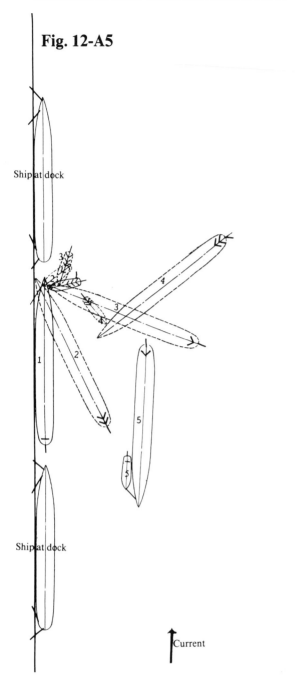

Fig. 12-A5

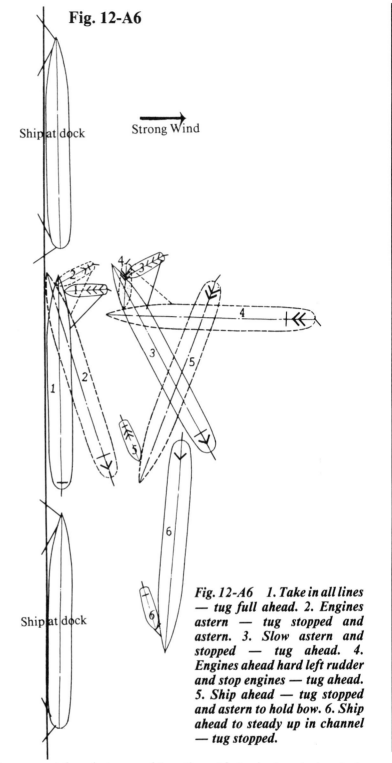

Fig. 12-A6

Fig. 12-A5   1. Take in stern lines — hold head and spring line — tug full ahead. 2. Engines astern — take in head lines — tug stopped and ahead. 3. Engines astern — tug ahead. 4. Engines ahead — hard left rudder — tug ahead. 5. Steady up in channel — tug stopped.

Fig. 12-A6   1. Take in all lines — tug full ahead. 2. Engines astern — tug stopped and astern. 3. Slow astern and stopped — tug ahead. 4. Engines ahead hard left rudder and stop engines — tug ahead. 5. Ship ahead — tug stopped and astern to hold bow. 6. Ship ahead to steady up in channel — tug stopped.

Water rushing by ships tied up at docks creates a turbulence the same as any other obstruction that interferes with the natural flow of water. So, if a light draft ship is sailing from a berth where there is a strong current, and there is a deep loaded ship secured at the up current end, there will be very little current effect felt until the ship moves away from the dock enough to feel the full force of the current.

Always, the draft of a ship, and the amount of her super-structure that is above the water line has to be taken into consideration. If she is deeply loaded, current, bottom and bank suction are the controlling factors. If she is light in the water, wind and current are the controlling factors.

The following illustrations suggest alternatives for turning at the dock when circumstances and conditions require such maneuvers.

If the ship is "flying light" with no ballast, and there is a gale blowing off the dock, the tug can breast her bow in to the dock while her stern comes away, and all lines

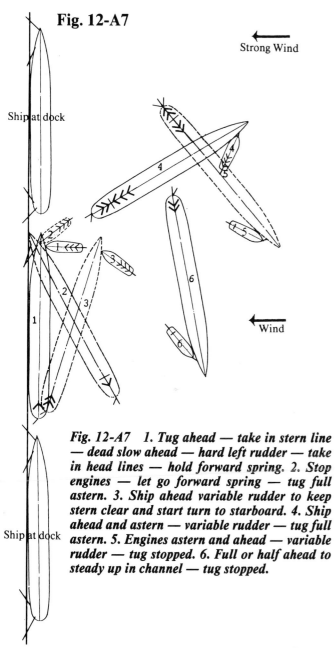

Fig. 12-A7 *1. Tug ahead — take in stern line — dead slow ahead — hard left rudder — take in head lines — hold forward spring. 2. Stop engines — let go forward spring — tug full astern. 3. Ship ahead variable rudder to keep stern clear and start turn to starboard. 4. Ship ahead and astern — variable rudder — tug full astern. 5. Engines astern and ahead — variable rudder — tug stopped. 6. Full or half ahead to steady up in channel — tug stopped.*

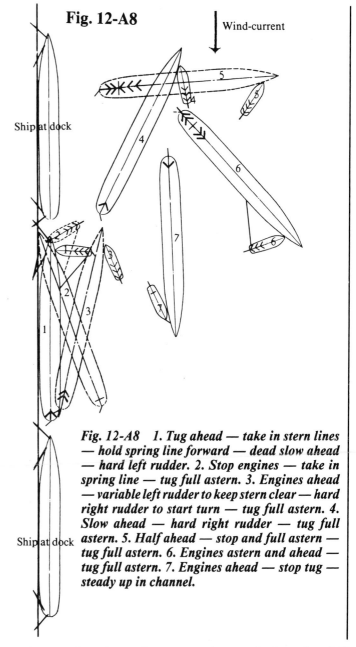

Fig. 12-A8 *1. Tug ahead — take in stern lines — hold spring line forward — dead slow ahead — hard left rudder. 2. Stop engines — take in spring line — tug full astern. 3. Engines ahead — variable left rudder to keep stern clear — hard right rudder to start turn — tug full astern. 4. Slow ahead — hard right rudder — tug full astern. 5. Half ahead — stop and full astern — tug full astern. 6. Engines astern and ahead — tug full astern. 7. Engines ahead — stop tug — steady up in channel.*

are taken in. The tug can be stopped, or backed if necessary while the ship is being blown out into the channel. The tug can then come ahead and turn her to head in the opposite direction.

The positive thing about turning in this manner is, that when the wind catches the opposite bow of the ship, the tug can be backed and act as a drag to keep her in position until she can gain enough headway to hold herself in position as she heads down the channel. (Figure 12-A6). (Page 70)

If there is a gale blowing on dock under the same circumstances, more of a problem will definitely exist.

It may as well be mentioned, that under extreme conditions, there is no such thing as dead slow or slow speed on either the ship's or tug's engines. It just will not work if the ship is sitting on top of the water and there is a gale of wind blowing. In many cases, both the ship's and tug's engines must be worked under full capacity in order to complete this maneuver without doing damage. It can be seen in Figure 12-A7 that, in this case, it is necessary to turn the ship on a right rudder while leaving the tug on the starboard bow.

Here again, if there is a strong head current and/or wind, it may be more desirable to sail the ship as illustrated in Figure 12-A8.

It generally will be best to leave the tug on the starboard bow, and turn on a right rudder after the ship is clear and has sufficient turning room. The tug will back alongside, but at the same time it will help keep the ship from gaining headway while she is coming ahead on her engines and turning with a hard right rudder. In most cases it will be found that the tug can be backed continuously until the ship has made her complete turn.

Figure 12-A9 illustrates sailing with a strong stern current and/or wind when it is necessary or desirable to leave the dock and turn on a right rudder, as is sometimes the case with a deep loaded vessel.

After the ship is clear of the dock the tug can move to the port bow and push her around to head into the wind and current.

SAILING FROM SLIP WITH SLACK WATER INTO CHANNEL AND CURRENT

If it were not for the vessel secured to the dock outside the slip as shown in Figure 12-B (Page 73), it is pos-

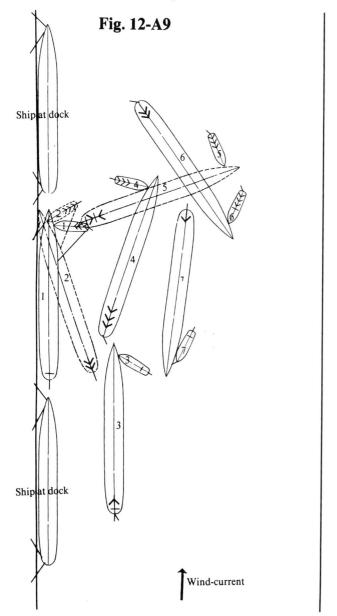

Fig. 12-A9

Ship at dock

Ship at dock

↑ Wind-current

Fig. 12-A9   1. Tug ahead — take in stern lines and head lines — hold forward spring. 2. Stop tug — engines astern — take in spring line — back tug if necessary to clear dock. 3. Engines ahead — hard right rudder — tug moved to port bow. 4. Full astern — tug full ahead. 5. Engines ahead and astern — tug full ahead. 6. Engines ahead — hard right rudder — tug ahead and stopped. 7. Engines ahead to steady up in channel — tug stopped.

sible that the ship would be able to sail by just moving along the dock until the current starts to swing her bow down stream while backing the tug to relieve some of the pressure on the dock, and by putting the engines full ahead with hard right rudder after her pivot point has passed the corner of the dock.

In this case however, it may be necessary to work the ship over to the opposite side of the slip in slack water before heading out into the current. It should be noted that when she starts out, there can be no stopping when she catches the current. If it appears that the tug will not be able to hold her bow, the starboard anchor can be put down and drug.

If there is any uncertainty about the ship being able to clear, she can be backed back into the calm water of the slip and the anchor put down before starting out of the slip.

Figure 12-B1 (Page 73), illustrates backing out of the slip and into a strong current on the starboard side.

As she backs out and the current starts to swing her around the corner of the dock, the tug can come up to her port bow and push as the ship continues moving astern. As she starts to become parallel to the outside dock and head into the current, the ship can keep her stern clear of the docks, while the tug continues to push her bow around and she turns on a right rudder and heads with the current.

In Figure 12-B2 (Page 73), the ship is sailing from the same position as shown in Figure 12-B1, but with the current catching her on the port side as she backs into the channel to head into the current.

Under most conditions, it will be found that it will not be necessary for the tug to put out a stern line to the ship as shown.

Figure 12-C (Page 74), illustrates leaving the slip from port side to the dock and heading into the current.

The tug would work the bow to the starboard side of the slip as close as possible, while the ship keeps her stern clear as she starts out of the slip. The tug backing alongside on the bow should keep the ship from making too much head way until the current catches her and she can come on out into the channel, full speed if necessary. Here again, it is easy to see that once the ship is committed to coming out of the slip, she must do just that. It should also be remembered that an anchor can be used if necessary.

In Figure 12-C1 (Page 74), the ship is leaving from starboard side to the dock and backing out of the slip with the current catching her on the port side.

As the current starts to swing the ship around the corner of the dock, the tug can come up on the starboard bow and push as the ship continues to move astern and head into the current.

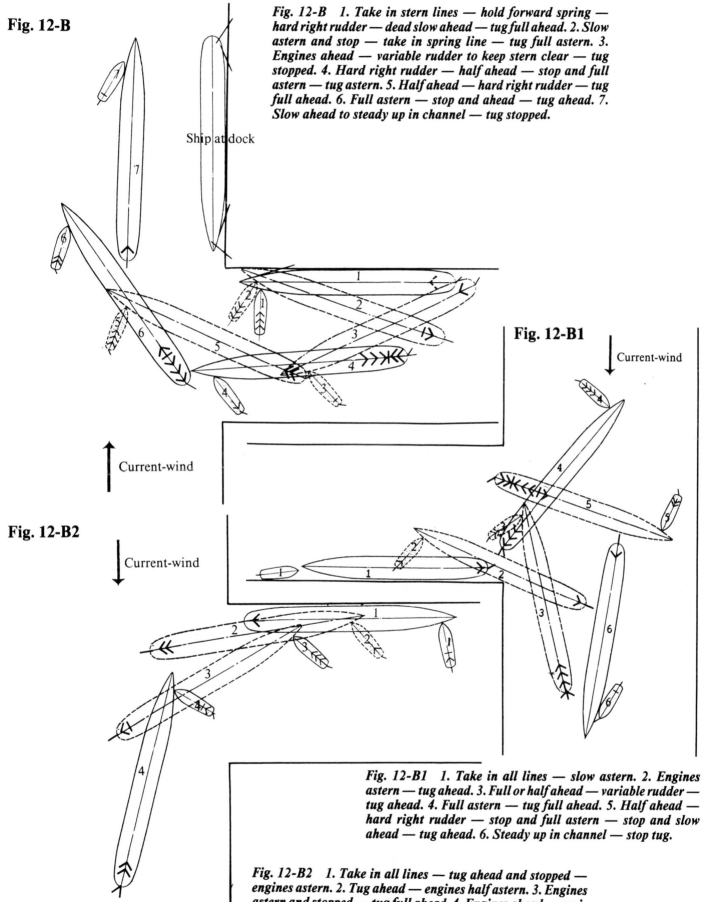

Fig. 12-B

Fig. 12-B   1. Take in stern lines — hold forward spring — hard right rudder — dead slow ahead — tug full ahead. 2. Slow astern and stop — take in spring line — tug full astern. 3. Engines ahead — variable rudder to keep stern clear — tug stopped. 4. Hard right rudder — half ahead — stop and full astern — tug astern. 5. Half ahead — hard right rudder — tug full ahead. 6. Full astern — stop and ahead — tug ahead. 7. Slow ahead to steady up in channel — tug stopped.

Ship at dock

Fig. 12-B1

Current-wind

Current-wind

Fig. 12-B2

Current-wind

Fig. 12-B1   1. Take in all lines — slow astern. 2. Engines astern — tug ahead. 3. Full or half ahead — variable rudder — tug ahead. 4. Full astern — tug full ahead. 5. Half ahead — hard right rudder — stop and full astern — stop and slow ahead — tug ahead. 6. Steady up in channel — stop tug.

Fig. 12-B2   1. Take in all lines — tug ahead and stopped — engines astern. 2. Tug ahead — engines half astern. 3. Engines astern and stopped — tug full ahead. 4. Engines ahead — variable rudder to steady up in channel — tug ahead and stopped.

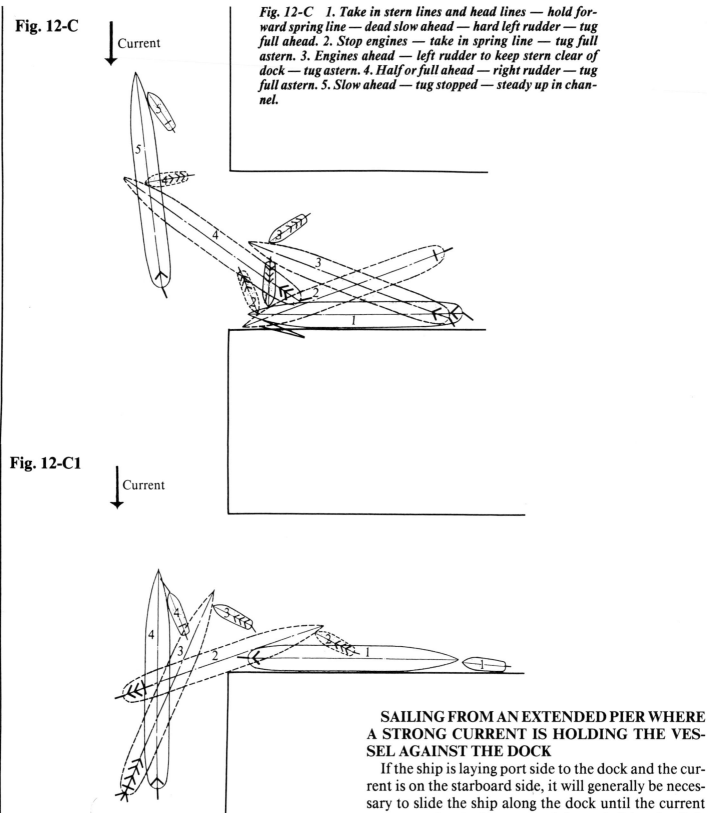

Fig. 12-C

Current

Fig. 12-C 1. Take in stern lines and head lines — hold forward spring line — dead slow ahead — hard left rudder — tug full ahead. 2. Stop engines — take in spring line — tug full astern. 3. Engines ahead — left rudder to keep stern clear of dock — tug astern. 4. Half or full ahead — right rudder — tug full astern. 5. Slow ahead — tug stopped — steady up in channel.

Fig. 12-C1

Current

Fig. 12-C1 1. Take in all lines — slow astern. 2. Tug full ahead — engines half astern and stopped. 3. Full ahead — variable rudder — tug full ahead. 4. Steady up in channel — tug stopped.

SAILING FROM AN EXTENDED PIER WHERE A STRONG CURRENT IS HOLDING THE VESSEL AGAINST THE DOCK

If the ship is laying port side to the dock and the current is on the starboard side, it will generally be necessary to slide the ship along the dock until the current starts to swing the bow around the end of the pier. It is best to use the ship's engines with a midship rudder, and the tug stopped, so that the ship's hull will maintain the same amount of pressure against the dock.

As she moves out into the channel and the force of the current starts to turn her around the end of the pier, the tug can push on the bow until the current is on the port quarter and side of her hull. Then the tug can be backed and the current will take her away from the end of the pier out into the channel. It should be noted however, that while all of this is going on, the ships engines will need to be put astern enough to keep her from gaining headway with the current. (Figure 12-D).

If the ship is head in and starboard side to the dock, with the current on the port side, she can back her stern out into the channel, while leaving the tug stopped until she starts to pivot around the end of the pier. At this time the tug can be backed until the current is well on the starboard bow. The tug can then be stopped and the ships engines put ahead at the necessary speed to head into the current and turn on a right rudder to head with the current.

Here again, it should be noted, that as the ship pivots around the end of the pier and she heads into the current, it will be necessary to come ahead on her engines enough to keep her from gaining sternway with the current. (Figure 12-D1).

SAILING WITH THE CURRENT HOLDING THE VESSEL OFF THE DOCK

As shown in the following illustrations, this is a touchy situation, and it all boils down to the amount of room there is for a vessel to maneuver. It's not a matter of off-docking, but a matter of getting headed in the right direction after the lines are let go and the ship is on her own.

If the ship is secured starboard side to the dock and headed toward the channel, and she is going to head into the current, the tug can be placed on the port bow and there is not much to it except for the fact that it will be necessary for the ship's engines to be worked ahead and astern as necessary while the tug is bringing the ship's bow into the current. It must be remembered that if the ship has too much headway, the tug will not be able to work at a right angle to the ship and consequently will not be able to push her bow up against the current as effectually as it can with the ship stopped in the water. (Figure 12-D2). (Page 76)

When the ship is going to head with the current after leaving the dock we still have the problem of how much room she has in which to maneuver.

When in confined quarters and leaving a pier with the current pushing the ship away from the dock and with the tug on the port bow as illustrated in Figure 12-D3 (Page 76), the tug will be backing the bow around while keeping the ship from making too much headway, but it will not stop the broadside movement caused by the current. If there is enough room this sort of maneuver will work fine, but if there is not it will be necessary to approach it from another angle and place

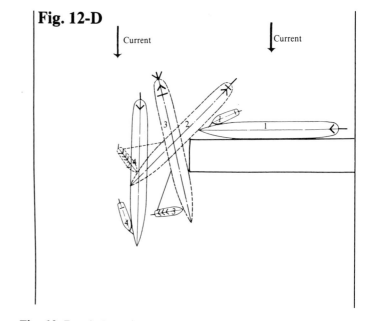

Fig. 12-D 1. Take in all lines — slow ahead — tug stopped. 2. Engines astern and stopped — tug full ahead. 3. Engines astern — tug astern. 4. Slow ahead — tug stopped.

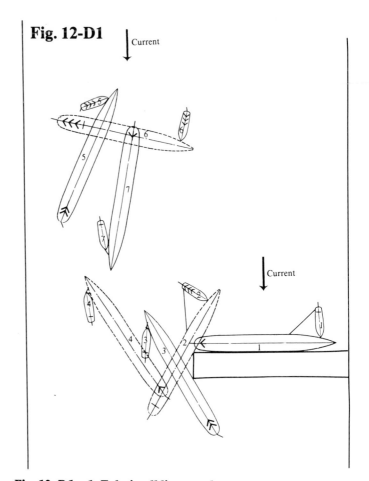

Fig. 12-D1 1. Take in all lines — slow astern — tug stopped. 2. Engines stopped — tug full astern. 3. Half ahead — right rudder — tug stopped. 4. Slow ahead — tug stopped. 5. Half ahead — hard right rudder — tug full ahead. 6. Full astern and stopped — tug full ahead. 7. Slow ahead — tug stopped — steady up in channel.

the tug on the port quarter of the ship as shown in Figure 12-D4.

The port anchor can be put out with one shot (90 feet) or more in the water depending on the depth of the harbor, before letting the lines go.

The tug should be able to hold the ship's stern up against the current as the bow comes around with it. It should be remembered however, that the anchor must drag and be picked up after the ship is under way or the ship will turn around with the current regardless of what the tug may do.

Figure 12-D5 illustrates sailing with the current running under the pier and pushing the ship away form the dock. If it is not too strong, and there is sufficient room, this procedure works well. However, with the tug laying broadside at a right angle to the ship and held by a

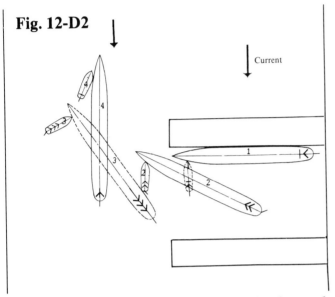

Fig. 12-D2   1. Take in all lines — slow ahead and stopped — tug slow ahead and stopped. 2. Half or full ahead — hard right rudder — tug half or full ahead. 3. Full astern — tug full ahead. 4. Engines ahead — steady up in channel — tug stopped.

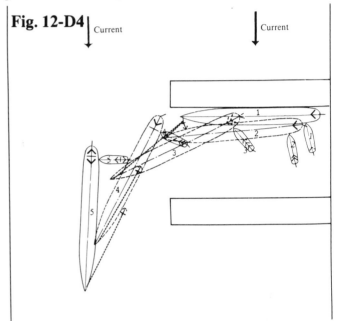

Fig. 12-D4   1. Drop port anchor — take in all lines — slow ahead — tug slow ahead. 2. Slow ahead — left rudder — slack anchor chain — tug half ahead. 3. Variable speed ahead — variable rudder — hold anchor chain — tug full ahead. 4. Slow ahead and stopped — tug ahead — heave anchor. 5. Engines astern — stop and slow ahead — tug holds stern in current — heave in anchor.

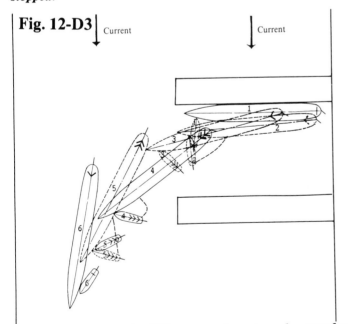

Fig. 12-D3   1. Take in all lines — engines stopped — tug slow astern. 2. Dead slow ahead — hard left rudder — tug slow astern. 3. Slow ahead — hard left rudder — tug half or full astern. 4. Half or full ahead — hard left rudder — tug full astern. 5. Half astern if necessary — tug full astern. 6. Slow ahead to steady up in channel — tug stopped.

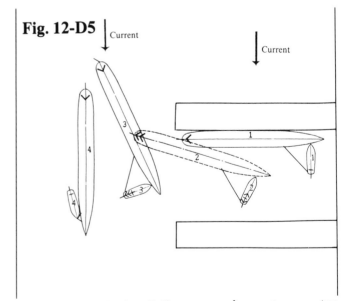

Fig. 12-D5   1. Take in all lines — engines astern — tug stopped. 2. Engines astern — tug astern or ahead to keep bow in position. 3. Engines ahead — right rudder — tug astern and stopped. 4. Slow ahead to steady up in channel — tug stopped.

stern line, the ship cannot gain good sternway or the tug's stern line is subject to break, or capsize the tug.

Sailing with the tug lashed up on the bow, is one of the best, and sometimes the only way, to sail in close quarters when the current is pushing the ship away from the dock as shown in Figure 12-D6.

In this manner, the ship can use as much engine speed astern as necessary to clear before drifting down against the other extended pier. Also, if necessary the tug can be backed to keep the ship from gaining excessive sternway, or it can come ahead with a hard right rudder to assist in turning as the ship clears.

When the ship is clear and straight in the channel, she must not gain headway until the tug can let its stern line go, and is able to fall alongside as the ship gets under way.

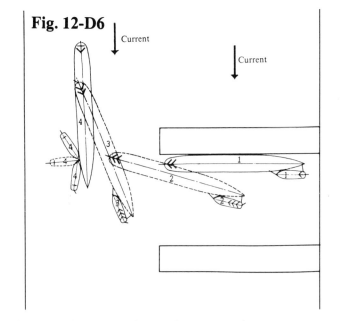

Fig. 12-D6

Fig. 12-D6   1. Take in all lines — engines astern — tug ahead. 2. Engines astern — tug full ahead with hard right rudder. 3. Engines ahead — right rudder — tug ahead with right rudder. 4. Engines stopped and ahead — tug stopped and take in stern line to fall alongside.

CHAPTER 13

MANEUVERING A SHIP EQUIPPED WITH BOW- THRUSTER AND ONE TUG ASSISTING

Maneuvering a ship equipped with a bow-thruster only is explained in Chapter 8.

No ship steers or handles well with a tug hanging on her quarter, and for that reason one should not be brought alongside until they are needed.

Figure 13-A illustrates turning in close quarters with a tug assisting on the starboard quarter.

As can be seen, the bow-thruster takes care of the bow and the tug does its thing on the stern. The approximate propeller speeds are shown, but it always depends upon the person handling the vessel as to what happens.

Figure 13-A1 (Page 78) is almost a repetition of docking a ship port side to the dock by using the ship's bow-thruster only, as illustrated in chapter 8, Figure 8-A.

However, the tug on the starboard quarter of the ship can push her stern in, or back to hold her stern off of another vessel, or to keep the ship's stern from coming along side the dock too hard.

When going starboard side to the dock however, a tug on the port quarter can be of real value as shown in Figure 13-A2. (Page 78).

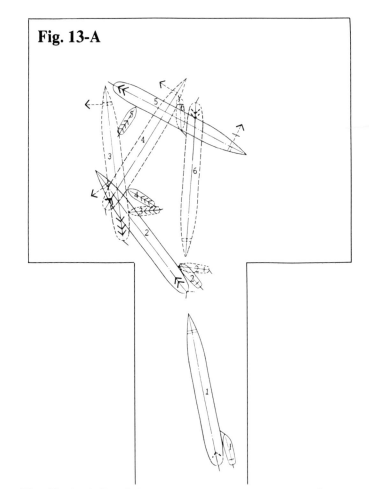

Fig. 13-A

Fig. 13-A   1. Dead slow ahead — tug stopped. 2. Half ahead — hard left and hard right rudder — thrust to starboard — tug stopped. 3. Full astern — thrust to starboard — tug full ahead. 4. Slow ahead — hard right rudder — thrust to starboard — tug full ahead. 5. Half astern — tug full ahead — thrust to starboard and stop bow-thruster. 6. Engines ahead to steady up in channel — tug stopped and let go or lay alongside.

Fig. 13-A1   Fig. 13-A2

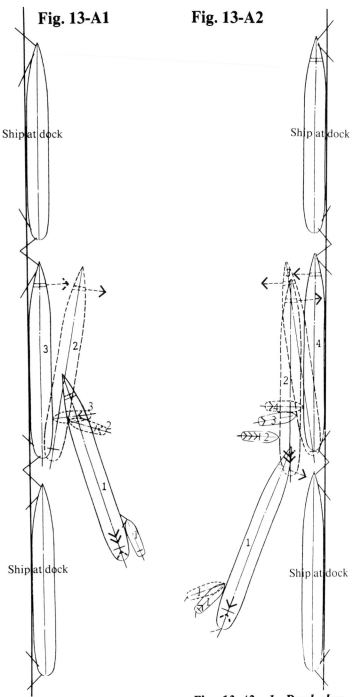

Ship at dock

Ship at dock

Ship at dock

Ship at dock

Fig. 13-A1 1. Dead slow ahead — stop and half astern — tug stopped. 2. Engines stopped — thrust to port — tug holds stern in position. 3. Thrust to port — tug slow ahead — secure in berth.

Fig. 13-A2 1. Dead slow ahead — left and midship rudder — slow astern — thrust to port — tug stopped and slow ahead. 2. Thrust to port — half astern — tug full ahead. 3. Stop engines — thrust to starboard — tug slow ahead. 4. Thrust to starboard — tug slow ahead — secure in berth.

The tug can be worked into position to hold the ship's stern in toward the dock when her engines are put astern so that lines can be put out and she is secured in her berth.

MOVING WITH HEAD CURRENT AND DOCKING HEAD IN AND PORT SIDE TO THE DOCK IN A SLIP WITH SLACK WATER

Figure 13-A3 (Page 79) is self explanatory. As the ship turns on a right rudder and her bow enters the slack water of the slip, she works her bow-thruster to hold the bow close to the dock, while the tug on her starboard quarter pushes her stern up against the current as she swings into place and is secured at her berth.

BACKING INTO SLIP AND DOCKING STARBOARD SIDE TO THE DOCK WITH STERN CURRENT

Figure 13-A4 (Page 79), maneuver is done just the opposite of what is shown in Figure 13-A3. While the ship backs into the current, she will be backing to port, and as the stern enters the slack water of the slip, the tug has to hold her stern in close to the dock while the bow-thruster brings her bow around against the current.

Depending on the draft of the ship and the force of the current, this too can be a touchy situation. Here again, if the bow-thruster has sufficient power it can keep the bow of the ship angled to the current so that the ship can back on into the slip.

Figure 13-A5 (Page 80), illustrates taking the ship into the slip stern first, either with a slack tide in the channel or with a stern current. Following this procedure with a strong head current cannot be recommended because it is very unlikely that the tug and the ships bow-thruster can stop the ships broadside movement when the current is at a right angle to the ships hull. However, with a following current the tug can fall around away from the ship's side and head into the slip while moving her stern first into the slip and holding her stern near the dock for putting out stern lines while the bow-thruster brings her alongside the dock.

There is one thing to consider when having a tug move a ship into a narrow slip on a hawser, and that is to make sure that the tug has enough room to come out of the slip when the ship is secured at her berth. When there is another vessel berthed on the opposite side of a narrow slip, it is somewhat embarrassing to find after your vessel is secured that the tug which assisted you on a hawser does not have room to get out of the slip between the two vessels.

DOCKING HEAD IN AND STARBOARD SIDE TO THE DOCK IN A SLIP WITH A HEAD CURRENT

In this situation the tug can put a line on the starboard quarter of the vessel as she approaches the slip.

The ship can use her bow-thruster as needed to land gently against the corner of the dock as near the mid-

Fig. 13-A3

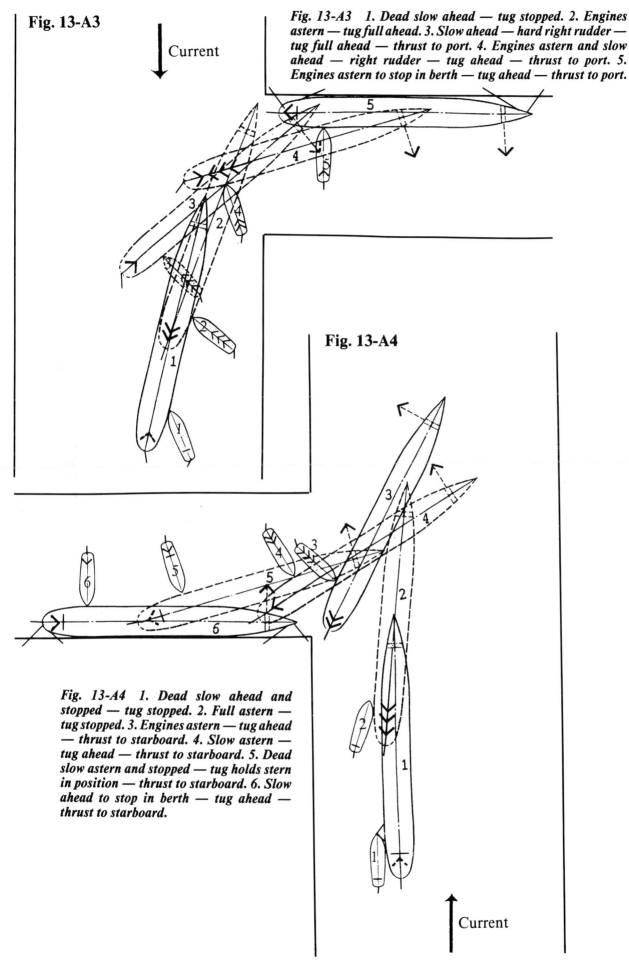

Current

Fig. 13-A3   1. Dead slow ahead — tug stopped. 2. Engines astern — tug full ahead. 3. Slow ahead — hard right rudder — tug full ahead — thrust to port. 4. Engines astern and slow ahead — right rudder — tug ahead — thrust to port. 5. Engines astern to stop in berth — tug ahead — thrust to port.

Fig. 13-A4

Fig. 13-A4   1. Dead slow ahead and stopped — tug stopped. 2. Full astern — tug stopped. 3. Engines astern — tug ahead — thrust to starboard. 4. Slow astern — tug ahead — thrust to starboard. 5. Dead slow astern and stopped — tug holds stern in position — thrust to starboard. 6. Slow ahead to stop in berth — tug ahead — thrust to starboard.

Current

ship section of her hull as possible. She can then use the bow-thruster to breast her bow into the slip, while the tug pushes her stern up into the current.

As she moves into the slip and loses the force of the current on her stern, the tug can let go and move to the port side to hold her against the dock while she is being secured. (Figure 13-A6) (Page 80).

Fig. 13-A5

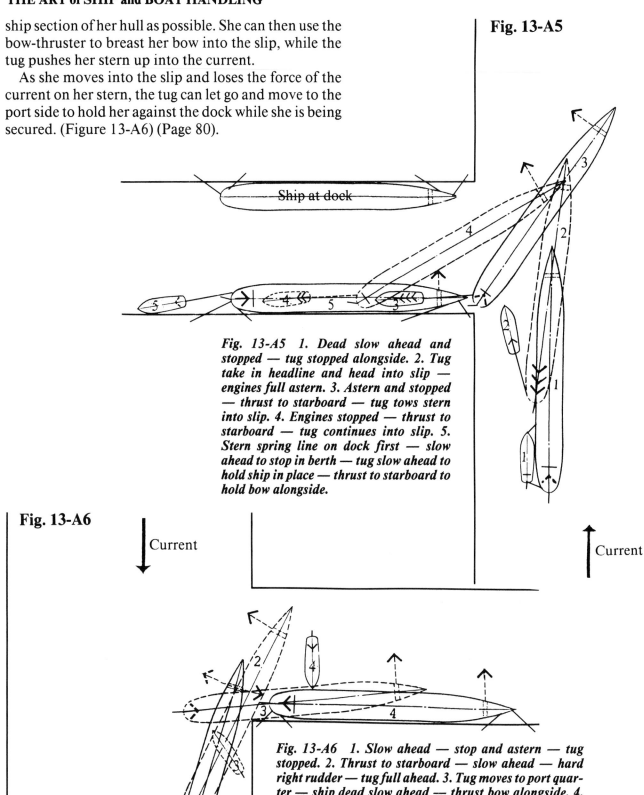

Fig. 13-A5 1. Dead slow ahead and stopped — tug stopped alongside. 2. Tug take in headline and head into slip — engines full astern. 3. Astern and stopped — thrust to starboard — tug tows stern into slip. 4. Engines stopped — thrust to starboard — tug continues into slip. 5. Stern spring line on dock first — slow ahead to stop in berth — tug slow ahead to hold ship in place — thrust to starboard to hold bow alongside.

Fig. 13-A6

Current

Current

Fig. 13-A6 1. Slow ahead — stop and astern — tug stopped. 2. Thrust to starboard — slow ahead — hard right rudder — tug full ahead. 3. Tug moves to port quarter — ship dead slow ahead — thrust bow alongside. 4. Slow astern to stop in berth — tug ahead — thrust to starboard to hold ship alongside.

HEADING INTO THE CURRENT AND GOING STERN FIRST AND PORT SIDE TO THE DOCK INSIDE A SLIP

As can be noted in the following diagrams, this procedure is opposite to the situation in Figure 13-A6.

In this case the tug would still put a line on the starboard quarter, but she would stay there. The vessel would use her bow-thruster to land gently against the corner of the dock as near the midship section of the hull as possible, and the tug would push her stern around into the slip, while the ship's bow-thruster holds her bow against the current as she backs into the slip, as shown in Figure 13-A7.

While illustration 13-A8 shows that the bow-thruster is unable to hold the bow against the current. The ship can continue to back on into the slip as the bow falls around with the current. As the current effect becomes less, the bow-thruster should be able to bring the bow alongside.

Fig. 13-A7 Current

Fig. 13-A7   1. Slow ahead — tug stopped. 2. Full astern — tug ahead. 3. Full astern — stop — slow ahead and slow astern — tug full ahead. 4. Thrust to port — full astern — tug ahead. 3. Dead slow ahead to stop in berth — tug slow ahead — thrust to port to hold ship alongside.

Fig. 13-A8 Current

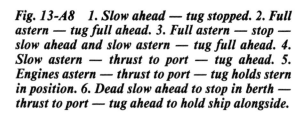

Fig. 13-A8   1. Slow ahead — tug stopped. 2. Full astern — tug full ahead. 3. Full astern — stop — slow ahead and slow astern — tug full ahead. 4. Slow astern — thrust to port — tug ahead. 5. Engines astern — thrust to port — tug holds stern in position. 6. Dead slow ahead to stop in berth — thrust to port — tug ahead to hold ship alongside.

CHAPTER 14

EFFECT OF TWO TUGS ALONGSIDE A SHIP UNDERWAY

As explained in chapter 10, a tug made fast alongside a ship underway and moving through the water has an effect on light draft vessels.

Two tugs alongside and made fast on the same side can cause a good bit of trouble when traversing and maneuvering in narrow congested channels, especially if they are allowed to lay at an angle to the ship while making steerage way as shown in Figure 14-A. With the tug on the starboard quarter acting as a right rudder and the one on the bow acting as a drag, the ship will have to carry considerable left rudder in order to stay on a straight course, which will then cause a broadside movement to port.

If both tugs are positioned alongside in line with the hull of the ship she will still take some left rudder, but should experience some broadside movement to starboard. (Figure 14-B).

Figure 14-C illustrates the effect of a tug made fast on the starboard bow and one made fast on the port quarter. With the tug on the quarter acting as a left rudder, and the one on the starboard bow acting as a drag, the ship will take right rudder and will experience a broadside movement to starboard.

If both tugs lay parallel she will steer somewhat better and experience very little if any broadside movement.

If, of course, the ship has a tug of the same size on each bow and they lay at the same angle to the ship's hull, they will act only as a drag and have no effect on the ship's steering or drift. (Figure 14-D).

Fig. 14-A   **Fig. 14-B**   **Fig. 14-C**   **Fig. 14-D**

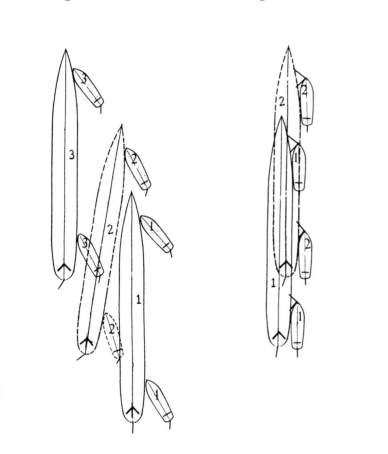

Fig. 14-A 1. Tugs made fast and laying at an angle on starboard side of ship. Note rudder angle and drift to port.

Fig. 14-B 1. Tugs on starboard side of ship laying parallel — minimal drift to starboard.

Fig. 14-C 1. Tugs on opposite sides laying at an angle. Note rudder angle and drift to starboard.

Fig. 14-D 1. Tugs made fast on each bow laying at same angle or parallel. No drift.

CHAPTER 15

HANDLING A SHIP WITH TWO TUGS ASSISTING

TURNING IN CHANNEL OR BASIN

Turning a ship with two tugs assisting is only a matter of applying pressure on the opposite sides of each end of the vessel as shown in Figure 15-A. If the ship backs to port, she would turn on a right rudder, and when she has safely completed the turn, the tug on the starboard quarter should let go and stand by in order to keep from interfering with the ship's steering.

DOCKING STARBOARD SIDE TO THE DOCK BETWEEN TWO SHIPS

The procedures shown here need little explanation. In Figure 15-B (Page 84), the same risk is taken as

Fig. 15-A

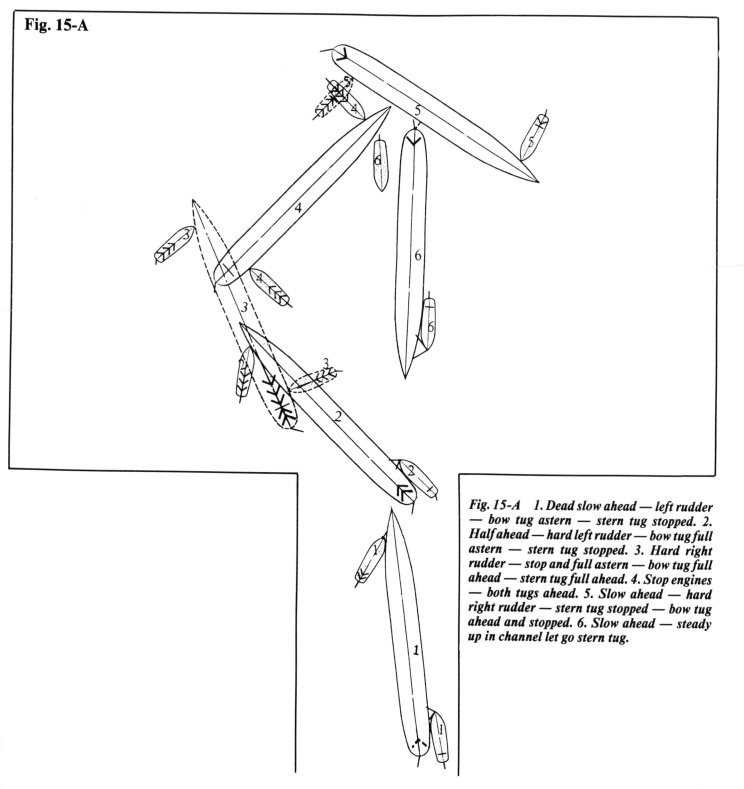

Fig. 15-A 1. Dead slow ahead — left rudder — bow tug astern — stern tug stopped. 2. Half ahead — hard left rudder — bow tug full astern — stern tug stopped. 3. Hard right rudder — stop and full astern — bow tug full ahead — stern tug full ahead. 4. Stop engines — both tugs ahead. 5. Slow ahead — hard right rudder — stern tug stopped — bow tug ahead and stopped. 6. Slow ahead — steady up in channel let go stern tug.

explained in Chapter 11 when docking in the same manner with one tug assisting, with the exception that there is no need to work the ship's engines against a spring line.

In slack water if the ship's engines can be depended upon to stop her head-way, and the tug on the port quarter can hold her stern while she is backing, there will be no problem and the tugs can push her alongside for securing. However, if there is any misjudgment in

the ship stopping her headway, or the ability of the tug on the quarter to keep her from backing to port, she will most likely ram the dock or the ship ahead, or both.

With a strong head current however, the situation changes somewhat as shown in Figure 15-B1.

The vessel can be stopped directly off of her berth and clear of the other vessels. She can then angle her bow toward the dock, while the current with the assistance of the tugs, takes her alongside. It will, of course, be necessary to use her engines to stay in position with the dock in order to keep from gaining sternway until she is alongside and at least head lines are out, or the tugs are in a position to hold her.

Figure 15-C (Page 85), illustrates the only really safe way to dock a ship under these conditions, especially if the ship is loaded. In fact, it is the safest way to dock a loaded ship even at an open dock.

If there is a strong stern current, the ship must be careful not to get her stern at too much of an angle to the dock or she will start to go broadside with the current and have to come ahead on her engines with a hard right rudder to avoid doing damage.

By keeping her stern at a slight angle toward the dock with the use of the tugs, she can use her engines to keep from gaining headway and the current and tugs can put her alongside for securing. (Figure 15-C1) (Page 85).

SAILING FROM CHANNEL BERTH

If the ship employs two tugs for sailing from this berth and it is necessary to turn in a basin or other turning area, it can be done as shown in Figure 15-D (Page 85). The tug on the port quarter would back the ship's stern away from the dock while the tug forward would breast the ship's bow in toward the dock, and then back her bow out into the channel.

The tug on the stern should then let go and come alongside the ship on the starboard quarter just before she is ready to turn.

In the event the ship backs to starboard, or for some reason it is necessary for her to turn on a left rudder, the tug that has let go from the port quarter can come alongside on the starboard bow, and the tug on the port bow can slide back to the port quarter for turning. (Figure 15-D1). (Page 85).

If there is room enough to turn off the dock, it can be done efficiently as shown in Figure 15-E (Page 86), when there is slack water or a stern current.

One of the tugs can put a hawser on the ship's stern and pull her around, while the tug on the port bow holds her off the dock and the ship uses her engines to back clear while turning.

When there is a strong head current, it may be necessary to off-dock as illustrated in Figure 15-E1 (Page 87), since the tug on the bow might not be able to hold the bow against the current to keep it off the dock and clear of the ship astern.

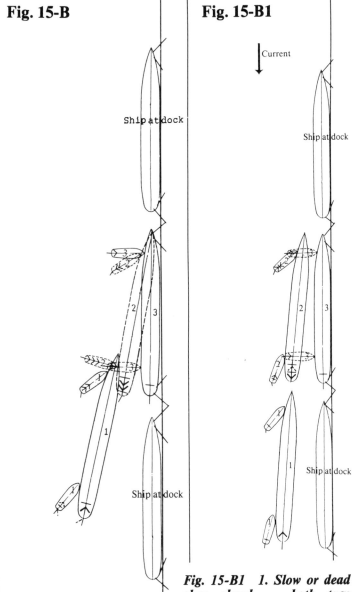

Fig. 15-B

Fig. 15-B1

Current

Ship at dock

Ship at dock

Ship at dock

Ship at dock

Fig. 15-B 1. Slow ahead and stopped — variable rudder — bow tug astern — tug aft stopped and ahead. 2. Engines astern and stopped — bow tug astern — tug aft ahead. 3. Engines stopped — both tugs ahead to hold vessel alongside for securing.

Fig. 15-B1 1. Slow or dead slow ahead — both tugs stopped —current on port bow. 2. Engines astern to stop a beam of berth — ahead and stopped to hold position against current — use tugs ahead and astern as necessary to keep current on port bow. 3. Both tugs ahead to hold vessel alongside — head lines and after spring out first — engines stopped.

Fig. 15-C

Fig. 15-C1

Fig. 15-D

Fig. 15-D1

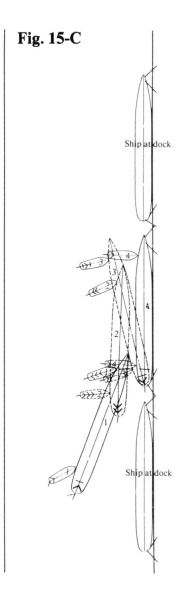

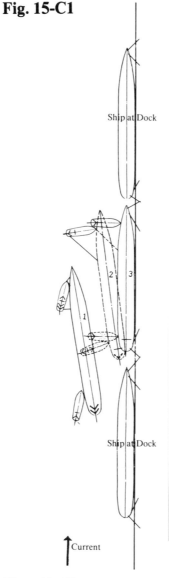

↑ Current

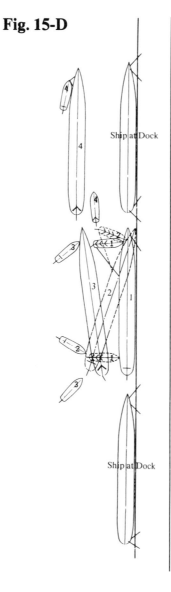

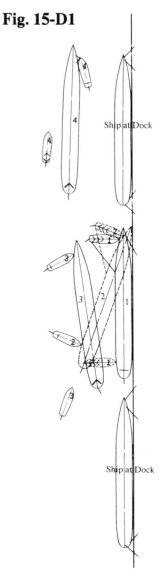

Fig. 15-C 1. Engines ahead and stopped — midships and hard left rudder — bow tug full astern — tug aft ahead. 2. Engines astern — bow tug astern — tug aft ahead. 3. Slow astern to stop at berth — tug aft holds stern in position — bow tug brings bow alongside. 4. Engines stopped — both tugs ahead to hold vessel alongside for securing.

Fig. 15-C1 1. Engines astern to stop abeam of berth — tugs hold ship at angle to current. 2. Engines astern to hold ship against current — tugs hold ship in position. 3. Engines stopped — stern and forward spring lines out first — tugs hold ship in place for securing.

Fig. 15-D 1. Take in stern and bow lines — hold forward spring — full ahead on bow tug — full astern on tug aft. 2. Stop tug aft — let go forward spring — full astern on bow tug. 3. Stop bow tug — steady up in channel — let go tug aft. 4. Tug number 4 stand by to make fast on starboard quarter for turning.

Fig. 15-D1 1. Take in stern and bow lines — hold forward spring — full ahead on bow tug — full astern on tug aft. 2. Stop tug aft. Let go forward spring — full astern on bow tug. 3. Stop bow tug — engines ahead to steady up in channel — let go tug aft. 4. Stern tug makes fast on starboard bow — tug on port bow stands by to make fast on port quarter for turning.

THE ART of SHIP and BOAT HANDLING

The ship would off dock in the same manner as if she were to continue to head into the current, but instead would continue to turn on a hard left rudder with the tug on the port bow backing full. The ship would keep her stern clear with her engines while the tug on the port quarter holds her stern up against the current and the bow comes around to where she is headed down stream.

HEADING IN AND DOCKING INSIDE SLIPS

With slack water and calm conditions there should never be a problem of heading into and docking either side to the dock in a slip, even a narrow one, with two tugs assisting. If however, the slip is so narrow that the tugs cannot work around broadside to the ship she must be careful not to gain too much headway, especially with a port backing ship going starboard side to the dock. The tugs pushing at an angle will tend to push her ahead and it will be necessary to back her engines until lines are on the dock. (See Figures 15-F and 15-F1) (Page 87).

SAILING FROM SLIP

Coming out of a slip and into a channel with slack water need not be illustrated because all that is necessary is to back or head out, and let the tugs head her in the direction she wishes to go as long as there are no obstructions.

However, if the ship has to come out and pass other vessels secured inside the slip, and there is not room enough for the tugs to work at a right angle to the ship, it can be done as shown in Figure 15-F2 (Page 88).

One of the tugs can lash up on the bow headed aft, and the other can put out a short hawser as near the center line of the ship as possible on the stern. The ship can hold a spring line forward and have the tug on the bow put its engines astern, while the tug on the hawser comes slow ahead to bring the ships stern clear. Then the bow tug can come ahead and steer the bow clear while the tug on the hawser tows her out into the channel and heads her in the direction she wishes to go.

DOCKING WITH HEAD CURRENT

When going port side to the dock with a strong head current the situation changes somewhat. The ship should steer in close to the opening of the slip while still heading into the current as nearly as possible until she can head her bow into the slack water of the slip. The tug on the stern will then do most of the work by pushing her stern up against the current. The tug on the bow should have no trouble taking care of that end because that part of her hull will be in slack water. (Figure 15-F3) (Page 88).

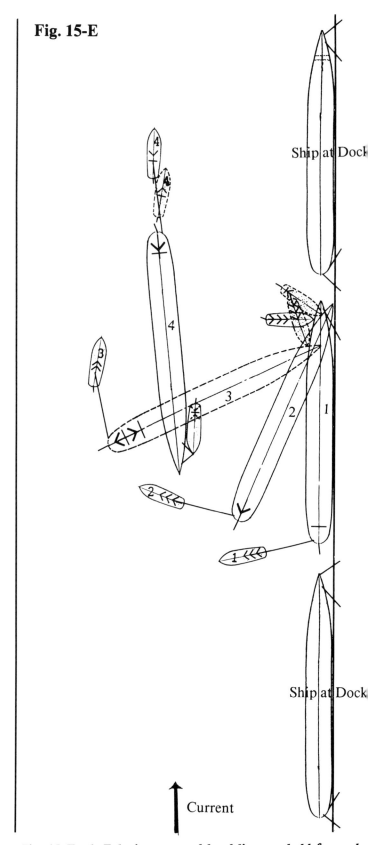

Fig. 15-E

Current

Fig. 15-E   1. Take in stern and head lines — hold forward spring — bow and stern tugs full ahead. 2. Engines slow astern — bow tug stopped and astern — take in spring line forward — stern tug ahead. 3. Engines astern and ahead — bow tug full ahead — stern tug ahead. 4. Slow ahead and stopped — bow tug ahead and astern to hold ship in position — stern tug let go and take in hawser.

Fig. 15-E1

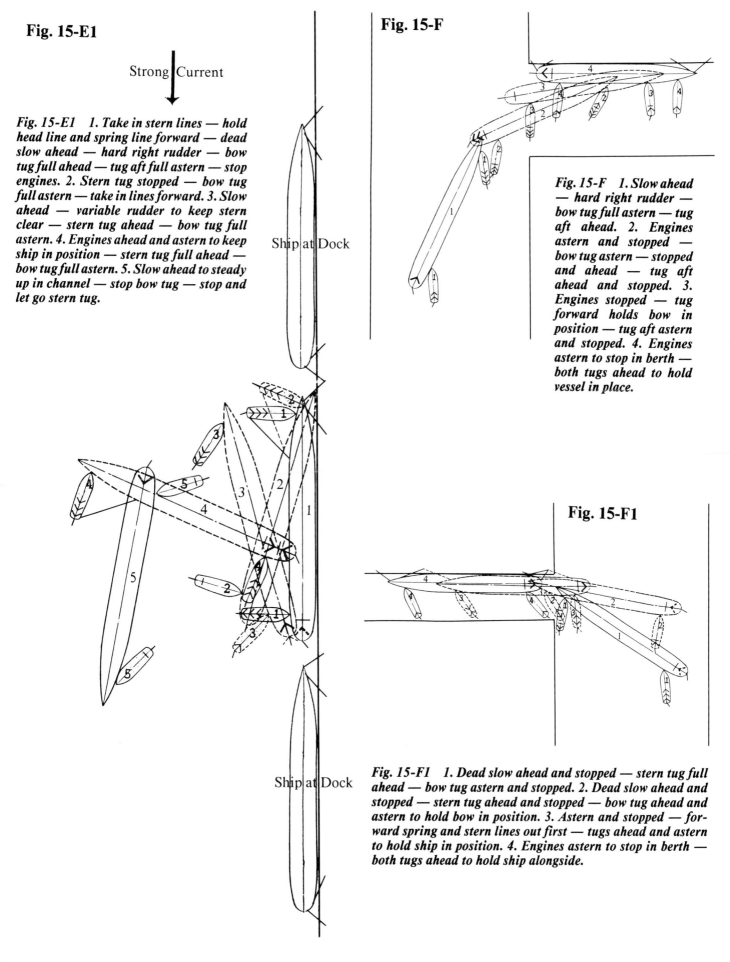

Strong Current

Fig. 15-E1   1. Take in stern lines — hold head line and spring line forward — dead slow ahead — hard right rudder — bow tug full ahead — tug aft full astern — stop engines. 2. Stern tug stopped — bow tug full astern — take in lines forward. 3. Slow ahead — variable rudder to keep stern clear — stern tug ahead — bow tug full astern. 4. Engines ahead and astern to keep ship in position — stern tug full ahead — bow tug full astern. 5. Slow ahead to steady up in channel — stop bow tug — stop and let go stern tug.

Ship at Dock

Ship at Dock

Fig. 15-F

Fig. 15-F   1. Slow ahead — hard right rudder — bow tug full astern — tug aft ahead. 2. Engines astern and stopped — bow tug astern — stopped and ahead — tug aft ahead and stopped. 3. Engines stopped — tug forward holds bow in position — tug aft astern and stopped. 4. Engines astern to stop in berth — both tugs ahead to hold vessel in place.

Fig. 15-F1

Fig. 15-F1   1. Dead slow ahead and stopped — stern tug full ahead — bow tug astern and stopped. 2. Dead slow ahead and stopped — stern tug ahead and stopped — bow tug ahead and astern to hold bow in position. 3. Astern and stopped — forward spring and stern lines out first — tugs ahead and astern to hold ship in position. 4. Engines astern to stop in berth — both tugs ahead to hold ship alongside.

Fig. 15-F2

Fig. 15-F2   1. Take in all stern lines — hold forward spring — bow tug full astern — stern tug slow ahead. 2. Bow tug ahead with left rudder to keep bow clear — stern tug ahead — let go forward spring. 3. Engines ahead — bow tug slow ahead — stern tug pull as directed.

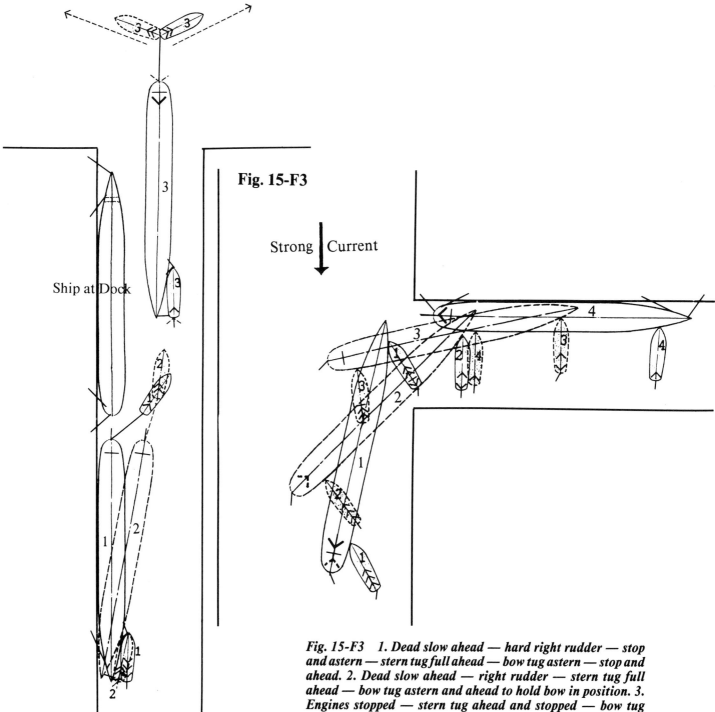

Fig. 15-F3

Strong Current

Ship at Dock

Fig. 15-F3   1. Dead slow ahead — hard right rudder — stop and astern — stern tug full ahead — bow tug astern — stop and ahead. 2. Dead slow ahead — right rudder — stern tug full ahead — bow tug astern and ahead to hold bow in position. 3. Engines stopped — stern tug ahead and stopped — bow tug astern and ahead. 4. Engines astern to stop in berth — both tugs ahead to hold ship alongside.

SAILING

It is not difficult when leaving from port side to the dock and backing into the channel with the current on the port side, if the ship is going to head with the current as shown in Figure 15-F4.

The tugs can both make fast on the starboard side to hold her against the current as she backs out, and when the bow is clear, the tug on the quarter can hold her stern while the current and the tug brings her bow around straight in the channel.

Some pilots prefer to have the stern tug tow the ship out with a hawser, but when this is done it is necessary for the ship to keep her propeller stopped while the tug backs down and takes in the hawser. (Figure 15-F4A) (Page 90).

Backing out with the current on the starboard side is shown in Figure 15-F5 (Page 90).

The stern tug can lay at the outside of the slip and put a line on the port quarter of the ship as she backs out. The bow tug can lay ahead of the ship facing aft, and when the current starts to break the stern around the corner of the dock, the tug can put a line on the port bow as it comes away from the dock and push her head into the current if she is going to get under way in that direction. The tug on the port quarter can hold the stern out in the channel.

ship backs out of the slip (Fig. 15-F6A) (Page 91).

DOCKING

With a head current going starboard side to the dock is another matter. The ship should stem the current and stay as close to the opening of the slip as possible, and let her hull rest against the corner of the dock as her bow heads into slack water.

One tug would be on the port bow, and the other would be on the starboard quarter to push her stern up against the current as she moves into the slip, or the tug aft can put up a hawser and pull the stern around as shown in Figures 15-F7 and 15-F7A (Page 92). It should be remembered, however, that when a tug is on a hawser all it can do is pull, and if anything happens such as engine or rudder failure on the tug, everything is all messed up. Also a lot depends on confidence in the tug captain's ability to keep the tug headed into the current so that it does not jack and fall around the stern of the ship as she starts to move into the slip.

Fig. 15-F4

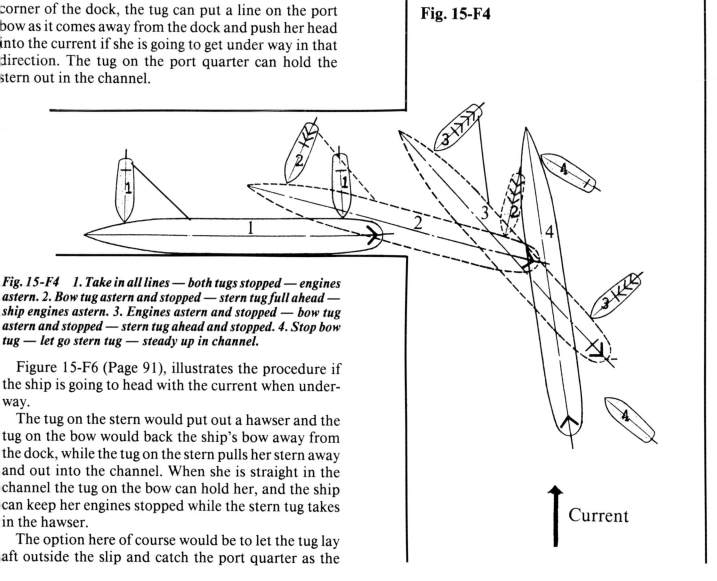

Fig. 15-F4 1. Take in all lines — both tugs stopped — engines astern. 2. Bow tug astern and stopped — stern tug full ahead — ship engines astern. 3. Engines astern and stopped — bow tug astern and stopped — stern tug ahead and stopped. 4. Stop bow tug — let go stern tug — steady up in channel.

Current

Figure 15-F6 (Page 91), illustrates the procedure if the ship is going to head with the current when underway.

The tug on the stern would put out a hawser and the tug on the bow would back the ship's bow away from the dock, while the tug on the stern pulls her stern away and out into the channel. When she is straight in the channel the tug on the bow can hold her, and the ship can keep her engines stopped while the stern tug takes in the hawser.

The option here of course would be to let the tug lay aft outside the slip and catch the port quarter as the

Fig. 15-F4-A

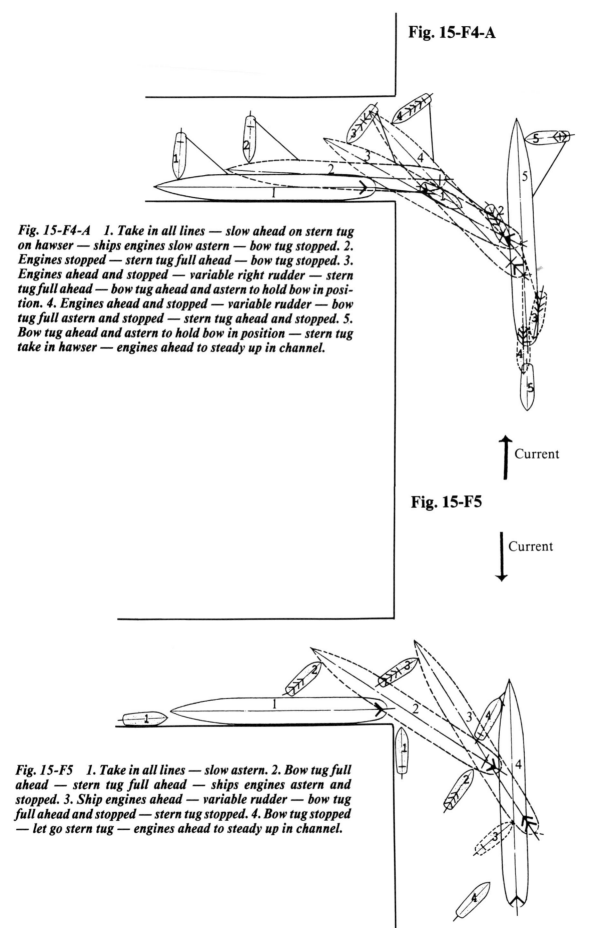

Fig. 15-F4-A *1. Take in all lines — slow ahead on stern tug on hawser — ships engines slow astern — bow tug stopped. 2. Engines stopped — stern tug full ahead — bow tug stopped. 3. Engines ahead and stopped — variable right rudder — stern tug full ahead — bow tug ahead and astern to hold bow in position. 4. Engines ahead and stopped — variable rudder — bow tug full astern and stopped — stern tug ahead and stopped. 5. Bow tug ahead and astern to hold bow in position — stern tug take in hawser — engines ahead to steady up in channel.*

Current

Fig. 15-F5

Current

Fig. 15-F5 *1. Take in all lines — slow astern. 2. Bow tug full ahead — stern tug full ahead — ships engines astern and stopped. 3. Ship engines ahead — variable rudder — bow tug full ahead and stopped — stern tug stopped. 4. Bow tug stopped — let go stern tug — engines ahead to steady up in channel.*

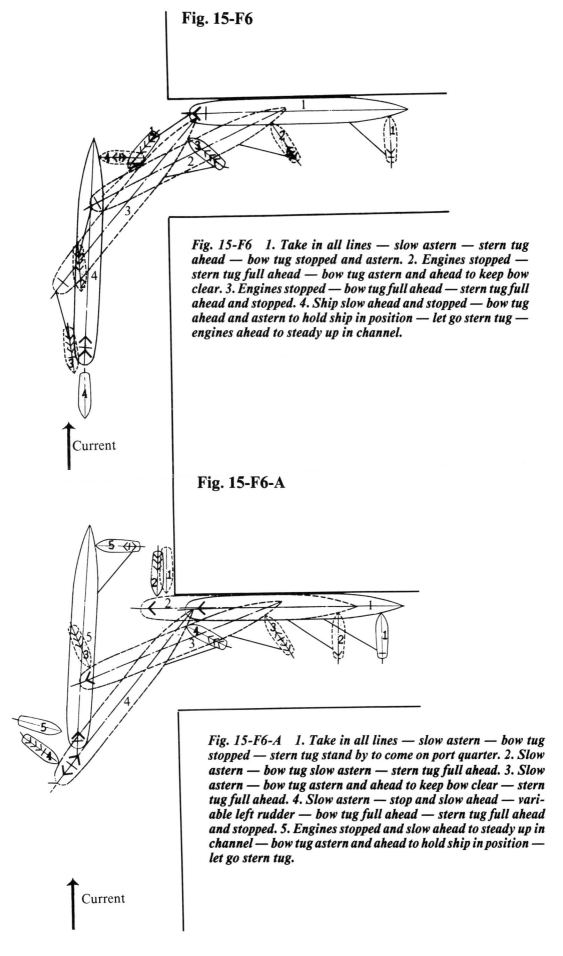

Fig. 15-F6

Fig. 15-F6 *1. Take in all lines — slow astern — stern tug ahead — bow tug stopped and astern. 2. Engines stopped — stern tug full ahead — bow tug astern and ahead to keep bow clear. 3. Engines stopped — bow tug full ahead — stern tug full ahead and stopped. 4. Ship slow ahead and stopped — bow tug ahead and astern to hold ship in position — let go stern tug — engines ahead to steady up in channel.*

Current

Fig. 15-F6-A

Fig. 15-F6-A *1. Take in all lines — slow astern — bow tug stopped — stern tug stand by to come on port quarter. 2. Slow astern — bow tug slow astern — stern tug full ahead. 3. Slow astern — bow tug astern and ahead to keep bow clear — stern tug full ahead. 4. Slow astern — stop and slow ahead — variable left rudder — bow tug full ahead — stern tug full ahead and stopped. 5. Engines stopped and slow ahead to steady up in channel — bow tug astern and ahead to hold ship in position — let go stern tug.*

Current

Fig. 15-F7

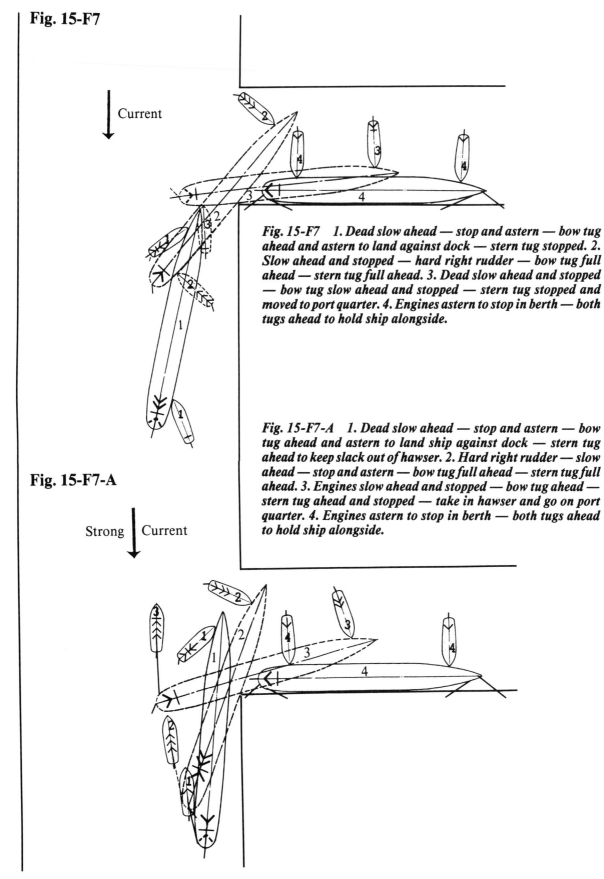

Current

Fig. 15-F7   1. Dead slow ahead — stop and astern — bow tug ahead and astern to land against dock — stern tug stopped. 2. Slow ahead and stopped — hard right rudder — bow tug full ahead — stern tug full ahead. 3. Dead slow ahead and stopped — bow tug slow ahead and stopped — stern tug stopped and moved to port quarter. 4. Engines astern to stop in berth — both tugs ahead to hold ship alongside.

Fig. 15-F7-A   1. Dead slow ahead — stop and astern — bow tug ahead and astern to land ship against dock — stern tug ahead to keep slack out of hawser. 2. Hard right rudder — slow ahead — stop and astern — bow tug full ahead — stern tug full ahead. 3. Engines slow ahead and stopped — bow tug ahead — stern tug ahead and stopped — take in hawser and go on port quarter. 4. Engines astern to stop in berth — both tugs ahead to hold ship alongside.

Fig. 15-F7-A

Strong Current

Fig. 15-F8

Fig. 15-F8   1. Dead slow ahead and stopped with bare steerage way — drop port anchor and slack off chain — bow tug astern — tug aft stopped. 2. Full astern and stopped — hold anchor chain — bow tug full astern — tug aft stopped and ahead. 3. Engines astern — stop and ahead — start heaving anchor — bow tug astern and stopped — stern tug ahead. 4. Engines dead slow ahead — bow tug ahead — stern tug ahead and stopped — let go and move to starboard quarter. 5. Engines stopped and astern to stop in berth — both tugs ahead to hold ship alongside.

Strong Current

Figure 15-F8 illustrates going port side to the dock with a strong stern current. In this illustration it is considered that there is not enough room for the vessel to turn before entering the slip.

Under these conditions, a prudent ship handler will put the port anchor down before heading her bow into the slip.

In many cases, the ship's stern will come around with the current anyway, so it is best to have her bow far enough into the slip so that her stern will clear, and the tug on the port quarter can let her hull ease down and rest against the corner of the dock as shown in Figure 15-F8A (Page 94).

If there is turning room in any reasonable vicinity of the slip, the ship should turn and approach heading into the current before entering the slip. In this manner she can let her hull rest against the corner of the dock and the tug aft can push her stern up against the current, or pull it around with a hawser as illustrated in Figure 15-F7A. (Page 92).

BACKING INTO SLIP AND DOCKING

Figure 15-G (Page 95), shows one of the most used methods of backing into a slip where the current is not strong and hazardous.

A port-backing ship of course, will start her stern toward the slip when backed if she is approaching with the slip on her port side, but she will not, if she is approaching the slip on her starboard.

With two tugs assisting however, this really does not make a great deal of difference because the tugs can keep her in position while backing into the slip and securing.

In a slip where there is not sufficient room for the tugs to work broadside at a ninety degree angle to the ship, it may be best to let the stern tug tow the ship into the slip on a hawser as shown in Figure 15-G1 (Page 95). The stern tug can come alongside and put out a short head line and then run out her hawser before approaching the slip. Before the ship backs her engines, the tug can let go its headline and swing around on the hawser to head into the slip. The tug on the bow can hold a short stern line to hold itself alongside the ship as much as necessary in order to clear as the ship is towed into the slip.

Another alternative in this situation would be to let the bow tug swing all the way around and lash up facing aft as shown in Figure 15-G2 (Page 96). If the tug is well lashed up, this procedure works well because it offers the ship a propeller and rudder on the bow, and the ship does not have to disturb the water in the slip by using her engines to excess.

TURNING AND DOCKING AT BERTH

When there is sufficient room, and a ship is to turn and dock at a designated berth, it is almost always more efficient and time saving to turn with the stern to her berth as illustrated in Figure 15-G3 (Page 97).

The reason this procedure is more effective is because of the hull design and the necessity of a vessel in ballast, or with normal seaworthy trim, to be heavier on the stern than on the bow. Also, because of the curvature of the hull on the stern, it is not possible in most cases for the tug to make fast far enough aft to have good pushing leverage.

If her stern is kept close to the dock while turning, the after spring or breast and stern lines can be put out.

Fig. 15-F8-A

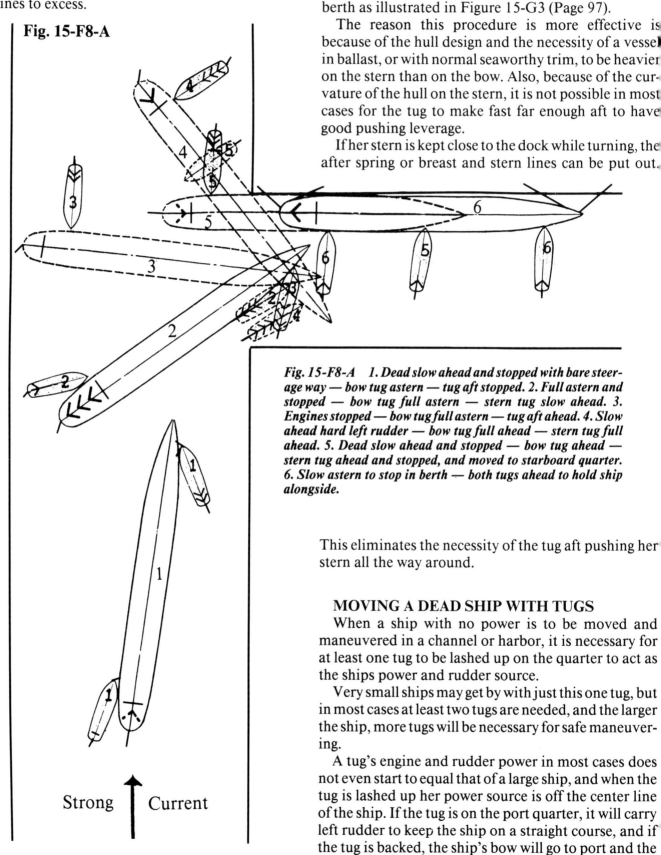

Fig. 15-F8-A 1. Dead slow ahead and stopped with bare steerage way — bow tug astern — tug aft stopped. 2. Full astern and stopped — bow tug full astern — stern tug slow ahead. 3. Engines stopped — bow tug full astern — tug aft ahead. 4. Slow ahead hard left rudder — bow tug full ahead — stern tug full ahead. 5. Dead slow ahead and stopped — bow tug ahead — stern tug ahead and stopped, and moved to starboard quarter. 6. Slow astern to stop in berth — both tugs ahead to hold ship alongside.

Strong Current

This eliminates the necessity of the tug aft pushing her stern all the way around.

MOVING A DEAD SHIP WITH TUGS

When a ship with no power is to be moved and maneuvered in a channel or harbor, it is necessary for at least one tug to be lashed up on the quarter to act as the ships power and rudder source.

Very small ships may get by with just this one tug, but in most cases at least two tugs are needed, and the larger the ship, more tugs will be necessary for safe maneuvering.

A tug's engine and rudder power in most cases does not even start to equal that of a large ship, and when the tug is lashed up her power source is off the center line of the ship. If the tug is on the port quarter, it will carry left rudder to keep the ship on a straight course, and if the tug is backed, the ship's bow will go to port and the

Fig. 15-G

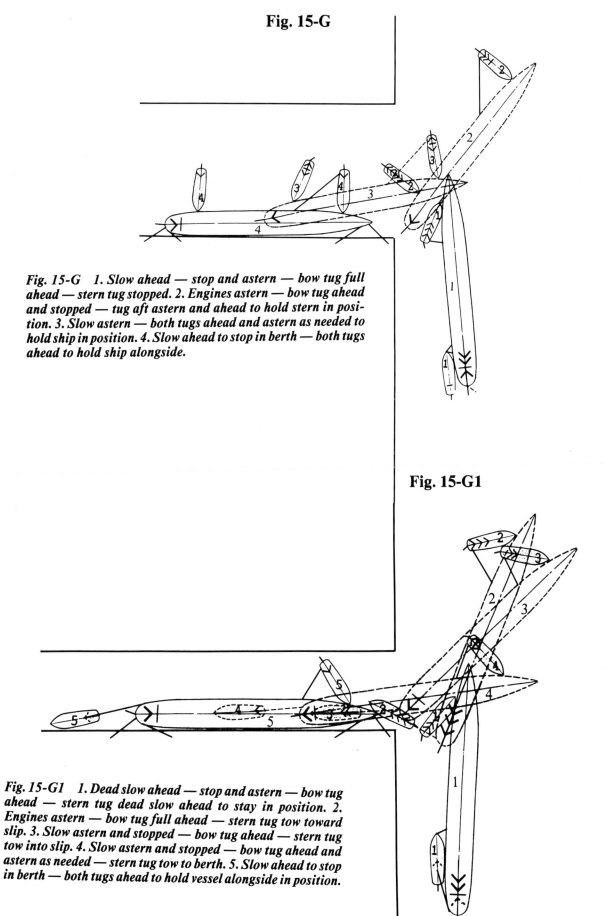

Fig. 15-G   1. Slow ahead — stop and astern — bow tug full ahead — stern tug stopped. 2. Engines astern — bow tug ahead and stopped — tug aft astern and ahead to hold stern in position. 3. Slow astern — both tugs ahead and astern as needed to hold ship in position. 4. Slow ahead to stop in berth — both tugs ahead to hold ship alongside.

Fig. 15-G1

Fig. 15-G1   1. Dead slow ahead — stop and astern — bow tug ahead — stern tug dead slow ahead to stay in position. 2. Engines astern — bow tug full ahead — stern tug tow toward slip. 3. Slow astern and stopped — bow tug ahead — stern tug tow into slip. 4. Slow astern and stopped — bow tug ahead and astern as needed — stern tug tow to berth. 5. Slow ahead to stop in berth — both tugs ahead to hold vessel alongside in position.

Fig. 15-G2

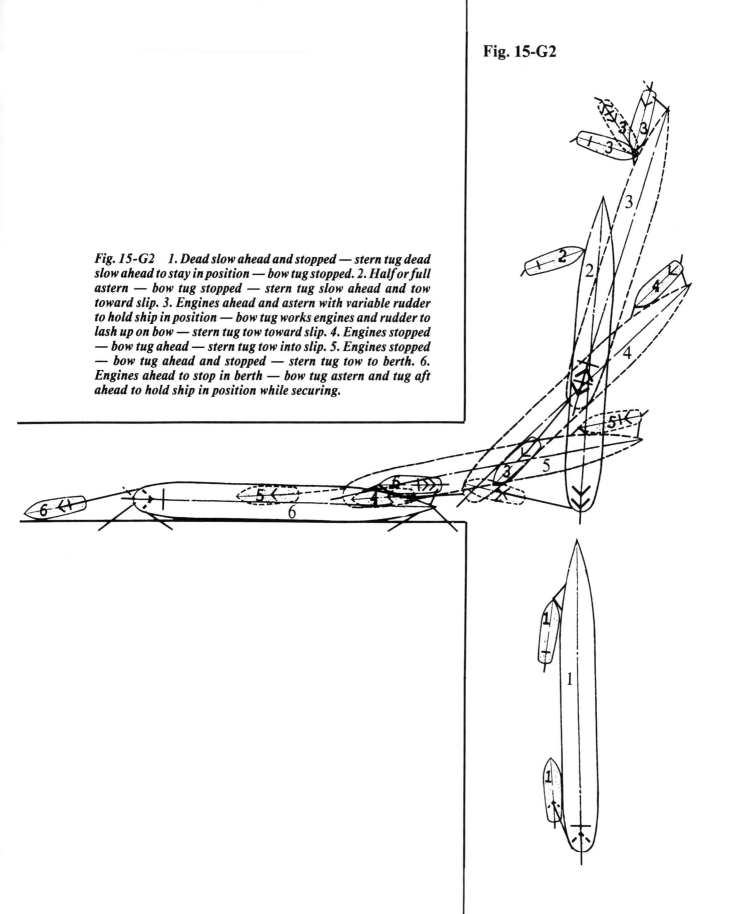

Fig. 15-G2   1. Dead slow ahead and stopped — stern tug dead slow ahead to stay in position — bow tug stopped. 2. Half or full astern — bow tug stopped — stern tug slow ahead and tow toward slip. 3. Engines ahead and astern with variable rudder to hold ship in position — bow tug works engines and rudder to lash up on bow — stern tug tow toward slip. 4. Engines stopped — bow tug ahead — stern tug tow into slip. 5. Engines stopped — bow tug ahead and stopped — stern tug tow to berth. 6. Engines ahead to stop in berth — bow tug astern and tug aft ahead to hold ship in position while securing.

Fig. 15-G3

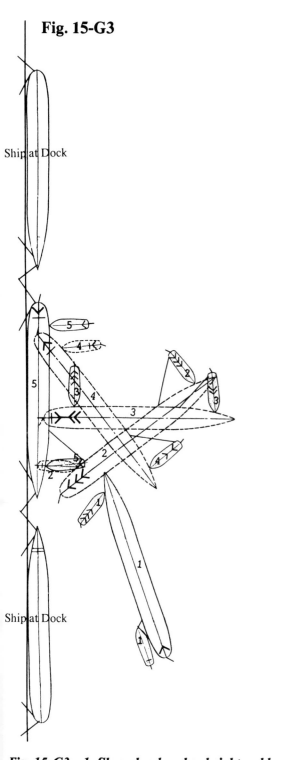

Ship at Dock

Ship at Dock

Fig. 15-G3   1. Slow ahead — hard right rudder — bow tug full ahead — stern tug stopped. 2. Full astern — bow tug full ahead — stern tug stopped. 3. Engines stopped — slow ahead and half astern — hard right and midship rudder — bow tug ahead — tug aft full astern. 4. Slow astern and stopped — bow tug ahead and astern to hold bow in position — stern tug ahead and stopped to keep stern in position — after spring and stern line out first. 5. Slow ahead to stop in berth — both tugs ahead to hold ship alongside.

stern will move to starboard. If the tug is lashed up on the starboard quarter, the reverse effect will be experienced. (Figure 15-H).

With two tugs it is a matter of choice and the existing conditions as to where the second tug is placed.

If both are lashed up with one on each quarter, the ship will act as a twin screw vessel, but then there is no help on the bow except the anchor, and if the ship is light (and they usually are) the tugs may not be able to control her drift, especially if there is a broadside wind as shown in Figure 15-H1.

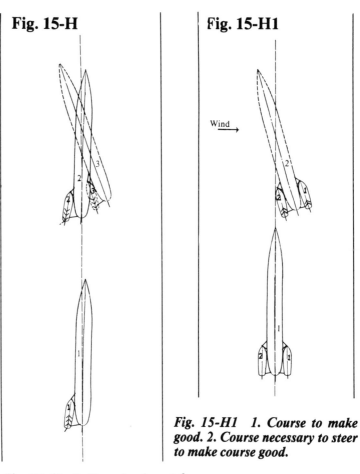

Fig. 15-H

Fig. 15-H1

Wind

Fig. 15-H1   1. Course to make good. 2. Course necessary to steer to make course good.

Fig. 15-H   1. Tug ahead — left rudder required. 2-3. Tug engines astern — ship goes to port.

If a tug is lashed up on the port quarter, and one is made fast on the port bow, the ship will steer better underway because of the tug's drag on the bow. But if it is necessary for the ship to stop, the bow tug will have to be put ahead when the tug lashed up is backed. This creates a problem because when the tug on the bow is put ahead, it will tend to cause the ship to gain headway and go broadside to the starboard instead of stopping. (Figure 15-H2).

When a ship is moving some distance and is using only two tugs, the procedure shown in Figure 15-H3 will prove to be effective and comparatively safe, especially if the ship is going port side to the dock at her destination. All that would be necessary is for the tug on the bow to change sides just before arriving at the berth.

The tug lashed up on the starboard quarter will be protected from the wash of meeting and passing traffic, and the tug on the port bow can come ahead to correct the off balance of the tug pushing and steering on the starboard quarter, and also help the ship make better headway. If the ship has to stop, both tugs can be backed and the ship kept on a straight heading with comparative ease, although she will most likely make some leeway to port.

When three tugs are used, a good procedure to follow is to have a tug lash up on each quarter, and the third tug on either bow, depending on how far the ship has to move and which side will be secured to the dock upon arrival at her berth. Of course, if the third tug is made fast on the starboard bow, it will be out of the way of oncoming and passing traffic. (Figure 15-H4).

When four tugs are used, the best way to handle it is to lash one up on each quarter, and have one make fast on each bow, which offers complete control of the vessel as shown in Figure 15-H5.

If the vessel is to proceed to sea under tow the thing to do is to let the towing vessel put out her towing hawser, and have the other tugs make fast as shown in Figure 15-H6 (Page 99).

About the only time five tugs are needed is on large heavy vessels and/or deeply loaded ones, or, when a large vessel is moving a good distance in a busy channel, and is proceeding to sea or to a drydock.

In either case, one tug would be on a hawser, and the rest alongside as shown in Figure 15-H7 (Page 99).

Fig. 15-H2

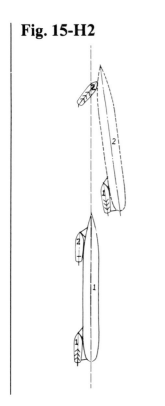

Fig. 15-H3

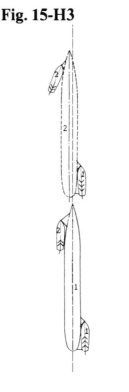

Fig. 15-H4

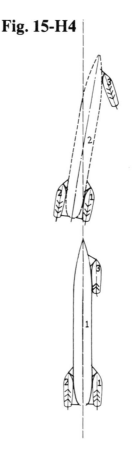

Fig. 15-H5

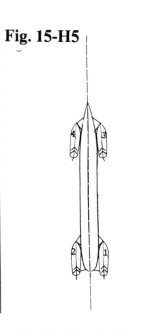

Fig. 15-H5   1. All tugs ahead — ship steady on course.

Fig. 15-H2   1. Stern tug full ahead — bow tug stopped to act as drag for steering. 2. Stern tug full astern — bow tug ahead to keep ship straight — Note broadside movement to starboard. Ship will maintain headway from tug pushing on bow.

Fig. 15-H3   1. Stern tug full ahead — bow tug ahead with left rudder to lay alongside, keep ship on course and gain headway. 2. Tug aft full astern — bow tug astern to stop headway and keep ship straight — Note broadside movement to port.

Fig. 15-H4 1. Stern tugs full ahead — bow tug half ahead with right rudder to lay alongside. 2. All tugs full astern to stop headway.

Fig. 15-H6   **Fig. 15-H7**   **Fig. 15-I**   **Fig. 15-J**

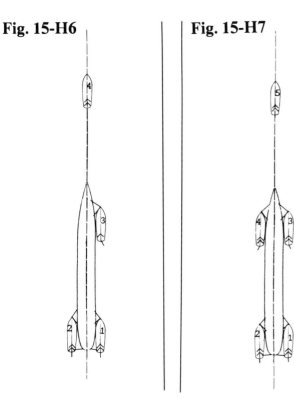

Fig. 15-I 1. Square ended barge balanced on port bow quarter of tug for even steering.

Fig. 15-J 1. Barge with model bow balanced on port bow quarter of tug under way.

Fig. 15-H6 1. All tugs ahead for making head-way.

Fig. 15-H7 1. Large vessel under way — all tugs ahead.

CHAPTER 16

VESSELS GOING ALONGSIDE ONE ANOTHER

Vessels of the same or similar size wishing to go alongside each other while under way, can do so efficiently if one vessel holds a straight course while the other maneuvers alongside. Even large ships can maneuver in this manner, but heavy duty cushioned fenders should be hung over the side so that the vessel's hulls do not scrape and rub together. The vessel which is holding a straight course should maintain a constant speed of just over the slow speed of the vessel doing the maneuvering so that this vessel can adjust her speed while coming alongside and not run past the vessel. When the vessels are alongside each other a head line, or breast line, leading forward can be put out from the maneuvering vessel and a short breast line aft to hold the vessels together while other lines are put out as necessary. The vessel which has done the maneuvering may put her engines on slow ahead or stopped as the situation requires.

The reason for keeping headway on the vessels is that the water passing between the two vessels forms a cushion for landing. All that is necessary is to drive one vessel up alongside the other.

TUG LASHED UP AND MOVING BARGES

This is somewhat different from moving a vessel which has her own power, or from vessels and barges where the tug fits into a notch or is made fast aft directly in the center of the vessel as do some coastal and river units that act as one vessel when made fast together.

As shown in Figure 15-I, the tug should be lashed up with her stern protruding well aft of the barge when possible, so that the tug's rudder and propeller power will not be interfered with by the wash from the barge hull.

The tug should balance the tow at an angle on her bow so that when under way, the tug will carry a midship rudder when steering a straight course. A square ended barge will have to be made fast at more of an angle to the tug than will a barge with a molded sharp bow, due to the water resistance on the square bow. Barges with a high rake bow, and barges with what is called spoon-bill bows will work much the same as the molded bow barge. When the square ended barge is properly made fast for good handling, the forward outboard corner will act more as a bow for displacing the water while moving ahead.

Figure 15-J depicts the difference in the angle that is needed when a tug is lashed up to a barge with a molded bow.

When two vessels are stopped in the water, it is best for one of them to do all the maneuvering. It will be found that even then the water displaced by the vessel's movement and the use of her engines will cause the stopped vessel to drift away if the maneuver is not accomplished on the first approach. If both try to maneuver alongside each other, the water will become more disturbed, making difficult matters worse, unless the vessels are equipped with bow-thrusters to hold their bow's together.

Offshore in open water where a sea and/or swell is running, it is much easier and safer to keep the vessel's sterns to the sea and/or swell, whichever is the greater. Many times it will be found that the seas build from one direction, while the swell is running from another. If the seas are not too heavy, large ships can generally maneuver alongside by heading into them, but smaller vessel cannot do so with safety.

It is much easier and safer for two small vessels to keep their sterns to the sea and swell in order to keep the vessels from rolling into each other. If the vessels have headway this is no problem. However, if both are stopped, the one waiting for the other to come alongside will in most cases, have to use her engines to keep her stern to the sea. This, of course, will add to the water disturbance while the other is trying to maneuver alongside. If a small vessel is at anchor and rolling badly, it is best for her to use her engines to put her stern to the sea if possible, if not, it is best for her to get under way and do so. (Figure's 16-A and 16-A1)

A large ship or other vessel such as a drilling rig under way can make a lee for a smaller vessel by putting the sea on the opposite bow or quarter. That is, if the smaller vessel is to come alongside on the starboard side, the seas should be put on the port quarter if possible, or the port bow if necessary. In either case, the seas should not be put so far abeam that the vessel will start to roll. (Figure 16-A2) (Page 101).

Fig. 16-A

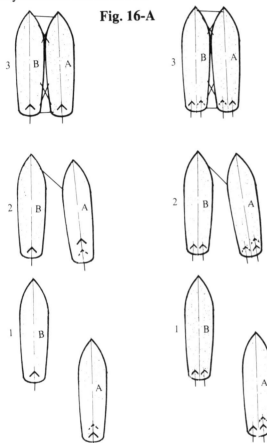

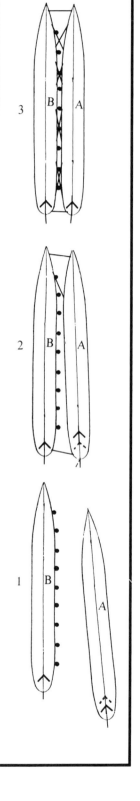

Fig. 16-A1

Fig. 16-A Single screw vessels 1. A — Engines ahead ⅓. B — Slow ahead — maintain course and speed. 2. A — Adjust speed to B — steer alongside and put out breast spring. 3. Secure vessels.

Twin screw vessels 1. B — Slow ahead both engines — maintain course and speed. A — Slow ahead port — ⅓ ahead starboard. 2. A — Dead slow ahead port — adjust speed to B with starboard engine — steer alongside B and put out breast spring. 3. Secure vessels. A — Dead slow ahead port — slow ahead starboard. B — Slow ahead port — dead slow ahead starboard.

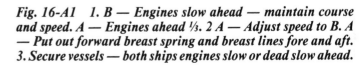

Fig. 16-A1 1. B — Engines slow ahead — maintain course and speed. A — Engines ahead ⅓. 2 A — Adjust speed to B. A — Put out forward breast spring and breast lines fore and aft. 3. Secure vessels — both ships engines slow or dead slow ahead.

Fig. 16-A 2

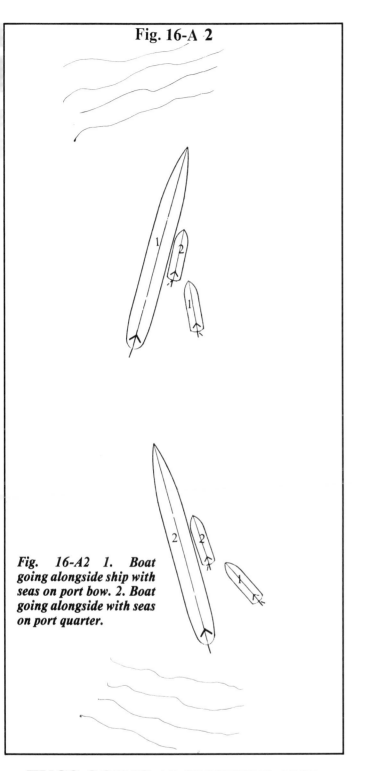

Fig. 16-A2 1. Boat going alongside ship with seas on port bow. 2. Boat going alongside with seas on port quarter.

TUGS GOING ALONGSIDE AND ASSISTING SHIPS

GOING ALONGSIDE ON THE BOW

Going alongside on the bow of a large vessel is no problem as long as the vessel has good steerage way (4 - 6 knots). The displacement wash around the bow as the ship moves through the water tends to force the tug away as she starts to come alongside, and the tug will take some rudder toward the ship. The faster the ship

is moving, the more rudder it will take to bring the tug alongside, and of course, a loaded ship has more displacement wash than a light one.

On twin screw tugs it is best to use the outboard engine to adjust speed while leaving the inboard engine stopped or slow ahead as the circumstances require. When the tug is alongside and a head line is out, she should lay parallel to the ships hull while the rest of the necessary lines are put out. If the ship is nearing her berth, or maneuvering in close quarters, the tug should stop her engines and wait for further orders from the ship. If the ship is making good headway, it is a good practice to come ahead on the tug's engines so as not to interfere with the ship's steering, and to avoid the possibility of breaking her headline. The tug should stay as near parallel to the ship's hull as possible. (Figure 16-B).

Fig. 16-B

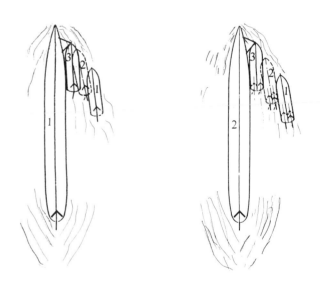

Fig. 16-B 1. Single screw tug going alongside and making fast on bow of ship underway. 2. Twin screw tug going on bow of ship under same conditions.

GOING ALONGSIDE ON THE QUARTER

When a tug is going on the quarter of a ship it is best to land the tug just forward of the counter (forward of where the hull starts to curve in toward the propeller) so that the suction effect caused by the water displacement rushing back in around the stern does not drag the tug under the counter and into the propeller. Here again, in most cases, rudder on the tug toward the ship will be necessary because of this suction effect caused by the water rushing around the ship's stern and catching the tug's stern as she nears the ship's hull. When the tug is alongside, she should lay as near parallel to the ship's hull as possible so as not to interfere with the ship's steering.

If the ship is moving too fast, the tug should go alongside further forward toward midship — or not at all until the ship has slowed down.

On large vessels the hull area alongside half way between the bow and stern is flat and not affected to any extent by bow wash or stern suction when underway. Pilot boats, personnel boats etc. should land in this area when possible. (Figure's 16-C and 16-D).

Fig. 16-C

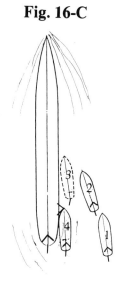

Fig. 16-D

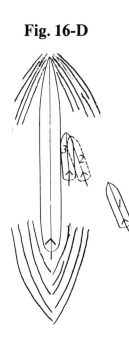

Fig. 16-C 1. Single screw tug going alongside and making fast on starboard quarter of ship under way.

Fig. 16-D 1. Single screw boat going alongside at the midship section of a ship underway.

PUTTING OUT A HAWSER ON THE STERN

When a tug is required to put a hawser on a vessel under way for the purpose of docking or moving stern first after the vessel is stopped, the tug should land on the quarter as shown in Figure 16-C, and put out a short head line to hold the tug parallel to the vessel for the same reason.

The hawser can then be put out to the quarter or stern chock of the vessel, while taking care to keep it clear of the ships propeller(s). Just before the ship is to stop her headway, the tug can let go her headline while coming ahead on her engines enough to keep the slack out of the hawser, and let the tug fall around to head in the opposite direction of the ship's heading, or head as directed by the ship's pilot.

If the ship is making too much headway, and does not stop when the tug falls around astern, the tug has no choice but to stay directly stern to stern with the ship. If she tries to work around at an angle to the ship, with

the ship making headway, there is a good possibility that the tug will capsize. (Figures 16-E and 16-F).

Fig. 16-E   **Fig. 16-F**

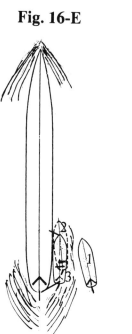

Fig. 16-E Tug putting towing hawser on ship under way.

Fig. 16-F Tug swinging around on hawser to tow ship astern.

the ship making headway, there is a good possibility that the tug will capsize. (Figures 16-E and 16-F).

When a ship is deep loaded, and the bow of a tug can fit flush against the quarter above the curvature of the hull, the tug can come up astern and put out a line to assist in docking and/or turning, as shown in Figure 16-G. When it is possible to place the tug aft in this position her efficiency in assisting the ship is greatly increased. However, most of the time the captain of the ship, or the pilot, will not be aware that the tug can work in this position, so it is left up to the tug's captain to inform them and have their permission before making fast in this manner. A good tug captain who takes his work seriously will do this, and in most cases it will be appreciated by both the ship's captain and pilot.

Fig. 16-G

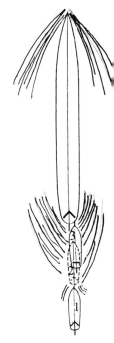

Fig. 16-G Tug making fast on stern counter of loaded ship.

PUTTING A TOWING HAWSER ON THE BOW OF A SHIP UNDER WAY

Putting a hawser out to the bow of a ship under way is not difficult as long as there is an understanding between the ship and the tug. It is important that the ship hold the same speed and if possible the same course, until the tug can complete the operation of running out and taking a strain on the hawser.

If this cooperation can be shown between the ship and the tug, the tug can work up under the flare of the bow while running parallel with the ship and maintaining a little more speed than the ship until the tug's stern starts to come even with the bow stem of the ship. The tug is then slowed to the speed of the ship while the hawser is put out.

This operation can be accomplished within a minute or so once the tug is close enough for a line to be passed over. It should never be necessary for the tug to touch the ship's bow if it is properly maneuvered. (Figure 16-H)

A tug should never run ahead of a ship under way and stop dead ahead and wait for the ship to come up to the tug. Even the most experienced tug captain cannot judge speed and distance that well, and it's the best way in the world to get run over and sunk.

CHAPTER 17

HANDLING SMALL SINGLE SCREW VESSELS IN HARBORS

The smaller class, single-screw vessels such as tugs, dispatch boats, commercial fishing vessels, some off-shore support craft, etc., react to their rudder and propeller basically the same as large ships. Of course, they are easier to handle simply because they are much smaller, and in most cases have more horsepower per tonnage weight ratio than do large ships, especially in the tug boat class.

It's like making a comparison of automobiles weighing three or four thousand pounds with one hundred and fifty to three hundred horsepower engines, to large trucks with three hundred and fifty to five hundred horsepower, and a gross weight load of sixty or seventy thousand pounds.

In the following diagrams and explanations, all vessels are considered to be standard, right-turning, fixed propellers.

Docking port side to the dock with slack water or a head current is just as easy as with a twin screw boat. The dock is approached at a slight angle, and when the engine is put astern she will back alongside. However, lines must be put out as she comes alongside or she will drift away from the dock. (Figure 17-A).

Fig. 16-H

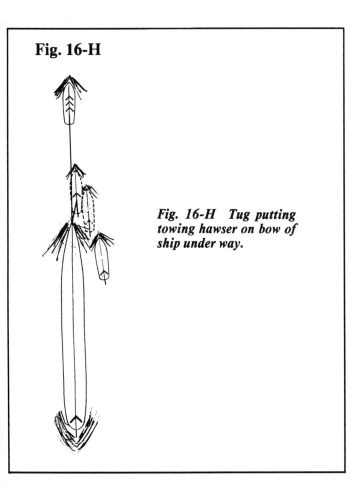

Fig. 16-H Tug putting towing hawser on bow of ship under way.

Fig. 17-A

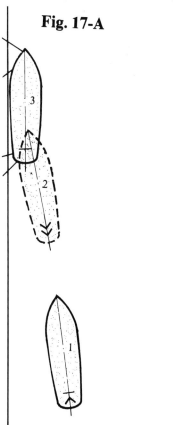

Fig. 17-A 1. Engine slow ahead and stopped. 2. Engine astern — midship rudder. 3. Engine stopped — secure at berth.

TURNING AND DOCKING STARBOARD SIDE TO THE DOCK

When there is sufficient turning room, the turning and broadside movement principle, illustrated in Chapter 1, can be used when turning and going starboard side to the dock when there is slack water or a current. However, the force of a head current must be considered and allowed for before making the turn, to insure that it does not carry the boat back past the berth while she is turning. When the current is on the stern, the stern should be at a little more of an angle toward the dock than what would be necessary with slack water. Running with the current she would, of course, make the turn a little before her berth is abeam so that she will not drift past her berth while turning. (Figure's 17-B and 17-B1) (Pages 104, 105).

Fig. 17-B

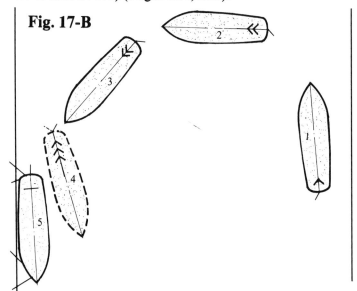

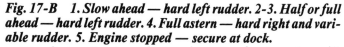

Fig. 17-B   1. Slow ahead — hard left rudder. 2-3. Half or full ahead — hard left rudder. 4. Full astern — hard right and variable rudder. 5. Engine stopped — secure at dock.

The faster the boat is turning, the further she will move broadside when stopped off her berth. However, the captain must be very sure of the boat's turning ability, and the engine's performance when coming astern, before making these turns on full speed, especially if she is going to dock between two other vessels.

A port backing boat will pivot much faster to port with good sternway, than she will when going ahead. If she is past her dock and is going to tie up starboard side to it, she can work into a position to where she will be laying at approximately a forty five degree angle with her stern toward the dock, and put her engine full astern, leaving the rudder hard left. With good sternway, her stern will be swinging very fast to port, and when she is almost abeam of her berth she can put her engine full ahead and she will go broadside for at least the width of the boat. (Figure 17-B2).

If there is not sufficient turning room to make a com-

plete turn, the vessel can be stopped and make a ninet[y] degree turn as illustrated in Figure 17-C. However, i[f]

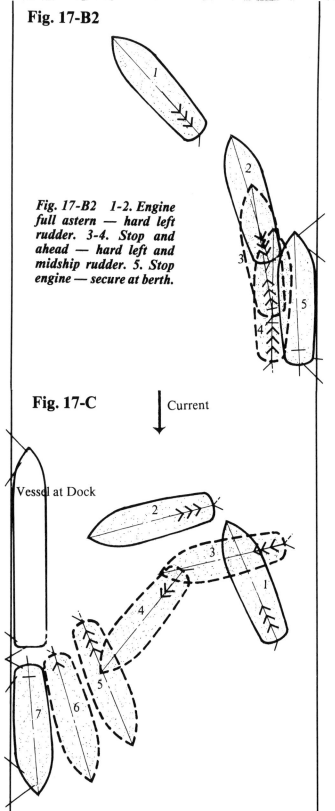

Fig. 17-B2

Fig. 17-B2   1-2. Engine full astern — hard left rudder. 3-4. Stop and ahead — hard left and midship rudder. 5. Stop engine — secure at berth.

Fig. 17-C

Current

Vessel at Dock

Fig. 17-C   1. Full ahead — hard left rudder. 2. Full astern — hard right rudder. 3. Full ahead — hard left rudder. 4. Half or slow ahead — hard left rudder. 5. Full astern — midship and hard right rudder. 6. Engine astern to hold position. 7. Stop engine — secure at berth.

Fig. 17-B1

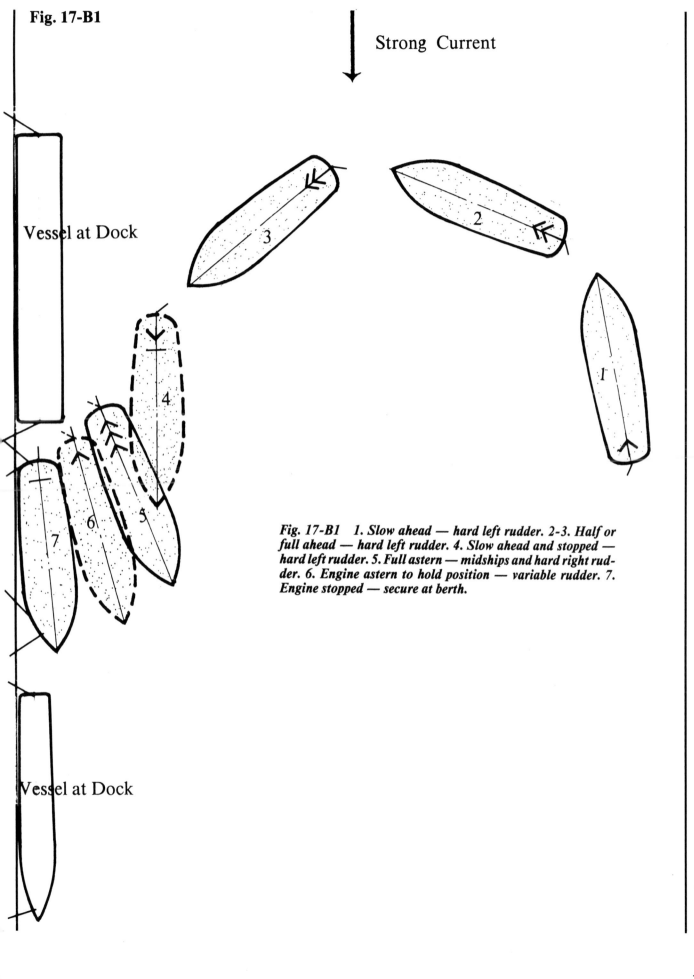

Strong Current

Vessel at Dock

Vessel at Dock

Fig. 17-B1   1. Slow ahead — hard left rudder. 2-3. Half or full ahead — hard left rudder. 4. Slow ahead and stopped — hard left rudder. 5. Full astern — midships and hard right rudder. 6. Engine astern to hold position — variable rudder. 7. Engine stopped — secure at berth.

Fig. 17-C1

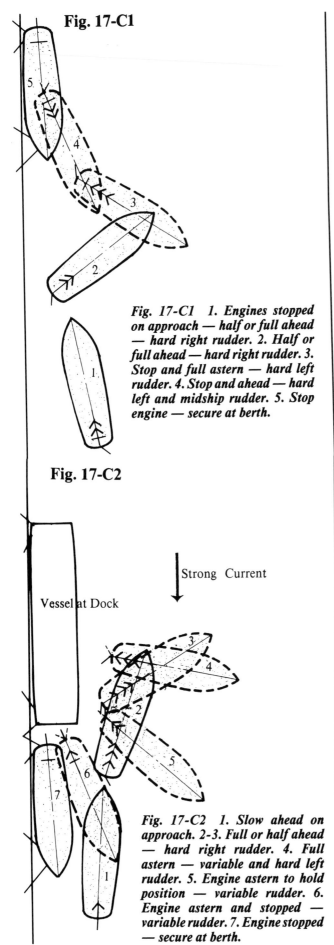

Fig. 17-C1 *1. Engines stopped on approach — half or full ahead — hard right rudder. 2. Half or full ahead — hard right rudder. 3. Stop and full astern — hard left rudder. 4. Stop and ahead — hard left and midship rudder. 5. Stop engine — secure at berth.*

Fig. 17-C2

Strong Current

Vessel at Dock

Fig. 17-C2 *1. Slow ahead on approach. 2-3. Full or half ahead — hard right rudder. 4. Full astern — variable and hard left rudder. 5. Engine astern to hold position — variable rudder. 6. Engine astern and stopped — variable rudder. 7. Engine stopped — secure at berth.*

there is a head current, the vessel must go far enough past the berth to allow for the current drift when it is broadside. Also, the vessel must be swung far enough so that the current will be slightly on the port quarter when she is backed.

In many cases, regardless of whether there is a current or not, it will be found that turning on a right rudder with her stern to the dock may be much easier and more effective as shown in diagrams 17-C1 and 17-C2.

GOING PORT SIDE TO THE DOCK WITH A STERN CURRENT

Figure's 17-D and 17-D1 (Page 107), illustrates going port side to the dock at an open berth, and also docking between two vessels with a stern current. Docking at an open berth is not very risky, because she can always come ahead with a left rudder if her stern swings toward the dock too fast when she is backed, and the current is on her starboard quarter. Or, she can come ahead with a right rudder if her bow is at too much of an angle to the dock and the current stays on

Fig. 17-D

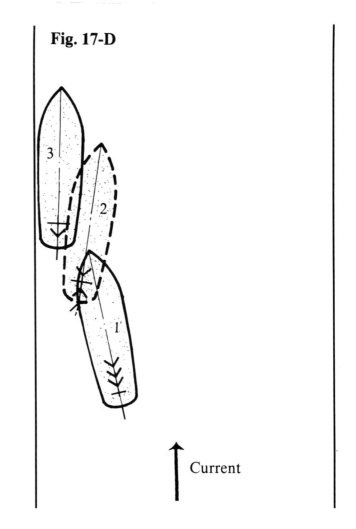

Current

Fig. 17-D *1. Engine stopped and full astern. 2. Slow ahead and astern — hard left and variable rudder. 3. Slow astern and stopped — secure at berth.*

her port quarter.

Docking between two vessels is another matter. She should maneuver so that she will be right abeam of her berth, with the current slightly on her starboard quarter or dead astern when she has stopped her headway. As it becomes necessary to kick her engines astern to keep from gaining headway, the current should come on her starboard quarter and carry her alongside where a stern line can be put out to hold her in position while she is secured.

If the current gets too far on her port quarter, it will be necessary to back away and start all over, or if it gets too far on the starboard quarter, she will have to come ahead and do the same.

GOING STARBOARD SIDE TO THE DOCK WITH A STERN CURRENT

Since the stern of the boat will go to port when she is backed, it will be necessary to have the current on the port quarter when she is backed to secure at her berth. Going to an open berth, is no more difficult than going port side to the dock. The only difference is, that the stern should go alongside the dock first, and a stern line put out to hold her in place against the current.

Docking between two vessels is a little more difficult. If the engine has to be backed with the current on her starboard quarter when she is abeam of her berth, it will not work and it will be necessary to back away and start all over.

If the current is kept at a slight angle on her port quarter, the current will carry her alongside where a stern line can be put out to hold her while she is secured. (Figure's 17-E and 17-E1) (Pages 107, 108).

SAILING

Sailing from an open berth is no problem at all in slack water or with a head current as shown in Figure 17-F (Page 108).

All that is necessary is to hold a short spring line aft and back down slow against it to breast the bow out. Then let the line go and come ahead on the engine with enough right rudder to keep the stern from scraping against the dock and she is underway.

If there are other vessels ahead and astern, and extending out into the channel to where the bow cannot swing clear, this will not work unless there is a head current.

With a head current, she can let go the spring line aft when her bow has swung out as far as possible, and hold herself in position with the engine and rudder until the current carries her clear as shown in Figure 17-F1. (Page 109)

If there is a stern current under the same conditions, it will be necessary to work the stern out enough to clear

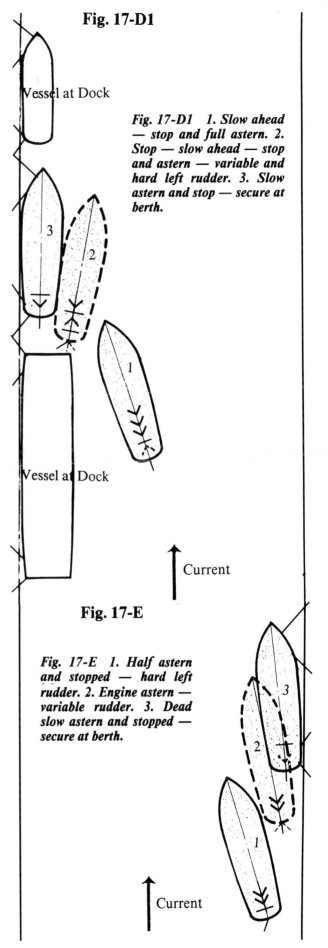

Fig. 17-D1

Vessel at Dock

Fig. 17-D1   1. Slow ahead — stop and full astern. 2. Stop — slow ahead — stop and astern — variable and hard left rudder. 3. Slow astern and stop — secure at berth.

Vessel at Dock

Current

Fig. 17-E

Fig. 17-E   1. Half astern and stopped — hard left rudder. 2. Engine astern — variable rudder. 3. Dead slow astern and stopped — secure at berth.

Current

any obstructions and put the engines full astern for a few seconds to gain sternway, while leaving her rudder hard right. (See Figure F-2) (Page 109). With good sternway, the rudder should hold her stern up into the current while her bow falls around to clear and get under way.

The same procedure would be followed when sailing with no current, but the stern may need to be worked out a little further into the channel. If necessary she can let the spring line go and come ahead and astern (back & fill) with a hard right rudder until she has moved broadside enough for her stern to clear.

If the vessel is moored starboard side to the dock with a stern current, and is going to turn, her stern can be worked out until clear as shown in Figure 17-F3 (Page 110). Her engines can then be put full astern with a hard left rudder. Since her stern will back hard to port, she should turn immediately off the dock and be under way headed into the current.

SAILING FROM PORT SIDE TO THE DOCK

Basically the same procedure is followed as in Figures 17-F, 17-F1, and 17-F2 (Page 109). Generally these maneuvers are easier because of the boat's ability to back to port. For this reason a different maneuver is used to turn and head into a current, or turning and getting underway with no current, as illustrated in Figure 17-G (Page 110).

The stern can be worked out into the channel by holding a spring line forward, until the stern and port quarter are well clear of all obstructions. As she backs clear, she will have started her swing to starboard and her engines can be put full ahead with a hard right rudder to turn and head in the opposite direction. If there is not sufficient room to make a complete turn, the engine can be stopped and backed as she continues to turn.

Under most conditions, all of the procedures shown here for sailing are proper. If the wind and/or current is off the dock it is that much better. With a little help, let these elements carry the vessel into the channel and clear while she is getting underway. If the wind and/or current is pressing the vessel against the dock this would be another matter, and she will need to work out at more of an angle to the dock than would otherwise be necessary.

MOVING ASTERN AND STEERING WITH RUDDER

Some single screw boats just will not steer with the rudder while moving astern, but most of them will, especially in the tug boat class. However, it takes quite a bit of practice and experimenting with an individual boat in most cases before this trick can be mastered.

Figure 17-H (Page 110), illustrates the normal procedure for this maneuver.

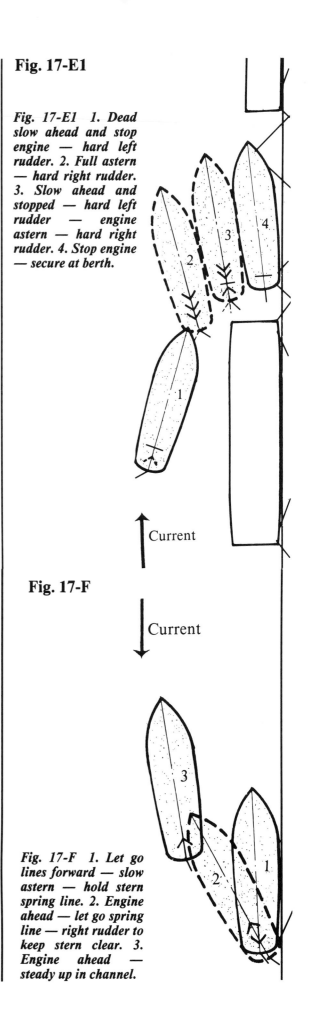

Fig. 17-E1

Fig. 17-E1 1. Dead slow ahead and stop engine — hard left rudder. 2. Full astern — hard right rudder. 3. Slow ahead and stopped — hard left rudder — engine astern — hard right rudder. 4. Stop engine — secure at berth.

Current

Fig. 17-F

Current

Fig. 17-F 1. Let go lines forward — slow astern — hold stern spring line. 2. Engine ahead — let go spring line — right rudder to keep stern clear. 3. Engine ahead — steady up in channel.

The boat should put the course she wishes to travel at an angle on her port quarter. The engine can be backed half or full astern with a hard right rudder for a short time to gain sternway. When this is done she will back to port, and when the stern starts to approach the direction she wishes to travel, the engine should be put on dead slow astern or stopped until the stern starts to answer the rudder. Before her stern starts to starboard, the rudder should be eased toward midship, and the engine can be put slow or dead slow astern to maintain sternway, while the stern can be kept straight by moving the rudder from right to midship. If there is any disturbance of the water however, she may sheer in either direction.

Although bow-thrusters would be extremely helpful in maneuvering in close quarters, very few of these type vessels are so equipped. Some of the larger single screw ocean going towing and commercial fishing vessels, etc., over one hundred feet in length are equipped with a bow-thruster.

Fig. 17-F2

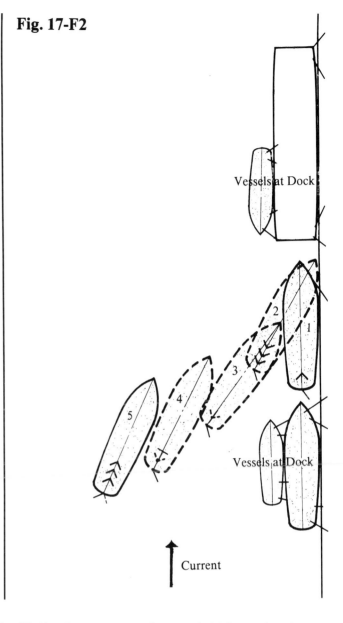

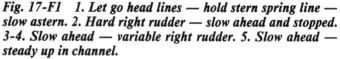

Fig. 17-F2   1. Let go stern lines — hold forward spring — slow ahead — hard right rudder. 2. Full astern — hard right rudder. 3. Dead slow astern — hard right rudder. 4. Dead slow astern and stopped — hard right rudder. 5. Engine ahead with left rudder to steady up in channel.

Fig. 17-F1

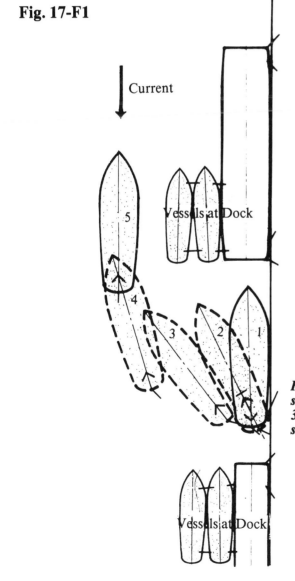

Fig. 17-F1   1. Let go head lines — hold stern spring line — slow astern. 2. Hard right rudder — slow ahead and stopped. 3-4. Slow ahead — variable right rudder. 5. Slow ahead — steady up in channel.

Fig. 17-F3

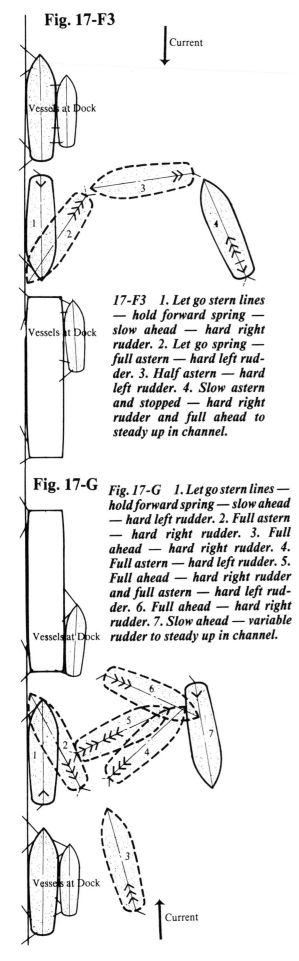

17-F3 1. Let go stern lines — hold forward spring — slow ahead — hard right rudder. 2. Let go spring — full astern — hard left rudder. 3. Half astern — hard left rudder. 4. Slow astern and stopped — hard right rudder and full ahead to steady up in channel.

Fig. 17-G

Fig. 17-G 1. Let go stern lines — hold forward spring — slow ahead — hard left rudder. 2. Full astern — hard right rudder. 3. Full ahead — hard right rudder. 4. Full astern — hard left rudder. 5. Full ahead — hard right rudder and full astern — hard left rudder. 6. Full ahead — hard right rudder. 7. Slow ahead — variable rudder to steady up in channel.

Fig. 17-H

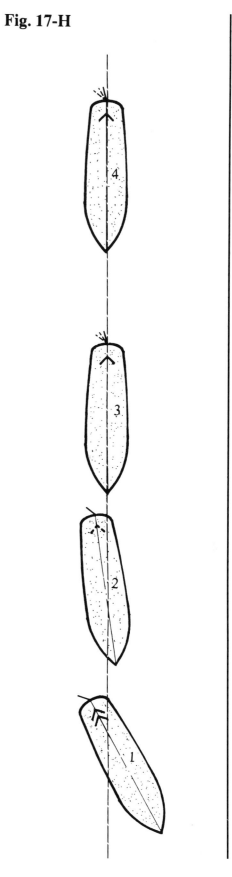

Fig. 17-H 1. Half or full astern — hard right rudder. 2. Dead slow astern — hard right rudder. 3-4. Slow astern — variable right rudder to steer straight course while moving astern.

CHAPTER 18

HANDLING TWIN SCREW VESSELS IN HARBORS AND CHANNELS

EFFECT OF TWO PROPELLERS ON VESSELS UNDER WAY AND MANEUVERING

Figures 18-A through Figure 18-A3 shows what happens with twin screw vessels under way. Although vessels will react differently according to types and sizes, the principle remains the same.

Notice the lines running from each propeller to the bow stem, which illustrates the angle of pressure from each one, regardless of the direction it may turn. The further the propellers are apart and away from the center line of the hull, increases this angle of pressure to the bow and makes her reaction to the propellers and rudders more pronounced when maneuvering or under way.

Of course both engines ahead or astern with midship rudder, will move the vessel directly ahead or astern providing there is no wind or current to interfere. But notice that in Figure 18-A the port engine ahead pushes the bow to starboard with the rudder's midship. If the port engine were backed, the stern would go to starboard and the bow to port. While in Figure 18-A1 left rudder on the vessel with the port engine going ahead causes a broadside movement along with headway.

This broadside movement is not predominant once good headway is achieved, but it does exist. Considerable left rudder would be required to keep the vessel on a straight course. If it were necessary to turn the vessel to port in confined quarters with only the port engine, it would be necessary to come ahead and astern (back & fill) in order to turn.

Figures 18-A2 and 18-A3 applies mostly to vessels with a wide beam such as offshore supply vessels, river boats, some crew boats etc., because their propellers are spaced well enough apart to give good leverage when working against each other with the rudders. Tugs of any size other than the inland pusher type, do not as a rule answer this method of maneuver well because of their V-hull, rounded bottom and deep draft, and by necessity, their propellers are placed too close together to offer good maneuvering leverage. Also, most tug boat propellers turn outboard, and when either is backed the rotation of the propeller tends to back the stern in the opposite direction, in addition to the force caused by the propellers being positioned off the center line of the boat.

In contrast to tug boats, most of the offshore supply boats and other flat bottom vessels, have inboard turning propellers which tends to back the stern away from the direction of the opposing propeller.

Notice Figure 18- A2 where the starboard engine is going astern and pulling the bow to starboard, while left turning propeller tends to back in that direction, and the port engine going ahead with a hard left rudder is pushing the stern to starboard also. In this illustration, the rudder pressure with the port engine ahead and the left turning starboard engine backing to starboard, is equal to the pull power on the bow by the starboard engine backing. In cases where there is disturbed water or currents, or the hull is near the bottom the starboard engine may pull the bow faster to starboard than

Fig. 18-A   **Fig. 18-A1**

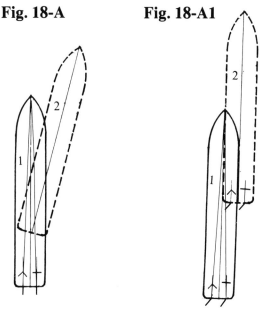

Fig. 18-A 1. Port engine slow ahead — starboard engine stopped — rudder midship. 2. Vessel turns to starboard.

Fig. 18-A1 1. Port engine slow ahead — starboard engine stopped — hard left rudder. 2. Vessel moves to starboard while making headway.

Fig. 18-A2

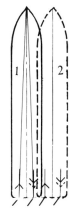

Fig. 18-A2 1. Port engine slow ahead — starboard engine ⅓ astern — with left variable rudder. 2. Vessel moves broadside to starboard.

the stern will move in that direction. This can be corrected by reversing the procedure and putting the starboard engine ahead and the port engine astern until the vessel is straightened up. Or if the vessel has headway, the starboard engine can be stopped and the port engine backing will straighten her up to keep from gaining more headway.

Figure 18-A3 illustrates broadside movement while moving ahead. Speed and movement must be adjusted with engines and rudders. If sufficient room is available, even many of the twin screw tugs will maneuver in this manner.

Fig. 18-A3

Fig. 18-A3 1. Port engine ⅓ ahead — starboard slow astern with variable left rudder. 2. Vessel moves broadside to starboard while making headway.

EXPERIENCES IN DOCKING

DOCKING WITH A HEAD CURRENT

Other than in slack water, docking head into the current at an open dock is one of the easiest ways to dock most vessels. The bow can be put at a slight angle to the current and dock and the current will do the rest.

There are exceptions however. Vessels with the bridge well forward on the bow, such as ore carriers, some cargo ships, and the offshore supply vessels have a characteristic all their own. The flare of the bow generally extends well aft of the bridge, and the edge of the dock will disappear under the bridge before her bow comes in contact with the dock. This makes it next to impossible to tell how far the hull is from the dock before her bow lands against it. (Figure 18-B).

Fig. 18-B

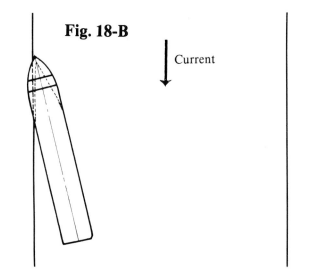

Current

Fig. 18-B Ships navigation bridge extending over dock.

It is best to dock these types of vessels broadside, or let the stern come alongside the dock first. Regardless of how large a ship is, she should never let the current get on the dock side of the ship's bow unless there is a bow line out to the dock, a tug made fast on the bow, or be equipped with a bow-thruster.

Offshore supply and other types of twin screw vessels, can fair somewhat better unless their bow is allowed to get the current at too much of an angle on the dockside bow. These vessels are much smaller, and have a square stern, and a greater beam to length ratio. A line can be put out on the dockside quarter aft. By coming ahead on the offshore engine with hard left rudder, the bow should come alongside. If more pressure is needed to bring the bow in, the dockside engine can be put astern. (Figures 18-B1 and 18-B2) (Page 113).

DOCKING WITH A STERN CURRENT

With a stern current, unless there are obstructions or some other circumstances that require it, there is absolutely no need to dock one of these vessels bow first, as shown in Figure 18-C (Page 113). All that is needed is to bring her stern alongside the dock at a slight angle and put a line out from the quarter. The current will do the rest, and if so desired, the offshore engine can be put dead slow ahead to make sure the stern line is tight while the vessel is secured.

DOCKING WITH AN OFFDOCK CURRENT OR WIND

With an offdock current and/or wind, smaller vessels can generally handle it as shown in Figures 18-D (Page 113) and 18-D1. After a stern line is out from the quar-

Fig. 18-B1

Current

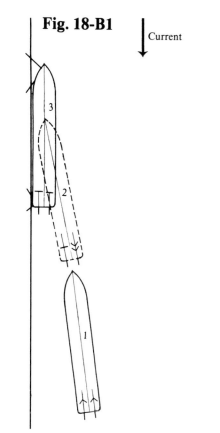

Fig. 18-B1   1. Both engine slow ahead. 2. Port engine stopped — starboard engine half astern. 3. Secure at berth.

Fig. 18-B2

Current

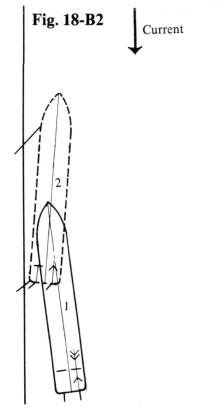

Fig. 18-B2   1. Port engine stopped — starboard engine slow ahead — stop and half astern. 2. Put out stern line and forward spring — starboard engine slow ahead — left rudder to bring vessel alongside.

Fig. 18-C

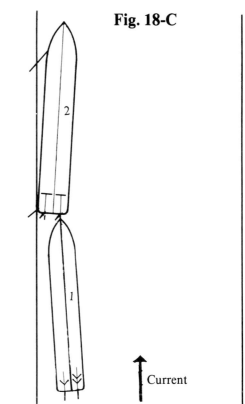

Current

18-C   1. Port engine slow astern — starboard engine half astern. 2. Put out stern and forward spring line — port engine may be backed or starboard engine dead slow ahead to bring vessel alongside.

Fig. 18-D

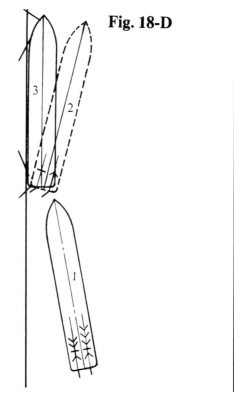

Fig. 18-D   1. Both engines slow ahead and stopped — starboard engine full astern — port engine half or slow astern. 2. Put out stern line — starboard engine ahead — port engine stopped — hard left rudder — if necessary, back port engine. 3. Secure at berth.

ter if the vessel cannot bring the bow alongside with her engines, it will be necessary to let go her stern lines and dock bow first. She can work her bow in close enough to the dock to get lines out and use her engines to work her stern alongside, while taking care not to break the forward lines.

Fig. 18-D1

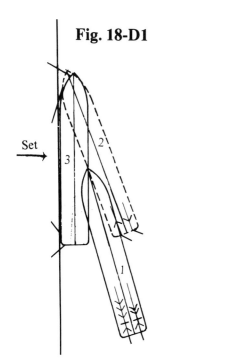

Fig. 18-D1   1. Both engines slow ahead and stopped — port engine full astern — starboard engine half or slow astern. 2. Put out spring and head lines — port engine ahead — starboard engine astern — hard right rudder. 3. Secure at berth.

DOCKING WITH AN ONDOCK CURRENT OR WIND SET

Docking with a strong current and/or wind broadside toward the dock is a matter of not coming alongside and landing too hard against the dock.

Figure 18-E illustrates the safest ways to dock the offshore supply vessels when there is a current running under the dock, and/or a gale blowing on dock and there are solid stringers or piles to land the stern against. Due to the lack of visibility forward over the bow, and over the side from the bridge, it is best to use the stern controls when the vessel is off the dock. By doing this, at least two thirds or more of the vessel's side rail and the stern can be seen. The stern can be landed first, with the bow angled away from the dock. When the stern is hard against the dock, the offdock engine can be backed and the dockside engine put ahead with midship rudder, or with the rudders hard over away from the dock, to keep her from falling alongside too fast.

Fig. 18-E

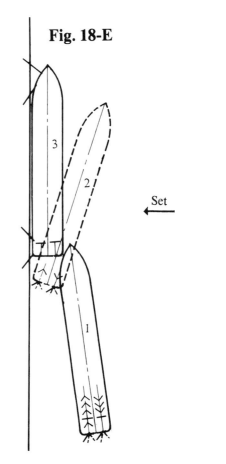

Fig. 18-E   1. Port engine slow ahead and stopped — variable rudder — port engine full or half ahead — starboard engine full or half astern. 2. Port engine slow or half ahead — starboard engine slow or half astern — variable rudder. 3. Secure at berth — stern and aft spring lines out first.

Most all vessels that work offshore have efficient anchors, but they are seldom used for maneuvering in harbors and channels, except for anchoring in fog, or when standing by. It should be remembered however, that they are there and should be used if necessary to keep from doing damage.

If there is good visibility forward from the bridge, the bow can sometimes be landed first. With the dockside engine going ahead and the offdock engine going astern, the rudders can be used from midships to hard left to let her bow fall gently against the dock. The engines would not have to be stopped, and she can use her rudders to keep the stern from falling alongside too fast. (Figure 18-E1) (Page 115).

When the on-dock set is not too strong, the vessel can stop several feet off the dock and parallel to it. When she starts to fall toward the dock, she can use her engines and rudders by backing her offdock engine and coming ahead on the dockside engine. Her rudders can be moved from midships to hard left to keep from landing too hard. This is the same procedure that would be used for taking her broadside away from the dock with

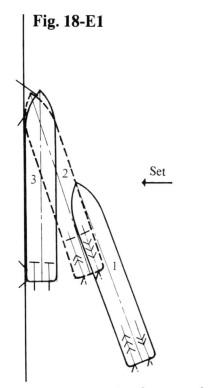

Fig. 18-E1

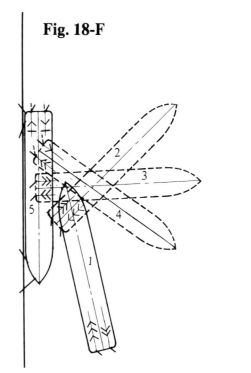

Fig. 18-F

Fig. 18-E1 1. Port engine full or half ahead — starboard engine half or slow astern — variable left rudder. 2. Port engine half or slow ahead — starboard engine full or half astern. 3. Secure at berth — forward head and spring lines out first.

Fig. 18-F 1. Port engine full or half ahead — starboard engine half or slow astern — hard right rudder. 2. Port engine — half or slow ahead — starboard engine full or half astern. 3. Port engine ahead — starboard engine astern — adjust speed to keep stern clear. 4. Port engine slow or half ahead — starboard engine half or full astern — midship and variable left rudder. 5. Port engine ahead — starboard engine astern — variable left rudder — secure at berth — stop engines.

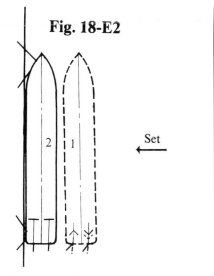

Fig. 18-E2

Fig. 18-E2 1. Ahead port — astern starboard — variable left rudder. 2. Engines stopped — secure at berth.

no set or current, and which is also shown in Figure 18-E1 for landing the bow first with an ondock set. (Figure 18-E2).

TURNING AND DOCKING

This maneuver is illustrated in Figure 18-F where the vessel turns at her berth and secures starboard side to the dock. Offshore supply vessels especially, handle well with this maneuver because the stern controls can be used, and in most cases the stern and side rail will be visible from the bridge.

As she approaches the dock where the bow will be secured when alongside, a sharp right turn is started by putting the starboard engine astern and leaving the port engine ahead with right rudder. The stern can be kept close to the dock as she turns by using engine speed and rudder angle.

With a little practice, this maneuver can be performed without stopping the engines at all until she is alongside and lines are out. All that will be needed is correct engine speed and rudder angle. This maneuver also works well in shallow water where the vessel's hull is near the bottom.

MANEUVERING IN SHALLOW WATER

Deep draft tug boats and similar type vessels, can in most cases steer the bow up to the dock at an angle and put out a spring line to hold the bow in while the stern is worked alongside with the engines.

The offshore supply type vessel however, has the problem of not being able to see over the bow or along-

Fig. 18-G

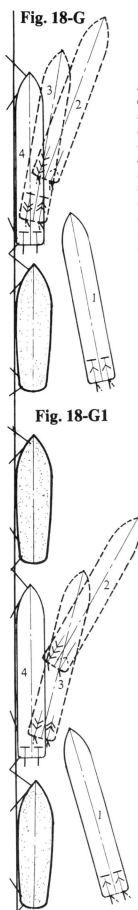

Fig. 18-G 1. Slow ahead and stopped — variable right rudder. 2. Port engine half or full astern — starboard engine slow, dead slow or stopped — variable right rudder. 3. Port engine astern — starboard engine ahead — adjust speed to hold position. Variable right rudder. 4. Secure at berth — stop engines.

Fig. 18-G1

Fig. 18-G1 1. Slow ahead and stopped — variable rudder. 2. Port engine full or half astern — starboard engine dead slow, slow ahead or stopped — hard right rudder. 3. Starboard engine half or full ahead — port engine half or slow astern — variable right rudder. 4. Stop engines and secure at berth.

side from the forward control station when approaching the dock. This makes it advisable in most cases to dock stern first when going to an open dock, or ahead of another vessel so that the stern controls can be used as shown in Figure 18-G. Also, this is beneficial because the propellers turning tend to wash the slush and silt away from the dock where the vessel is to secure.

If docking between two vessels, it will be necessary to keep the bow at more of an angle away from the dock to make sure that the bow does not fall down against the vessel ahead before it is clear. (Figure 18-G1).

THE BENEFIT OF A BOW-THRUSTER

The standard bow-thruster is a great help on offshore supply vessels and the larger tugs for maneuvering in close quarters, and in the open sea for running anchors, and for working around drilling rigs, platforms, etc.. They do a good job of helping overcome seas and cross currents in this area. However, one should first learn to work without them so when they break down (and they will) the function of the vessel will not be interfered with to any great extent.

In calm water and weather with good depth, it is a matter of choice as to how the bow-thruster is used. Notice in Figure 18-H where the rudders are hard over to push the stern up to the dock by backing the offshore

Fig. 18-H

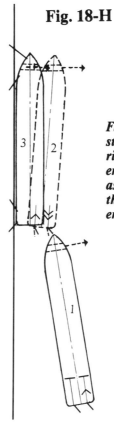

Fig. 18-H 1. Port engine stopped — starboard engine ahead and stopped — right rudder — thrust to port. 2. Port engine ahead — starboard engine astern — variable right rudder — thrust to port. 3. Secure at berth — stop engines and thruster.

Set

Fig. 18-H1

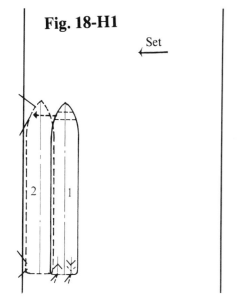

Set →

Fig. 18-H1   1. Port engine ahead — starboard engine astern — variable left rudder — thrust to port. 2. Stop engines and thruster — secure at berth. Note: If thruster can hold bow, engine directions may be changed with the starboard engine going ahead and the port engine astern to hold vessel against set.

Fig. 18-I

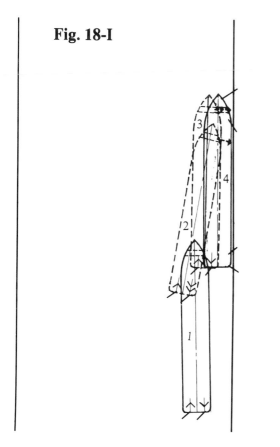

Fig. 18-I   1. Port engine slow ahead — starboard engine slow astern — hard left rudder — thruster stopped. 2. Slow ahead port — half or full astern starboard — hard left rudder — thrust bow to port. 3. Slow ahead port — slow astern starboard — thrust slow to port. 4. Secure at berth — stop engines and thruster.

engine and coming ahead on the inshore one, while the bow-thruster pushes the bow in. This is the best procedure if the vessel's stern is dragging or near the bottom, or if there is a set away from the dock.

Figure 18-H1 shows the set on dock, so the procedure is reversed and the vessel is allowed to drift slowly in against the dock. During this maneuver the main engines nor the bow-thruster engine may not need to be stopped until the vessel is alongside. The main engines and rudders can keep her in position, while the bow-thruster can keep the bow from coming alongside too fast.

Vessels equipped with bow-thrusters seem to maneuver a little differently from vessels not so equipped, as shown in Figure 18-I. Depending on the draft and trim, the bow will sometimes move toward the dock faster than the stern when the engines and rudders are set for the vessel to move broadside. This can be corrected in one of two ways. If the bow-thruster is not working or cannot be used, the correction can be made by reversing the direction of both engines for a few seconds to straighten the vessel up parallel to the dock. If the bow-thruster can be used it can hold the bow off the dock until the stern and bow are parallel to the dock as the vessel moves broadside and secures.

Figure 18-J (Page 118), shows the procedure for turning and docking in shallow water or against the current or set. When the vessel is almost turned, it is necessary to change the direction her propellers are turning. In this illustration the vessel is turning to starboard and docking starboard side to the dock. When she starts making the turn with a hard right rudder, the port engine is going ahead and the starboard engine is going astern, with the bow-thruster pushing the bow to starboard. Generally it will not be necessary to stop the bow-thruster until the vessel is alongside and secured, but as the starboard quarter comes around at a good angle to the dock, the rudders should be put hard left and starboard engine should be put ahead and the port engine astern to bring her stern alongside with the bow.

SAILING — WITH AND WITHOUT A BOW-THRUSTER

Many of the channels and harbors that these smaller vessels frequent are not large enough to accommodate large ships, and are only suited for use by these smaller vessels. Therefore, the small vessel in a narrow shallow channel feels the same effects as a large ship in a wider and deeper channel.

When sailing a twin screw vessel headed into the current there is no need to hold any lines for final cast off when nothing is moored close up. However, if she is loaded and her hull is near the bottom, it will not hurt to hold the short breast or spring line aft until the bow

Fig. 18-J

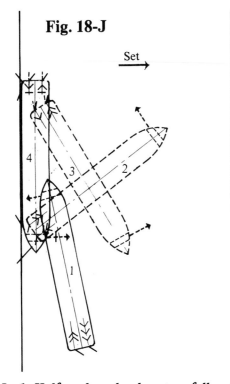

Fig. 18-J   1. Half or slow ahead port — full or half astern starboard — hard right rudder — thrust bow to starboard. 2. Adjust port engine ahead and starboard engine astern to keep stern clear — hard right rudder — thrust bow to starboard. 3. Starboard engine ahead — port engine astern — variable left rudder — thrust to starboard. 4. Ahead on starboard — astern on port — variable right rudder — thrust to starboard — secure at berth — stop engines and thruster.

Fig. 8-K

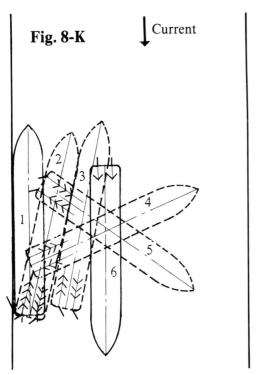

Fig. 18-K   1. Hold stern spring line — ahead port — astern starboard. 2. Hard left rudder — full ahead port — full astern starboard. 3-4-5. Ahead port — astern starboard — right rudder. 6. Slow ahead to steady up in channel.

is away from the dock.

When the bow is allowed to come away from the dock first, care must be taken not to let the stern get over or under the dock where the rudders, propellers and hull may be damaged. When conditions permit, this is the ideal way to sail when headed into the current or in calm dead water, especially if the vessel is loaded with her hull near the bottom. She can, in most cases, be kept on a continuous turn if she is going to head with the current, and all that is necessary is to keep her stern clear of the dock as shown in Figure 18-K. Notice in this diagram, the starboard engine is backing and the port engine is going ahead with hard left rudders. If the port engine and rudders can keep her stern clear of the dock, the only thing necessary to do is change the rudder angle and adjust the speed of the engines until she is completely turned and headed with the current. If her stern will not clear in this manner, it will be necessary to reverse the direction of the engines until it is, and then put them back in the same direction as before to complete the turn.

Figure 18-K1 (Page 119), illustrates the benefit of a bow-thruster when following the above procedure.

With a head current, if for some reason it is necessary for the vessel to sail with her bow toward the dock, it can be done as illustrated in Figure 18-K2 (Page 119).

A forward spring from the bow can be held to work against as long as it can be thrown off, but this should not be necessary. In most cases the vessel can be held in place by coming ahead on the starboard engine and astern on the port engine with hard left rudder, as shown in this diagram. With her bow against the dock, the stern should be worked out as far as possible, keeping enough pressure against the dock to keep the bow from sliding with the current. When her stern is clear, both engines can be backed with the rudder midship. When the bow is clear, the starboard engine can be put full ahead with a hard left rudder, while continuing to back the port engine until she is headed with the current.

Figure 18-K2-A and 18-K2-B (Page 120), illustrates the benefit of a bow-thruster in the same situation. If it is desired to work the vessel off the dock before turning, she can move broadside off the dock until clear and turn on the spot in either direction. The bow-thruster can push the bow around while the engines and rudders turn the stern.

Sailing from a berth where the current is running at a right angle and pressing the vessel against the dock is illustrated in Figure 18-K3 (Page 121), when she is proceeding in the same direction. She should work the stern out as far as possible by coming ahead on the starboard and astern on the port engine with a hard left rudder. She should then back both engines full speed

Fig. 18-K1

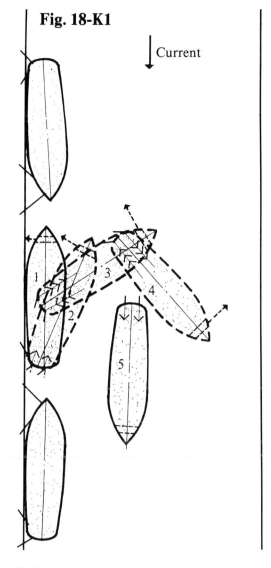

↓ Current

Fig. 18-K1   1. Hold spring line aft — thrust bow to starboard. 2. Let go stern spring line — both engines ahead — hard left rudder — thrust bow to starboard. 3-4. Port engine ahead — starboard engine astern — hard right rudder. 5. Both engines ahead — steady up in channel.

for a few seconds to gain sternway and clear the dock, while putting her rudder midship and then hard right. When she is clear, the port engine can be put full ahead and the starboard engine half or slow astern as required to straighten her up and get headway while holding up against the broadside current. If she wishes to turn and head in the opposite direction, the procedure would be the same as in Figure 18-K2.

The benefit of a bow-thruster is shown in Figure 18-K3-A (Page 121). It should be able to push the bow out against the current, while the starboard engine is put astern and the port engine ahead with a hard right rudder. When the bow is clear, both engines can be put ahead with enough left rudder and power to move the stern away from the dock and she will be under way.

Sailing from port side to the dock and heading with a stern current is illustrated in Figure 18-K4 (Page 121). The stern would be swung away from the dock and the engines backed until she is clear, then the engines can be put ahead with sufficient right rudder to straighten her out with the current.

It should be remembered, that when one engine is used the stern will swing away from that engine when it is backed, and toward it when it is going ahead.

A vessel equipped with a bow-thruster would sail in basically the same way, unless she would rather go broadside away from the dock. In this case she would let the bow-thruster push the bow away from the dock while the port engine is backed, and the starboard engine is put ahead with a hard left rudder to move her stern away as shown in Figure 18-K4-A. (Page 121).

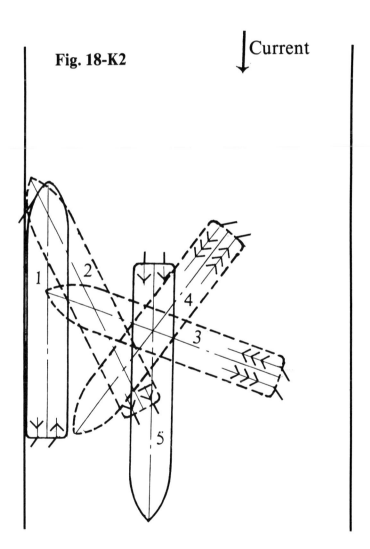

↓ Current

Fig. 18-K2

Fig. 18-K2   1. Hold spring line forward — starboard engine ahead — port engine astern — hard left rudder. 2. Both engines astern — let go forward spring — rudder midship. 3-4. Ahead on starboard engine — astern on port — hard left rudder. 5. Both engines ahead to steady up in channel.

Fig. 18-K2-A

Fig. 18-K2-B

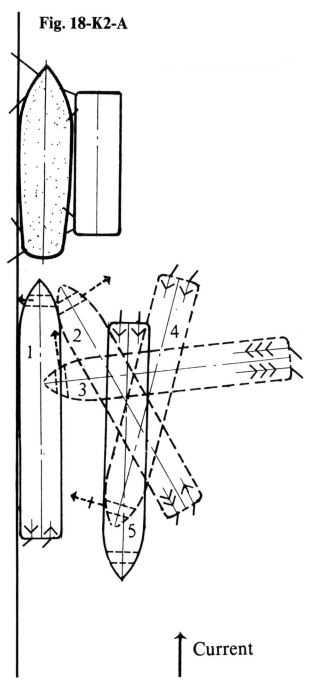

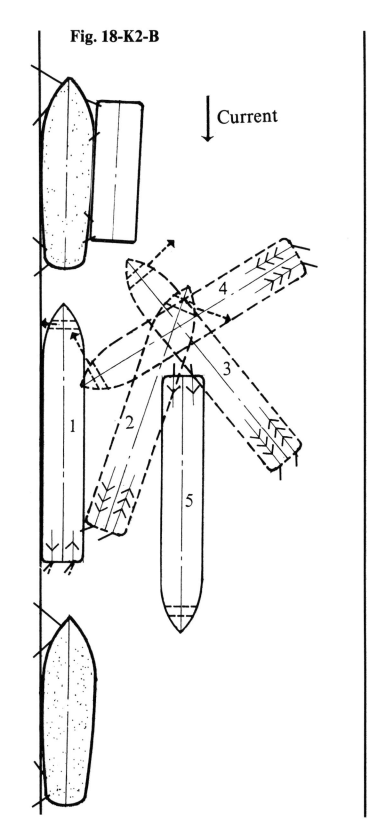

↓ Current

↑ Current

Fig. 18-K2-A   1. Starboard engine ahead — port engine astern — hard left rudder — thrust bow to starboard. 2. Slow ahead starboard — half astern port — hard left rudder — thrust bow to port. 3. Full ahead starboard — full astern port — hard left rudder — thrust to port. 4. Both engines ahead — variable left rudder — thrust bow to port. 5. Slow ahead to steady up in channel — stop bow-thruster.

Fig. 18-K2-B   1. Thrust bow to starboard — starboard engine ahead — port engine astern — variable left rudder. 2-3-4. Thrust to port — starboard engine ahead — port engine astern — hard left rudder. 5. Both engines ahead to steady up in channel. Stop bow-thruster.

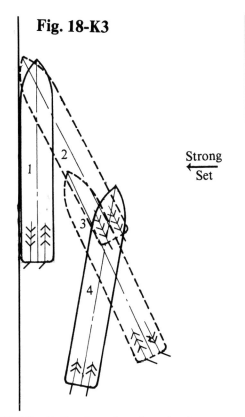

Fig. 18-K3

Strong
← Set

Fig. 18-K3   1. Starboard engine ahead — port engine astern — hard left rudder. 2. Both engines full astern — rudder midship. 3. Full ahead port — half astern starboard — hard right rudder. 4. Both engines ahead to steady up in channel.

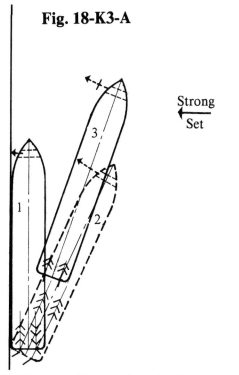

Fig. 18-K3-A

Strong
← Set

Fig. 18-K3-A   1. Port engine ahead — starboard engine astern — hard right rudder — thrust bow to starboard — adjust engine speed to keep from gaining headway. 2. Both engines ahead — left rudder to clear stern — thrust bow to starboard. 3. Reduce speed to steady up in channel and stop bow-thruster.

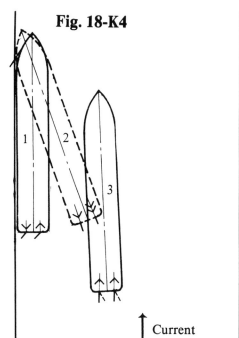

Fig. 18-K4

↑ Current

Fig. 18-K4   1. Hold forward spring — slow ahead starboard — slow astern port — hard left rudder. 2. Half astern starboard — slow astern port — let go forward spring — rudder midship. 3. Ahead on both engines — variable rudder to steady up in channel.

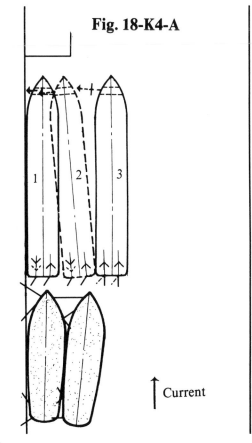

Fig. 18-K4-A

↑ Current

Fig. 18-K4-A   1-2. Ahead starboard — astern port — thrust bow to starboard — adjust engine speed to keep from gaining way — adjust rudder angle and bow-thruster speed to put current on port quarter. 3. Ahead on both engines to steady up in channel — stop bow-thruster.

CHAPTER 19

EXPLANATION OF HANDLING VESSELS OFFSHORE

Handling vessels offshore is somewhat different from working in close and confined quarters with banks, docks and a limited depth of water. Freed from these confinements, vessels will react more readily to propellers and rudders except in bad and severe weather, where they feel the sea regardless of how they are positioned.

The smaller the vessel, the more pronounced is the effect of the sea. Most small vessels will be safe enough running in a fairly heavy broadside sea if properly trimmed and not top heavy with too much gear or cargo. They are uncomfortable to be sure, even a large ship is. However, it is not much more uncomfortable than trying to run with the sea on either bow quarter and going nowhere. Large ships can put the seas on the bow and ride fairly well, but this is not so with a small vessel. A small vessel in a heavy sea that may endanger its cargo machinery and equipment, should either head into, or put her stern to the sea until the weather subsides. If time is not important it is much more comfortable to do this with any small vessel.

If it is desirable not to get too far off course, the vessel can run back and forth with her head into the sea for a time, then turn and head with the stern to the sea for the same distance. If there are no stationary objects on which the distance run can be determined, she will of course have to head into the seas for a longer period of time than when running before them.

Currents at sea are just as pronounced and dangerous, and at times more so than inshore currents. Much of the time the direction of the current cannot be determined until the vessel has arrived at her destination. If due care is not taken to determine the direction and force of the current before attempting to dock, the vessel can find herself in all kinds of trouble.

Remember that offshore there is no bank or bulkhead to interfere with the current's movement or direction as is the case inshore. The only comparison that can be made, is a finger pier extending out into the channel with nothing to obstruct the flow, even though the current will be flowing with the direction of the channel.

When a vessel is committed to dock with the current flowing under a rig, that in most cases, is exactly what is going to happen. In this case, it is not a matter of not

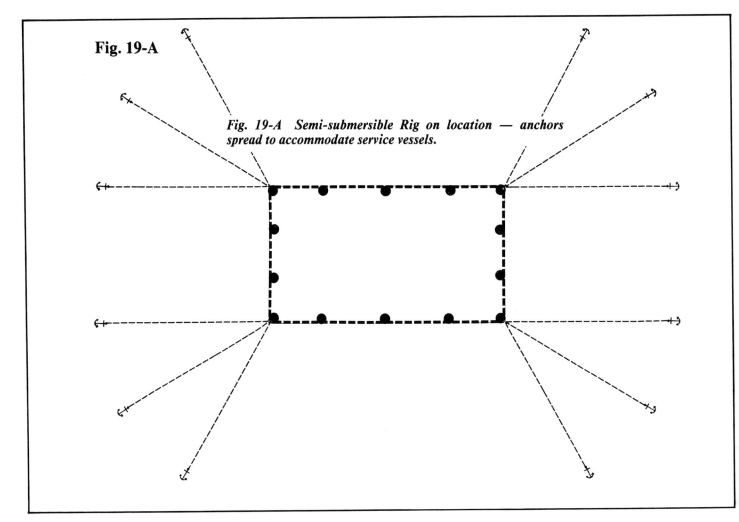

Fig. 19-A

Fig. 19-A Semi-submersible Rig on location — anchors spread to accommodate service vessels.

being able to dock, but a matter of not docking too fast. This can cause a problem when docking at semi-submersible rigs, drillships and lay barges which have anchor chains or cables leading out broadside from the bow and stern. This leaves the approaching vessel no way of working her way out once she has been committed. Deep draft drillships and other large deep draft vessels anchored on each end with the current abeam do offer some backwash. In most cases this is insufficient to keep from doing damage when the approach is not done in a manner to offset the current.

Remember that the current does not necessarily run in the direction which the wind may be blowing, or from the direction from which the seas build up. Every situation should be studied as it presents itself before committing the vessel to go alongside.

Figure 19-A (Page 122), illustrates the general direction of the anchor cables leading from a semi-submersible drilling rig.

Figure 19-B illustrates the general direction of the anchor cables leading from drilling ships.

Of course the best holding position for the anchors is for them to be placed straight ahead and astern, and at forty five and ninety degree angles on the bow and stern respectively. The size of the rig determines the angle at which the beam anchors are positioned. On smaller rigs it is generally necessary for these anchors to be spread further apart toward the bow and stern in order to accommodate service vessels.

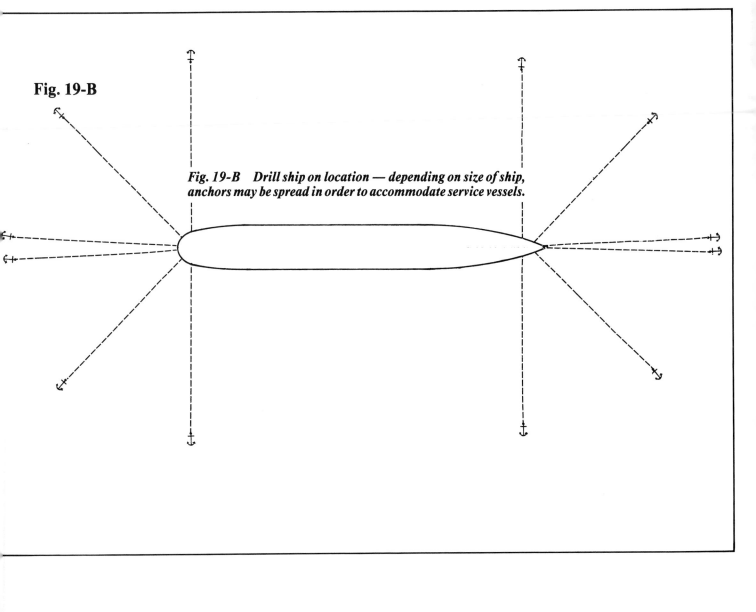

Fig. 19-B

Fig. 19-B   Drill ship on location — depending on size of ship, anchors may be spread in order to accommodate service vessels.

CHAPTER 20

MANEUVERING AT OFFSHORE PLATFORMS

APPROACHING A PLATFORM WITH THE CURRENT RUNNING UNDERNEATH

When approaching a platform or rig with the current or set running underneath, it is best to approach with caution while keeping the vessel headed as nearly as possible in the same direction in which the current or set is running.

If the direction of this set is uncertain, and there is bad weather with rough seas, it is always wise and good seamanship to lay off or circle the rig in order to determine the direction of the set before committing the vessel to go alongside. There are times however, it seems more often than not, that a vessel will be required to work and land against the set in order to place it in the proper position for loading or discharging. Most of these platforms and some rigs have piles or protective structures for vessels to land against. This should be located before the vessel prepares to go alongside and secure. The direction of the current and set can easily be determined by observing the direction the water is running around the legs of the platform, and the anchor buoys. When boats are anchored or hanging off of a rig with one line, their anchor chains or lines will generally be headed in the direction of the current.

When the set is running at an angle under the rig, a vessel should approach with the set on her stern until the bow is close to, or touching, the docking area. With the vessel docking port side to the rig as shown in Figure 20-A, putting the starboard engine full astern should pick the bow up against the current but the stern will start to swing rapidly toward the rig. The rudders then should be put hard left with the starboard engine ahead and the port engine astern with the bow against the rig. Her stern can be allowed to fall alongside slowly by use of the rudder while she is held in place with the engines.

Because of the poor visibility forward and alongside from the forward control station on most supply vessels, it is easier in most cases to use the stern controls and dock them stern first as shown in Figure 20-A1 (Page 125). The stern is made to land softly by using left rudder and putting the port engine astern and the starboard engine ahead. As soon as the stern touches, the rudder angle is changed along with the engines. The starboard engine is put astern and the port engine ahead with right rudder to let the bow fall alongside slowly.

Of course, this is why a bow-thruster is so beneficial

to this type of vessel. If the current is not too strong, she would most likely be able to dock broadside with no trouble, and in any case she would be more able to control her bow as she comes alongside.

Fig. 20-A

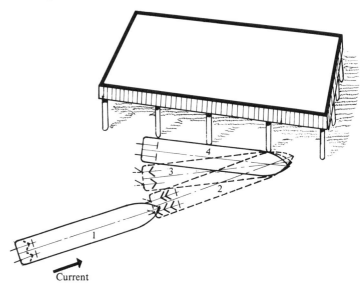

Fig. 20-A   1. Dead slow ahead and stopped. 2. Full astern starboard — half astern port and stop both engines when bow is against platform leg. 3. Starboard engine ahead — port engine astern — variable left rudder to let stern come alongside. 4. Stop engines and secure to rig.

When it is necessary to go port side to the rig with the current running at an angle on the starboard bow, the maneuver is basically the same as shown in figure 20-A1. It is best to turn the vessel so that she is almost headed into the current, and let the port quarter land against the docking area first. (Figure 20-B) (Page 125). Then if the bow starts falling alongside too fast, the starboard engine can be backed and the port engine put ahead with a hard right rudder. Here again, is where a bow-thruster is a real asset. If the force of the current is uncertain, the above is still the best procedure to follow, and the bow-thruster can help keep the bow from coming alongside too fast. However, emphasis is put on handling vessels without a bow-thruster, because if one learns to handle them without a thruster, they can certainly handle them with one.

The procedure in Figure 20-C (Page 126), is nothing more that what is shown in Figure 1-A at the beginning of this book. In this case, we have a twin screw supply vessel where the rudders and propellers can assist in this broadside movement. This maneuver can be successful even against a fair current running under the rig abeam. When the turn is started and the vessel has a

Fig. 20-A1

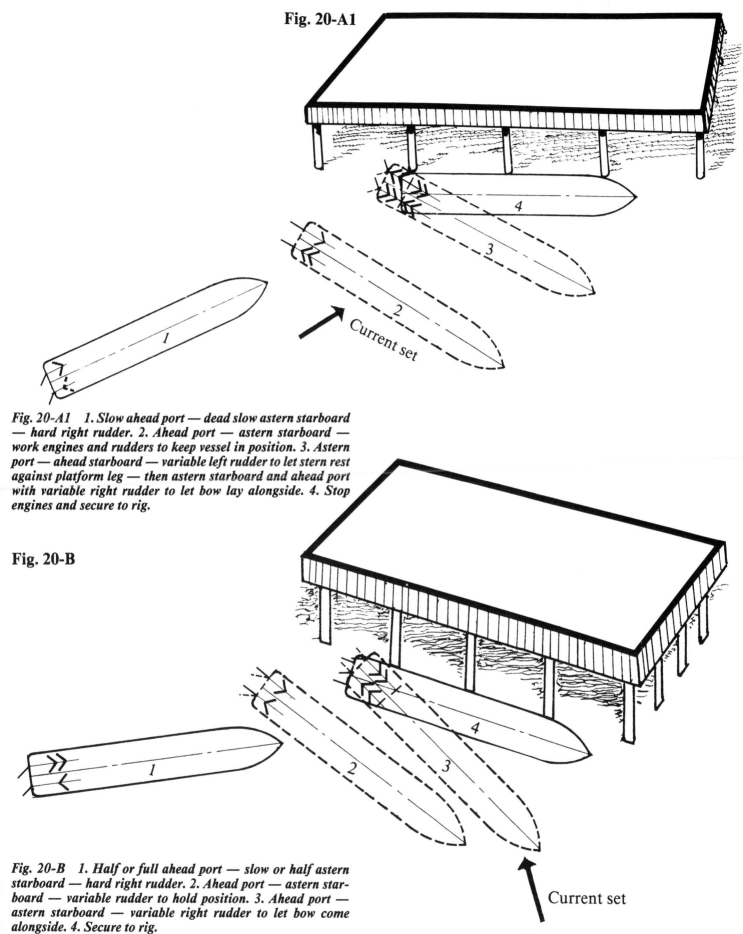

Fig. 20-A1   1. Slow ahead port — dead slow astern starboard — hard right rudder. 2. Ahead port — astern starboard — work engines and rudders to keep vessel in position. 3. Astern port — ahead starboard — variable left rudder to let stern rest against platform leg — then astern starboard and ahead port with variable right rudder to let bow lay alongside. 4. Stop engines and secure to rig.

Fig. 20-B

Fig. 20-B   1. Half or full ahead port — slow or half astern starboard — hard right rudder. 2. Ahead port — astern starboard — variable rudder to hold position. 3. Ahead port — astern starboard — variable right rudder to let bow come alongside. 4. Secure to rig.

Fig. 20-C

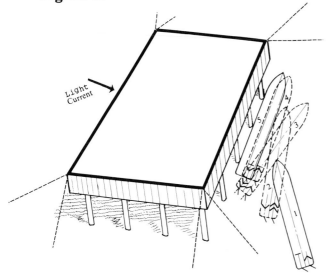

Fig. 20-C 1. Slow or half ahead starboard — port engine stopped — hard right rudder. 2. Half or full ahead starboard — slow or half astern port — hard right rudder. 3. Slow or half ahead starboard — half or full astern port — variable rudder to hold position. 4. Ahead starboard — astern port — variable rudder to bring vessel alongside. 5. Secure to rig and stop engines.

good swing, it works best if the port engine can be stopped, and the turn continued with the starboard engine ahead for a short distance before putting the port engine astern.

When the current is running strong underneath a rig and the vessel cannot be walked broadside against it, the vessel should continue on as if to make a circle, as shown in Figure 20-D (Page 126). Or, if an effort has been made to make a broadside landing, just work her around to that approximate position to where she would be on the circle. Then proceed to back her up to the rig so that a short stern line can be put out. It is best to have the port engine coming astern, and the starboard engine ahead if the vessel will hold her stern up against the current. This will keep her bow at a better angle for working alongside with the starboard engine ahead and hard left rudder when the stern line is out. If more pressure is needed to bring the bow alongside, the port engine can be put astern or ahead. If the bow will still not come alongside against the force of the current, another stern line can be put out forward of the stern chock on the vessel to give more leverage to the rudders and propellers. (Fig. 20-D1) (Page 127).

Fig. 20-D

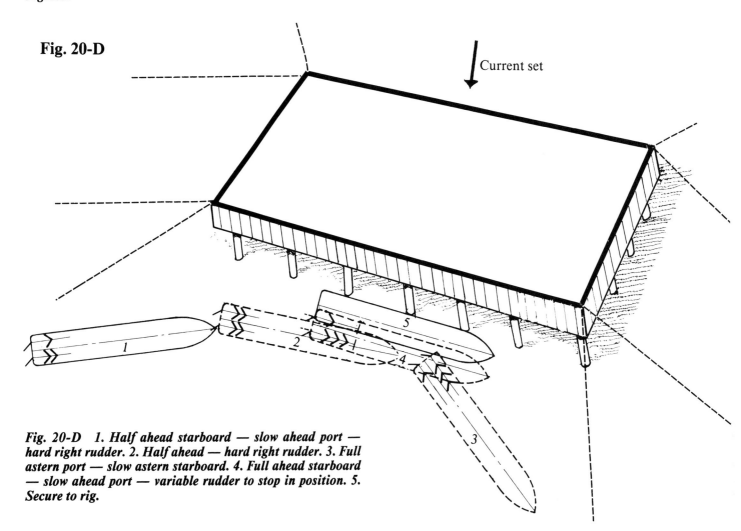

Fig. 20-D 1. Half ahead starboard — slow ahead port — hard right rudder. 2. Half ahead — hard right rudder. 3. Full astern port — slow astern starboard. 4. Full ahead starboard — slow ahead port — variable rudder to stop in position. 5. Secure to rig.

Fig. 20-D1

Fig. 20-D1   1. Half ahead starboard — slow ahead port — hard right rudder. 2. Full astern starboard — slow ahead port — variable rudder and stop engines. 3. Put out stern line and make fast — slow ahead starboard — port engine stopped or astern — left rudder. 4. Secure at rig and stop engines.

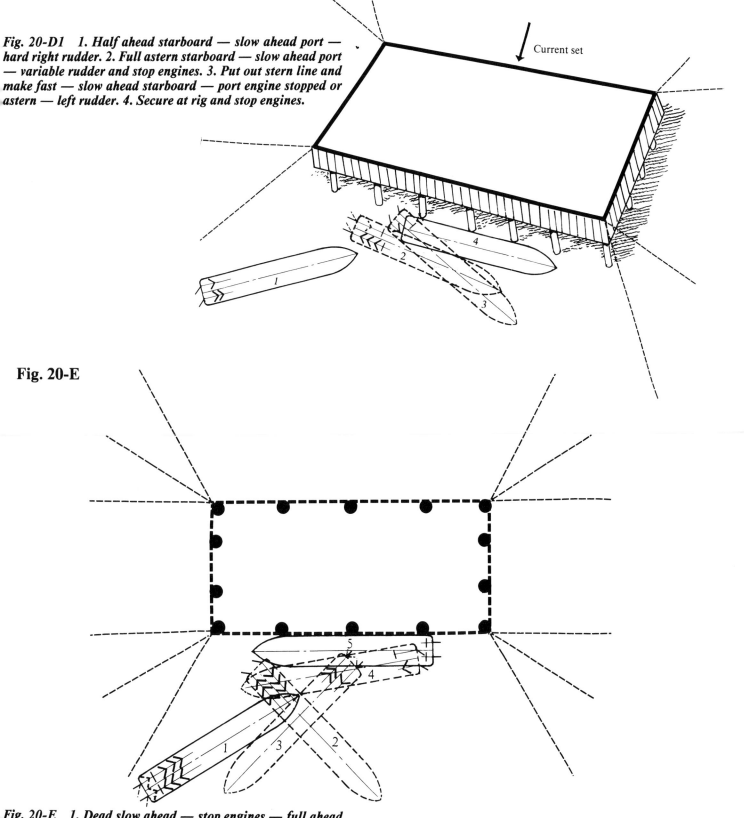

Current set

Fig. 20-E

Fig. 20-E   1. Dead slow ahead — stop engines — full ahead port — full astern starboard — hard right rudder. 2. Full ahead port — full astern starboard — hard right rudder. 3. Half or full astern starboard — slow or half ahead port — variable left rudder to keep stern in position. 4. Ahead port — stop starboard — variable rudder to bring vessel alongside. 5. Stop and secure at rig.

Working the oil patch and knowing what to expect is next to impossible. The only expectation worthwhile is to "expect the unexpected." This explains the maneuver illustrated in Figure 20-E (Page 127). In vessel 1, it is obvious she is shaped up to secure port side to the rig. However, before she can get alongside, the rig decides it wants her to secure starboard side to.

It will generally be necessary to carry out this maneuver with some full speed on the engines. First, the starboard engine should be put full astern to stop the vessel's headway and start her swinging to starboard. When the head-way is stopped, and maybe a little stern-way has begun, the port engine can be put full ahead with hard right rudder to complete the necessary turn before backing up to the rig as shown in almost the opposite manner as explained in Figure 20-D. (Page 127).

CHAPTER 21

APPROACHING AND MAKING FAST TO RIGS USING STERN MOORING LINES

Most all jack-up and semi- submersible rigs have mooring lines which are passed down by crane to vessels where it is necessary to secure with their stern to the rig. This is comparatively easy as long as set and drift are taken into consideration. In this manner, supply vessels can secure in much heavier weather than they can in a broadside position.

If there is a strong current and wind, the vessel's stern will lay toward it and there is not much that can be done about it if an anchor cannot be put out before securing. If there are chocks and bits aft that are forward of the propellers on a vessel which is making fast in this manner, she can hold herself up against a fairly strong set. However, most supply vessels are not constructed with their aft mooring bits placed this far forward. Only tug boats seem to claim this accommodation.

In many areas now, an anchor cannot be dropped without having a survey vessel spot the place where the anchor can be dropped, because of pipe lines laying on the bottom. This is done with special vessels which are committed to stay secured for long periods of time doing service or repair work, etc.. However, this service is not generally available to supply vessels. If the vessel cannot lay at an angle that will keep her clear of the rigs structure, it will be necessary for her to cast off the lines and wait until she can.

Fig. 21-A

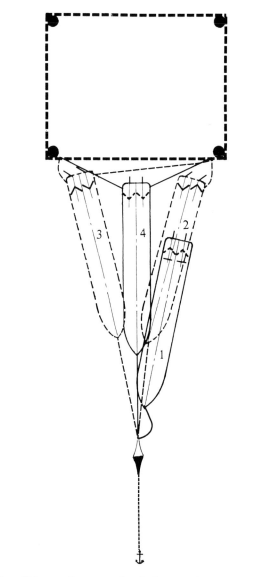

1. Put head line on buoy — dead slow or slow astern and stop — slack head line. 2. Take port stern line and pay out — ahead starboard — astern port — hard left rudder — hold head line. 3. Take starboard stern line — ahead port — astern starboard — left rudder. 4. Make stern lines fast in position — dead slow ahead and heave slack out of head line.

Some rigs have mooring buoys anchored with concrete forms or blocks that will not hang up or damage the pipe lines if it is drug over them. These buoys usually are placed away from the rig to hold the vessel's bow out so that the vessel will lay at a right angle to the rig or nearly so, when the vessel backs up to the rig and the stern lines are made fast.

These buoys are better than nothing, but should be watched closely. If possible, the engines should be kept on slow ahead to keep as much strain as possible off of the buoy, because in strong currents and heavy seas they will drag, or possible part the line attached to them from the vessel. (Figure 21-A).

Fig. 21-A1

Current set

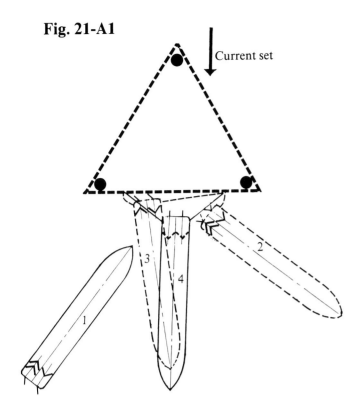

Fig. 21-B

Current set

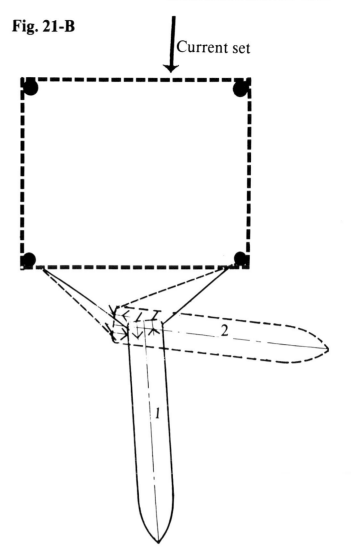

Fig. 21-A1   1. Ahead port — astern starboard — hard right rudder. 2. Ahead port — astern starboard — variable rudder — take port stern line. 3. Ahead port — astern starboard — take starboard line — variable right rudder. 4. Take in excess slack on lines and make fast in position — engines slow or dead slow ahead.

Figure 21-A1 shows the way a vessel will lay with a line from each quarter to the rig. When the lines are made fast and tight, the vessel should keep both engines working slow or dead slow ahead so that she will lie steady with the set with midship rudder.

Under some conditions, depending on the location of the crane used in loading or discharging the vessel, it may be required to swing against the set so that the crane can reach the proper place on deck. In this case the rudders can be put hard over toward the set on the port side, and if necessary more power can be put on the starboard engine. The port engine can be stopped and/or backed to bring the vessel around against the current until the work is completed. She should then fall back with the set to ease the strain on the lines. (Figure 21-B).

Figure 21-C (Page 130), illustrates only one way of taking the stern lines from a rig. This maneuver may vary depending on conditions. If the sea is calm and there is only tidal current, it is easy to back directly into the current up to the rig. The line that will be put out on the current side, should be made fast first so that the vessel can hold herself off the rig's leg structure while the off current line is made fast.

Fig. 21-B   1. Ahead starboard — astern port — hard left rudder to swing to port. 2. Ahead starboard — astern port — variable rudder to hold position.

In bad weather with rough seas it is difficult to determine the exact direction of the current, and because of the design of the supply vessels with a square stern and flat bottom, they do not back well into a heavy sea. Therefore, it is easier and safer to take the stern lines where the set is greatest as shown here.

Fig. 21-C

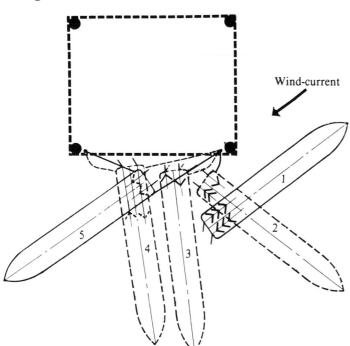

Wind-current

Fig. 21-C   1. Full ahead port — full astern starboard — hard right rudder. 2. Ahead port — astern starboard — variable rudder to hold position — take port stern line and pay out. 3. Ahead port — astern starboard — variable rudder — pay out port stern line. 4. Ahead port — astern starboard — take starboard stern line and pay out — hold port stern line. 5. Hold stern lines with vessel in position — dead slow ahead to lay with current.

CHAPTER 22

ANCHORING AND MOORING STERN FIRST TO A RIG

When there are no pipe lines on the bottom to worry about and the anchor is allowed to be dropped before securing with stern lines to the rig, it is always safer to do so. Especially if the vessel is expected to stay in that position for some time.

If asked, the rig will sometimes inform the vessel as to how long she will be needed, but it is not customary for a rig to show this courtesy unless asked, and much of the time the rig itself does not know because of the type of cargo the vessel may be carrying. Therefore, it is generally best to put the anchor out unless advised otherwise.

The ocean tidal currents generally run back and forth in opposite directions for designated periods of time. This information can be found in the tide tables for the area. However, bad weather and severe disturbances can change this at any time. Therefore, if the vessel has

an anchor out she will generally have no problem.

When the anchor is put out, it should be placed well away from the rig, as shown in Figure 22-A. The depth of the water will designate the distance, but a good rule of thumb is about five times the water depth. The main thing is to make certain that it will not drag under a strain.

Only trained personnel should be used in letting the anchor go and paying out the chain. Most supply vessels do not have adequate communications from the bridge to the bow, and the operator will be working from the stern controls and away from the anchor windlass area. The personnel operating the windlass must be able to pay the chain out so that the anchor is

Fig. 22-A

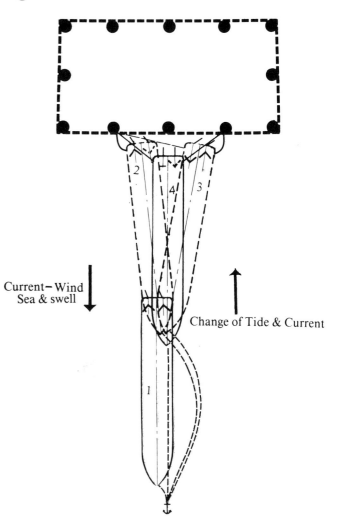

Current–Wind
Sea & swell

Change of Tide & Current

Fig. 22-A   1. Drop anchor and pay out chain — slow astern — right rudder. 2. Take starboard stern line and pay out — ahead port — astern starboard — right rudder — hold anchor chain. 3. Hold starboard stern line — take port stern line and pay out — ahead starboard — astern port — left rudder. 4. Take excess slack out of starboard stern line — make stern lines fast — heave anchor chain tight and stop engines — or leave on dead slow ahead.

Fig. 22-B

Fig. 22-B   1. Drop anchor and pay out chain — slow astern. 2. Slow astern starboard — dead slow ahead port — stern should move to port. 3. Take port stern line — ahead starboard — astern port — left rudder — hold anchor chain and slack off port stern line. 4. Hold port stern line — take starboard line and slack off easy. 5. Hold stern lines with vessel in position — heave anchor chain tight and stop engines, or leave on dead slow ahead with midship rudder.

Change of Tide & Current

Tidal Current-Wind-Sea & Swell

not dragged and the chain does not pile up on the bottom as she moves astern to make fast to the rig.

Notice the procedure taken in backing up to the rig and making the stern lines fast. The stern is swung to starboard as it approaches the rig and the starboard mooring line is taken first. The port engine is ahead and starboard engine astern with a right rudder. The line to the starboard quarter is slacked off so that the line to the port quarter can be taken on board and both lines are then made fast so that the vessel will lay in the proper position. One or both engines should work ahead with rudder midship, to keep a strain on the lines while the slack is heaved out of the anchor chain and the windlass brake set.

It is always best to anchor a vessel so that her stern or bow will lie in the direction of the sea and swell when she is made fast to a rig, as shown in Figure 22-B. Supply vessels are designed with a square stern and flat bot-

tom, and the sea running under the stern shakes them badly, especially when they have a light draft. However, this is better than having one roll her decks under the water when there are people on deck discharging cargo. Also, if the stern lines should break, all that might be lost would be any hose that might be attached for supplying liquids to the rig.

When a supply boat is anchored and made fast to a rig heading into the sea, she will lay much better minus most of the pounding that is experienced with a stern sea. However, the sea and swell ahead presents a potentially dangerous problem. If the anchor should drag or anything give way forward, the rig will be right behind the vessel. Good judgement and prudent seamanship would advise keeping the engines running, and one or both of them working slow ahead, with a mate on watch at all times when made fast under these conditions.

Figure 22-C shows what happens when the anchor is put out at a right angle to the rig with the current, sea and swell running at a different angle. The tidal currents are more dependable than the sea and swell which is built up mostly by weather. The seas calm relatively fast after a blow, but the swell that builds up before and during a blow last for some time. Depending on the extremity of the weather, swells build up well ahead of a bad weather disturbance. The vessel will give to the greatest force regardless of whether it is wind and seas, or tidal currents.

If both forces are approximately the same and coming from different directions, she will try to lay at an angle to both and become restless, swinging from one direction of force to the other.

If there is a heavy swell with no wind and the tidal current is running at an angle to the swell, she will swing with the current and roll with the swell unless there are lines to the rig to prevent her from doing so.

There is not an effective way to beat a broadside current with the sea and swell coming from the same direction. Figure 22-D illustrates what seems to be the safest and most efficient all-around procedure, especially if the vessel is to be secured for a long period of time.

If circumstances permit, the anchor chain can be slacked off to allow the vessel to swing around more with the set, where she will probably ride better. However, if this is done, the safest procedure would be the same as shown in Figure 22-C with the vessel headed into the sea. One or both engines should be kept running with the rudders slightly toward the rig, so if a line from the stern should break, the stern will not go into the rig.

The maneuver shown in Figure 22-E can be effective when the sea and swell are running contrary and at an angle to the current. When backing up to the rig the vessel should keep her stern angled up into the current so that the anchor chain will pay out in as straight a line as

Fig. 22-C

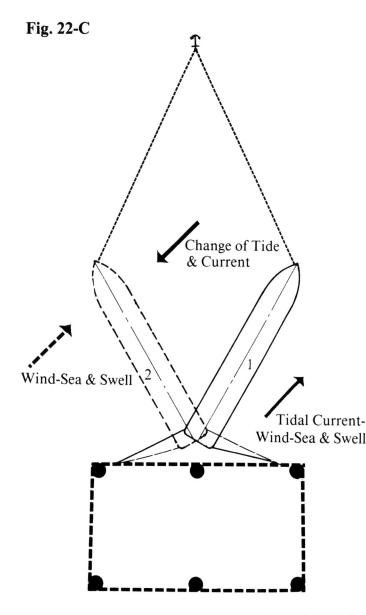

Fig. 22-C 1. Tidal Current — Wind — Sea and Swell 2. Wind — Sea and Swell 3. Change of Tide and Current

Fig. 22-D

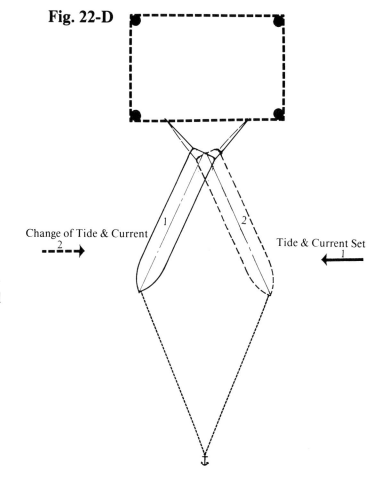

Fig. 22-D   Tide and Current Set Change of Tide and Current

possible toward where the bow will be when she is made fast. Always, the stern line on the current or weather side should be taken from the rig and made fast first, so that it can hold the stern in position while the other stern line is taken and made fast.

When circumstances require that a vessel lie at a right angle to a rig for loading etc., or when the sea and swell are running at a right angle to the current, the procedure shown in Figure 22-F can be used effectively.

The vessel should be maneuvered so that the anchor chain is kept in as straight a line as possible toward the bow location when at a right angle and made fast to the rig. If the vessel is allowed to fall down in front of the rig before she has backed her stern up to it, the anchor chain will most likely hold the bow in much the same way as if the anchor were set straight out from the rig.

However, because of the change in tidal current and possible weather changes, this procedure can only be recommended when the vessel is going to be secured to the rig for a limited time only.

Fig. 22-E

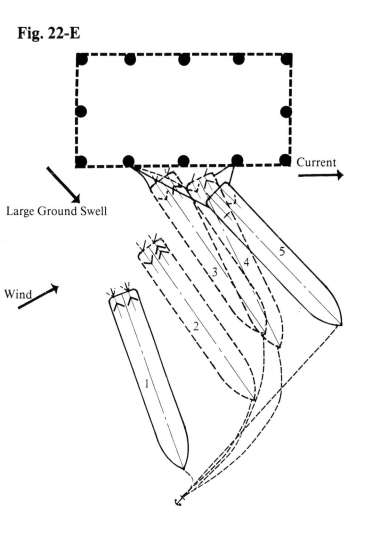

Fig. 22-F

Fig. 22-E   1. Drop anchor and pay out chain — slow astern — variable rudder. 2. Astern port — ahead starboard — variable rudder — pay out anchor chain, but hold strain. 3. Take starboard stern line and pay out — ahead starboard — astern port — variable rudder and speed. 4. Astern port — ahead starboard — variable rudder and speed to hold position — take port stern line — hold anchor chain. 5. Stop starboard — dead slow ahead port — hold stern lines with vessel in position — slack anchor chain to lay with stern toward swell — leave one or both engines on dead slow ahead.

Fig. 22-F   1. Drop port anchor and pay out chain — engines slow astern. 2. Astern port — ahead starboard — variable left rudder — pay out, but keep excess slack out of anchor chain. 3. Take starboard stern line and slack off — ahead starboard — eastern port — variable left rudder — hold stern in position with engines, and bow in position with anchor. 4. Ahead starboard — astern port — left rudder — take port stern line. 5. Adjust stern lines to hold stern in position — hold bow in position with anchor — keep one or both engines ahead.

CHAPTER 23

RUNNING ANCHORS WITH TUG FOR LAY BARGES, ETC.

There is little to say about this operation. The most important thing is to be able to handle a tug well, and this has been covered.

A tug employed in this work really takes a beating, to both her engines and hull, because the operation is generally full astern and full ahead, and the anchor buoys bang up the stern counter, quarter bulwarks and hull. As long as the barge is laying or dredging pipe, she is moving over the ground and does not like this movement to be interrupted to move anchors, which is right and proper.

This operation however, is somewhat dangerous to a tug's deck personnel in the best of conditions — and becomes extremely so in bad weather. Since a barge is held down with anchors and cable all around it, it does not feel the heavy seas like the smaller tug, and the barge crew does not, in most cases, understand the difficulty and danger of trying to put a line on a buoy which is jumping all over the place. So it is generally left up to the tug captain to decide when it is too rough to continue. In most cases, a jet or lay barge does not want its operation interfered with until it is too rough for the barge to work.

A tug tending a lay barge should have a double winch with a towing cable on one drum and what is called a "trunk line" on the other drum.

Fig. 23

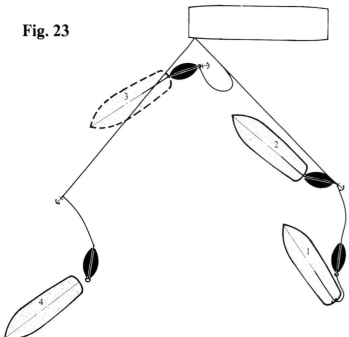

1. Attach pendent wire. 2. Heave up anchor and move toward barge. 3. Turn and move toward new anchor location. 4. Drop anchor and buoy.

The trunk line is only long enough to feed out through a center chock, or post, and around the quarter to the buoy, as shown in Figure 23. The trunk line will have a trip hook on the end to which another short line made fast on deck can be attached so that it will release when the anchor is moved and dropped. The anchor buoy has a hole through the center through which a wire pendant is run and attached to the anchor. The trunk cable is hooked into the eye of this pendant and heaved in on the drum with the trunk cable. The buoy hangs over the stern of the tug while the anchor is heaved off the bottom and moved.

When the anchor is respotted and the pendant line is paid out to where the tug's trunk line is on deck, the short line mentioned above is attached to the trip hook, and as the buoy pendant line goes over the side the hook is released.

When picking up anchors, the tug should take care not to put too much strain on the buoy pendant wire until the anchor is off of the bottom in order to prevent breaking it. Where there is a soft sandy or shell bottom, this is not much of a problem if the anchor has not been laying long enough to work itself deep. However, on a sticky clay bottom, the anchor will cling to it, and too much strain can break the wire.

When a pendant wire breaks, it generally causes a delay in the barge's progress, since the anchor cable will have to be stripped. This is accomplished by a large shackle being attached to the tug's towing cable and the anchor cable near the barge. The tug then slacks some cable off the towing drum and moves down the cable toward the anchor. At the same time, the large shackle slides down the anchor cable to the anchor, where the tug heaves in on its towing drum to break the anchor free from the bottom. The barge then heaves the tug and anchor alongside to replace the pendant.

CHAPTER 24

HANDLING ANCHORS FOR DRILL SHIPS AND SEMI- SUBMERSIBLE DRILLING RIGS WITH TOWING SUPPLY VESSEL

This procedure is altogether different to handling anchors for lay barges with tugs.

The towing supply vessels are larger than the tugs and generally have more horsepower because they have to work under more strenuous conditions.

Drill ships and other deep water rigs that are held in place by anchors, generally lay in one place for long periods of time and their anchors sink deep into the ocean floor.

The anchor buoys also are larger than the lay barge buoys and in most cases the anchor pendant wire does not run through the buoy. It is shackled to the buoy so that it must be taken on deck before unshackling the pendant wire and taken to the towing winch cable for heaving the anchor up.

The towing/supply vessels will have one or more small air or hydraulic driven winches for moving the buoys out of the way so that the pendant cable will be clear for heaving.

Some of these drilling vessels have wire cable running to the anchors and some of them have chain. Some are equipped to carry their anchor cable or chain on board, while others depend on the towing supply vessel to carry them. Some towing supply vessels are equipped with anchor chain lockers to store most of the chain used by these drilling vessels. The chain is stored in these lockers, and the anchors placed on deck and transported to the new location where they are put back out. (Figure 24-A).

When picking up anchors for these rigs, great care must be taken not to put too much strain on the pendant wires. A good strain should be taken and held while the anchor works up from the bottom. The longer

the rig has been in the same location, the deeper the anchors will be sunk into the ocean floor. It can take hours on end to heave one up through the tons of mud or clay. There is no doubt that the towing winch on these vessels will break a two inch wire cable pendant, and if you put too much strain on it, that will be exactly what happens. Stripping anchors on a lay barge is nothing compared to stripping an anchor on one of these rigs which has been anchored in deep water for a long period of time. It can cost many hours, and even days of production time, not to mention the frustration and the possibility of injury to personnel.

CHAPTER 25

PUTTING TOWING HAWSER ON RIGS

Figure 25-A (Page 136) illustrates different maneuvers practiced in putting a hawser out to a rig waiting to be towed when there is a beam current and set.

Circumstances and the direction the rig wishes to move when under way will dictate the direction the towing vessels will head while getting under way. The rig will generally advise if the tug is allowed to put a hard strain on the hawser while it is preparing to get underway. However, most experienced tug captains will keep their vessel in a position to where excessive strain on the hawser will not be necessary.

Maneuvers B and D illustrate heading into the set when putting out the hawser, while maneuvers A and C illustrate heading with the set. Weather and other conditions at the time will dictate which maneuver to follow.

Figure 25-B (Page 137) illustrates basically the same thing, but with the current & set running at a different angle. Maneuver A is subject to put the most strain on the hawser, and B should cause less strain because of the working angle, while C should cause no excessive strain at all since the set will be carrying her into position.

Figure 25-C (Page 138) illustrates one of the most dangerous conditions in which to maneuver. Position A of course is the safest because if anything happens the tug should drift by and away from the rig. In maneuver B however this is not the case. In the event of mechanical failure or human error the tug will drift into and/or under the rig and will most likely cause extensive, or even fatal damage.

Good seamanship suggests that only one vessel at a time should make fast to a rig so that the first one to make fast can stay out of the way of the other, etc.. The

Fig. 24-A

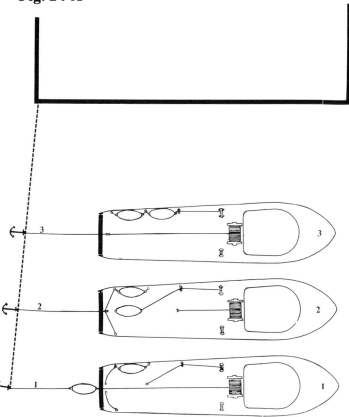

1. Heave buoy on deck. 2. Disconnect buoy and store on deck. 3. Heave up anchor.

Fig. 25-A

Fig. 25-A A1 — Slow or dead slow ahead starboard — dead slow or slow astern port — variable rudder to keep stern clear — make fast and pay out hawser. A2 — Half or full ahead starboard — half or full astern port — left rudder — pay out hawser. A3 — Half or full ahead starboard — full or half astern port — hard left rudder — pay out hawser. A4 — Half or slow ahead starboard — slow or dead slow astern port — left rudder — hold hawser. 5A — Dead slow or slow ahead — variable rudder to hold position.

B1 — Dead slow or slow ahead port — stop starboard — variable rudder to keep stern clear — make fast and pay out hawser. B2 — Dead slow or slow ahead — variable rudder to hold up against set — pay out hawser. B3 — Hold hawser — dead slow or slow ahead — variable rudder to hold position.

C1 — Put out and slack off hawser — starboard engine dead slow or slow ahead — port engine stopped — variable rudder. C2 — Full or half ahead starboard — full or half astern port — hard left rudder — pay out hawser. C3 — Half or slow ahead starboard — half or slow astern port — variable rudder — pay out hawser. C4 — Hold hawser — dead slow or slow ahead — variable rudder to hold position.

D1 — Slow or dead slow ahead port — starboard engine stopped — variable rudder to keep stern clear — put out and slack off hawser. D2 — Slow or dead slow ahead — variable rudder — pay out hawser. D3 — Hold hawser — dead slow or slow ahead — variable rudder to hold position.

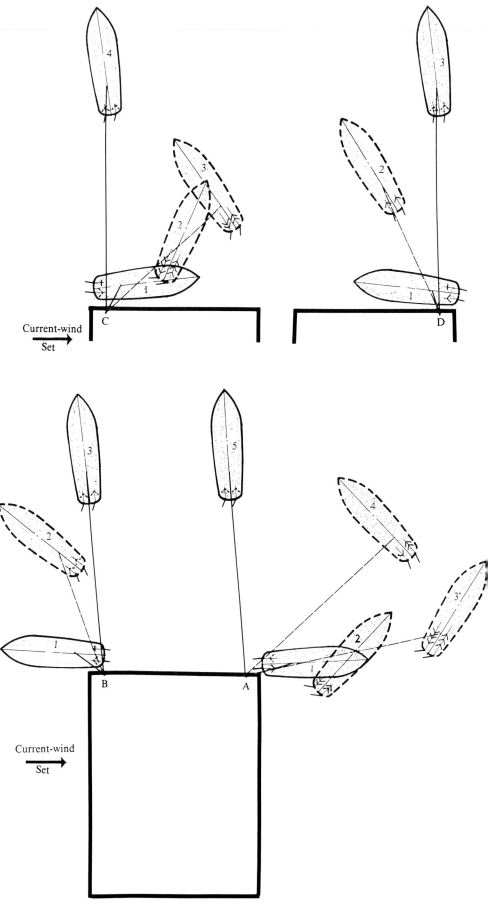

Current-wind Set

Current-wind Set

Fig. 25-B

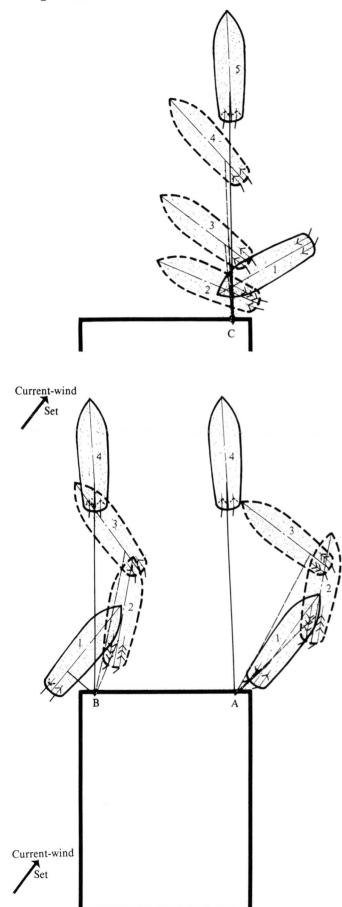

Fig. 25-B   A1 — Put out and slack off hawser — slow ahead starboard — slow astern port — hard left rudder. A2 — Full or half ahead starboard — full or half astern port — hard left rudder — pay out hawser. A3 — Half or slow ahead starboard — slow or half astern port — variable rudder — pay out hawser. A4 — Hold hawser — dead slow or slow ahead — variable rudder to hold position.

B1 — Put out and slack off hawser — slow or dead slow ahead starboard — dead slow or slow astern port — variable rudder to keep stern clear — B2 — Full or half ahead starboard — full or half astern port — left rudder — pay out hawser — B3 — Slow or half ahead starboard — slow or half astern port — variable left rudder — pay out hawser. B4 — Hold hawser — dead slow or slow ahead — variable rudder to hold position.

C1 — Dead slow ahead — right rudder — C2 — Slow or dead slow ahead port — half or full astern starboard — variable rudder to keep stern clear — put out and slack off hawser — C3-C4 — Dead slow or slow ahead — variable rudder — pay out hawser — C5 — Hold hawser — dead slow or slow ahead — variable rudder to hold position.

Current-wind
Set

Current-wind
Set

Fig. 25-C

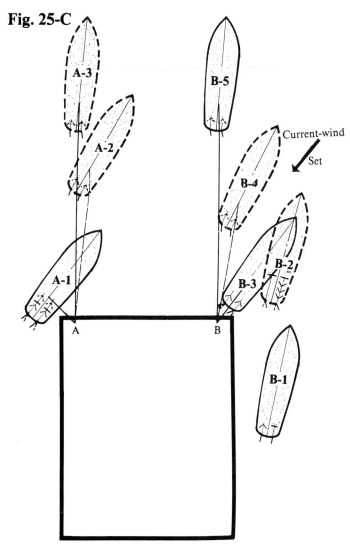

Current-wind

Set

Fig. 25-C A1 — Dead slow or slow ahead and stopped — put out and slack off hawser — variable rudder to keep stern clear — dead slow or slow ahead — A2 — dead slow or slow ahead — variable right rudder — pay out hawser — A3 — Hold hawser — dead slow or slow ahead — variable rudder to hold in position.

B1 — Slow ahead port — starboard engine stopped — hold up for set — B2 — Starboard engine astern — port engine stopped — hard right and midship rudder — B3 — Put out and slack off hawser — slow ahead — variable left and midship rudder — B4 — Dead slow or slow ahead — variable right rudder — pay out hawser — B5 — Hold hawser — dead slow or slow ahead — variable right rudder to hold in position.

tug making fast first should pay out the hawser and move clear for the other tug(s) to make fast. When circumstances permit, the tug on the down current side will generally be the first to put out a hawser so that her propeller wash will not interfere with the other tugs as they maneuver into place.

Figure 25-C1 (Page 139), illustrates tugs placing hawsers on a rig for towing. Tugs A, B, & C will put out their hawsers, with tug A being the first to put out a hawser and move out of the way for tugs B & C to put out their hawsers in that order. Tug D can then put out a hawser and work into position while A, B & C falls around with the current to be in position with tug D.

UNDERWAY AND PUTTING RIG ON LOCATION

Figure 25-D (Page 140), illustrates approaching and placing a square rig on location. Direct tug orders will come from the rig itself, concerning the heading and speed of the tugs. This is general procedure and the way it happens in most cases.

Just before arriving at the location site, the two tugs towing on the inside will turn loose and put hawsers out on "B" and "C" corners of the rig as shown in step 1. As the rig approaches the location buoy these tugs fall around to a forty five degree heading to the stern of the rig, while the tugs on the forward part of the rig will spread out to a forty five degree angle on the bow. This leaves the tugs pulling in a direct line from each other by the time the location buoy is approached as shown in step 3. The rig spotter in all cases direct the heading and speed of the tugs while placing the rig on location.

On occasion a rig will be underway when it is necessary for another tug to put out a towing hawser as shown in Figure 25-E (Page 141).

In most all cases it will be necessary to maneuver between two other tugs because there will be one on each corner for the purpose of keeping the rig straight while under tow.

This creates a dangerous situation to say the least and due caution should be taken. If at all possible, the rig should be maneuvered so that the sea and swell will be on the stern. If this is not possible, the tugs should head the rig into the sea and swell. The tugs which are towing should spread apart and slow down while keeping just enough power to keep their towing hawsers off of the bottom or from letting them fall around out of control.

It is not difficult to see that mechanical failure or human error here can cause a real problem.

Figure 25-E1 (Page 141), illustrates three tugs putting towing hawsers on a triangle type jackup rig with the current running broadside.

Tug A would be the first to put out a hawser, and then drift broadside to the rig, keeping just enough strain on the hawser to stay out of the way. Tug B would then put out a hawser and head into the current while keeping enough strain on the hawser to offset the pull on the rig by tug A. Tug C would then put out a hawser and head in the direction the rig is facing. Tug A then works

Fig. 25-C1

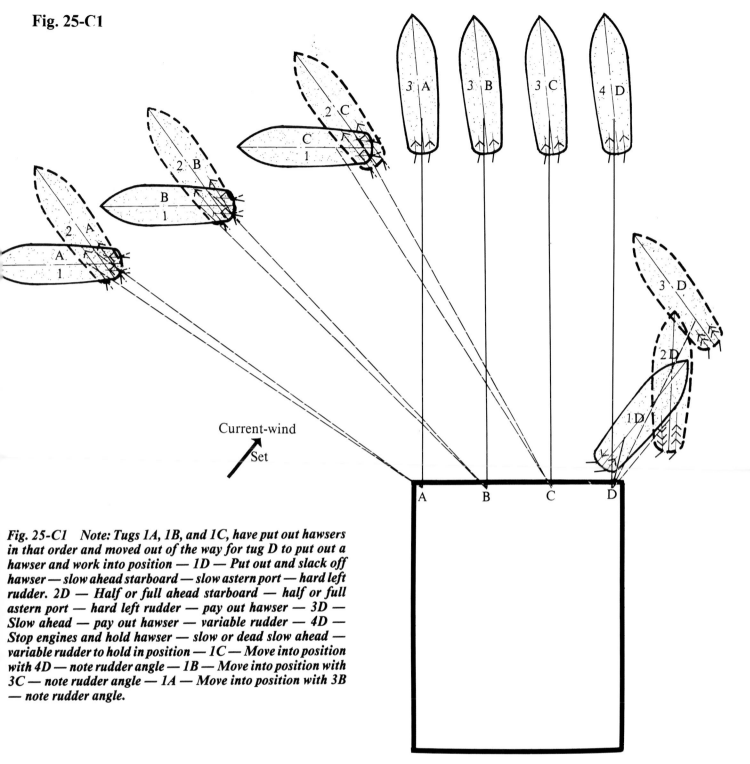

Fig. 25-C1   Note: Tugs 1A, 1B, and 1C, have put out hawsers in that order and moved out of the way for tug D to put out a hawser and work into position — 1D — Put out and slack off hawser — slow ahead starboard — slow astern port — hard left rudder. 2D — Half or full ahead starboard — half or full astern port — hard left rudder — pay out hawser — 3D — Slow ahead — pay out hawser — variable rudder — 4D — Stop engines and hold hawser — slow or dead slow ahead — variable rudder to hold in position — 1C — Move into position with 4D — note rudder angle — 1B — Move into position with 3C — note rudder angle — 1A — Move into position with 3B — note rudder angle.

around alongside tug C while tug B holds a strain on the hawser to offset the strain placed on the rig by tug A. Tug B can then let the current carry her around to head in the same direction as tugs A and C.

When a triangle type jackup rig has only a short distance to move, they will generally have the tugs make fast as illustrated in Figure 25-F (Page 142).

They will tow as shown in step 1, and the tugs towing from the aft corners will fall around when the rig is nearing location in step 2. They should be in the proper position to pull in the direction ordered when the rig is ready to be placed on location.

Fig. 25-D

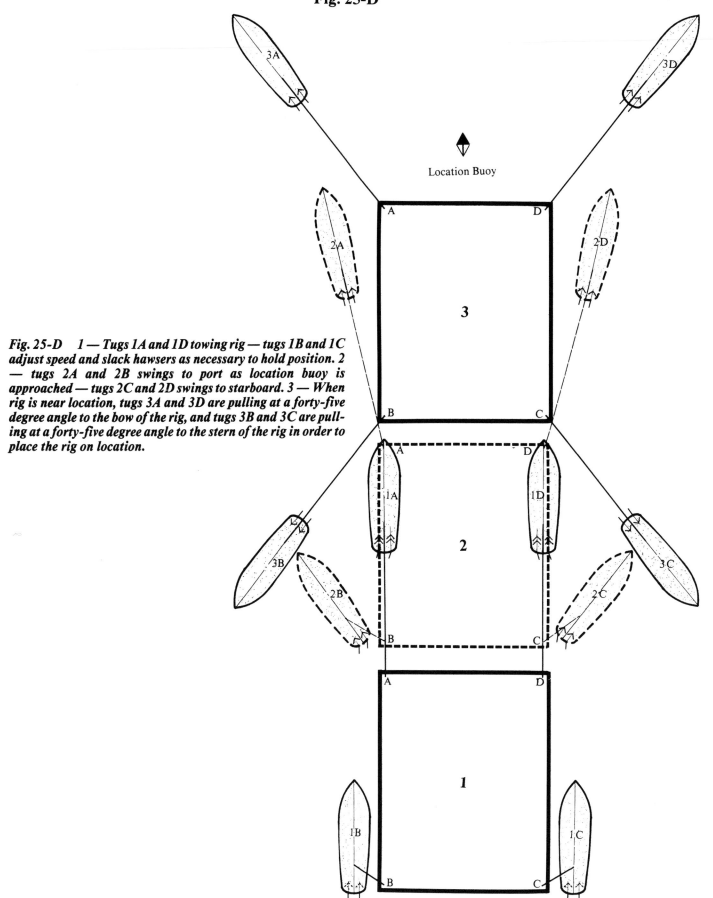

Fig. 25-D   1 — Tugs 1A and 1D towing rig — tugs 1B and 1C adjust speed and slack hawsers as necessary to hold position. 2 — tugs 2A and 2B swings to port as location buoy is approached — tugs 2C and 2D swings to starboard. 3 — When rig is near location, tugs 3A and 3D are pulling at a forty-five degree angle to the bow of the rig, and tugs 3B and 3C are pulling at a forty-five degree angle to the stern of the rig in order to place the rig on location.

Fig. 25-E

Fig. 25-E   Putting out hawser to rig under way. Tugs A, B, and D, are spread at an angle to allow tug C to put out hawser. 1C — Engines ahead as rig approaches — make fast and pay out hawser. 2C — Dead slow ahead — pay out hawser — steady on course. 3C — Hold hawser — engines ahead — tug in position for towing.

Fig. 25-E1   Note: Tugs making fast for towing long distance. 1A — Put out hawser and head with current to make room for 1B and 1C — dead slow on one engine to keep strain off of rig. 1B — Put out hawser and head into current to make room for 1C — slow ahead, or as directed to keep strain off of rig while 1A works into position with 3C. 1C — Put out hawser and work into position — dead slow or slow ahead as directed. 1A — Ahead starboard — astern port — hard left rudder — move into position with 3C or as directed. 2B — Slow ahead — variable rudder to move in position with 3C or as directed.

Fig. 25-E1

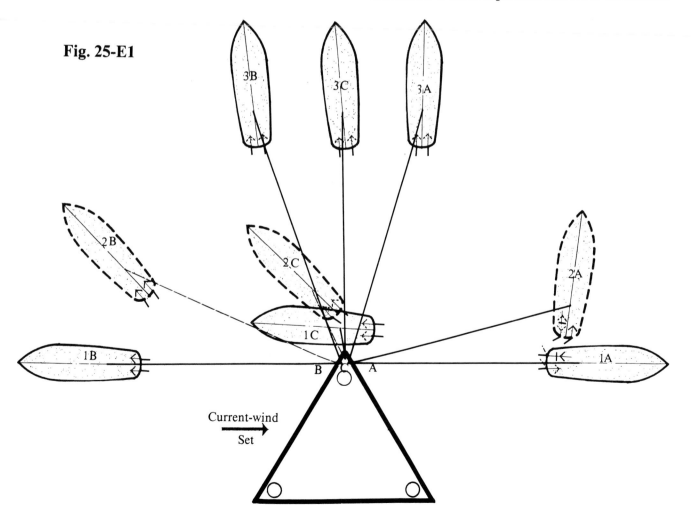

Current-wind
Set

Fig. 25-F

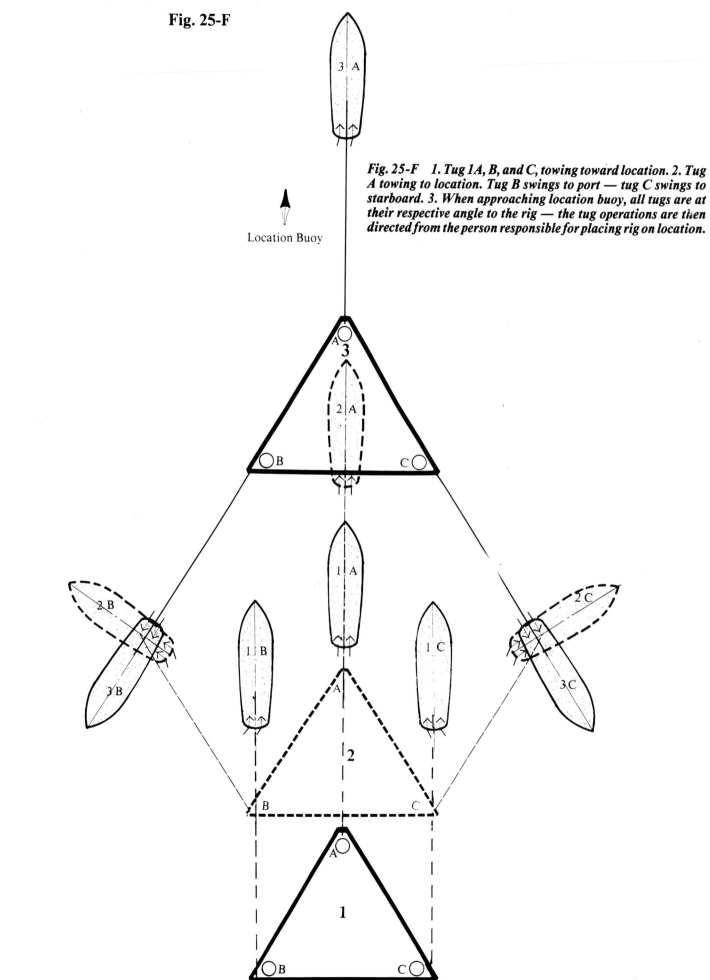

Location Buoy

Fig. 25-F   1. Tug 1A, B, and C, towing toward location. 2. Tug A towing to location. Tug B swings to port — tug C swings to starboard. 3. When approaching location buoy, all tugs are at their respective angle to the rig — the tug operations are then directed from the person responsible for placing rig on location.

CHAPTER 26

HANDLING FERRY BOATS

Some of these vessels are about the easiest thing around to handle and maneuver. Some, however, are not.

They are generally designed to travel only one specific route which may leave them with limited maneuverability.

Those constructed with two engines and rudders on each end with independent controls should never be a problem in handling. You can go either way or broadside at a pretty good clip or at a snail's pace by working the engines and rudders against each other.

Those that have only one shaft running straight through from one end to the other and turned by one or more engines are another story. One propeller is going ahead and the other backing all the time with the one rudder on each end acting in conjunction with each other. This type is far more likely to damage their landing and themselves.

A cross-current generally exists in channels and harbors where ferries are used and most of the landings have "Y" bulkhead slips constructed for protection from these currents once the vessel is inside, and most landings have pile clusters to land against while approaching.

Fig. 26

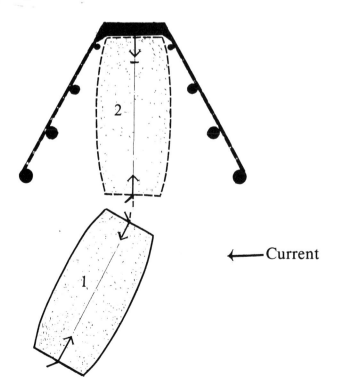

←—Current

In approaching the landing with a cross current it will be necessary to approach at an angle to offset the current as would be necessary with any other vessel.

Ferry boats that are required to land broadside to the ramp are mostly twin screw type with engines and rudders only on one end. They will be found mostly on rivers like the Mississippi where the current flows constantly from the same direction. This type of vessel will act somewhat differently because of the hull design, but should be handled basically as any other twin screw vessel while better understanding their particular maneuvering capabilities. (Figure 26).

CHAPTER 27

OPERATION OF OUTBOARD, AND INBOARD/OUTBOARD MOTOR BOATS

Unlike boats with inboard motors that have fixed rudders and propellers, the outboard and the inboard/outboard motor boats operate somewhat differently because the propeller serves both as propulsion and rudder power. On the outboard the whole motor and propeller shaft swings on a pivot, while on the inboard/outboard, only the shaft and propeller turn on a pivot which gives the same effect as an outboard engine.

Outboard motor boats equipped with a steering wheel steer the same as inboard motor boats, or your car when going ahead. When the steering wheel is turned to the left, the steering cables will pull the engine to face to the right and the bow of the boat will go to the left in the opposite direction the engine is facing. However when backing, the bow will turn in the same direction the engine is facing.

If the boat does not have a steering wheel, the steering procedure is changed. If making a left turn, the handle on the motor is pushed to the right and the bow will go to the left when going ahead as shown in Figure 27-A (Page 144) and if the engine is backed the bow will go to the right as shown in Figure 27-B (Page 144).

The vertical propeller shaft housing on these boats is formed to resemble a balanced rudder, which is found on some larger vessels. This allows them to be steered with the engine stopped, as long as they have fair headway. These boats however tend to slow down and lose steerage way soon after the engines are stopped.

Some of the very small outboard and trolling motors swing 360 degrees and have no reverse. These motors must be turned to face the direction the stern is to trav-

Fig. 27-A

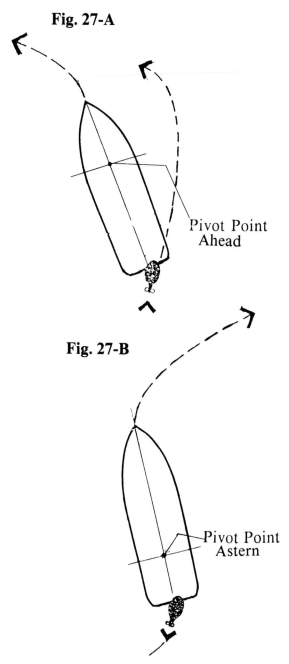

Pivot Point
Ahead

Fig. 27-B

Pivot Point
Astern

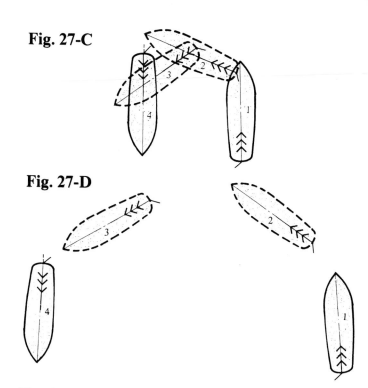

Fig. 27-C

Fig. 27-D

Fig. 27-C Turning ability of outboard and inboard/ outboard boats.

Fig. 27-D Turning ability of inboard motor boats with fixed rudder.

el, when moving astern. When going ahead they steer the same as any other outboard with no steering wheel.

Figures 27-C and 27-D illustrates the difference in the turning circle of the single engine outboard, or stern driven boat and the single engine inboard with fixed rudder. The outboard type makes the turn much shorter because the propeller is pushing at an angle to the keel, instead of in a direct line with it.

WORKING WITH SINGLE SCREW INBOARD BOATS

ANCHORING WITH WIND AND CURRENT

On sea coast where jetties extend out from the shore-line to protect channels and harbors, tidal and river currents are much more pronounced between the jetties than on the outside of them. Some of the ground swell will be running on the outside however, which can make a small craft very uncomfortable. Depending on the velocity of the wind, the draft of the vessel, and the amount of superstructure above the water line, one can sometimes be made to lay head into the swell by fashioning a bridle as shown in Figure 27-E (Page 145). After enough anchor line has been put out to hold, a line leading from aft can be made fast to a bite in the anchor line. The anchor line can then be slacked off until she is headed into the swell. Of course, if the wind should shift or calm down, she will fall around broadside to the swell.

Using two anchors as shown in Figure 27-F (Page 145), is the most efficient way to lay head into the swell. The bow anchor should be put out first, and then the boat backed into position to put the stern anchor out. This eliminates the chance of backing over the stern anchor line and getting it fowled in the propeller(s).

The amount of anchor line to be put out in order to hold the boat safely depends on several factors, but from five to nine times the depth of water is a good rule of thumb. Size of vessel, type and size of anchor, type of bottom, weather conditions, length of time to be anchored, etc. all should be taken into consideration Under any conditions, it is always best to put out enough anchor line to be sure that an anchor will not

Fig. 27-E

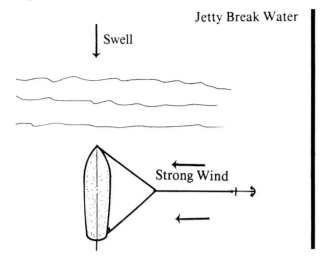

Fig. 27-E Strong Wind Swell Jetty Break Water Laying at anchor head into swell

Fig. 27-F

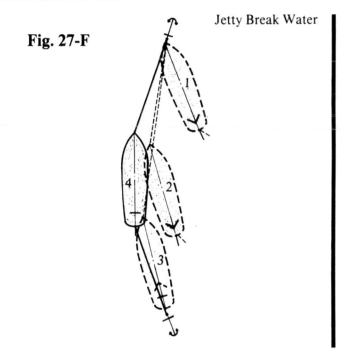

Fig. 27-F 1. Drop and pay out anchor line — engine astern — variable rudder. 2. Keep bow headed into swell. 3. Drop stern anchor — engines slow ahead and stopped — pay out anchor line to position #4 — heave on bow anchor line. 4. Make fast anchor lines to head into swell.

drag, especially if the boat will drag into a shoal or dangerous area.

A few feet of chain attached between the anchor and anchor line increases the holding ability of the anchor a great deal. The weight of the chain tends to keep the anchor stock near the bottom so that the anchor will dig in before dragging.

MOORING TO DOCK USING ONE OR MORE ANCHORS

Where docks are constructed on pilings or pontoons and the current is free to run underneath, a boat can be safely moored with the use of one anchor. Figure 27-G illustrates this process with the thought in mind that the vessel will be left unattended. Of course in this case, it will be necessary to have a dingy or some other form of transportation to get ashore after the boat is moored. In this illustration the bow line is put ashore first and slacked off, while the boat backs away and a stern anchor is dropped. She then moves back toward the dock and adjusts the lines so that an equal strain is placed on each of them. In some areas it may be possi-

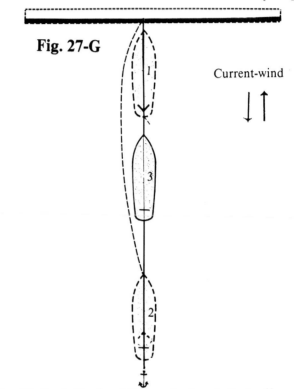

Fig. 27-G

Current-wind

Fig. 27-G 1. Put head line on dock and slack off — engine slow astern. 2. Stop engine and dead slow ahead — drop starboard anchor and pay out line — heave on bow line. 3. Make fast in place.

ble to put the anchor out from the bow and back up to the dock where two stern lines may be secured and a long gangway put ashore for disembarking as shown in Figure 27-H (Page 146).

Mooring parallel to the dock can be accomplished as shown in Figure 27-I (Page 146). First the bow anchor is put out, and the boat is backed into position and the stern anchor dropped. The boat then is backed into position to put out the stern line to the dock, taking care to keep the stern backing away from the stern anchor line. The stern anchor line should be tended at all times during this maneuver, and as soon as the stern line is on the dock, the slack should be taken out of the stern anchor line. The stern line should be slacked until the stern is in position and a bow line is put out. Now, with the four lines out, the boat can be worked into position with the lines tight and made fast.

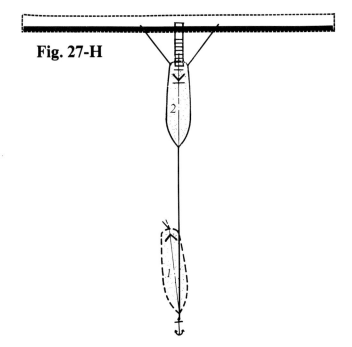

Fig. 27-H

Fig. 27-H 1. Drop anchor — slow astern — variable right rudder. 2. Put out stern lines and make fast — dead slow ahead — heave anchor line tight and stop engine. Note: When boat is left unattended, gangway should be removed.

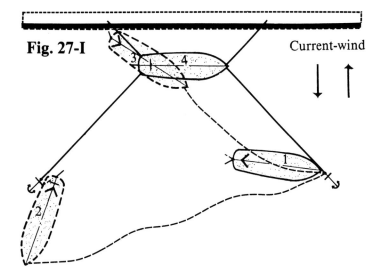

Fig. 27-I

Current-wind

Fig. 27-I 1. Drop bow anchor and pay out line — engine astern with variable rudder. 2. Engine stopped — drop stern anchor off of starboard quarter and pay out line — engine slow astern. 3. Put out port stern line and slack off — engine slow ahead to move into position. 4. Put out port head line and make fast lines to dock — take slack out of anchor lines and make fast — stop engine.

DOCKING AND OFF-DOCKING ALONGSIDE IN STALLS — LEAVING BOATS CENTERED IN MIDDLE OF STALLS

In Figure 27-J the boat is docking stern first with a head current or wind in stall A. While she is still headed almost into the set, a line is put out from the starboard side forward to the end of the stall. As the engine comes astern she will fall alongside for mooring lines to be put out. In stall B, the boat is docking head in under the same conditions. As the bow approaches the dock at an angle, a spring line can be put out and surged off until she is in place. By coming ahead on the engine with a right rudder the boat will lay alongside to be secured.

Stall C represents a larger boat secured which may be left unattended. When a boat is to be left for long periods of time, the lines should be left with enough slack to allow the boat to work up and down with the waves. Any rise and fall of the water must be taken into consideration.

Fig. 27-J

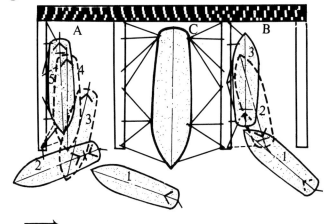

Wind-current

Fig. 27-J 1A. Slow ahead — left rudder. 2. Slow ahead — stop and astern — put out starboard breast line. 3. Engine astern — midship rudder. 4. Put out head line and aft spring. 5. Put out all lines and secure — stop engine.

1B. Engine ahead — right rudder. 2. Engine astern — put out spring line — head line and stern line. 3. Dead slow ahead — right rudder — put out all lines and secure — stop engine. C. Large boat secured to be left unattended.

In Figure 27-K (Page 147), the boat in stall A is sailing. All lines are taken in except a stern spring line. When the engine is given a kick astern the bow will come away and the spring line can be taken in. The engine ahead with right rudder will keep the stern clear, and when the turn around the end of the stall is started the engine can be given more speed and she will be clear.

In stall B the boat is backing out to get under way. Only a spring line forward is held and the engine is giv-

CHAPTER TWENTY-SEVEN

Fig. 27-K

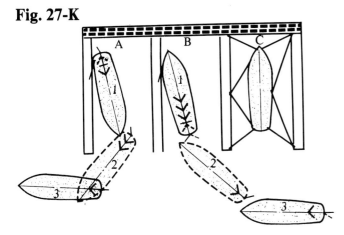

Fig. 27-K   1A. Dead slow astern — hold aft spring line — stop and let go spring line — slow ahead — right rudder. 2. More speed ahead — hard right rudder. 3. Slow speed — steady up under way.

1B. Hold forward spring — dead slow ahead — left rudder — stop — let go spring — right rudder — engine astern. 2. Slow astern or stopped — right rudder. 3. Engine ahead — steady up under way. C. Boat secured — illustrating two different ways of securing spring lines.

en a kick ahead with left rudder. As the stern comes away, the engine is stopped and put astern with right rudder, while taking in the spring line. When she has gained fair sternway, the engine is put on slow astern or stopped so that the stern will swing to the rudder. When she is clear of the stall the engine can be put ahead with left rudder to steady up.

The boat in stall C illustrates two different ways of putting out spring lines. Either way will work and it is mainly a matter of choice, however because the lines on the starboard side are longer, they will allow for more rise and fall of the water without having slack.

Crossing mooring lines so that they will chafe against each other should be avoided.

MOORING BETWEEN PILING AND DOCK

In Figure 27-L the boat going to dock A is moving with the current and securing stern first. Using a fender, she should let her starboard bow rest against the dock and put the starboard head line out. The port headline should be taken down the deck and put on the piling, then made fast on the port bow quarter. With a strain on that line and the engine coming astern, the starboard bow line can be slacked off and the stern lines put out. Then the engine can be put ahead to hold her

in place if necessary in order to move the port head line to the bow chock.

The boat going to dock B will maneuver the same way, except the piling will be used to land the bow against. She will back against the port bow line leading to the dock. There is a possibility also that the stern will try to fall more to starboard as shown.

The boat heading into the current and going to dock C will put her port bow line out first from the bow quarter. When she backs around and puts out her port stern line, she should have no trouble putting out the starboard bow and stern lines since the current will hold her in position.

Fig. 27-L

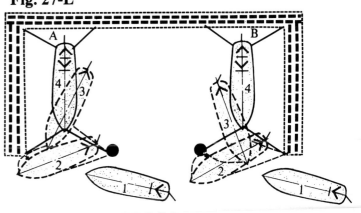

Current-wind

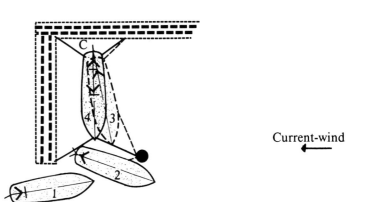

Current-wind

Fig. 27-L   1A-B. Slow ahead and stop — hard left rudder. 2. Engine astern — put out starboard bow line and port breast line. 3. Slow astern — variable rudder — take up slack in port breast line and pay out starboard bow line. 4. Hold port breast line — put out stern lines and make fast — slow ahead — shift port breast line to bow — adjust lines and make fast — stop engine.

1C. Slow ahead and stopped — right rudder. 2. Engine astern — put out port breast line — variable right and left rudder. 3. Slow astern — put out port and starboard stern lines — stop engine and make fast. 4. Slow ahead — put out starboard bow line and shift port breast to port bow chock — stop and secure.

TURNING AND DOCKING IN CLOSE QUARTERS

Running with a fair current and turning and docking in a narrow channel can be easily accomplished as shown in Figure 27-M.

The distance run past the dock you are going to will depend on the speed of the current. When the boat starts to gain sternway, make sure the rudder is hard left against the rudder stop, especially if the engine is going to be left full astern while turning. The water pressure against the rudder can cause the rudder to go hard over, even with power steering. This can damage or break the steering gear or cables. The helm or steering wheel can also break an arm.

With good stern-way it may be necessary to come ahead on the engine before the rudder can be brought back to midship and put hard right for docking.

TWIN SCREW CRAFT

Handling twin screw vessels is explained in chapter 18. They will turn in their own length, and can maneuver in and out of close quarters much easier than one

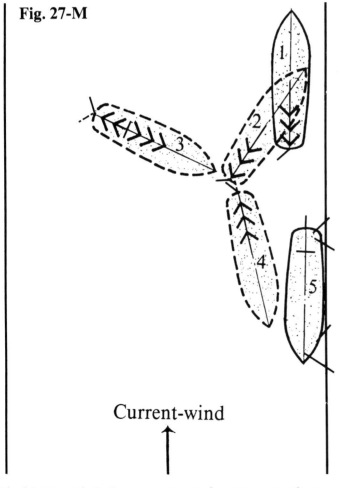

Fig. 27-M

Current-wind

Fig. 27-M   1-2. Full astern — hard left rudder. 3. Half astern — stop and full ahead — hard right rudder. 4. Full astern — hard right and midship rudder. 5. Stop and secure in berth.

with a single propeller. It should be remembered that most small vessels will have more horse power per weight ratio than do larger vessels. The deep draft vessel will not act as lively as one with a shallow draft. A boat with high freeboard and superstructure will be effected as much or more by high winds than by currents. A boat with low freeboard and superstructure will be affected more by strong currents than by high winds. The twin screw outboard, or so called stern driven boats, do not act exactly as the fixed propeller-rudder type. This is because the propellers rotate horizontally to push or back at an angle to the keel and center line of the boat. They can however be maneuvered in basically the same manner.

CHAPTER 28

SAFETY AND COMMON SENSE

There is nothing more enjoyable and relaxing than a day on a good boat in good weather. Out of the way places can be explored that are inaccessible in any other way, or you can just cruise the coast line or the open water. It should be remembered however, that the same applies here as with any equipment. A boat is just as safe as the operator and the rig itself. U.S. Coast Guard and local safety rules and regulations should be followed to the letter before even thinking of leaving the dock.

Before leaving the dock advise someone ashore of your destination and how long you expect to be gone. A boat going any distance needs a compass which should be mounted in line with the keel and adjusted for error. All courses to your destination should be recorded rather than depending on memory. If you were to encounter fog, heavy rain or simply get lost, reverse your compass courses to return to your dock.

In addition to required lights, anchor and line, fire extinguisher, oars or paddles, sufficient life preservers, etc., it is suggested that a half dozen or so distress flares (whether required or not) be included, along with a water proof flash light and water proof container of matches, a small set of mechanic tools including a small hammer, screw driver and pliers, and a spare propeller to be kept on board. Also on today's market there are approved battery powered radio distress signal devices that can be carried along if there is trouble and quick assistance is needed.

On small pleasure boats with only one motor, it has been found that it pays to carry a small outboard motor for a spare that can be bracketed down under the bow out of the way, or made fast to the transom out of the way of the main motor. An electric trolling motor beats nothing, but if you have some distance to travel and the battery runs down, you will still be out of luck. Of course there are the oars or paddles, but they are a very hard way to get anywhere.

NEVER, never leave your boat and try to swim for help unless you are absolutely sure and double sure you can make it. Many people have been lost that way.

Some people get a thrill out of going just as fast as a boat will go whether they are going anywhere or not, and there is nothing wrong with this as long as time and place are taken into consideration. If a boat has been pulling one or more skiers and they are in the water, the boat's engine(s) should be stopped and turned completely off before coming too close to them. The person in the water can then swim up to the boat to be picked up, rather than taking a chance on cutting them up with the boat's propeller(s).

One should never go faster than a slow moderate speed where there are other small pleasure boats nearby unless there is a designated speed area.

Going at high speed in unknown, secluded areas is asking for serious trouble. Floating debris such as logs and stumps should always be avoided. The most dangerous debris are those floating just under the water. Trees that may have limbs just under the surface that cannot be seen could punch a hole in your boat or worse. In a split second your fun day can turn into a day of disaster if someone is permanently injured or worse.

If you are going offshore into unprotected water, a frequent glance at the weather is one of the best safeguards you can take.

One never wants to get caught offshore in a heavy squall with a small boat if it can be avoided, and at certain times of the year these squalls can make up very fast.

If a squall is seen making up, it is far better and safer to run in to shore and go back out after it has passed than to get caught in open water. However, if you should be caught, don't try to run full speed. That chance is gone, and if it is really rough with heavy seas, it will be necessary to head into them at slow speed until it passes or run with the seas on your stern with just enough speed to keep the water from breaking over the stern.

If your engine stops, you will need to get something over the bow to act as a drag to keep the bow into the sea as much as possible. You can tie anything to your anchor that is available (not life preservers, unless there are plenty of spares other than the ones you should have on), but any object that will submerge and not drift as fast as your boat.

Above everything else, DON'T PANIC! If you feel yourself doing this, just pause and consider a moment. There are things that can be done that you may not have considered. If your boat should fill up with water and sink, just hang on to the boat. Anything that will float can be tied together for additional buoyancy, but don't leave your boat unless it sinks altogether. Remember, there are flares and if you can get them lit they will burn. If you have the battery operated distress device, it will be sending signals. In either case if you don't panic and tire yourself out, they will be looking for you soon, anyway, especially if you have followed all the rules and regulations.

SUGGESTION

There is a cliche among professional ship and boat handlers worthy of mention because it is in line with safe and efficient operation. It is as follows.

There are times to, and times not to! Which in literal terms mean, there are times when full ahead is better than full astern, or vice versa. Slow ahead may be a better alternative than full ahead, or sometimes ten degrees of rudder is better than hard over rudder, etc.

Another saying is that one should never maneuver a vessel into any position that a safe way out cannot be seen before this decision is made. If there is confusion and one is not sure of proceeding safely, the vessel should be stopped and/or anchored, or even turned around and headed in the other direction until a safe maneuver can be determined.

If these cliches are mastered and practiced, one can then consider themselves a professional ship or boat handler.

MARLINESPIKE SEAMANSHIP

Illustrated here are some common knots, bends, hitches, and splices.

Bowline

The bowline is considered a knot second in usefulness only to the square knot. The bowline will not slip, does not pinch or kink the rope as much as some other knots, and does not jam and become difficult to untie. By tying a bowline with a small loop and passing the line through the loop the running bowline is obtained. This is an excellent form of running noose.

Overhand

The simple overhand knot is used to keep the end of a rope from unlaying.

Two Half Hitches

Two half hitches are used for making a line fast to a bollard, ring, timber, or stanchion. Note that the knot consists of a turn around the fixed object and a clove hitch around the standing part of the line.

Figure Eight

The figure eight knot. This does not jam.

Correct Method of Making Fast to a Cleat

Correct method for making fast to a cleat is shown. The half hitch which completes the fastening is taken with the free part of the line. The line can then be freed without taking up slack in the standing part.

Square or Reef Knot

The square or reef knot is a most useful and common knot. The rope manipulated by the right hand (this is the rope leading from the left side of the sketch and terminating in the arrow in A) is turned over the other rope in tying both the first and second half of the knot.

Incorrect Method of Making Fast to a Cleat

Common incorrect method of making fast to a cleat is shown. The half hitch is taken with the standing part of the line and the line consequently can not be freed without taking up slack in the standing part. Accidents have been caused by the use of this type of fastening on lines which must be freed quickly.

Sheet or Becket Bend

The sheet or becket bend is used for tying two lines together. It will not slip even if there is great difference in the sizes of the lines.

Fisherman's Bend

The fisherman's bend, also called the anchor bend, is made by taking two round turns around the ring, then passing the end under both turns to form a half hitch around the standing part of the line. For further security, a second half hitch is taken around the standing part only.

Clove Hitch

The clove hitch is used for making a line fast temporarily to a pile or a bollard.